MYTHS OF BABYLONIA AND ASSYRIA
Donald A. Mackenzie

Preface

This volume deals with the myths and legends of Babylonia and Assyria, and as these reflect the civilization in which they developed, a historical narrative has been provided, beginning with the early Sumerian Age and concluding with the periods of the Persian and Grecian Empires. Over thirty centuries of human progress are thus passed under review.

During this vast interval of time the cultural influences emanating from the Tigro-Euphrates valley reached far-distant shores along the intersecting avenues of trade, and in consequence of the periodic and widespread migrations of peoples who had acquired directly or indirectly the leavening elements of Mesopotamian civilization. Even at the present day traces survive in Europe of the early cultural impress of the East; our "Signs of the Zodiac", for instance, as well as the system of measuring time and space by using 60 as a basic numeral for calculation, are inheritances from ancient Babylonia.

As in the Nile Valley, however, it is impossible to trace in Mesopotamia the initiatory stages of prehistoric culture based on the agricultural mode of life. What is generally called the "Dawn of History" is really the beginning of a later age of progress; it is necessary to account for the degree of civilization attained at the earliest period of which we have knowledge by postulating a remoter age of culture of much longer duration than that which separates the "Dawn" from the age in which we now live. Although Sumerian (early Babylonian) civilization presents distinctively local features which justify the application of the term "indigenous" in the broad sense, it is found, like that of Egypt, to be possessed of certain elements which suggest exceedingly remote influences and connections at present obscure. Of special interest in this regard is Professor Budge's mature and well-deliberated conclusion that "both the Sumerians and early Egyptians derived their primeval gods from some common but exceedingly ancient source". The prehistoric burial customs of these separate peoples are also remarkably similar and they resemble closely in turn those of the Neolithic Europeans. The cumulative effect of such evidence forces us to regard as not wholly satisfactory and conclusive the hypothesis of cultural influence. A remote racial connection is possible, and is certainly worthy of consideration when so high an authority as Professor Frazer, author of *The Golden Bough*, is found prepared to admit that the widespread "homogeneity of beliefs" may have been due to "homogeneity of race". It is shown (Chapter 1) that certain ethnologists have accumulated data which establish a racial kinship between the Neolithic Europeans, the proto-Egyptians, the Sumerians, the southern Persians, and the Aryo-Indians.

Throughout this volume comparative notes have been compiled in dealing with Mesopotamian beliefs with purpose to assist the reader towards the study of linking myths and legends. Interesting parallels have been gleaned from various religious literatures in Europe, Egypt, India, and elsewhere. It will be found that certain relics of Babylonian intellectual life, which have a distinctive geographical significance, were shared by peoples in other cultural areas where they were similarly overlaid with local colour. Modes of thought were the products of modes of life and were influenced in their development by human experiences. The influence of environment on the growth of culture has long been recognized, but consideration must also be given to the choice of environment by peoples who had adopted distinctive habits of life. Racial units migrated from cultural areas to districts suitable for colonization and carried with them a heritage of immemorial beliefs and customs which were regarded as being quite as indispensable for their welfare as their implements and domesticated animals.

When consideration is given in this connection to the conservative element in primitive religion, it is not surprising to find that the growth of religious myths was not so spontaneous in early civilizations of the highest order as has hitherto been assumed. It seems clear that in each great local mythology we have to deal, in the first place, not with symbolized ideas so much as symbolized folk beliefs of remote antiquity, and, to a certain degree, of common inheritance. It may not be found possible to arrive at a conclusive solution of the most widespread, and therefore the most ancient folk myths, such as, for instance, the Dragon Myth, or the myth of the culture hero. Nor, perhaps, is it necessary that we should concern ourselves greatly regarding the origin of the idea of the dragon, which in one country symbolized fiery drought and in another overwhelming river floods.

The student will find footing on surer ground by following the process which exalts the dragon of the folk tale into the symbol of evil and primordial chaos. The Babylonian Creation Myth, for instance, can be shown to be a localized and glorified legend in which the hero and his tribe are displaced by the war god and his fellow deities whose welfare depends on his prowess. Merodach kills the dragon, Tiamat, as the heroes of Eur-Asian folk stories kill grisly hags, by casting his weapon down her throat.

He severed her inward parts, he pierced her heart,
He overcame her and cut off her life;
He cast down her body and stood upon it ...

And with merciless club he smashed her skull.

He cut through the channels of her blood,

And he made the north wind to bear it away into secret places.

Afterwards

He divided the flesh of the *Ku-pu* and devised a cunning plan.

Mr. L.W. King, from whose scholarly *Seven Tablets of Creation* these lines are quoted, notes that "Ku-pu" is a word of uncertain meaning. Jensen suggests "trunk, body". Apparently Merodach obtained special knowledge after dividing, and perhaps eating, the "Ku-pu". His "cunning plan" is set forth in detail: he cut up the dragon's body:

He split her up like a flat fish into two halves.

He formed the heavens with one half and the earth with the other, and then set the universe in order. His power and wisdom as the Demiurge were derived from the fierce and powerful Great Mother, Tiamat.

In other dragon stories the heroes devise their plans after eating the dragon's heart. According to Philostratus,[1] Apollonius of Tyana was worthy of being remembered for two things--his bravery in travelling among fierce robber tribes, not then subject to Rome, and his wisdom in learning the language of birds and other animals as the Arabs do. This accomplishment the Arabs acquired, Philostratus explains, by eating the hearts of dragons. The "animals" who utter magic words are, of course, the Fates. Siegfried of the *Nibelungenlied*, after slaying the Regin dragon, makes himself invulnerable by bathing in its blood. He obtains wisdom by eating the heart: as soon as he tastes it he can understand the language of birds, and the birds reveal to him that Mimer is waiting to slay him. Sigurd similarly makes his plans after eating the heart of the Fafner dragon. In Scottish legend Finn-mac-Coul obtains the power to divine secrets by partaking of a small portion of the seventh salmon associated with the "well dragon", and Michael Scott and other folk heroes become great physicians after tasting the juices of the middle part of the body of the white snake. The hero of an Egyptian folk tale slays a "deathless snake" by cutting it in two parts and putting sand between the parts. He then obtains from the box, of which it is the guardian, the book of spells; when he reads a page of the spells he knows what the birds of the sky, the fish of the deep, and the beasts of the hill say; the book gives him power to enchant "the heaven and the earth, the abyss, the mountains and the sea".[2]

Magic and religion were never separated in Babylonia; not only the priests but also the gods performed magical ceremonies. Ea, Merodach's father, overcame Apsu, the husband of the dragon Tiamat, by means of spells: he was "the great magician of the gods". Merodach's division of the "Ku-pu" was evidently an act of contagious magic; by eating or otherwise disposing of the vital part of the fierce and wise mother dragon, he became endowed with her attributes, and was able to proceed with the work of creation. Primitive peoples in our own day, like the Abipones of Paraguay, eat the flesh of fierce and cunning animals so that their strength, courage, and wisdom may be increased.

The direct influence exercised by cultural contact, on the other hand, may be traced when myths with an alien geographical setting are found among peoples whose experiences could never have given them origin. In India, where the dragon symbolizes drought and the western river deities are female, the Manu fish and flood legend resembles closely the Babylonian, and seems to throw light upon it. Indeed, the Manu myth appears to have been derived from the lost flood story in which Ea figured prominently in fish form as the Preserver. The Babylonian Ea cult and the Indian Varuna cult had apparently much in common, as is shown.

Throughout this volume special attention has been paid to the various peoples who were in immediate contact with, and were influenced by, Mesopotamian civilization. The histories are traced in outline of the Kingdoms of Elam, Urartu (Ancient Armenia), Mitanni, and the Hittites, while the story of the rise and decline of the Hebrew civilization, as narrated in the Bible and referred to in Mesopotamian inscriptions, is related from the earliest times until the captivity in the Neo-Babylonian period and the restoration during the age of the Persian Empire. The struggles waged between the great Powers for the control of trade routes, and the periodic migrations of pastoral warrior folks who determined the fate of empires, are also dealt with, so that light may be thrown on the various processes and influences associated with the developments of local religions and mythologies. Special chapters, with comparative notes, are devoted to the Ishtar-Tammuz myths, the Semiramis legends, Ashur and his symbols, and the origin and growth of astrology and astronomy.

The ethnic disturbances which occurred at various well-defined periods in the Tigro-Euphrates valley were not always favourable to the advancement of knowledge and the growth of culture. The invaders who absorbed Sumerian civilization may have secured more settled conditions by welding together political units, but seem to have exercised a retrogressive

2

influence on the growth of local culture. "Babylonian religion", writes Dr. Langdon, "appears to have reached its highest level in the Sumerian period, or at least not later than 2000 B.C. From that period onward to the first century B.C. popular religion maintained with great difficulty the sacred standards of the past." Although it has been customary to characterize Mesopotamian civilization as Semitic, modern research tends to show that the indigenous inhabitants, who were non-Semitic, were its originators. Like the proto-Egyptians, the early Cretans, and the Pelasgians in southern Europe and Asia Minor, they invariably achieved the intellectual conquest of their conquerors, as in the earliest times they had won victories over the antagonistic forces of nature. If the modern view is accepted that these ancient agriculturists of the goddess cult were of common racial origin, it is to the most representative communities of the widespread Mediterranean race that the credit belongs of laying the foundations of the brilliant civilizations of the ancient world in southern Europe, and Egypt, and the valley of the Tigris and Euphrates.

[1] *Life of Apollonius of Tyana*, i, 20.
[2] *Egyptian Tales* (Second Series), W.M. Flinders Petrie, pp. 98 *et seq.*

Introduction

Ancient Babylonia has made stronger appeal to the imagination of Christendom than even Ancient Egypt, because of its association with the captivity of the Hebrews, whose sorrows are enshrined in the familiar psalm:

By the rivers of Babylon, there we sat down;
Yea, we wept, when we remembered Zion.
We hanged our harps upon the willows....

In sacred literature proud Babylon became the city of the anti-Christ, the symbol of wickedness and cruelty and human vanity. Early Christians who suffered persecution compared their worldly state to that of the oppressed and disconsolate Hebrews, and, like them, they sighed for Jerusalem--the new Jerusalem. When St. John the Divine had visions of the ultimate triumph of Christianity, he referred to its enemies--the unbelievers and persecutors--as the citizens of the earthly Babylon, the doom of which he pronounced in stately and memorable phrases:

Babylon the great is fallen, is fallen,
And is become the habitation of devils,
And the hold of every foul spirit,
And a cage of every unclean and hateful bird....

For her sins have reached unto heaven
And God hath remembered her iniquities....
The merchants of the earth shall weep and mourn over her,
For no man buyeth their merchandise any more.

"At the noise of the taking of Babylon", cried Jeremiah, referring to the original Babylon, "the earth is moved, and the cry is heard among the nations.... It shall be no more inhabited forever; neither shall it be dwelt in from generation to generation." The Christian Saint rendered more profound the brooding silence of the desolated city of his vision by voicing memories of its beauty and gaiety and bustling trade:

The voice of harpers, and musicians, and of pipers and trumpeters shall be heard no more at all in thee;
And no craftsman, of whatsoever craft he be, shall be found any more in thee;
And the light of a candle shall shine no more at all in thee;
And the voice of the bridegroom and of the bride shall be heard no more at all in thee:
For thy merchants were the great men of the earth;
For by thy sorceries were all nations deceived.
And in her was found the blood of prophets, and of saints,
And of all that were slain upon the earth.[3]

So for nearly two thousand years has the haunting memory of the once-powerful city pervaded Christian literature, while its broken walls and ruined temples and palaces lay buried deep in desert sand. The history of the ancient land of which it was the capital survived in but meagre and fragmentary form, mingled with accumulated myths and legends. A slim volume contained all that could be derived from references in the Old Testament and the compilations of classical writers.

It is only within the past half-century that the wonderful story of early Eastern civilization has been gradually pieced together by excavators and linguists, who have thrust open the door of the past and probed the hidden secrets of long ages. We now know more about "the land of Babel" than did not only the Greeks and Romans, but even the Hebrew writers who foretold its destruction. Glimpses are being afforded us of its life and manners and customs for some thirty centuries before the captives of Judah uttered lamentations on the banks of its reedy canals. The sites of some of the ancient cities of Babylonia and Assyria were identified by European officials and travellers in the East early in the nineteenth century, and a few relics found their way to Europe. But before Sir A.H. Layard set to work as an excavator in the "forties", "a case scarcely three feet square", as he himself wrote, "enclosed all that remained not only of the great city of Nineveh, but of Babylon itself".[4]

Layard, the distinguished pioneer Assyriologist, was an Englishman of Huguenot descent, who was born in Paris. Through his mother he inherited a strain of Spanish blood. During his early boyhood he resided in Italy, and his education, which began there, was continued in schools in France, Switzerland, and England. He was a man of scholarly habits and fearless and independent character, a charming writer, and an accomplished fine-art critic; withal he was a great traveller, a strenuous politician, and an able diplomatist. In 1845, while sojourning in the East, he undertook the exploration of ancient Assyrian cities. He first set to work at Kalkhi, the Biblical Calah. Three years previously M.P.C. Botta, the French consul at Mosul, had begun to investigate the Nineveh mounds; but these he abandoned for a mound near Khorsabad which proved to be the site of the city erected by "Sargon the Later", who is referred to by Isaiah. The relics discovered by Botta and his successor, Victor Place, are preserved in the Louvre.

At Kalkhi and Nineveh Layard uncovered the palaces of some of the most famous Assyrian Emperors, including the Biblical Shalmaneser and Esarhaddon, and obtained the colossi, bas reliefs, and other treasures of antiquity which formed the nucleus of the British Museum's unrivalled Assyrian collection. He also conducted diggings at Babylon and Niffer (Nippur). His work was continued by his assistant, Hormuzd Rassam, a native Christian of Mosul, near Nineveh. Rassam studied for a time at Oxford.

The discoveries made by Layard and Botta stimulated others to follow their example. In the "fifties" Mr. W.K. Loftus engaged in excavations at Larsa and Erech, where important discoveries were made of ancient buildings, ornaments, tablets, sarcophagus graves, and pot burials, while Mr. J.E. Taylor operated at Ur, the seat of the moon cult and the birthplace of Abraham, and at Eridu, which is generally regarded as the cradle of early Babylonian (Sumerian) civilization.

In 1854 Sir Henry Rawlinson superintended diggings at Birs Nimrud (Borsippa, near Babylon), and excavated relics of the Biblical Nebuchadrezzar. This notable archaeologist began his career in the East as an officer in the Bombay army. He distinguished himself as a political agent and diplomatist. While resident at Baghdad, he devoted his leisure time to cuneiform studies. One of his remarkable feats was the copying of the famous trilingual rock inscription of Darius the Great on a mountain cliff at Behistun, in Persian Kurdistan. This work was carried out at great personal risk, for the cliff is 1700 feet high and the sculptures and inscriptions are situated about 300 feet from the ground.

Darius was the first monarch of his line to make use of the Persian cuneiform script, which in this case he utilized in conjunction with the older and more complicated Assyro-Babylonian alphabetic and syllabic characters to record a portion of the history of his reign. Rawlinson's translation of the famous inscription was an important contribution towards the decipherment of the cuneiform writings of Assyria and Babylonia.

Twelve years of brilliant Mesopotamian discovery concluded in 1854, and further excavations had to be suspended until the "seventies" on account of the unsettled political conditions of the ancient land and the difficulties experienced in dealing with Turkish officials. During the interval, however, archaeologists and philologists were kept fully engaged studying the large amount of material which had been accumulated. Sir Henry Rawlinson began the issue of his monumental work *The Cuneiform Inscriptions of Western Asia* on behalf of the British Museum.

Goodspeed refers to the early archaeological work as the "Heroic Period" of research, and says that the "Modern Scientific Period" began with Mr. George Smith's expedition to Nineveh in 1873.

George Smith, like Henry Schliemann, the pioneer investigator of pre-Hellenic culture, was a self-educated man of humble origin. He was born at Chelsea in 1840. At fourteen he was apprenticed to an engraver. He was a youth of studious habits and great originality, and interested himself intensely in the discoveries which had been made by Layard and other explorers. At the British Museum, which he visited regularly to pore over the Assyrian inscriptions, he attracted the attention of Sir Henry Rawlinson. So greatly impressed was Sir Henry by the young man's enthusiasm and remarkable intelligence that he allowed him the use of his private room and provided casts and squeezes of inscriptions to assist him in his studies.

4

Smith made rapid progress. His earliest discovery was the date of the payment of tribute by Jehu, King of Israel, to the Assyrian Emperor Shalmaneser. Sir Henry availed himself of the young investigator's assistance in producing the third volume of *The Cuneiform Inscriptions.*

In 1867 Smith received an appointment in the Assyriology Department of the British Museum, and a few years later became famous throughout Christendom as the translator of fragments of the Babylonian Deluge Legend from tablets sent to London by Rassam. Sir Edwin Arnold, the poet and Orientalist, was at the time editor of the*Daily Telegraph*, and performed a memorable service to modern scholarship by dispatching Smith, on behalf of his paper, to Nineveh to search for other fragments of the Ancient Babylonian epic. Rassam had obtained the tablets from the great library of the cultured Emperor Ashur-bani-pal, "the great and noble Asnapper" of the Bible,[5]who took delight, as he himself recorded, in

The wisdom of Ea,[6] the art of song, the treasures of science.

This royal patron of learning included in his library collection, copies and translations of tablets from Babylonia. Some of these were then over 2000 years old. The Babylonian literary relics were, indeed, of as great antiquity to Ashur-bani-pal as that monarch's relics are to us.

The Emperor invoked Nebo, god of wisdom and learning, to bless his "books", praying:

Forever, O Nebo, King of all heaven and earth,
Look gladly upon this Library
Of Ashur-bani-pal, his (thy) shepherd, reverencer of thy divinity.[7]

Mr. George Smith's expedition to Nineveh in 1873 was exceedingly fruitful of results. More tablets were discovered and translated. In the following year he returned to the ancient Assyrian city on behalf of the British Museum, and added further by his scholarly achievements to his own reputation and the world's knowledge of antiquity. His last expedition was made early in 1876; on his homeward journey he was stricken down with fever, and on 19th August he died at Aleppo in his thirty-sixth year. So was a brilliant career brought to an untimely end.

Rassam was engaged to continue Smith's great work, and between 1877 and 1882 made many notable discoveries in Assyria and Babylonia, including the bronze doors of a Shalmaneser temple, the sun temple at Sippar; the palace of the Biblical Nebuchadrezzar, which was famous for its "hanging gardens"; a cylinder of Nabonidus, King of Babylon; and about fifty thousand tablets.

M. de Sarzec, the French consul at Bassorah, began in 1877 excavations at the ancient Sumerian city of Lagash (Shirpula), and continued them until 1900. He found thousands of tablets, many has reliefs, votive statuettes, which worshippers apparently pinned on sacred shrines, the famous silver vase of King Entemena, statues of King Gudea, and various other treasures which are now in the Louvre.

The pioneer work achieved by British and French excavators stimulated interest all over the world. An expedition was sent out from the United States by the University of Pennsylvania, and began to operate at Nippur in 1888. The Germans, who have displayed great activity in the domain of philological research, are at present represented by an exploring party which is conducting the systematic exploration of the ruins of Babylon. Even the Turkish Government has encouraged research work, and its excavators have accumulated a fine collection of antiquities at Constantinople. Among the archaeologists and linguists of various nationalities who are devoting themselves to the study of ancient Assyrian and Babylonian records and literature, and gradually unfolding the story of ancient Eastern civilization, those of our own country occupy a prominent position. One of the most interesting discoveries of recent years has been new fragments of the Creation Legend by L.W. King of the British Museum, whose scholarly work, *The Seven Tablets of Creation*, is the standard work on the subject.

The archaeological work conducted in Persia, Asia Minor, Palestine, Cyprus, Crete, the Aegean, and Egypt has thrown, and is throwing, much light on the relations between the various civilizations of antiquity. In addition to the Hittite discoveries, with which the name of Professor Sayce will ever be associated as a pioneer, we now hear much of the hitherto unknown civilizations of Mitanni and Urartu (ancient Armenia), which contributed to the shaping of ancient history. The Biblical narratives of the rise and decline of the Hebrew kingdoms have also been greatly elucidated.

In this volume, which deals mainly with the intellectual life of the Mesopotamian peoples, a historical narrative has been provided as an appropriate setting for the myths and legends. In this connection the reader must be reminded that the chronology of the early period is still uncertain. The approximate dates which are given, however, are those now generally adopted by most European and American authorities. Early Babylonian history of the Sumerian period begins some time prior to 3000 B.C; Sargon of Akkad flourished about 2650 B.C., and Hammurabi not long before or after 2000 B.C. The inflated system of dating which places Mena of Egypt as far back as 5500 B.C. and Sargon at about 3800 B.C. has been abandoned by the majority of prominent archaeologists, the exceptions including Professor Flinders Petrie. Recent discoveries appear to support the new chronological system. "There is a growing conviction", writes Mr. Hawes, "that Cretan evidence, especially in the eastern part of the island, favours the minimum (Berlin) system of Egyptian chronology, according to which the Sixth (Egyptian) Dynasty began at *c.* 2540 B.C. and the Twelfth at *c.* 2000 B.C.[8] Petrie dates the beginning of the Twelfth Dynasty at *c.* 3400 B.C.

To students of comparative folklore and mythology the myths and legends of Babylonia present many features of engrossing interest. They are of great antiquity, yet not a few seem curiously familiar. We must not conclude, however, that because a European legend may bear resemblances to one translated from a cuneiform tablet it is necessarily of Babylonian origin. Certain beliefs, and the myths which were based upon them, are older than even the civilization of the Tigro-Euphrates valley. They belong, it would appear, to a stock of common inheritance from an uncertain cultural centre of immense antiquity. The problem involved has been referred to by Professor Frazer in the *Golden Bough*. Commenting on the similarities presented by certain ancient festivals in various countries, he suggests that they may be due to "a remarkable homogeneity of civilization throughout Southern Europe and Western Asia in prehistoric times. How far", he adds, "such homogeneity of civilization may be taken as evidence of homogeneity of race is a question for the ethnologist."[9]

In Chapter I the reader is introduced to the ethnological problem, and it is shown that the results of modern research tend to establish a remote racial connection between the Sumerians of Babylonia, the prehistoric Egyptians, and the Neolithic (Late Stone Age) inhabitants of Europe, as well as the southern Persians and the "Aryans" of India.

Comparative notes are provided in dealing with the customs, religious beliefs, and myths and legends of the Mesopotamian peoples to assist the student towards the elucidation and partial restoration of certain literary fragments from the cuneiform tablets. Of special interest in this connection are the resemblances between some of the Indian and Babylonian myths. The writer has drawn upon that "great storehouse" of ancient legends, the voluminous Indian epic, the *Mahabharata*, and it is shown that there are undoubted links between the Garuda eagle myths and those of the Sumerian Zu bird and the Etana eagle, while similar stories remain attached to the memories of "Sargon of Akkad" and the Indian hero Karna, and of Semiramis (who was Queen Sammu-ramat of Assyria) and Shakuntala. The Indian god Varuna and the Sumerian Ea are also found to have much in common, and it seems undoubted that the Manu fish and flood myth is a direct Babylonian inheritance, like the Yuga (Ages of the Universe) doctrine and the system of calculation associated with it. It is of interest to note, too, that a portion of the Gilgamesh epic survives in the *Ramayana* story of the monkey god Hanuman's search for the lost princess Sita; other relics of similar character suggest that both the Gilgamesh and Hanuman narratives are derived in part from a very ancient myth. Gilgamesh also figures in Indian mythology as Yama, the first man, who explored the way to the Paradise called "The Land of Ancestors", and over which he subsequently presided as a god. Other Babylonian myths link with those found in Egypt, Greece, Scandinavia, Iceland, and the British Isles and Ireland. The Sargon myth, for instance, resembles closely the myth of Scyld (Sceaf), the patriarch, in the *Beowulf* epic, and both appear to be variations of the Tammuz-Adonis story. Tammuz also resembles in one of his phases the Celtic hero Diarmid, who was slain by the "green boar" of the Earth Mother, as was Adonis by the boar form of Ares, the Greek war god.

In approaching the study of these linking myths it would be as rash to conclude that all resemblances are due to homogeneity of race as to assume that folklore and mythology are devoid of ethnological elements. Due consideration must be given to the widespread influence exercised by cultural contact. We must recognize also that the human mind has ever shown a tendency to arrive quite independently at similar conclusions, when confronted by similar problems, in various parts of the world.

But while many remarkable resemblances may be detected between the beliefs and myths and customs of widely separated peoples, it cannot be overlooked that pronounced and striking differences remain to be accounted for. Human experiences varied in localities because all sections of humanity were not confronted in ancient times by the same problems in their everyday lives. Some peoples, for instance, experienced no great difficulties regarding the food supply, which might be provided for them by nature in lavish abundance; others were compelled to wage a fierce and constant conflict against hostile forces in inhospitable environments with purpose to secure adequate sustenance and their meed of enjoyment. Various habits of life had to be adopted in various parts of the world, and these produced various habits of thought.

6

Consequently, we find that behind all systems of primitive religion lies the formative background of natural phenomena. A mythology reflects the geography, the fauna and flora, and the climatic conditions of the area in which it took definite and permanent shape.

In Babylonia, as elsewhere, we expect, therefore, to find a mythology which has strictly local characteristics--one which mirrors river and valley scenery, the habits of life of the people, and also the various stages of progress in the civilization from its earliest beginnings. Traces of primitive thought--survivals from remotest antiquity--should also remain in evidence. As a matter of fact Babylonian mythology fulfils our expectations in this regard to the highest degree.

Herodotus said that Egypt was the gift of the Nile: similarly Babylonia may be regarded as the gift of the Tigris and Euphrates--those great shifting and flooding rivers which for long ages had been carrying down from the Armenian Highlands vast quantities of mud to thrust back the waters of the Persian Gulf and form a country capable of being utilized for human habitation. The most typical Babylonian deity was Ea, the god of the fertilizing and creative waters.

He was depicted clad in the skin of a fish, as gods in other geographical areas were depicted wearing the skins of animals which were regarded as ancestors, or hostile demons that had to be propitiated. Originally Ea appears to have been a fish--the incarnation of the spirit of, or life principle in, the Euphrates River. His centre of worship was at Eridu, an ancient seaport, where apparently the prehistoric Babylonians (the Sumerians) first began to utilize the dried-up beds of shifting streams to irrigate the soil. One of the several creation myths is reminiscent of those early experiences which produced early local beliefs:

O thou River, who didst create all things,
When the great gods dug thee out,
They set prosperity upon thy banks,
Within thee Ea, the king of the Deep, created his dwelling.[10]

The Sumerians observed that the land was brought into existence by means of the obstructing reeds, which caused mud to accumulate. When their minds began to be exercised regarding the origin of life, they conceived that the first human beings were created by a similar process:

Marduk (son of Ea) laid a reed upon the face of the waters,
He formed dust and poured it out beside the reed ...
He formed mankind.[11]

Ea acquired in time, as the divine artisan, various attributes which reflected the gradual growth of civilization: he was reputed to have taught the people how to form canals, control the rivers, cultivate the fields, build their houses, and so on.

But although Ea became a beneficent deity, as a result of the growth of civilization, he had also a demoniac form, and had to be propitiated. The worshippers of the fish god retained ancient modes of thought and perpetuated ancient superstitious practices.

The earliest settlers in the Tigro-Euphrates valley were agriculturists, like their congeners, the proto-Egyptians and the Neolithic Europeans. Before they broke away from the parent stock in its area of characterization they had acquired the elements of culture, and adopted habits of thought which were based on the agricultural mode of life. Like other agricultural communities they were worshippers of the "World Mother", the Creatrix, who was the giver of all good things, the "Preserver" and also the "Destroyer"--the goddess whose moods were reflected by natural phenomena, and whose lovers were the spirits of the seasons.

In the alluvial valley which they rendered fit for habitation the Sumerians came into contact with peoples of different habits of life and different habits of thought. These were the nomadic pastoralists from the northern steppe lands, who had developed in isolation theories regarding the origin of the Universe which reflected their particular experiences and the natural phenomena of their area of characterization. The most representative people of this class were the "Hatti" of Asia Minor, who were of Alpine or Armenoid stock. In early times the nomads were broken up into small tribal units, like Abraham and his followers, and depended for their food supply on the prowess of the males. Their chief deity was the sky and mountain god, who was the "World Father", the creator, and the wielder of the thunder hammer, who waged war against the demons of storm or drought, and ensured the food supply of his worshippers.

The fusion in Babylonia of the peoples of the god and goddess cults was in progress before the dawn of history, as was the case in Egypt and also in southern Europe. In consequence independent Pantheons came into existence in the various city States in the Tigro-Euphrates valley. These were mainly a reflection of city politics: the deities of each influential section had to receive recognition. But among the great masses of the people ancient customs associated with agriculture continued in practice, and, as Babylonia depended for its prosperity on

7

its harvests, the force of public opinion tended, it would appear, to perpetuate the religious beliefs of the earliest settlers, despite the efforts made by conquerors to exalt the deities they introduced.

Babylonian religion was of twofold character. It embraced temple worship and private worship. The religion of the temple was the religion of the ruling class, and especially of the king, who was the guardian of the people. Domestic religion was conducted in homes, in reed huts, or in public places, and conserved the crudest superstitions surviving from the earliest times. The great "burnings" and the human sacrifices in Babylonia, referred to in the Bible, were, no doubt, connected with agricultural religion of the private order, as was also the ceremony of baking and offering cakes to the Queen of Heaven, condemned by Jeremiah, which obtained in the streets of Jerusalem and other cities. Domestic religion required no temples. There were no temples in Crete: the world was the "house" of the deity, who had seasonal haunts on hilltops, in groves, in caves, &c. In Egypt Herodotus witnessed festivals and processions which are not referred to in official inscriptions, although they were evidently practised from the earliest times.

Agricultural religion in Egypt was concentrated in the cult of Osiris and Isis, and influenced all local theologies. In Babylonia these deities were represented by Tammuz and Ishtar. Ishtar, like Isis, absorbed many other local goddesses.

According to the beliefs of the ancient agriculturists the goddess was eternal and undecaying. She was the Great Mother of the Universe and the source of the food supply. Her son, the corn god, became, as the Egyptians put it, "Husband of his Mother". Each year he was born anew and rapidly attained to manhood; then he was slain by a fierce rival who symbolized the season of pestilence-bringing and parching sun heat, or the rainy season, or wild beasts of prey. Or it might be that he was slain by his son, as Cronos was by Zeus and Dyaus by Indra. The new year slew the old year.

The social customs of the people, which had a religious basis, were formed in accordance with the doings of the deities; they sorrowed or made glad in sympathy with the spirits of nature. Worshippers also suggested by their ceremonies how the deities should act at various seasons, and thus exercised, as they believed, a magical control over them.

In Babylonia the agricultural myth regarding the Mother goddess and the young god had many variations. In one form Tammuz, like Adonis, was loved by two goddesses--the twin phases of nature--the Queen of Heaven and the Queen of Hades. It was decreed that Tammuz should spend part of the year with one goddess and part of the year with the other. Tammuz was also a Patriarch, who reigned for a long period over the land and had human offspring. After death his spirit appeared at certain times and seasons as a planet, star, or constellation. He was the ghost of the elder god, and he was also the younger god who was born each year.

In the Gilgamesh epic we appear to have a form of the patriarch legend--the story of the "culture hero" and teacher who discovered the path which led to the land of ancestral spirits. The heroic Patriarch in Egypt was Apuatu, "the opener of the ways", the earliest form of Osiris; in India he was Yama, the first man, "who searched and found out the path for many".

The King as Patriarch was regarded during life as an incarnation of the culture god: after death he merged in the god. "Sargon of Akkad" posed as an incarnation of the ancient agricultural Patriarch: he professed to be a man of miraculous birth who was loved by the goddess Ishtar, and was supposed to have inaugurated a New Age of the Universe.

The myth regarding the father who was superseded by his son may account for the existence in Babylonian city pantheons of elder and younger gods who symbolized the passive and active forces of nature.

Considering the persistent and cumulative influence exercised by agricultural religion it is not surprising to find, as has been indicated, that most of the Babylonian gods had Tammuz traits, as most of the Egyptian gods had Osirian traits. Although local or imported deities were developed and conventionalized in rival Babylonian cities, they still retained traces of primitive conceptions. They existed in all their forms--as the younger god who displaced the elder god and became the elder god, and as the elder god who conciliated the younger god and made him his active agent; and as the god who was identified at various seasons with different heavenly bodies and natural phenomena. Merodach, the god of Babylon, who was exalted as chief of the National pantheon in the Hammurabi Age, was, like Tammuz, a son, and therefore a form of Ea, a demon slayer, a war god, a god of fertility, a corn spirit, a Patriarch, and world ruler and guardian, and, like Tammuz, he had solar, lunar, astral, and atmospheric attributes. The complex characters of Merodach and Tammuz were not due solely to the monotheistic tendency: the oldest deities were of mystical character, they represented the "Self Power" of Naturalism as well as the spirit groups of Animism.

8

The theorizing priests, who speculated regarding the mysteries of life and death and the origin of all things, had to address the people through the medium of popular beliefs. They utilized floating myths for this purpose. As there were in early times various centres of culture which had rival pantheons, the adapted myths varied greatly. In the different forms in which they survive to us they reflect, not only aspects of local beliefs, but also grades of culture at different periods. We must not expect, however, to find that the latest form of a myth was the highest and most profound. The history of Babylonian religion is divided into periods of growth and periods of decadence. The influence of domestic religion was invariably opposed to the new and high doctrines which emanated from the priesthood, and in times of political upheaval tended to submerge them in the debris of immemorial beliefs and customs. The retrogressive tendencies of the masses were invariably reinforced by the periodic invasions of aliens who had no respect for official deities and temple creeds.

We must avoid insisting too strongly on the application of the evolution theory to the religious phenomena of a country like Babylonia.

The epochs in the intellectual life of an ancient people are not comparable to geological epochs, for instance, because the forces at work were directed by human wills, whether in the interests of progress or otherwise. The battle of creeds has ever been a battle of minds. It should be recognized, therefore, that the human element bulks as prominently in the drama of Babylon's religious history as does the prince of Denmark in the play of *Hamlet*. We are not concerned with the plot alone. The characters must also receive attention. Their aspirations and triumphs, their prejudices and blunders, were the billowy forces which shaped the shoreland of the story and made history.

Various aspects of Babylonian life and culture are dealt with throughout this volume, and it is shown that the growth of science and art was stimulated by unwholesome and crude superstitions. Many rank weeds flourished beside the brightest blossoms of the human intellect that wooed the sun in that fertile valley of rivers. As in Egypt, civilization made progress when wealth was accumulated in sufficient abundance to permit of a leisured class devoting time to study and research. The endowed priests, who performed temple ceremonies, were the teachers of the people and the patrons of culture. We may think little of their religious beliefs, regarding which after all we have only a superficial knowledge, for we have yet discovered little more than the fragments of the shell which held the pearl, the faded petals that were once a rose, but we must recognize that they provided inspiration for the artists and sculptors whose achievements compel our wonder and admiration, moved statesmen to inaugurate and administer humanitarian laws, and exalted Right above Might.

These civilizations of the old world, among which the Mesopotamian and the Nilotic were the earliest, were built on no unsound foundations. They made possible "the glory that was Greece and the grandeur that was Rome", and it is only within recent years that we have begun to realize how incalculable is the debt which the modern world owes to them.

---

[3] *Revelation*, xviii. The Babylon of the Apocalypse is generally believed to symbolize or be a mystic designation of Rome.

[4] *Nineveh and Its Remains*, vol. i, p. 17.

[5] *Ezra*, iv, 10.

[6] The culture god.

[7] Langdon's *Sumerian and Babylonian Psalms*, p. 179.

[8] *Crete the Forerunner of Greece*, p. 18.

[9] *The Scapegoat vol.*, p. 409 (3rd edition).

[10] *The Seven Tablets of Creation*, L. W. King, p. 129.

[11] *Ibid*, pp. 133-4.

Chapter I. The Races and Early Civilization of Babylonia

Abstract

Prehistoric Babylonia--The Confederacies of Sumer and Akkad--Sumerian Racial Affinities--Theories of Mongolian and Ural-Altaic Origins--Evidence of Russian Turkestan--Beginnings of Agriculture--Remarkable Proofs from Prehistoric Egyptian Graves--Sumerians and the Mediterranean Race--Present-day Types in Western Asia--The Evidence of Crania--Origin of the Akkadians--The Semitic Blend--Races in Ancient Palestine--Southward Drift of Armenoid Peoples--The Rephaims of the Bible--Akkadians attain Political Supremacy in Northern Babylonia--Influence of Sumerian Culture--Beginnings of Civilization--Progress in the Neolithic Age--Position of Women in Early Communities--Their Legal Status in Ancient Babylonia--Influence in Social and Religious Life--The "Woman's Language"--Goddess who inspired Poets.

Before the dawn of the historical period Ancient Babylonia was divided into a number of independent city states similar to those which existed in pre-Dynastic Egypt. Ultimately these were grouped into loose confederacies. The northern cities were embraced in the territory known as Akkad, and the southern in the land of Sumer, or Shumer. This division had a racial as well as a geographical significance. The Akkadians were "late comers" who had achieved political ascendency in the north when the area they occupied was called Uri, or Kiuri, and Sumer was known as Kengi. They were a people of Semitic speech with pronounced Semitic affinities. From the earliest times the sculptors depicted them with abundant locks, long full beards, and the prominent distinctive noses and full lips, which we usually associate with the characteristic Jewish type, and also attired in long, flounced robes, suspended from their left shoulders, and reaching down to their ankles. In contrast, the Sumerians had clean-shaven faces and scalps, and noses of Egyptian and Grecian rather than Semitic type, while they wore short, pleated kilts, and went about with the upper part of their bodies quite bare like the Egyptian noblemen of the Old Kingdom period. They spoke a non-Semitic language, and were the oldest inhabitants of Babylonia of whom we have any knowledge. Sumerian civilization was rooted in the agricultural mode of life, and appears to have been well developed before the Semites became numerous and influential in the land. Cities had been built chiefly of sun-dried and fire-baked bricks; distinctive pottery was manufactured with much skill; the people were governed by humanitarian laws, which formed the nucleus of the Hammurabi code, and had in use a system of cuneiform writing which was still in process of development from earlier pictorial characters. The distinctive feature of their agricultural methods was the engineering skill which was displayed in extending the cultivatable area by the construction of irrigating canals and ditches. There are also indications that they possessed some knowledge of navigation and traded on the Persian Gulf. According to one of their own traditions Eridu, originally a seaport, was their racial cradle. The Semitic Akkadians adopted the distinctive culture of these Sumerians after settlement, and exercised an influence on its subsequent growth.

Much controversy has been waged regarding the original home of the Sumerians and the particular racial type which they represented. One theory connects them with the lank-haired and beardless Mongolians, and it is asserted on the evidence afforded by early sculptural reliefs that they were similarly oblique-eyed. As they also spoke an agglutinative language, it is suggested that they were descended from the same parent stock as the Chinese in an ancient Parthian homeland. If, however, the oblique eye was not the result of faulty and primitive art, it is evident that the Mongolian type, which is invariably found to be remarkably persistent in racial blends, did not survive in the Tigris and Euphrates valleys, for in the finer and more exact sculpture work of the later Sumerian period the eyes of the ruling classes are found to be similar to those of the Ancient Egyptians and southern Europeans. Other facial characteristics suggest that a Mongolian racial connection is highly improbable; the prominent Sumerian nose, for instance, is quite unlike the Chinese, which is diminutive. Nor can far-reaching conclusions be drawn from the scanty linguistic evidence at our disposal. Although the languages of the Sumerians and long-headed Chinese are of the agglutinative variety, so are those also which are spoken by the broad-headed Turks and Magyars of Hungary, the broad-headed and long-headed, dark and fair Finns, and the brunet and short-statured Basques with pear-shaped faces, who are regarded as a variation of the Mediterranean race with distinctive characteristics developed in isolation. Languages afford no sure indication of racial origins or affinities.

Another theory connects the Sumerians with the broad-headed peoples of the Western Asian plains and plateaus, who are vaguely grouped as Ural-Altaic stock and are represented by the present-day Turks and the dark variety of Finns. It is assumed that they migrated southward in remote times in consequence of tribal pressure caused by changing climatic conditions, and abandoned a purely pastoral for an agricultural life. The late Sumerian sculpture work again presents difficulties in this connection, for the faces and bulging occiputs suggest rather a long-headed than a broad-headed type, and the theory no longer obtains that new habits of life alter skull forms which are usually associated with other distinctive traits in the structure of skeletons. These broad-headed nomadic peoples of the Steppes are allied to Tatar stock, and distinguished from the pure Mongols by their abundance of wavy hair and beard. The fact that the Sumerians shaved their scalps and faces is highly suggestive in this connection. From the earliest times it has been the habit of most peoples to emphasize their racial characteristics so as to be able, one may suggest, to distinguish readily a friend from a foeman. At any rate this fact is generally recognized by ethnologists. The Basques, for instance, shave their pointed chins and sometimes grow short side whiskers to increase the distinctive pear-shape which is given to their faces by their prominent temples. In contrast, their neighbours, the Andalusians, grow chin whiskers to broaden their already rounded chins, and to distinguish them markedly from the Basques.[12] Another example of similar character is afforded in Asia Minor, where the skulls of the children of long-headed Kurds are narrowed, and those of the children of broad-headed Armenians made flatter behind as a result of systematic pressure applied by using cradle boards. In this way these rival peoples accentuate their contrasting head forms, which at times may, no doubt, show a tendency towards variation as a result of the crossment of types. When it is found, therefore, that the Sumerians, like the Ancient Egyptians, were in the habit of shaving, their ethnic affinities should be looked for among a naturally glabrous rather than a heavily-bearded people.

A Central Asiatic source for Sumerian culture has also been urged of late with much circumstantial detail. It breaks quite fresh and interesting ground. Recent scientific expeditions in Russian and Chinese Turkestan have accumulated important archaeological data which clearly establish that vast areas of desert country were at a remote period most verdurous and fruitful, and thickly populated by organized and apparently progressive communities. From these ancient centres of civilization wholesale migrations must have been impelled from time to time in consequence of the gradual encroachment of wind-distributed sand and the increasing shortage of water. At Anau in Russian Turkestan, where excavations were conducted by the Pumpelly expedition, abundant traces were found of an archaic and forgotten civilization reaching back to the Late Stone Age. The pottery is decorated with geometric designs, and resembles somewhat other Neolithic specimens found as far apart as Susa, the capital of ancient Elam, on the borders of Babylonia, Boghaz Köi in Asia Minor, the seat of Hittite administration, round the Black Sea to the north, and at points in the southern regions of the Balkan Peninsula. It is suggested that these various finds are scattered evidences of early racial drifts from the Central Asian areas which were gradually being rendered uninhabitable. Among the Copper Age artifacts at Anau are clay votive statuettes resembling those which were used in Sumeria for religious purposes. These, however, cannot be held to prove a racial connection, but they are important in so far as they afford evidence of early trade relations in a hitherto unsuspected direction, and the long distances over which cultural influence extended before the dawn of history. Further we cannot go. No inscriptions have yet been discovered to render articulate this mysterious Central Asian civilization, or to suggest the original source of early Sumerian picture writing. Nor is it possible to confirm Mr. Pumpelly's view that from the Anau district the Sumerians and Egyptians first obtained barley and wheat, and some of their domesticated animals. If, as Professor Elliot Smith believes, copper was first used by the Ancient Egyptians, it may be, on the other hand, that a knowledge of this metal reached Anau through Sumeria, and that the elements of the earlier culture were derived from the same quarter by an indirect route. The evidence obtainable in Egypt is of interest in this connection. Large quantities of food have been taken from the stomachs and intestines of sun-dried bodies which have lain in their pre-Dynastic graves for over sixty centuries. This material has been carefully examined, and has yielded, among other things, husks of barley and millet, and fragments of mammalian bones, including those, no doubt, of the domesticated sheep and goats and cattle painted on the pottery.[13] It is therefore apparent that at an extremely remote period a knowledge of agriculture extended throughout Egypt, and we have no reason for supposing that it was not shared by the contemporary inhabitants of Sumer.

The various theories which have been propounded regarding the outside source of Sumerian culture are based on the assumption that it commenced abruptly and full grown. Its rude beginnings cannot be traced on the banks of the Tigris and Euphrates, but although no specimens of the earliest form of picture writing have been recovered from the ruins of Sumerian and Akkadian cities, neither have any been found elsewhere. The possibility remains, therefore, that early Babylonian culture was indigenous. "A great deal of ingenuity has been displayed by many scholars", says Professor Elliot Smith, "with the object of bringing these Sumerians from somewhere else as immigrants into Sumer; but no reasons have been advanced to show that they had not been settled at the head of the Persian Gulf for long generations before they first appeared on the stage of history. The argument that no early remains have been found is futile, not only because such a country as Sumer is no more favourable to the preservation of such evidence than is the Delta of the Nile, but also upon the more general grounds that negative statements of this sort cannot be assigned a positive evidence for an immigration."[14] This distinguished ethnologist is frankly of opinion that the Sumerians were the congeners of the pre-Dynastic Egyptians of the Mediterranean or Brown race, the eastern branch of which reaches to India and the western to the British Isles and Ireland. In the same ancient family are included the Arabs, whose physical characteristics distinguish them from the Semites of Jewish type.

Some light may be thrown on the Sumerian problem by giving consideration to the present-day racial complexion of Western Asia. The importance of evidence of this character has been emphasized elsewhere. In Egypt, for instance, Dr. C.S. Myers has ascertained that the modern peasants have skull forms which are identical with those of their pre-Dynastic ancestors.

Mr. Hawes has also demonstrated that the ancient inhabitants of Crete are still represented on that famous island. But even more remarkable is the fact that the distinctive racial type which occupied the Palaeolithic caves of the Dordogne valley in France continues to survive in their vicinity after an interval of over twenty thousand years.[15] It is noteworthy, therefore, to find that in south-western Asia at the present day one particular racial type predominates over all others. Professor Ripley, who summarizes a considerable mass of data in this connection, refers to it as the "Iranian", and says: "It includes the Persians and Kurds, possibly the Ossetes in the Caucasus, and farther to the east a large number of Asiatic tribes, from the Afghans to the Hindus. These peoples are all primarily long-headed and dark brunets. They incline to slenderness of habit, although varying in stature according to circumstances. In them we recognize at once undoubted congeners of our Mediterranean race in Europe. The area of their extension runs off into Africa, through the Egyptians, who are clearly of the same race. Not only the modern peoples, but the Ancient Egyptians and the Phoenicians also have been traced to the same source. By far the largest portion of this part of Western Asia is inhabited by this eastern branch of the Mediterranean race." The broad-headed type "occurs sporadically among a few ethnic remnants in Syria and Mesopotamia".[16] The exhaustive study of thousands of ancient crania in London and Cambridge collections has shown that Mediterranean peoples, having alien traits, the result of early admixture, were distributed between Egypt and the Punjab.[17] Where blending took place, the early type, apparently, continued to predominate; and it appears to be reasserting itself in our own time in Western Asia, as elsewhere. It seems doubtful, therefore, that the ancient Sumerians differed racially from the pre-Dynastic inhabitants of Egypt and the Pelasgians and Iberians of Europe. Indeed, the statuettes from Tello, the site of the Sumerian city of Lagash, display distinctively Mediterranean skull forms and faces. Some of the plump figures of the later period suggest, however, "the particular alien strain" which in Egypt and elsewhere "is always associated with a tendency to the development of fat", in contrast to "the lean and sinewy appearance of most representatives of the Brown race".[18] This change may be accounted for by the presence of the Semites in northern Babylonia.

Whence, then, came these invading Semitic Akkadians of Jewish type? It is generally agreed that they were closely associated with one of the early outpourings of nomadic peoples from Arabia, a country which is favourable for the production of a larger population than it is able to maintain permanently, especially when its natural resources are restricted by a succession of abnormally dry years. In tracing the Akkadians from Arabia, however, we are confronted at the outset with the difficulty that its prehistoric, and many of its present-day, inhabitants are not of the characteristic Semitic type. On the Ancient Egyptian pottery and monuments the Arabs are depicted as men who closely resembled the representatives of the Mediterranean race in the Nile valley and elsewhere. They shaved neither scalps nor faces as did the historic Sumerians and Egyptians, but grew the slight moustache and chin-tuft beard like the Libyans on the north and the majority of the men whose bodies have been preserved in pre-Dynastic graves in the Nile valley. "If", writes Professor Elliot Smith, "the generally accepted view is true, that Arabia was the original home of the Semites, the Arab must have undergone a profound change in his physical characters after he left his homeland and before he reached Babylonia." This authority is of opinion that the Arabians first migrated into Palestine and northern Syria, where they mingled with the southward-migrating Armenoid peoples from Asia Minor. "This blend of Arabs, kinsmen of the proto-Egyptians and Armenoids, would then form the big-nosed, long-bearded Semites, so familiar not only on the ancient Babylonian and Egyptian monuments, but also in the modern Jews."[19] Such a view is in accord with Dr. Hugo Winckler's contention that the flow of Arabian migrations was northwards towards Syria ere it swept through Mesopotamia. It can scarcely be supposed that these invasions of settled districts did not result in the fusion and crossment of racial types and the production of a sub-variety with medium skull form and marked facial characteristics.

Of special interest in this connection is the evidence afforded by Palestine and Egypt. The former country has ever been subject to periodic ethnic disturbances and changes. Its racial history has a remote beginning in the Pleistocene Age. Palaeolithic flints of Chellean and other primitive types have been found in large numbers, and a valuable collection of these is being preserved in a French museum at Jerusalem. In a northern cave fragments of rude pottery, belonging to an early period in the Late Stone Age, have been discovered in association with the bones of the woolly rhinoceros. To a later period belong the series of Gezer cave dwellings, which, according to Professor Macalister, the well-known Palestinian authority, "were occupied by a non-Semitic people of low stature, with thick skulls and showing evidence of the great muscular strength that is essential to savage life".[20] These people are generally supposed to be representatives of the Mediterranean race, which Sergi has found to have been widely distributed throughout Syria and a part of Asia Minor.[21] An interesting problem, however, is raised by the fact that, in one of the caves, there are evidences that the dead were cremated. This was not a Mediterranean custom, nor does it appear to have prevailed outside the Gezer area. If, however, it does not indicate that the kinsmen of the Ancient Egyptians came into contact with the remnants of an earlier people, it may be that the dead of a later people were burned there. The possibility that unidentified types may have contributed to the Semitic blend, however, remains. The Mediterraneans mingled in Northern Syria and Asia Minor with the broad-headed Armenoid peoples who are represented in Europe by the Alpine race. With them they ultimately formed the great Hittite confederacy. These Armenoids were moving southwards at the very dawn of Egyptian history, and nothing is known of their conquests and settlements. Their pioneers, who were probably traders, appear to have begun to enter the Delta region before the close of the Late Stone Age.[22] The earliest outpourings of migrating Arabians may have been in progress about the same time. This early southward drift of Armenoids might account for the presence in southern Palestine, early in the Copper Age, of the tall race referred to in the Bible as the Rephaim or Anakim, "whose power was broken only by the Hebrew invaders".[23] Joshua drove them out of Hebron,[24] in the neighbourhood of which Abraham had purchased a burial cave from Ephron, the Hittite.[25] Apparently a system of land laws prevailed in Palestine at this early period. It is of special interest for us to note that in Abraham's day and afterwards, the landed proprietors in the country of the Rephaim were identified with the aliens from Asia Minor--the tall variety in the Hittite confederacy.

Little doubt need remain that the Arabians during their sojourn in Palestine and Syria met with distinctive types, and if not with pure Armenoids, at any rate with peoples having Armenoid traits. The consequent multiplication of tribes, and the gradual pressure exercised by the constant stream of immigrants from Arabia and Asia Minor, must have kept this part of Western Asia in a constant state of unrest. Fresh migrations of the surplus stock were evidently propelled towards Egypt in one direction, and the valleys of the Tigris and Euphrates in another. The Semites of Akkad were probably the conquerors of the more highly civilized Sumerians, who must have previously occupied that area. It is possible that they owed their success to the possession of superior weapons. Professor Elliot Smith suggests in this connection that the Arabians had become familiar with the use of copper as a result of contact with the Egyptians in Sinai. There is no evidence, however, that the Sumerians were attacked before they had begun to make metal weapons. It is more probable that the invading nomads had superior military organization and considerable experience in waging war against detached tribal units. They may have also found some of the northern Sumerian city states at war with one another and taken advantage of their unpreparedness to resist a common enemy. The rough Dorians who overran Greece and the fierce Goths who shattered the power of Rome were similarly in a lower state of civilization than the peoples whom they subdued.

The Sumerians, however, ultimately achieved an intellectual conquest of their conquerors. Although the leaders of invasion may have formed military aristocracies in the cities which they occupied, it was necessary for the great majority of the nomads to engage their activities in new directions after settlement. The Semitic Akkadians, therefore, adopted Sumerian habits of life which were best suited for the needs of the country, and they consequently came under the spell of Sumerian modes of thought. This is shown by the fact that the native speech of ancient Sumer continued long after the dawn of history to be the language of Babylonian religion and culture, like Latin in Europe during the Middle Ages. For centuries the mingling peoples must have been bilingual, as are many of the inhabitants of Ireland, Wales, and the Scottish Highlands in the present age, but ultimately the language of the Semites became the prevailing speech in Sumer and Akkad. This change was the direct result of the conquests and the political supremacy achieved by the northern people. A considerable period elapsed, however, ere this consummation was reached and Ancient Babylonia became completely Semitized. No doubt its brilliant historical civilization owed much of its vigour and stability to the organizing genius of the Semites, but the basis on which it was established had been laid by the ingenious and imaginative Sumerians who first made the desert to blossom like the rose.

The culture of Sumer was a product of the Late Stone Age, which should not be regarded as necessarily an age of barbarism. During its vast periods there were great discoveries and great inventions in various parts of Asia, Africa, and Europe. The Neoliths made pottery and bricks; we know that they invented the art of spinning, for spindle-whorls are found even in the Gezer caves to which we have referred, while in Egypt the pre-Dynastic dead were sometimes wrapped in finely woven linen: their deftly chipped flint implements are eloquent of artistic and mechanical skill, and undoubted mathematical ability must be credited to the makers of smoothly polished stone hammers which are so perfectly balanced that they revolve on a centre of gravity. In Egypt and Babylonia the soil was tilled and its fertility increased by irrigation. Wherever man waged a struggle with Nature he made rapid progress, and consequently we find that the earliest great civilizations were rooted in the little fields of the Neolithic farmers. Their mode of life necessitated a knowledge of Nature's laws; they had to take note of the seasons and measure time. So Egypt gave us the Calendar, and Babylonia the system of dividing the week into seven days, and the day into twelve double hours.

The agricultural life permitted large communities to live in river valleys, and these had to be governed by codes of laws; settled communities required peace and order for their progress and prosperity. All great civilizations have evolved from the habits and experiences of settled communities. Law and religion were closely associated, and the evidence afforded by the remains of stone circles and temples suggests that in the organization and division of labour the influence of religious teachers was pre-eminent. Early rulers, indeed, were priest-kings -- incarnations of the deity who owned the land and measured out the span of human life.

We need not assume that Neolithic man led an idyllic existence; his triumphs were achieved by slow and gradual steps; his legal codes were, no doubt, written in blood and his institutions welded in the fires of adversity. But, disciplined by laws, which fostered humanitarian ideals, Neolithic man, especially of the Mediterranean race, had reached a comparatively high state of civilization long ages before the earliest traces of his activities can be obtained. When this type of mankind is portrayed in Ancient Sumeria, Ancient Egypt, and Ancient Crete we find that the faces are refined and intellectual and often quite modern in aspect. The skulls show that in the Late Stone Age the human brain was fully developed and that the racial types were fixed. In every country in Europe we still find the direct descendants of the ancient Mediterranean race, as well as the descendants of the less highly cultured conquerors who swept westward out of Asia at the dawn of the Bronze Age; and everywhere there are evidences of crossment of types in varying degrees. Even the influence of Neolithic intellectual life still remains. The comparative study of mythology and folk beliefs reveals that we have inherited certain modes of thought from our remote ancestors, who were the congeners of the Ancient Sumerians and the Ancient Egyptians. In this connection it is of interest, therefore, to refer to the social ideals of the early peoples who met and mingled on the southern plains of the Tigris and Euphrates, and especially the position occupied by women, which is engaging so much attention at the present day.

It would appear that among the Semites and other nomadic peoples woman was regarded as the helpmate rather than the companion and equal of man. The birth of a son was hailed with joy; it was "miserable to have a daughter", as a Hindu sage reflected; in various countries it was the custom to expose female children after birth and leave them to die. A wife had no rights other than those accorded to her by her husband, who exercised over her the power of life and death. Sons inherited family possessions; the daughters had no share allotted to them, and could be sold by fathers and brothers. Among the peoples who observed "male right", social life was reflected in the conception of controlling male deities, accompanied by shadowy goddesses who were often little else than figures of speech.

The Ancient Sumerians, on the other hand, like the Mediterranean peoples of Egypt and Crete, reverenced and exalted motherhood in social and religious life. Women were accorded a legal status and marriage laws were promulgated by the State. Wives could possess private property in their own right, as did the Babylonian Sarah, wife of Abraham, who owned the Egyptian slave Hagar.[26] A woman received from her parents a marriage dowry, and in the event of separation from her husband she could claim its full value. Some spinsters, or wives, were accustomed to enter into business partnerships with men or members of their own sex, and could sue and be sued in courts of law. Brothers and sisters were joint heirs of the family estate. Daughters might possess property over which their fathers exercised no control: they could also enter into legal agreements with their parents in business matters, when they had attained to years of discretion. Young women who took vows of celibacy and lived in religious institutions could yet make business investments, as surviving records show. There is only one instance of a Sumerian woman ascending the throne, like Queen Hatshepsut of Egypt. Women, therefore, were not rigidly excluded from official life. Dungi II, an early Sumerian king, appointed two of his daughters as rulers of conquered cities in Syria and Elam. Similarly Shishak, the Egyptian Pharaoh, handed over the city of Gezer, which he had subdued, to his daughter, Solomon's wife.[27] In the religious life of ancient Sumeria the female population exercised an undoubted influence, and in certain temples there were priestesses. The oldest hymns give indication of the respect shown to women by making reference to mixed assemblies as "females and males", just as present-day orators address themselves to "ladies and gentlemen". In the later Semitic adaptations of these productions, it is significant to note, this conventional reference was altered to "male and female". If influences, however, were at work to restrict the position of women they did not meet with much success, because when Hammurabi codified existing laws, the ancient rights of women received marked recognition.

There were two dialects in ancient Sumeria, and the invocatory hymns were composed in what was known as "the women's language". It must not be inferred, however, that the ladies of Sumeria had established a speech which differed from that used by men. The reference would appear to be to a softer and homelier dialect, perhaps the oldest of the two, in which poetic emotion found fullest and most beautiful expression. In these ancient days, as in our own, the ideal of womanhood was the poet's chief source of inspiration, and among the hymns the highest reach of poetic art was attained in the invocation of Ishtar, the Babylonian Venus. The following hymn is addressed to that deity in her Valkyrie-like character as a goddess of war, but her more feminine traits are not obscured:--

HYMN TO ISHTAR

To thee I cry, O lady of the gods,
Lady of ladies, goddess without peer,
Ishtar who shapes the lives of all mankind,
Thou stately world queen, sovran of the sky,
And lady ruler of the host of heaven--
Illustrious is thy name.... O light divine,
Gleaming in lofty splendour o'er the earth--
Heroic daughter of the moon, oh! hear;
Thou dost control our weapons and award
In battles fierce the victory at will--
crown'd majestic Fate. Ishtar most high,
Who art exalted over all the gods,
Thou bringest lamentation; thou dost urge
With hostile hearts our brethren to the fray;
The gift of strength is thine for thou art strong;
Thy will is urgent, brooking no delay;
Thy hand is violent, thou queen of war
Girded with battle and enrobed with fear...
Thou sovran wielder of the wand of Doom,
The heavens and earth are under thy control.

Adored art thou in every sacred place,
In temples, holy dwellings, and in shrines,
Where is thy name not lauded? where thy will
Unheeded, and thine images not made?
Where are thy temples not upreared? O, where
Art thou not mighty, peerless, and supreme?

Anu and Bel and Ea have thee raised
To rank supreme, in majesty and pow'r,
They have established thee above the gods
And all the host of heaven... O stately queen,
At thought of thee the world is filled with fear,
The gods in heaven quake, and on the earth
All spirits pause, and all mankind bow down
With reverence for thy name.... O Lady Judge,

Thy ways are just and holy; thou dost gaze
On sinners with compassion, and each morn
Leadest the wayward to the rightful path.

Now linger not, but come! O goddess fair,
O shepherdess of all, thou drawest nigh
With feet unwearied... Thou dost break the bonds
Of these thy handmaids... When thou stoopest o'er
The dying with compassion, lo! they live;
And when the sick behold thee they are healed.

Hear me, thy servant! hearken to my pray'r,
For I am full of sorrow and I sigh
In sore distress; weeping, on thee I wait.

Be merciful, my lady, pity take
And answer, "'Tis enough and be appeased".

How long must my heart sorrow and make moan
And restless be? How long must my dark home
Be filled with mourning and my soul with grief?
O lioness of heaven, bring me peace
And rest and comfort. Hearken to my pray'r!
Is anger pity? May thine eyes look down
With tenderness and blessings, and behold
Thy servant. Oh! have mercy; hear my cry
And unbewitch me from the evil spells,
That I may see thy glory... Oh! how long
Shall these my foes pursue me, working ill,
And robbing me of joy?... Oh! how long
Shall demons compass me about and cause
Affliction without end?... I thee adore--
The gift of strength is thine and thou art strong--
The weakly are made strong, yet I am weak...
O hear me! I am glutted with my grief--
This flood of grief by evil winds distressed;
My heart hath fled me like a bird on wings,
And like the dove I moan. Tears from mine eyes
Are falling as the rain from heaven falls,
And I am destitute and full of woe.

     *   *   *   *   *

What have I done that thou hast turned from me?
Have I neglected homage to my god
And thee my goddess? O deliver me
And all my sins forgive, that I may share
Thy love and be watched over in thy fold;
And may thy fold be wide, thy pen secure.

     *   *   *   *   *

How long wilt thou be angry? Hear my cry,
And turn again to prosper all my ways--
O may thy wrath be crumbled and withdrawn
As by a crumbling stream. Then smite my foes,
And take away their power to work me ill,
That I may crush them. Hearken to my pray'r!
And bless me so that all who me behold
May laud thee and may magnify thy name,
While I exalt thy power over all--
Ishtar is highest! Ishtar is the queen!
Ishtar the peerless daughter of the moon!

[12] *The Races of Europe*, W.Z. Ripley, p. 203.
[13] *The Ancient Egyptians*, by Elliot Smith, p. 41 *et seq.*
[14] *The Ancient Egyptians*, p. 140.
[15] *Crete the Forerunner of Greece*, C. H. and H. B. Hawes, 1911, p. 23 *et seq.*
[16] *The Races of Europe*, W. Z. Ripley, p. 443 *et seq.*
[17] *The Ancient Egyptians*, pp. 144-5.
[18] *The Ancient Egyptians*, p. 114.
[19] *The Ancient Egyptians*, p. 136.
[20] *A History of Palestine*, R.A.S. Macalister, pp. 8-16.
[21] *The Mediterranean Race* (1901 trans.), G. Sergi, p. 146 *et seq.*
[22] *The Ancient Egyptians*, p. 130.
[23] *A History of Civilization in Palestine*, p. 20 et seq.

[24] *Joshua*, xi. 21.

[25] *Genesis*, xxiii.

[26] *Genesis*, xvi. 8, 9.

[27] *1 Kings*, xvi. 16.

Chapter II. The Land of Rivers and the God of the Deep

Abstract

Fertility of Ancient Babylonia--Rivers, Canals, Seasons, and Climate--Early Trade and Foreign Influences--Local Religious Cults--Ea, God of the Deep, identical with Oannes of Berosus--Origin as a Sacred Fish--Compared with Brahma and Vishnu--Flood Legends in Babylonia and India--Fish Deities in Babylonia and Egypt--Fish God as a Corn God--The River as Creator--Ea an Artisan God, and links with Egypt and India--Ea as the Hebrew Jah--Ea and Varuna are Water and Sky Gods--The Babylonian Dagan and Dagon of the Philistines--Deities of Water and Harvest in Phoenicia, Greece, Rome, Scotland, Scandinavia, Ireland, and Egypt--Ea's Spouse Damkina--Demons of Ocean in Babylonia and India--Anu, God of the Sky--Enlil, Storm and War God of Nippur, like Adad, Odin, &c.--Early Gods of Babylonia and Egypt of common origin--Ea's City as Cradle of Sumerian Civilization.

Ancient Babylonia was for over four thousand years the garden of Western Asia. In the days of Hezekiah and Isaiah, when it had come under the sway of the younger civilization of Assyria on the north, it was "a land of corn and wine, a land of bread and vineyards, a land of oil olive and of honey[28]". Herodotus found it still flourishing and extremely fertile. "This territory", he wrote, "is of all that we know the best by far for producing grain; it is so good that it returns as much as two hundredfold for the average, and, when it bears at its best, it produces three hundredfold. The blades of the wheat and barley there grow to be full four fingers broad; and from millet and sesame seed, how large a tree grows, I know myself, but shall not record, being well aware that even what has already been said relating to the crops produced has been enough to cause disbelief in those who have not visited Babylonia[29]." To-day great tracts of undulating moorland, which aforetime yielded two and three crops a year, are in summer partly barren wastes and partly jungle and reedy swamp. Bedouins camp beside sandy heaps which were once populous and thriving cities, and here and there the shrunken remnants of a people once great and influential eke out precarious livings under the oppression of Turkish tax-gatherers who are scarcely less considerate than the plundering nomads of the desert.

This historic country is bounded on the east by Persia and on the west by the Arabian desert. In shape somewhat resembling a fish, it lies between the two great rivers, the Tigris and the Euphrates, 100 miles wide at its broadest part, and narrowing to 35 miles towards the "tail" in the latitude of Baghdad; the "head" converges to a point above Basra, where the rivers meet and form the Shatt-el-Arab, which pours into the Persian Gulf after meeting the Karun and drawing away the main volume of that double-mouthed river. The distance from Baghdad to Basra is about 300 miles, and the area traversed by the Shatt-el-Arab is slowly extending at the rate of a mile every thirty years or so, as a result of the steady accumulation of silt and mud carried down by the Tigris and Euphrates. When Sumeria was beginning to flourish, these two rivers had separate outlets, and Eridu, the seat of the cult of the sea god Ea, which now lies 125 miles inland, was a seaport at the head of the Persian Gulf. A day's journey separated the river mouths when Alexander the Great broke the power of the Persian Empire.

In the days of Babylonia's prosperity the Euphrates was hailed as "the soul of the land" and the Tigris as "the bestower of blessings". Skilful engineers had solved the problem of water distribution by irrigating sun-parched areas and preventing the excessive flooding of those districts which are now rendered impassable swamps when the rivers overflow. A network of canals was constructed throughout the country, which restricted the destructive tendencies of the Tigris and Euphrates and developed to a high degree their potentialities as fertilizing agencies. The greatest of these canals appear to have been anciently river beds. One, which is called Shatt en Nil to the north, and Shatt el Kar to the south, curved eastward from Babylon, and sweeping past Nippur, flowed like the letter **S** towards Larsa and then rejoined the river. It is believed to mark the course followed in the early Sumerian period by the Euphrates river, which has moved steadily westward many miles beyond the sites of ancient cities that were erected on its banks. Another important canal, the Shatt el Hai, crossed the plain from the Tigris to its sister river, which lies lower at this point, and does not run so fast. Where the artificial canals were constructed on higher levels than the streams which fed them, the water was raised by contrivances known as "shaddufs"; the buckets or skin bags were roped to a weighted beam, with the aid of which they were swung up by workmen and emptied into the canals. It is possible that this toilsome mode of irrigation was substituted in favourable parts by the primitive water wheels which are used in our own day by the inhabitants of the country who cultivate strips of land along the river banks.

In Babylonia there are two seasons--the rainy and the dry. Rain falls from November till March, and the plain is carpeted in spring by patches of vivid green verdure and brilliant wild flowers. Then the period of drought ensues; the sun rapidly burns up all vegetation, and everywhere the eye is wearied by long stretches of brown and yellow desert. Occasional sandstorms darken the heavens, sweeping over sterile wastes and piling up the shapeless mounds which mark the sites of ancient cities. Meanwhile the rivers are increasing in volume, being fed by the melting snows at their mountain sources far to the north. The swift Tigris, which is 1146 miles long, begins to rise early in March and reaches its highest level in May; before the end of June it again subsides. More sluggish in movement, the Euphrates, which is 1780 miles long, shows signs of rising a fortnight later than the Tigris, and is in flood for a more extended period; it does not shrink to its lowest level until early in September. By controlling the flow of these mighty rivers, preventing disastrous floods, and storing and distributing surplus water, the ancient Babylonians developed to the full the natural resources of their country, and made it--what it may once again become--one of the fairest and most habitable areas in the world. Nature conferred upon them bountiful rewards for their labour; trade and industries flourished, and the cities increased in splendour and strength. Then as now the heat was great during the long summer, but remarkably dry and unvarying, while the air was ever wonderfully transparent under cloudless skies of vivid blue. The nights were cool and of great beauty, whether in brilliant moonlight or when ponds and canals were jewelled by the lustrous displays of clear and numerous stars which glorified that homeland of the earliest astronomers.

Babylonia is a treeless country, and timber had to be imported from the earliest times. The date palm was probably introduced by man, as were certainly the vine and the fig tree, which were widely cultivated, especially in the north. Stone, suitable for building, was very scarce, and limestone, alabaster, marble, and basalt had to be taken from northern Mesopotamia, where the mountains also yield copper and lead and iron. Except Eridu, where ancient workers quarried sandstone from its sea-shaped ridge, all the cities were built of brick, an excellent clay being found in abundance. When brick walls were cemented with bitumen they were given great stability. This resinous substance is found in the north and south. It bubbles up through crevices of rocks on river banks and forms small ponds. Two famous springs at modern Hit, on the Euphrates, have been drawn upon from time immemorial. "From one", writes a traveller, "flows hot water black with bitumen, while the other discharges intermittently bitumen, or, after a rainstorm, bitumen and cold water.... Where rocks crop out in the plain above Hit, they are full of seams of bitumen."[30] Present-day Arabs call it "kiyara", and export it for coating boats and roofs; they also use it as an antiseptic, and apply it to cure the skin diseases from which camels suffer.

Sumeria had many surplus products, including corn and figs, pottery, fine wool and woven garments, to offer in exchange for what it most required from other countries. It must, therefore, have had a brisk and flourishing foreign trade at an exceedingly remote period. No doubt numerous alien merchants were attracted to its cities, and it may be that they induced or encouraged Semitic and other raiders to overthrow governments and form military aristocracies, so that they themselves might obtain necessary concessions and achieve a degree of political ascendancy. It does not follow, however, that the peasant class was greatly affected by periodic revolutions of this kind, which brought little more to them than a change of rulers. The needs of the country necessitated the continuance of agricultural methods and the rigid observance of existing land laws; indeed, these constituted the basis of Sumerian prosperity. Conquerors have ever sought reward not merely in spoil, but also the services of the conquered. In northern Babylonia the invaders apparently found it necessary to conciliate and secure the continued allegiance of the tillers of the soil. Law and religion being closely associated, they had to adapt their gods to suit the requirements of existing social and political organizations. A deity of pastoral nomads had to receive attributes which would give him an agricultural significance; one of rural character had to be changed to respond to the various calls of city life. Besides, local gods could not be ignored on account of their popularity. As a result, imported beliefs and religious customs must have been fused and absorbed according to their bearing on modes of life in various localities. It is probable that the complex character of certain deities was due to the process of adjustment to which they were subjected in new environments.

The petty kingdoms of Sumeria appear to have been tribal in origin. Each city was presided over by a deity who was the nominal owner of the surrounding arable land, farms were rented or purchased from the priesthood, and pasture was held in common. As in Egypt, where we find, for instance, the artisan god Ptah supreme at Memphis, the sun god Ra at Heliopolis, and the cat goddess Bast at Bubastis, the various local Sumerian and Akkadian deities had distinctive characteristics, and similarly showed a tendency to absorb the attributes of their rivals. The chief deity of a state was the central figure in a pantheon, which had its political aspect and

18

influenced the growth of local theology. Cities, however, did not, as a rule, bear the names of deities, which suggests that several were founded when Sumerian religion was in its early animistic stages, and gods and goddesses were not sharply defined from the various spirit groups.

A distinctive and characteristic Sumerian god was Ea, who was supreme at the ancient sea-deserted port of Eridu. He is identified with the Oannes of Berosus,[31] who referred to the deity as "a creature endowed with reason, with a body like that of a fish, with feet below like those of a man, with a fish's tail". This description recalls the familiar figures of Egyptian gods and priests attired in the skins of the sacred animals from whom their powers were derived, and the fairy lore about swan maids and men, and the seals and other animals who could divest themselves of their "skin coverings" and appear in human shape. Originally Ea may have been a sacred fish. The Indian creative gods Brahma and Vishnu had fish forms. In Sanskrit literature Manu, the eponymous "first man", is instructed by the fish to build a ship in which to save himself when the world would be purged by the rising waters. Ea befriended in similar manner the Babylonian Noah, called Pir-napishtim, advising him to build a vessel so as to be prepared for the approaching Deluge. Indeed the Indian legend appears to throw light on the original Sumerian conception of Ea. It relates that when the fish was small and in danger of being swallowed by other fish in a stream it appealed to Manu for protection. The sage at once lifted up the fish and placed it in a jar of water. It gradually increased in bulk, and he transferred it next to a tank and then to the river Ganges. In time the fish complained to Manu that the river was too small for it, so he carried it to the sea. For these services the god in fish form instructed Manu regarding the approaching flood, and afterwards piloted his ship through the weltering waters until it rested on a mountain top.[32]

If this Indian myth is of Babylonian origin, as appears probable, it may be that the spirit of the river Euphrates, "the soul of the land", was identified with a migrating fish. The growth of the fish suggests the growth of the river rising in flood. In Celtic folk tales high tides and valley floods are accounted for by the presence of a "great beast" in sea, loch, or river. In a class of legends, "specially connected with the worship of Atargatis", wrote Professor Robertson Smith, "the divine life of the waters resides in the sacred fish that inhabit them. Atargatis and her son, according to a legend common to Hierapolis and Ascalon, plunged into the waters--in the first case the Euphrates, in the second the sacred pool at the temple near the town--and were changed into fishes". The idea is that "where a god dies, that is, ceases to exist in human form, his life passes into the waters where he is buried; and this again is merely a theory to bring the divine water or the divine fish into harmony with anthropomorphic ideas. The same thing was sometimes effected in another way by saying that the anthropomorphic deity was born from the water, as Aphrodite sprang from sea foam, or as Atargatis, in another form of the Euphrates legend, ... was born of an egg which the sacred fishes found in the Euphrates and pushed ashore."[33]

As "Shar Apsi", Ea was the "King of the Watery Deep". The reference, however, according to Jastrow, "is not to the salt ocean, but the sweet waters flowing under the earth which feed the streams, and through streams and canals irrigate the fields".[34] As Babylonia was fertilized by its rivers, Ea, the fish god, was a fertilizing deity. In Egypt the "Mother of Mendes" is depicted carrying a fish upon her head; she links with Isis and Hathor; her husband is Ba-neb-Tettu, a form of Ptah, Osiris, and Ra, and as a god of fertility he is symbolized by the ram. Another Egyptian fish deity was the god Rem, whose name signifies "to weep"; he wept fertilizing tears, and corn was sown and reaped amidst lamentations. He may be identical with Remi, who was a phase of Sebek, the crocodile god, a developed attribute of Nu, the vague primitive Egyptian deity who symbolized the primordial deep. The connection between a fish god and a corn god is not necessarily remote when we consider that in Babylonia and Egypt the harvest was the gift of the rivers.

The Euphrates, indeed, was hailed as a creator of all that grew on its banks.

O thou River who didst create all things,
When the great gods dug thee out,
They set prosperity upon thy banks,
Within thee Ea, the King of the Deep, created his dwelling...
Thou judgest the cause of mankind!
O River, thou art mighty! O River, thou art supreme!
O River, thou art righteous![35]

In serving Ea, the embodiment or the water spirit, by leading him, as the Indian Manu led the Creator and "Preserver" in fish form, from river to water pot, water pot to pond or canal, and then again to river and ocean, the Babylonians became expert engineers and experienced agriculturists, the makers of bricks, the builders of cities, the framers of laws. Indeed, their civilization was a growth of Ea worship. Ea was their instructor. Berosus states that, as

Oannes, he lived in the Persian Gulf, and every day came ashore to instruct the inhabitants of Eridu how to make canals, to grow crops, to work metals, to make pottery and bricks, and to build temples; he was the artisan god--Nun-ura, "god of the potter"; Kuski-banda, "god of goldsmiths", &c.--the divine patron of the arts and crafts. "Ea knoweth everything", chanted the hymn maker. He taught the people how to form and use alphabetic signs and instructed them in mathematics: he gave them their code of laws. Like the Egyptian artisan god Ptah, and the linking deity Khnumu, Ea was the "potter or moulder of gods and man". Ptah moulded the first man on his potter's wheel: he also moulded the sun and moon; he shaped the universe and hammered out the copper sky. Ea built the world "as an architect builds a house".[36] Similarly the Vedic Indra, who wielded a hammer like Ptah, fashioned the universe after the simple manner in which the Aryans made their wooden dwellings.[37]

Like Ptah, Ea also developed from an artisan god into a sublime Creator in the highest sense, not merely as a producer of crops. His word became the creative force; he named those things he desired to be, and they came into existence. "Who but Ea creates things", exclaimed a priestly poet. This change from artisan god to creator (Nudimmud) may have been due to the tendency of early religious cults to attach to their chief god the attributes of rivals exalted at other centres.

Ea, whose name is also rendered Aa, was identified with Ya, Ya'u, or Au, the Jah of the Hebrews. "In Ya-Daganu, 'Jah is Dagon'", writes Professor Pinches, "we have the elements reversed, showing a wish to identify Jah with Dagon, rather than Dagon with Jah; whilst another interesting name, Au-Aa, shows an identification of Jah with Aa, two names which have every appearance of being etymologically connected." Jah's name "is one of the words for 'god' in the Assyro-Babylonian language".[38]

Ea was "Enki", "lord of the world", or "lord of what is beneath"; Amma-ana-ki, "lord of heaven and earth"; Sa-kalama, "ruler of the land", as well as Engur, "god of the abyss", Naqbu, "the deep", and Lugal-ida, "king of the river". As rain fell from "the waters above the firmament", the god of waters was also a sky and earth god.

The Indian Varuna was similarly a sky as well as an ocean god before the theorizing and systematizing Brahmanic teachers relegated him to a permanent abode at the bottom of the sea. It may be that Ea-Oannes and Varuna were of common origin.

Another Babylonian deity, named Dagan, is believed to be identical with Ea. His worship was certainly of great antiquity. "Hammurabi", writes Professor Pinches, "seems to speak of the Euphrates as being 'the boundary of Dagan', whom he calls his creator. In later inscriptions the form Daguna, which approaches nearer to the West Semitic form (Dagon of the Philistines), is found in a few personal names.[39]

It is possible that the Philistine deity Dagon was a specialized form of ancient Ea, who was either imported from Babylonia or was a sea god of more than one branch of the Mediterranean race. The authorities are at variance regarding the form and attributes of Dagan. Our knowledge regarding him is derived mainly from the Bible. He was a national rather than a city god. There are references to a Beth-dagon[40], "house or city of Dagon"; he had also a temple at Gaza, and Samson destroyed it by pulling down the two middle pillars which were its main support.[41] A third temple was situated in Ashdod. When the captured ark of the Israelites was placed in it the image of Dagon "fell on his face", with the result that "the head of Dagon and both the palms of his hands were cut off upon the threshold; only the stump of Dagon was left".[42] A further reference to "the threshold of Dagon" suggests that the god had feet like Ea-Oannes. Those who hold that Dagon had a fish form derive his name from the Semitic "dag = a fish", and suggest that after the idol fell only the fishy part (dāgo) was left. On the other hand, it was argued that Dagon was a corn god, and that the resemblance between the words Dagan and Dagon are accidental. Professor Sayce makes reference in this connection to a crystal seal from Phoenicia in the Ashmolean Museum, Oxford, bearing an inscription which he reads as Baal-dagon. Near the name is an ear of corn, and other symbols, such as the winged solar disc, a gazelle, and several stars, but there is no fish. It may be, of course, that Baal-dagon represents a fusion of deities. As we have seen in the case of Ea-Oannes and the deities of Mendes, a fish god may also be a corn god, a land animal god and a god of ocean and the sky. The offering of golden mice representing "your mice that mar the land",[43] made by the Philistines, suggests that Dagon was the fertilizing harvest god, among other things, whose usefulness had been impaired, as they believed, by the mistake committed of placing the ark of Israel in the temple at Ashdod. The Philistines came from Crete, and if their Dagon was imported from that island, he may have had some connection with Poseidon, whose worship extended throughout Greece. This god of the sea, who is somewhat like the Roman Neptune, carried a lightning trident and caused earthquakes. He was a brother of Zeus, the sky and atmosphere deity, and had bull and horse forms. As a horse he pursued Demeter, the earth and corn goddess, and, like Ea, he instructed mankind, but especially in the art of training horses. In his train were the Tritons, half men, half fishes, and the water fairies, the Nereids. Bulls, boars, and rams were offered to this sea god of fertility. Amphitrite was his spouse.

An obscure god Shony, the Oannes of the Scottish Hebrides, received oblations from those who depended for their agricultural prosperity on his gifts of fertilizing seaweed. He is referred to in Martin's *Western Isles*, and is not yet forgotten. The Eddic sea god Njord of Noatun was the father of Frey, the harvest god. Dagda, the Irish corn god, had for wife Boann, the goddess of the river Boyne. Osiris and Isis of Egypt were associated with the Nile. The connection between agriculture and the water supply was too obvious to escape the early symbolists, and many other proofs of this than those referred to could be given.

Ea's "faithful spouse" was the goddess Damkina, who was also called Nin-ki, "lady of the earth". "May Ea make thee glad", chanted the priests. "May Damkina, queen of the deep, illumine thee with her countenance; may Merodach (Marduk), the mighty overseer of the Igigi (heavenly spirits), exalt thy head." Merodach was their son: in time he became the Bel, or "Lord", of the Babylonian pantheon.

Like the Indian Varuna, the sea god, Ea-Oannes had control over the spirits and demons of the deep. The "ferryman" who kept watch over the river of death was called Arad-Ea, "servant of Ea". There are also references to sea maidens, the Babylonian mermaids, or Nereids. We have a glimpse of sea giants, which resemble the Indian Danavas and Daityas of ocean, in the chant:

> Seven are they, seven are they,
> In the ocean deep seven are they,
> Battening in heaven seven are they,
> Bred in the depths of ocean....
> Of these seven the first is the south wind,
> The second a dragon with mouth agape....[44]
> A suggestion of the Vedic Vritra and his horde of monsters.

These seven demons were also "the messengers of Anu", who, although specialized as a sky god in more than one pantheon, appears to have been closely associated with Ea in the earliest Sumerian period. His name, signifying "the high one", is derived from "ana", "heaven"; he was the city god of Erech (Uruk). It is possible that he was developed as an atmospheric god with solar and lunar attributes. The seven demons, who were his messengers, recall the stormy Maruts, the followers of Indra. They are referred to as

> Forcing their way with baneful windstorms,
> Mighty destroyers, the deluge of the storm god,
> Stalking at the right hand of the storm god.[45]

When we deal with a deity in his most archaic form it is difficult to distinguish him from a demon. Even the beneficent Ea is associated with monsters and furies. "Evil spirits", according to a Babylonian chant, were "the bitter venom of the gods". Those attached to a deity as "attendants" appear to represent the original animistic group from which he evolved. In each district the character of the deity was shaped to accord with local conditions.

At Nippur, which was situated on the vague and shifting boundary line between Sumer and Akkad, the chief god was Enlil, whose name is translated "lord of mist", "lord of might", and "lord of demons" by various authorities. He was a storm god and a war god, and "lord of heaven and earth", like Ea and Anu. An atmospheric deity, he shares the attributes of the Indian Indra, the thunder and rain god, and Vayu, the wind god; he also resembles the Semitic Adad or Rimman, who links with the Hittite Tarku. All these are deities of tempest and the mountains--Wild Huntsmen in the Raging Host. The name of Enlil's temple at Nippur has been translated as "mountain house", or "like a mountain", and the theory obtained for a time that the god must therefore have been imported by a people from the hills. But as the ideogram for "mountain" and "land" was used in the earliest times, as King shows, with reference to foreign countries,[46] it is more probable that Enlil was exalted as a world god who had dominion over not only Sumer and Akkad, but also the territories occupied by the rivals and enemies of the early Babylonians.

Enlil is known as the "older Bel" (lord), to distinguish him from Bel Merodach of Babylon. He was the chief figure in a triad in which he figured as earth god, with Anu as god of the sky and Ea as god of the deep. This classification suggests that Nippur had either risen in political importance and dominated the cities of Erech and Eridu, or that its priests were influential at the court of a ruler who was the overlord of several city states.

Associated with Bel Enlil was Beltis, later known as "Beltu--the lady". She appears to be identical with the other great goddesses, Ishtar, Nana, Zerpanitum, &c., a "Great Mother", or consort of an early god with whom she was equal in power and dignity.

In the later systematized theology of the Babylonians we seem to trace the fragments of a primitive mythology which was vague in outline, for the deities were not sharply defined, and existed in groups. Enneads were formed in Egypt by placing a local god at the head of a group of eight elder deities. The sun god Ra was the chief figure of the earliest pantheon of this character at Heliopolis, while at Hermopolis the leader was the lunar god Thoth. Professor Budge is of opinion that "both the Sumerians and the early Egyptians derived their primeval gods from some common but exceedingly ancient source", for he finds in the Babylonian and Nile valleys that there is a resemblance between two early groups which "seems to be too close to be accidental".[47]

The Egyptian group comprises four pairs of vague gods and goddesses--Nu and his consort Nut, Hehu and his consort Hehut, Kekui and his consort Kekuit, and Kerh and his consort Kerhet. "Man always has fashioned", he says, "and probably always will fashion, his god or gods in his own image, and he has always, having reached a certain stage in development, given to his gods wives and offspring; but the nature of the position taken by the wives of the gods depends upon the nature of the position of women in the households of those who write the legends and the traditions of the gods. The gods of the oldest company in Egypt were, the writer believes, invented by people in whose households women held a high position, and among whom they possessed more power than is usually the case with Oriental peoples."[48]

We cannot say definitely what these various deities represent. Nu was the spirit of the primordial deep, and Nut of the waters above the heavens, the mother of moon and sun and the stars. The others were phases of light and darkness and the forces of nature in activity and repose.

Nu is represented in Babylonian mythology by Apsu-Rishtu, and Nut by Mummu-Tiamat or Tiawath; the next pair is Lachmu and Lachamu, and the third, Anshar and Kishar. The fourth pair is missing, but the names of Anu and Ea (as Nudimmud) are mentioned in the first tablet of the Creation series, and the name of a third is lost. Professor Budge thinks that the Assyrian editors substituted the ancient triad of Anu, Ea, and Enlil for the pair which would correspond to those found in Egypt. Originally the wives of Anu and Ea may have made up the group of eight primitive deities.

There can be little doubt but that Ea, as he survives to us, is of later characterization than the first pair of primitive deities who symbolized the deep. The attributes of this beneficent god reflect the progress, and the social and moral ideals of a people well advanced in civilization. He rewarded mankind for the services they rendered to him; he was their leader and instructor; he achieved for them the victories over the destructive forces of nature. In brief, he was the dragon slayer, a distinction, by the way, which was attached in later times to his son Merodach, the Babylonian god, although Ea was still credited with the victory over the dragon's husband.

When Ea was one of the pre-Babylonian group--the triad of Bel-Enlil, Anu, and Ea--he resembled the Indian Vishnu, the Preserver, while Bel-Enlil resembled Shiva, the Destroyer, and Anu, the father, supreme Brahma, the Creator and Father of All, the difference in exact adjustment being due, perhaps, to Sumerian political conditions.

Ea, as we have seen, symbolized the beneficence of the waters; their destructive force was represented by Tiamat or Tiawath, the dragon, and Apsu, her husband, the arch-enemy of the gods. We shall find these elder demons figuring in the Babylonian Creation myth, which receives treatment in a later chapter.

The ancient Sumerian city of Eridu, which means "on the seashore", was invested with great sanctity from the earliest times, and Ea, the "great magician of the gods", was invoked by workers of spells, the priestly magicians of historic Babylonia. Excavations have shown that Eridu was protected by a retaining wall of sandstone, of which material many of its houses were made. In its temple tower, built of brick, was a marble stairway, and evidences have been forthcoming that in the later Sumerian period the structure was lavishly adorned. It is referred to in the fragments of early literature which have survived as "the splendid house, shady as the forest", that "none may enter". The mythological spell exercised by Eridu in later times suggests that the civilization of Sumeria owed much to the worshippers of Ea. At the sacred city the first man was created: there the souls of the dead passed towards the great Deep. Its proximity to the sea--Ea was Nin-bubu, "god of the sailor"--may have brought it into contact with other peoples and other early civilizations. Like the early Egyptians, the early Sumerians may have been in touch with Punt (Somaliland), which some regard as the cradle of the Mediterranean race. The Egyptians obtained from that sacred land incense-bearing trees which had magical potency. In a fragmentary Babylonian charm there is a reference to a sacred tree or bush at Eridu. Professor Sayce has suggested that it is the Biblical "Tree of Life" in the Garden of Eden. His translations of certain vital words, however, is sharply questioned by Mr. R. Campbell Thompson of the

British Museum, who does not accept the theory.[49] It may be that Ea's sacred bush or tree is a survival of tree and water worship.

If Eridu was not the "cradle" of the Sumerian race, it was possibly the cradle of Sumerian civilization. Here, amidst the shifting rivers in early times, the agriculturists may have learned to control and distribute the water supply by utilizing dried-up beds of streams to irrigate the land. Whatever successes they achieved were credited to Ea, their instructor and patron; he was Nadimmud, "god of everything".

[28] *2 Kings*, xviii, 32.

[29] *Herodotus*, i, 193.

[30] Peter's *Nippur*, i, p. 160.

[31] A Babylonian priest of Bel Merodach. In the third century a.c. he composed in Greek a history of his native land, which has perished. Extracts from it are given by Eusebius, Josephus, Apollodorus, and others.

[32] *Indian Myth and Legend*, pp. 140, 141.

[33] *The Religion of the Semites*, pp. 159, 160.

[34] *Religion of Babylonia and Assyria*, M. Jastrow, p. 88.

[35] *The Seven Tablets of Creation*, L.W. King, vol. i, p. 129.

[36] *Religious Belief in Babylonia and Assyria*, M. Jastrow, p. 88.

[37] *Cosmology of the Rigveda*, Wallis, and *Indian Myth and Legend*, p. 10.

[38] *The Old Testament in the Light of the Historical Records and Legends of Assyria and Babylonia*, T.G. Pinches, pp. 59-61.

[39] *The Religion of Babylonia and Assyria*, T.G. Pinches, pp. 91, 92.

[40] *Joshua*, xv, 41; xix, 27.

[41] *Judges*, xvi, 14.

[42] *I Sam.*, v, 1-9.

[43] *I Sam.*, vi, 5.

[44] *The Devils and Evil Spirits of Babylonia*, R. Campbell Thompson, London, 1903, vol. i, p. xlii.

[45] *The Devils and Evil Spirits of Babylonia*, R. C. Thompson, vol. i, p. xliii.

[46] *A History of Sumer and Akkad*, L. W. King, p. 54.

[47] *The Gods of the Egyptians*, E. Wallis Budge, vol. i, p. 290.

[48] *The Gods of the Egyptians*, vol. i, p. 287.

[49] *The Devils and Evil Spirits of Babylonia*, vol. i, *Intro*. See also Sayce's *The Religion of Ancient Egypt and Babylonia* (Gifford Lectures, 1902), p. 385, and Pinches' *The Old Testament in the Light of Historical Records*, &c., p. 71.

Chapter III. Rival Pantheons and Representative Deities

Abstract

Why Different Gods were Supreme at Different Centres--Theories regarding Origin of Life--Vital Principle in Water--Creative Tears of Weeping Deities--Significance of widespread Spitting Customs--Divine Water in Blood and Divine Blood in Water--Liver as the Seat of Life--Inspiration derived by Drinking Mead, Blood, &c.--Life Principle in Breath--Babylonian Ghosts as "Evil Wind Gusts"--Fire Deities--Fire and Water in Magical Ceremonies--Moon Gods of Ur and Harran--Moon Goddess and Babylonian "Jack and Jill"--Antiquity of Sun Worship--Tammuz and Ishtar--Solar Gods of War, Pestilence, and Death--Shamash as the "Great Judge"--His Mitra Name--Aryan Mitra or Mithra and linking Babylonian Deities--Varuna and Shamash Hymns compared--The Female Origin of Life--Goddesses of Maternity--The Babylonian Thor--Deities of Good and Evil.

In dealing with the city cults of Sumer and Akkad, consideration must be given to the problems involved by the rival mythological systems. Pantheons not only varied in detail, but were presided over by different supreme gods. One city's chief deity might be regarded as a secondary deity at another centre. Although Ea, for instance, was given first place at Eridu, and was so pronouncedly Sumerian in character, the moon god Nannar remained supreme at Ur, while the sun god, whose Semitic name was Shamash, presided at Larsa and Sippar. Other deities were similarly exalted in other states.

As has been indicated, a mythological system must have been strongly influenced by city politics. To hold a community in sway, it was necessary to recognize officially the various gods worshipped by different sections, so as to secure the constant allegiance of all classes to their rulers. Alien deities were therefore associated with local and tribal deities, those of the nomads with those of the agriculturists, those of the unlettered folks with those of the learned people. Reference has been made to the introduction of strange deities by conquerors. But these were not always imposed upon a community by violent means. Indications are not awanting that the worshippers of alien gods were sometimes welcomed and encouraged to settle in certain states. When they came as military allies to assist a city folk against a fierce enemy, they were naturally much admired and praised, honoured by the women and the bards, and rewarded by the rulers.

In the epic of Gilgamesh, the Babylonian Hercules, we meet with Ea-bani, a Goliath of the wilds, who is entreated to come to the aid of the besieged city of Erech when it seemed that its deities were unable to help the people against their enemies.

The gods of walled-round Erech
To flies had turned and buzzed in the streets;
The winged bulls of walled-round Erech
Were turned to mice and departed through the holes.

Ea-bani was attracted to Erech by the gift of a fair woman for wife. The poet who lauded him no doubt mirrored public opinion. We can see the slim, shaven Sumerians gazing with wonder and admiration on their rough heroic ally.

All his body was covered with hair,
His locks were like a woman's,
Thick as corn grew his abundant hair.
He was a stranger to the people and in that land.
Clad in a garment like Gira, the god,
He had eaten grass with the gazelles,
He had drunk water with savage beasts.
His delight was to be among water dwellers.

Like the giant Alban, the eponymous ancestor of a people who invaded prehistoric Britain, Ea-bani appears to have represented in Babylonian folk legends a certain type of foreign settlers in the land. No doubt the city dwellers, who were impressed by the prowess of the hairy and powerful warriors, were also ready to acknowledge the greatness of their war gods, and to admit them into the pantheon. The fusion of beliefs which followed must have stimulated thought and been productive of speculative ideas. "Nowhere", remarks Professor Jastrow, "does a high form of culture arise without the commingling of diverse ethnic elements."

We must also take into account the influence exercised by leaders of thought like En-we-dur-an-ki, the famous high priest of Sippar, whose piety did much to increase the reputation of the cult of Shamesh, the sun god. The teachings and example of Buddha, for instance, revolutionized Brahmanic religion in India.

A mythology was an attempt to solve the riddle of the Universe, and to adjust the relations of mankind with the various forces represented by the deities. The priests systematized existing folk beliefs and established an official religion. To secure the prosperity of the State, it was considered necessary to render homage unto whom homage was due at various seasons and under various circumstances.

The religious attitude of a particular community, therefore, must have been largely dependent on its needs and experiences. The food supply was a first consideration. At Eridu, as we have seen, it was assured by devotion to Ea and obedience to his commands as an instructor. Elsewhere it might happen, however, that Ea's gifts were restricted or withheld by an obstructing force--the raging storm god, or the parching, pestilence-bringing deity of the sun. It was necessary, therefore, for the people to win the favour of the god or goddess who seemed most powerful, and was accordingly considered to be the greatest in a particular district. A rain god presided over the destinies of one community, and a god of disease and death over another; a third exalted the war god, no doubt because raids were frequent and the city owed its strength and prosperity to its battles and conquests. The reputation won by a particular god throughout Babylonia would depend greatly on the achievements of his worshippers and the progress of the city civilization over which he presided. Bel-Enlil's fame as a war deity was probably due to the political supremacy of his city of Nippur; and there was probably good reason for attributing to the sun god a pronounced administrative and legal character; he may have controlled the destinies of exceedingly well organized communities in which law and order and authority were held in high esteem.

In accounting for the rise of distinctive and rival city deities, we should also consider the influence of divergent conceptions regarding the origin of life in mingled communities. Each foreign element in a community had its own intellectual life and immemorial tribal traditions, which reflected ancient habits of life and perpetuated the doctrines of eponymous ancestors. Among the agricultural classes, the folk religion which entered so intimately into their customs and labours must have remained essentially Babylonish in character. In cities, however, where official religions were formulated, foreign ideas were more apt to be imposed, especially when embraced by influential teachers. It is not surprising, therefore, to find that in Babylonia, as in Egypt, there were differences of opinion regarding the origin of life and the particular natural element which represented the vital principle.

One section of the people, who were represented by the worshippers of Ea, appear to have believed that the essence of life was contained in water. The god of Eridu was the source of the "water of life". He fertilized parched and sunburnt wastes through rivers and irrigating canals, and conferred upon man the sustaining "food of life". When life came to an end--

Food of death will be offered thee...
Water of death will be offered thee...

Offerings of water and food were made to the dead so that the ghosts might be nourished and prevented from troubling the living. Even the gods required water and food; they were immortal because they had drunk ambrosia and eaten from the plant of life. When the goddess Ishtar was in the Underworld, the land of the dead, the servant of Ea exclaimed--

"Hail! lady, may the well give me of its waters, so that I may drink."

The goddess of the dead commanded her servant to "sprinkle the lady Ishtar with the water of life and bid her depart". The sacred water might also be found at a confluence of rivers. Ea bade his son, Merodach, to "draw water from the mouth of two streams", and "on this water to put his pure spell".

The worship of rivers and wells which prevailed in many countries was connected with the belief that the principle of life was in moisture. In India, water was vitalized by the intoxicating juice of the Soma plant, which inspired priests to utter prophecies and filled their hearts with religious fervour. Drinking customs had originally a religious significance. It was believed in India that the sap of plants was influenced by the moon, the source of vitalizing moisture and the hiding-place of the mead of the gods. The Teutonic gods also drank this mead, and poets were inspired by it. Similar beliefs obtained among various peoples. Moon and water worship were therefore closely associated; the blood of animals and the sap of plants were vitalized by the water of life and under control of the moon.

The body moisture of gods and demons had vitalizing properties. When the Indian creator, Prajápati, wept at the beginning, "that (the tears) which fell into the water became the air. That which he wiped away, upwards, became the sky."[50] The ancient Egyptians believed that all men were born from the eyes of Horus except negroes, who came from other parts of his body.[51] The creative tears of Ra, the sun god, fell as shining rays upon the earth. When this god grew old saliva dripped from his mouth, and Isis mixed the vitalizing moisture with dust, and thus made the serpent which bit and paralysed the great solar deity.[52]

Other Egyptian deities, including Osiris and Isis, wept creative tears. Those which fell from the eyes of the evil gods produced poisonous plants and various baneful animals. Orion, the Greek giant, sprang from the body moisture of deities. The weeping ceremonies in connection with agricultural rites were no doubt believed to be of magical potency; they encouraged the god to weep creative tears.

Ea, the god of the deep, was also "lord of life" (Enti), "king of the river" (Lugal-ida), and god of creation (Nudimmud). His aid was invoked by means of magical formulae. As the "great magician of the gods" he uttered charms himself, and was the patron of all magicians. One spell runs as follows:

I am the sorcerer priest of Ea...
To revive the ... sick man
The great lord Ea hath sent me;
He hath added his pure spell to mine,
He hath added his pure voice to mine,
He hath added his pure spittle to mine.

R.C. Thompson's Translation.

Saliva, like tears, had creative and therefore curative qualities; it also expelled and injured demons and brought good luck. Spitting ceremonies are referred to in the religious literature of Ancient Egypt. When the Eye of Ra was blinded by Set, Thoth spat in it to restore vision. The sun god Tum, who was linked with Ra as Ra-Tum, spat on the ground, and his saliva became the gods Shu and Tefnut. In the Underworld the devil serpent Apep was spat upon to curse it, as was also its waxen image which the priests fashioned.[53]

Several African tribes spit to make compacts, declare friendship, and to curse.

Park, the explorer, refers in his *Travels* to his carriers spitting on a flat stone to ensure a good journey. Arabian holy men and descendants of Mohammed spit to cure diseases. Mohammed spat in the mouth of his grandson Hasen soon after birth. Theocritus,

Sophocles, and Plutarch testify to the ancient Grecian customs of spitting to cure and to curse, and also to bless when children were named. Pliny has expressed belief in the efficacy of the fasting spittle for curing disease, and referred to the custom of spitting to avert witchcraft. In England, Scotland, and Ireland spitting customs are not yet obsolete. North of England boys used to talk of "spitting their sauls" (souls). When the Newcastle colliers held their earliest strikes they made compacts by spitting on a stone. There are still "spitting stones" in the north of Scotland. When bargains are made in rural districts, hands are spat upon before they are shaken. The first money taken each day by fishwives and other dealers is spat upon to ensure increased drawings. Brand, who refers to various spitting customs, quotes *Scot's Discovery of Witchcraft* regarding the saliva cure for king's evil, which is still, by the way, practised in the Hebrides. Like Pliny, Scot recommended ceremonial spitting as a charm against witchcraft.[54] In China spitting to expel demons is a common practice. We still call a hasty person a "spitfire", and a calumniator a "spit-poison".

The life principle in trees, &c., as we have seen, was believed to have been derived from the tears of deities. In India sap was called the "blood of trees", and references to "bleeding trees" are still widespread and common. "Among the ancients", wrote Professor Robertson Smith, "blood is generally conceived as the principle or vehicle of life, and so the account often given of sacred waters is that the blood of the deity flows in them. Thus as Milton writes:

> Smooth Adonis from his native rock
> Ran purple to the sea, supposed with blood
> Of Thammuz yearly wounded.

Paradise Lost, i, 450.

The ruddy colour which the swollen river derived from the soil at a certain season was ascribed to the blood of the god, who received his death wound in Lebanon at that time of the year, and lay buried beside the sacred source."[55]

In Babylonia the river was regarded as the source of the life blood and the seat of the soul. No doubt this theory was based on the fact that the human liver contains about a sixth of the blood in the body, the largest proportion required by any single organ. Jeremiah makes "Mother Jerusalem" exclaim: "My liver is poured upon the earth for the destruction of the daughter of my people", meaning that her life is spent with grief.

Inspiration was derived by drinking blood as well as by drinking intoxicating liquors--the mead of the gods. Indian magicians who drink the blood of the goat sacrificed to the goddess Kali, are believed to be temporarily possessed by her spirit, and thus enabled to prophesy.[56] Malayan exorcists still expel demons while they suck the blood from a decapitated fowl.[57]

Similar customs were prevalent in Ancient Greece. A woman who drank the blood of a sacrificed lamb or bull uttered prophetic sayings.[58]

But while most Babylonians appear to have believed that the life principle was in blood, some were apparently of opinion that it was in breath--the air of life. A man died when he ceased to breathe; his spirit, therefore, it was argued, was identical with the atmosphere--the moving wind--and was accordingly derived from the atmospheric or wind god. When, in the Gilgamesh epic, the hero invokes the dead Ea-bani, the ghost rises up like a "breath of wind". A Babylonian charm runs:

> The gods which seize on men
>   Came forth from the grave;
> The evil wind gusts
>   Have come forth from the grave,
> To demand payment of rites and the pouring out of libations
>   They have come forth from the grave;
> All that is evil in their hosts, like a whirlwind,
>   Hath come forth from the grave.[59]

The Hebrew "nephesh ruach" and "neshamah" (in Arabic "ruh" and "nefs") pass from meaning "breath" to "spirit".[60] In Egypt the god Khnumu was "Kneph" in his character as an atmospheric deity. The ascendancy of storm and wind gods in some Babylonian cities may have been due to the belief that they were the source of the "air of life". It is possible that this conception was popularized by the Semites. Inspiration was perhaps derived from these deities by burning incense, which, if we follow evidence obtained elsewhere, induced a prophetic trance. The gods were also invoked by incense. In the Flood legend the Babylonian Noah burned incense. "The gods smelled a sweet savour and gathered like flies over the sacrificer." In Egypt devotees who inhaled the breath of the Apis bull were enabled to prophesy.

26

In addition to water and atmospheric deities Babylonia had also its fire gods, Girru, Gish Bar, Gibil, and Nusku. Their origin is obscure. It is doubtful if their worshippers, like those of the Indian Agni, believed that fire, the "vital spark", was the principle of life which was manifested by bodily heat. The Aryan fire worshippers cremated their dead so that the spirits might be transferred by fire to Paradise. This practice, however, did not obtain among the fire worshippers of Persia, nor, as was once believed, in Sumer or Akkad either. Fire was, however, used in Babylonia for magical purposes. It destroyed demons, and put to flight the spirits of disease. Possibly the fire-purification ceremonies resembled those which were practised by the Canaanites, and are referred to in the Bible. Ahaz "made his son to pass through the fire, according to the abominations of the heathen".[61] Ezekiel declared that "when ye offer your gifts, when ye make your sons to pass through the fire, ye pollute yourselves with all your idols".[62] In *Leviticus* it is laid down: "Thou shalt not let any of thy seed pass through the fire to Moloch".[63] It may be that in Babylonia the fire-cleansing ceremony resembled that which obtained at Beltane (May Day) in Scotland, Germany, and other countries. Human sacrifices might also have been offered up as burnt offerings. Abraham, who came from the Sumerian city of Ur, was prepared to sacrifice Isaac, Sarah's first-born. The fire gods of Babylonia never achieved the ascendancy of the Indian Agni; they appear to have resembled him mainly in so far as he was connected with the sun. Nusku, like Agni, was also the "messenger of the gods". When Merodach or Babylon was exalted as chief god of the pantheon his messages were carried to Ea by Nusku. He may have therefore symbolized the sun rays, for Merodach had solar attributes. It is possible that the belief obtained among even the water worshippers of Eridu that the sun and moon, which rose from the primordial deep, had their origin in the everlasting fire in Ea's domain at the bottom of the sea. In the Indian god Varuna's ocean home an "Asura fire" (demon fire) burned constantly; it was "bound and confined", but could not be extinguished. Fed by water, this fire, it was believed, would burst forth at the last day and consume the universe.[64] A similar belief can be traced in Teutonic mythology. The Babylonian incantation cult appealed to many gods, but "the most important share in the rites", says Jastrow, "are taken by fire and water--suggesting, therefore, that the god of water--more particularly Ea--and the god of fire ... are the chief deities on which the ritual itself hinges". In some temples there was a *bit rimki*, a "house of washing", and a *bit nuri*, a "house of light".[65]

It is possible, of course, that fire was regarded as the vital principle by some city cults, which were influenced by imported ideas. If so, the belief never became prevalent. The most enduring influence in Babylonian religion was the early Sumerian; and as Sumerian modes of thought were the outcome of habits of life necessitated by the character of the country, they were bound, sooner or later, to leave a deep impress on the minds of foreign peoples who settled in the Garden of Western Asia. It is not surprising, therefore, to find that imported deities assumed Babylonian characteristics, and were identified or associated with Babylonian gods in the later imperial pantheon.

Moon worship appears to have been as ancient as water worship, with which, as we have seen, it was closely associated. It was widely prevalent throughout Babylonia. The chief seat of the lunar deity, Nannar or Sin, was the ancient city of Ur, from which Abraham migrated to Harran, where the "Baal" (the lord) was also a moon god. Ur was situated in Sumer, in the south, between the west bank of the Euphrates and the low hills bordering the Arabian desert, and not far distant from sea-washed Eridu. No doubt, like that city, it had its origin at an exceedingly remote period. At any rate, the excavations conducted there have afforded proof that it flourished in the prehistoric period.

As in Arabia, Egypt, and throughout ancient Europe and elsewhere, the moon god of Sumeria was regarded as the "friend of man". He controlled nature as a fertilizing agency; he caused grass, trees, and crops to grow; he increased flocks and herds, and gave human offspring. At Ur he was exalted above Ea as "the lord and prince of the gods, supreme in heaven, the Father of all"; he was also called "great Anu", an indication that Anu, the sky god, had at one time a lunar character. The moon god was believed to be the father of the sun god: he was the "great steer with mighty horns and perfect limbs".

His name Sin is believed to be a corruption of "Zu-ena", which signifies "knowledge lord".[66] Like the lunar Osiris of Egypt, he was apparently an instructor of mankind; the moon measured time and controlled the seasons; seeds were sown at a certain phase of the moon, and crops were ripened by the harvest moon. The mountains of Sinai and the desert of Sin are called after this deity.

As Nannar, which Jastrow considers to be a variation of "Narnar", the "light producer", the moon god scattered darkness and reduced the terrors of night. His spirit inhabited the lunar stone, so that moon and stone worship were closely associated; it also entered trees and crops, so that moon worship linked with earth worship, as both linked with water worship.

27

The consort of Nannar was Nin-Uruwa, "the lady of Ur", who was also called Nin-gala. She links with Ishtar as Nin, as Isis of Egypt linked with other mother deities. The twin children of the moon were Mashu and Mashtu, a brother and sister, like the lunar girl and boy of Teutonic mythology immortalized in nursery rhymes as Jack and Jill.

Sun worship was of great antiquity in Babylonia, but appears to have been seasonal in its earliest phases. No doubt the sky god Anu had his solar as well as his lunar attributes, which he shared with Ea. The spring sun was personified as Tammuz, the youthful shepherd, who was loved by the earth goddess Ishtar and her rival Eresh-ki-gal, goddess of death, the Babylonian Persephone. During the winter Tammuz dwelt in Hades, and at the beginning of spring Ishtar descended to search for him among the shades.[67] But the burning summer sun was symbolized as a destroyer, a slayer of men, and therefore a war god. As Ninip or Nirig, the son of Enlil, who was made in the likeness of Anu, he waged war against the earth spirits, and was furiously hostile towards the deities of alien peoples, as befitted a god of battle. Even his father feared him, and when he was advancing towards Nippur, sent out Nusku, messenger of the gods, to soothe the raging deity with soft words. Ninip was symbolized as a wild bull, was connected with stone worship, like the Indian destroying god Shiva, and was similarly a deity of Fate. He had much in common with Nin-Girsu, a god of Lagash, who was in turn regarded as a form of Tammuz.

Nergal, another solar deity, brought disease and pestilence, and, according to Jensen, all misfortunes due to excessive heat. He was the king of death, husband of Eresh-ki-gal, queen of Hades. As a war god he thirsted for human blood, and was depicted as a mighty lion. He was the chief deity of the city of Cuthah, which, Jastrow suggests, was situated beside a burial place of great repute, like the Egyptian Abydos.

The two great cities of the sun in ancient Babylonia were the Akkadian Sippar and the Sumerian Larsa. In these the sun god, Shamash or Babbar, was the patron deity. He was a god of Destiny, the lord of the living and the dead, and was exalted as the great Judge, the lawgiver, who upheld justice; he was the enemy of wrong, he loved righteousness and hated sin, he inspired his worshippers with rectitude and punished evildoers. The sun god also illumined the world, and his rays penetrated every quarter: he saw all things, and read the thoughts of men; nothing could be concealed from Shamash. One of his names was Mitra, like the god who was linked with Varuna in the Indian *Rigveda*. These twin deities, Mitra and Varuna, measured out the span of human life. They were the source of all heavenly gifts: they regulated sun and moon, the winds and waters, and the seasons.[68]

These did the gods establish in royal power over themselves, because they were wise and the children of wisdom, and because they excelled in power.--*Prof. Arnold's trans. of Rigvedic Hymn.*

Mitra and Varuna were protectors of hearth and home, and they chastised sinners. "In a striking passage of the *Mahabharata*" says Professor Moulton, "one in which Indian thought comes nearest to the conception of conscience, a kingly wrongdoer is reminded that the sun sees secret sin."[69]

In Persian mythology Mitra, as Mithra, is the patron of Truth, and "the Mediator" between heaven and earth[70]. This god was also worshipped by the military aristocracy of Mitanni, which held sway for a period over Assyria. In Roman times the worship of Mithra spread into Europe from Persia. Mithraic sculptures depict the deity as a corn god slaying the harvest bull; on one of the monuments "cornstalks instead of blood are seen issuing from the wound inflicted with the knife[71]". The Assyrian word "metru" signifies rain[70]. As a sky god Mitra may have been associated, like Varuna, with the waters above the firmament. Rain would therefore be gifted by him as a fertilizing deity. In the Babylonian Flood legend it is the sun god Shamash who "appointed the time" when the heavens were to "rain destruction" in the night, and commanded Pir-napishtim, "Enter into the midst of thy ship and shut thy door". The solar deity thus appears as a form of Anu, god of the sky and upper atmosphere, who controls the seasons and the various forces of nature. Other rival chiefs of city pantheons, whether lunar, atmospheric, earth, or water deities, were similarly regarded as the supreme deities who ruled the Universe, and decreed when man should receive benefits or suffer from their acts of vengeance.

It is possible that the close resemblances between Mithra and Mitra of the Aryan-speaking peoples of India and the Iranian plateau, and the sun god of the Babylonians--the Semitic Shamash, the Sumerian Utu--were due to early contact and cultural influence through the medium of Elam. As a solar and corn god, the Persian Mithra links with Tammuz, as a sky and atmospheric deity with Anu, and as a god of truth, righteousness, and law with Shamash. We seem to trace in the sublime Vedic hymns addressed by the Indian Aryans to Mitra and Varuna the impress of Babylonian religious thought:

Whate'er exists within this earth, and all within the sky,

Yea, all that is beyond, King Varuna perceives....

Rigveda, iv, 16.[72]

O Varuna, whatever the offence may be
That we as men commit against the heavenly folk,
When through our want of thought we violate thy laws,
Chastise us not, O god, for that iniquity.

Rigveda, vii, 89.[73]

Shamash was similarly exalted in Babylonian hymns:
The progeny of those who deal unjustly will not prosper.
What their mouth utters in thy presence
Thou wilt destroy, what issues from their mouth thou wilt dissipate.
Thou knowest their transgressions, the plan of the wicked thou rejectest.
All, whoever they be, are in thy care....
He who takes no bribe, who cares for the oppressed,
Is favoured by Shamash,--his life shall be prolonged.[74]

The worshippers of Varuna and Mitra in the Punjab did not cremate their dead like those who exalted the rival fire god Agni. The grave was the "house of clay", as in Babylonia. Mitra, who was identical with Yama, ruled over departed souls in the "Land of the Pitris" (Fathers), which was reached by crossing the mountains and the rushing stream of death.[75] As we have seen, the Babylonian solar god Nergal was also the lord of the dead.

As Ma-banda-anna, "the boat of the sky", Shamash links with the Egyptian sun god Ra, whose barque sailed over the heavens by day and through the underworld of darkness and death during the night. The consort of Shamash was Aa, and his attendants were Kittu and Mesharu, "Truth" and "Righteousness".

Like the Hittites, the Babylonians had also a sun goddess: her name was Nin-sun, which Jastrow renders "the annihilating lady". At Erech she had a shrine in the temple of the sky god Anu.

We can trace in Babylonia, as in Egypt, the early belief that life in the Universe had a female origin. Nin-sun links with Ishtar, whose Sumerian name was Nana. Ishtar appears to be identical with the Egyptian Hathor, who, as Sekhet, slaughtered the enemies of the sun god Ra. She was similarly the goddess of maternity, and is depicted in this character, like Isis and other goddesses of similar character, suckling a babe. Another Babylonian lady of the gods was Ama, Mama, or Mami, "the creatress of the seed of mankind", and was "probably so called as the 'mother' of all things".[76]

A characteristic atmospheric deity was Ramman, the Rimmon of the Bible, the Semitic Addu, Adad, Hadad, or Dadu. He was not a presiding deity in any pantheon, but was identified with Enlil at Nippur. As a hammer god, he was imported by the Semites from the hills. He was a wind and thunder deity, a rain bringer, a corn god, and a god of battle like Thor, Jupiter, Tarku, Indra, and others, who were all sons of the sky.

In this brief review of the representative deities of early Babylonia, it will be seen that most gods link with Anu, Ea, and Enlil, whose attributes they symbolized in various forms. The prominence accorded to an individual deity depended on local conditions, experiences, and influences. Ceremonial practices no doubt varied here and there, but although one section might exalt Ea and another Shamash, the religious faith of the people as a whole did not differ to any marked extent; they served the gods according to their lights, so that life might be prolonged and made prosperous, for the land of death and "no return" was regarded as a place of gloom and misery.

When the Babylonians appear before us in the early stages of the historical period they had reached that stage of development set forth so vividly in the *Orations* of Isocrates: "Those of the gods who are the source to us of good things have the title of Olympians; those whose department is that of calamities and punishments have harsher titles: to the first class both private persons and states erect altars and temples; the second is not worshipped either with prayers or burnt sacrifices, but in their case we perform ceremonies of riddance".[77]

The Sumerians, like the Ancient Egyptians, developed their deities, who reflected the growth of culture, from vague spirit groups, which, like ghosts, were hostile to mankind. Those spirits who could be propitiated were exalted as benevolent deities; those who could not be bargained with were regarded as evil gods and goddesses. A better understanding of the character of Babylonian deities will therefore be obtained by passing the demons and evil spirits under review.

[50] *Indian Myth and Legend*, p. 100.

[51] Maspero's *Dawn of Civilization*, p. 156 *et seq*.

[52] *Egyptian Myth and Legend*, p. I *et seq*. The saliva of the frail and elderly was injurious.

[53] *Osiris and the Egyptian Resurrection*, E. Wallis Budge, vol. ii, p. 203 *et seq*.

[54] *Brana's Popular Antiquities*, vol. iii, pp. 259-263 (1889 ed.).

[55] *The Religion of the Semites*, pp. 158, 159.

[56] *Castes and Tribes of Southern India*, E. Thurston, iv, 187.

[57] *Omens and Superstitions of Southern India*, E. Thurston (1912), pp. 245, 246.

[58] Pausanias, ii, 24, 1.

[59] *Devils and Evil Spirits of Babylonia*, R.C. Thompson, vol. ii, tablet Y.

[60] *Animism*, E. Clodd, p. 37.

[61] *2 Kings*, xvi, 3.

[62] *Ezekiel*, xx, 31.

[63] *Leviticus*, xviii, 21.

[64] *Indian Myth and Legend*, p. 65.

[65] *Religious Belief in Babylonia and Assyria*, M. Jastrow, pp. 312, 313.

[66] *The Religion of Babylonia and Assyria*, T.G. Pinches, p. 81.

[67] In early times two goddesses searched for Tammuz at different periods.

[68] *Indian Myth and Legend*, p. 30.

[69] *Early Religious Poetry of Persia*, p. 35.

[70] *Early Religious Poetry of Persia*, p. 37.

[71] *The Golden Bough* (Spirits of the Corn and Wild, vol. ii, p. 10), 3rd edition.

[72] *Indian Wisdom*, Sir Monier Monier-Williams.

[73] *A History of Sanskrit Literature*, Professor Macdonell.

[74] *Religious Belief and Practice in Babylonia and Assyria*, M. Jastrow, pp. 111, 112.

[75] *Indian Myth and Legend*, pp. xxxii, and 38 *et seq*.

[76] *The Religion of Babylonia and Assyria*, T.G. Pinches, p. 94.

[77] *The Religion of Ancient Greece*, J.E. Harrison, p. 46, and Isoc. *Orat.*, v, 117

Chapter IV. Demons, Fairies, and Ghosts

Abstract

Spirits in Everything and Everywhere--The Bringers of Luck and Misfortune-- Germ Theory Anticipated--Early Gods indistinguishable from Demons--Repulsive form of Ea-- Spirit Groups as Attendants of Deities--Egyptian, Indian, Greek, and Germanic parallels--Elder Gods as Evil Gods--Animal Demons--The Babylonian "Will-o'-the-Wisp"--"Foreign Devils"-- Elves and Fairies--Demon Lovers--"Adam's first wife, Lilith"--Children Charmed against Evil Spirits--The Demon of Nightmare--Ghosts as Enemies of the Living--The Vengeful Dead Mother in Babylonia, India, Europe, and Mexico--Burial Contrast--Calling Back the Dead--Fate of Childless Ghosts--Religious Need for Offspring--Hags and Giants and Composite Monsters-- Tempest Fiends--Legend of Adapa and the Storm Demon--Wind Hags of Ancient Britain-- Tyrolese Storm Maidens--Zu Bird Legend and Indian Garuda Myth--Legend of the Eagle and the Serpent--The Snake Mother Goddess--Demons and the Moon God--Plague Deities-- Classification of Spirits, and Egyptian, Arabian, and Scottish parallels--Traces of Progress from Animism to Monotheism.

The memorable sermon preached by Paul to the Athenians when he stood "in the midst of Mars' hill", could have been addressed with equal appropriateness to the ancient Sumerians and Akkadians. "I perceive", he declared, "that in all things ye are too superstitious.... God that made the world and all things therein, seeing that he is Lord of heaven and earth, dwelleth not in temples made with hands; neither is worshipped with men's hands as though he needed any thing, seeing he giveth to all life, and breath, and all things ... for in him we live, and move, and have our being; as certain also of your own poets have said, For we are also his offspring. Forasmuch then as we are the offspring of God, we ought not to think that the Godhead is like unto gold, or silver, or stone, graven by art and man's device."[78]

Babylonian temples were houses of the gods in the literal sense; the gods were supposed to dwell in them, their spirits having entered into the graven images or blocks of stone. It is probable that like the Ancient Egyptians they believed a god had as many spirits as he had attributes. The gods, as we have said, appear to have evolved from early spirit groups. All the world swarmed with spirits, which inhabited stones and trees, mountains and deserts, rivers and

30

ocean, the air, the sky, the stars, and the sun and moon. The spirits controlled Nature: they brought light and darkness, sunshine and storm, summer and winter; they were manifested in the thunderstorm, the sandstorm, the glare of sunset, and the wraiths of mist rising from the steaming marshes. They controlled also the lives of men and women. The good spirits were the source of luck. The bad spirits caused misfortunes, and were ever seeking to work evil against the Babylonian. Darkness was peopled by demons and ghosts of the dead. The spirits of disease were ever lying in wait to clutch him with cruel invisible hands.

Some modern writers, who are too prone to regard ancient peoples from a twentieth-century point of view, express grave doubts as to whether "intelligent Babylonians" really believed that spirits came down in the rain and entered the soil to rise up before men's eyes as stalks of barley or wheat. There is no reason for supposing that they thought otherwise. The early folks based their theories on the accumulated knowledge of their age. They knew nothing regarding the composition of water or the atmosphere, of the cause of thunder and lightning, or of the chemical changes effected in soils by the action of bacteria. They attributed all natural phenomena to the operations of spirits or gods. In believing that certain demons caused certain diseases, they may be said to have achieved distinct progress, for they anticipated the germ theory. They made discoveries, too, which have been approved and elaborated in later times when they lit sacred fires, bathed in sacred waters, and used oils and herbs to charm away spirits of pestilence. Indeed, many folk cures, which were originally associated with magical ceremonies, are still practised in our own day. They were found to be effective by early observers, although they were unable to explain why and how cures were accomplished, like modern scientific investigators.

In peopling the Universe with spirits, the Babylonians, like other ancient folks, betrayed that tendency to symbolize everything which has ever appealed to the human mind. Our painters and poets and sculptors are greatest when they symbolize their ideals and ideas and impressions, and by so doing make us respond to their moods. Their "beauty and their terror are sublime". But what may seem poetic to us, was invariably a grim reality to the Babylonians. The statue or picture was not merely a work of art but a manifestation of the god or demon. As has been said, they believed that the spirit of the god inhabited the idol; the frown of the brazen image was the frown of the wicked demon. They entertained as much dread of the winged and human-headed bulls guarding the entrance to the royal palace as do some of the Arab workmen who, in our own day, assist excavators to rescue them from sandy mounds in which they have been hidden for long centuries.

When an idol was carried away from a city by an invading army, it was believed that the god himself had been taken prisoner, and was therefore unable any longer to help his people.

In the early stages of Sumerian culture, the gods and goddesses who formed groups were indistinguishable from demons. They were vaguely defined, and had changing shapes. When attempts were made to depict them they were represented in many varying forms. Some were winged bulls or lions with human heads; others had even more remarkable composite forms. The "dragon of Babylon", for instance, which was portrayed on walls of temples, had a serpent's head, a body covered with scales, the fore legs of a lion, hind legs of an eagle, and a long wriggling serpentine tail. Ea had several monster forms. The following description of one of these is repulsive enough:--

> The head is the head of a serpent,
> From his nostrils mucus trickles,
> His mouth is beslavered with water;
> The ears are like those of a basilisk,
> His horns are twisted into three curls,
> He wears a veil in his head band,
> The body is a suh-fish full of stars,
> The base of his feet are claws,
> The sole of his foot has no heel,
> His name is Sassu-wunnu,
> A sea monster, a form of Ea.

> *R.C. Thompson's Translation.*[79]

Even after the gods were given beneficent attributes to reflect the growth of culture, and were humanized, they still retained many of their savage characteristics. Bel Enlil and his fierce son, Nergal, were destroyers of mankind; the storm god desolated the land; the sky god deluged it with rain; the sea raged furiously, ever hungering for human victims; the burning sun struck down its victims; and the floods played havoc with the dykes and houses of human beings.

31

In Egypt the sun god Ra was similarly a "producer of calamity", the composite monster god Sokar was "the lord of fear".[80] Osiris in prehistoric times had been "a dangerous god", and some of the Pharaohs sought protection against him in the charms inscribed in their tombs.[81] The Indian Shiva, "the Destroyer", in the old religious poems has also primitive attributes of like character.

The Sumerian gods never lost their connection with the early spirit groups. These continued to be represented by their attendants, who executed a deity's stern and vengeful decrees. In one of the Babylonian charms the demons are referred to as "the spleen of the gods"--the symbols of their wrathful emotions and vengeful desires. Bel Enlil, the air and earth god, was served by the demons of disease, "the beloved sons of Bel", which issued from the Underworld to attack mankind. Nergal, the sulky and ill-tempered lord of death and destruction, who never lost his demoniac character, swept over the land, followed by the spirits of pestilence, sunstroke, weariness, and destruction. Anu, the sky god, had "spawned" at creation the demons of cold and rain and darkness. Even Ea and his consort, Damkina, were served by groups of devils and giants, which preyed upon mankind in bleak and desolate places when night fell. In the ocean home of Ea were bred the "seven evil spirits" of tempest--the gaping dragon, the leopard which preyed upon children, the great Beast, the terrible serpent, &c.

In Indian mythology Indra was similarly followed by the stormy Maruts, and fierce Rudra by the tempestuous Rudras. In Teutonic mythology Odin is the "Wild Huntsman in the Raging Host". In Greek mythology the ocean furies attend upon fickle Poseidon. Other examples of this kind could be multiplied.

As we have seen (Chapter II) the earliest group of Babylonian deities consisted probably of four pairs of gods and goddesses as in Egypt. The first pair was Apsu-Rishtu and Tiamat, who personified the primordial deep. Now the elder deities in most mythologies--the "grandsires" and "grandmothers" and "fathers" and "mothers"--are ever the most powerful and most vengeful. They appear to represent primitive "layers" of savage thought. The Greek Cronos devours even his own children, and, as the late Andrew Lang has shown, there are many parallels to this myth among primitive peoples in various parts of the world.

Lang regarded the Greek survival as an example of "the conservatism of the religious instinct".[82] The grandmother of the Teutonic deity Tyr was a fierce giantess with nine hundred heads; his father was an enemy of the gods. In Scotland the hag-mother of winter and storm and darkness is the enemy of growth and all life, and she raises storms to stop the grass growing, to slay young animals, and prevent the union of her son with his fair bride. Similarly the Babylonian chaos spirits, Apsu and Tiamat, the father and mother of the gods, resolve to destroy their offspring, because they begin to set the Universe in order. Tiamat, the female dragon, is more powerful than her husband Apsu, who is slain by his son Ea. She summons to her aid the gods of evil, and creates also a brood of monsters--serpents, dragons, vipers, fish men, raging hounds, &c.--so as to bring about universal and enduring confusion and evil. Not until she is destroyed can the beneficent gods establish law and order and make the earth habitable and beautiful.

But although Tiamat was slain, the everlasting battle between the forces of good and evil was ever waged in the Babylonian world. Certain evil spirits were let loose at certain periods, and they strove to accomplish the destruction of mankind and his works. These invisible enemies were either charmed away by performing magical ceremonies, or by invoking the gods to thwart them and bind them.

Other spirits inhabited the bodies of animals and were ever hovering near. The ghosts of the dead and male and female demons were birds, like the birds of Fate which sang to Siegfried. When the owl raised its melancholy voice in the darkness the listener heard the spirit of a departed mother crying for her child. Ghosts and evil spirits wandered through the streets in darkness; they haunted empty houses; they fluttered through the evening air as bats; they hastened, moaning dismally, across barren wastes searching for food or lay in wait for travellers; they came as roaring lions and howling jackals, hungering for human flesh. The "shedu" was a destructive bull which might slay man wantonly or as a protector of temples. Of like character was the "lamassu", depicted as a winged bull with human head, the protector of palaces; the "alu" was a bull-like demon of tempest, and there were also many composite, distorted, or formless monsters which were vaguely termed "seizers" or "overthrowers", the Semitic "labashu" and "ach-chazu", the Sumerian "dimmea" and "dimme-kur". A dialectic form of "gallu" or devil was "mulla". Professor Pinches thinks it not improbable that "mulla" may be connected with the word "mula", meaning "star", and suggests that it referred to a "will-o'-the-wisp".[83] In these islands, according to an old rhyme,

> Some call him Robin Good-fellow,
> Hob-goblin, or mad Crisp,

And some againe doe tearme him oft
　　By name of Will the Wisp.
Other names are "Kitty", "Peg", and "Jack with a lantern". "Poor Robin" sang:
I should indeed as soon expect
That Peg-a-lantern would direct
Me straightway home on misty night
As wand'ring stars, quite out of sight.

In Shakespeare's *Tempest*[84] a sailor exclaims: "Your fairy, which, you say, is a harmless fairy, has done little better than played the Jack with us". Dr. Johnson commented that the reference was to "Jack with a lantern". Milton wrote also of the "wandering fire",
Which oft, they say, some evil spirit attends,
Hovering and blazing with delusive light,
Misleads th' amaz'd night wand'rer from his way
To bogs and mires, and oft through pond or pool;
There swallowed up and lost from succour far.[85]

"When we stick in the mire", sang Drayton, "he doth with laughter leave us." These fires were also "fallen stars", "death fires", and "fire drakes":
So have I seen a fire drake glide along
Before a dying man, to point his grave,
And in it stick and hide.[86]

Pliny referred to the wandering lights as stars.[87] The Sumerian "mulla" was undoubtedly an evil spirit. In some countries the "fire drake" is a bird with gleaming breast: in Babylonia it assumed the form of a bull, and may have had some connection with the bull of Ishtar. Like the Indian "Dasyu" and "Dasa",[88] Gallu was applied in the sense of "foreign devil" to human and superhuman adversaries of certain monarchs. Some of the supernatural beings resemble our elves and fairies and the Indian Rakshasas. Occasionally they appear in comely human guise; at other times they are vaguely monstrous. The best known of this class is Lilith, who, according to Hebrew tradition, preserved in the Talmud, was the demon lover of Adam. She has been immortalized by Dante Gabriel Rossetti:
Of Adam's first wife Lilith, it is told
(The witch he loved before the gift of Eve)
That, ere the snake's, her sweet tongue could deceive,
And her enchanted hair was the first gold.
And still she sits, young while the earth is old,
And, subtly of herself contemplative,
Draws men to watch the bright web she can weave,
Till heart and body and life are in its hold.
The rose and poppy are her flowers; for where
Is he not found, O Lilith, whom shed scent
And soft shed kisses and soft sleep shall snare?
Lo! as that youth's eyes burned at thine, so went
Thy spell through him, and left his straight neck bent
And round his heart one strangling golden hair.

Lilith is the Babylonian Lilithu, a feminine form of Lilu, the Sumerian Lila. She resembles Surpanakha of the *Ramayana*, who made love to Rama and Lakshmana, and the sister of the demon Hidimva, who became enamoured of Bhima, one of the heroes of the *Mahabharata*,[89] and the various fairy lovers of Europe who lured men to eternal imprisonment inside mountains, or vanished for ever when they were completely under their influence, leaving them demented. The elfin Lilu similarly wooed young women, like the Germanic Laurin of the "Wonderful Rose Garden",[90] who carried away the fair lady Kunhild to his underground dwelling amidst the Tyrolese mountains, or left them haunting the place of their meetings, searching for him in vain:
A savage place! as holy and enchanted
As ere beneath the waning moon was haunted
By woman wailing for her demon lover...
His flashing eyes, his floating hair!
Weave a circle round him thrice,
And close your eyes with holy dread,
For he on honey dew hath fed
And drunk the milk of Paradise.

Coleridge's Kubla Khan.

33

Another materializing spirit of this class was Ardat Lili, who appears to have wedded human beings like the swan maidens, the mermaids, and Nereids of the European folk tales, and the goddess Ganga, who for a time was the wife of King Shantanu of the *Mahabharata*.[91]

The Labartu, to whom we have referred, was a female who haunted mountains and marshes; like the fairies and hags of Europe, she stole or afflicted children, who accordingly had to wear charms round their necks for protection. Seven of these supernatural beings were reputed to be daughters of Anu, the sky god.

The Alu, a storm deity, was also a spirit which caused nightmare. It endeavoured to smother sleepers like the Scandinavian hag Mara, and similarly deprived them of power to move. In Babylonia this evil spirit might also cause sleeplessness or death by hovering near a bed. In shape it might be as horrible and repulsive as the Egyptian ghosts which caused children to die from fright or by sucking out the breath of life.

As most representatives of the spirit world were enemies of the living, so were the ghosts of dead men and women. Death chilled all human affections; it turned love to hate; the deeper the love had been, the deeper became the enmity fostered by the ghost. Certain ghosts might also be regarded as particularly virulent and hostile if they happened to have left the body of one who was ceremonially impure. The most terrible ghost in Babylonia was that of a woman who had died in childbed. She was pitied and dreaded; her grief had demented her; she was doomed to wail in the darkness; her impurity clung to her like poison. No spirit was more prone to work evil against mankind, and her hostility was accompanied by the most tragic sorrow. In Northern India the Hindus, like the ancient Babylonians, regard as a fearsome demon the ghost of a woman who died while pregnant, or on the day of the child's birth.[92] A similar belief prevailed in Mexico. In Europe there are many folk tales of dead mothers who return to avenge themselves on the cruel fathers of neglected children.

A sharp contrast is presented by the Mongolian Buriats, whose outlook on the spirit world is less gloomy than was that of the ancient Babylonians. According to Mr. Jeremiah Curtin, this interesting people are wont to perform a ceremony with purpose to entice the ghost to return to the dead body--a proceeding which is dreaded in the Scottish Highlands.[93] The Buriats address the ghost, saying: "You shall sleep well. Come back to your natural ashes. Take pity on your friends. It is necessary to live a real life. Do not wander along the mountains. Do not be like bad spirits. Return to your peaceful home.... Come back and work for your children. How can you leave the little ones?" If it is a mother, these words have great effect; sometimes the spirit moans and sobs, and the Buriats tell that there have been instances of it returning to the body.[94] In his *Arabia Deserta*[95] Doughty relates that Arab women and children mock the cries of the owl. One explained to him: "It is a wailful woman seeking her lost child; she has become this forlorn bird". So do immemorial beliefs survive to our own day.

The Babylonian ghosts of unmarried men and women and of those without offspring were also disconsolate night wanderers. Others who suffered similar fates were the ghosts of men who died in battle far from home and were left unburied, the ghosts of travellers who perished in the desert and were not covered over, the ghosts of drowned men which rose from the water, the ghosts of prisoners starved to death or executed, the ghosts of people who died violent deaths before their appointed time. The dead required to be cared for, to have libations poured out, to be fed, so that they might not prowl through the streets or enter houses searching for scraps of food and pure water. The duty of giving offerings to the dead was imposed apparently on near relatives. As in India, it would appear that the eldest son performed the funeral ceremony: a dreadful fate therefore awaited the spirit of the dead Babylonian man or woman without offspring. In Sanskrit literature there is a reference to a priest who was not allowed to enter Paradise, although he had performed rigid penances, because he had no children.[96]

There were hags and giants of mountain and desert, of river and ocean. Demons might possess the pig, the goat, the horse, the lion, or the ibis, the raven, or the hawk. The seven spirits of tempest, fire, and destruction rose from the depths of ocean, and there were hosts of demons which could not be overcome or baffled by man without the assistance of the gods to whom they were hostile. Many were sexless; having no offspring, they were devoid of mercy and compassion. They penetrated everywhere:

The high enclosures, the broad enclosures, like a flood
  they pass through,
From house to house they dash along.
No door can shut them out;
No bolt can turn them back.
Through the door, like a snake, they glide,

Through the hinge, like the wind, they storm,
Tearing the wife from the embrace of the man,
Driving the freedman from his family home.[97]
These furies did not confine their unwelcomed attentions to mankind alone:
They hunt the doves from their cotes,
And drive the birds from their nests,
And chase the marten from its hole....
Through the gloomy street by night they roam,
Smiting sheepfold and cattle pen,
Shutting up the land as with door and bolt.

     R.C. Thompson's Translation.

The Babylonian poet, like Burns, was filled with pity for the animals which suffered in the storm:

List'ning the doors an' winnocks rattle,
I thought me o' the ourie cattle,
Or silly sheep, wha bide this brattle
  O' winter war....
Ilk happing bird, wee, helpless thing!
That in the merry months o' spring
Delighted me to hear thee sing,
  What comes o' thee?
Whare wilt thou cow'r thy chittering wing,
  And close thy e'e?

According to Babylonian belief, "the great storms directed from heaven" were caused by demons. Mankind heard them "loudly roaring above, gibbering below".[98] The south wind was raised by Shutu, a plumed storm demon resembling Hraesvelgur of the Icelandic Eddas:

Corpse-swallower sits at the end of heaven,
  A Jötun in eagle form;
From his wings, they say, comes the wind which fares
  Over all the dwellers of earth.[99]

The northern story of Thor's fishing, when he hooked and wounded the Midgard serpent, is recalled by the Babylonian legend of Adapa, son of the god Ea. This hero was engaged catching fish, when Shutu, the south wind, upset his boat. In his wrath Adapa immediately attacked the storm demon and shattered her pinions. Anu, the sky god, was moved to anger against Ea's son and summoned him to the Celestial Court. Adapa, however, appeared in garments of mourning and was forgiven. Anu offered him the water of life and the bread of life which would have made him immortal, but Ea's son refused to eat or drink, believing, as his father had warned him, that the sky god desired him to partake of the bread of death and to drink of the water of death.

     Another terrible atmospheric demon was the south-west wind, which caused destructive storms and floods, and claimed many human victims like the Icelandic "corpse swallower". She was depicted with lidless staring eyes, broad flat nose, mouth gaping horribly, and showing tusk-like teeth, and with high cheek bones, heavy eyebrows, and low bulging forehead.

     In Scotland the hag of the south-west wind is similarly a bloodthirsty and fearsome demon. She is most virulent in the springtime. At Cromarty she is quaintly called "Gentle Annie" by the fisher folks, who repeat the saying: "When Gentle Annie is skyawlan (yelling) roond the heel of Ness (a promontory) wi' a white feather on her hat (the foam of big billows) they (the spirits) will be harrying (robbing) the crook"--that is, the pot which hangs from the crook is empty during the spring storms, which prevent fishermen going to sea. In England the wind hag is Black Annis, who dwells in a Leicestershire hill cave. She may be identical with the Irish hag Anu, associated with the "Paps of Anu". According to Gaelic lore, this wind demon of spring is the "Cailleach" (old wife). She gives her name in the Highland calendar to the stormy period of late spring; she raises gale after gale to prevent the coming of summer. Angerboda, the Icelandic hag, is also a storm demon, but represents the east wind. A Tyrolese folk tale tells of three magic maidens who dwelt on Jochgrimm mountain, where they "brewed the winds". Their demon lovers were Ecke, "he who causes fear"; Vasolt, "he who causes dismay"; and the scornful Dietrich in his mythical character of Donar or Thunor (Thor), the thunderer.

     Another Sumerian storm demon was the Zu bird, which is represented among the stars by Pegasus and Taurus. A legend relates that this "worker of evil, who raised the head of evil", once aspired to rule the gods, and stole from Bel, "the lord" of deities, the Tablets of Destiny, which gave him his power over the Universe as controller of the fates of all. The Zu bird escaped with the Tablets and found shelter on its mountain top in Arabia. Anu called on Ramman, the thunderer, to attack the Zu bird, but he was afraid; other gods appear to have shrunk from the conflict. How the rebel was overcome is not certain, because the legend survives in fragmentary form. There is a reference, however, to the moon god setting out towards the mountain in Arabia with purpose to outwit the Zu bird and recover the lost Tablets. How he fared it is impossible to ascertain. In another legend--that of Etana--the mother serpent, addressing the sun god, Shamash, says:

> Thy net is like unto the broad earth;
> Thy snare is like unto the distant heaven!
> Who hath ever escaped from thy net?
> Even Zu, the worker of evil, who raised the head
> of evil [did not escape]!

L.W. King's Translation.

In Indian mythology, Garuda, half giant, half eagle, robs the Amrita (ambrosia) of the gods which gives them their power and renders them immortal. It had assumed a golden body, bright as the sun. Indra, the thunderer, flung his bolt in vain; he could not wound Garuda, and only displaced a single feather. Afterwards, however, he stole the moon goblet containing the Amrita, which Garuda had delivered to his enemies, the serpents, to free his mother from bondage. This Indian eagle giant became the vehicle of the god Vishnu, and, according to the *Mahabharata*, "mocked the wind with his fleetness".

It would appear that the Babylonian Zu bird symbolized the summer sandstorms from the Arabian desert. Thunder is associated with the rainy season, and it may have been assumed, therefore, that the thunder god was powerless against the sandstorm demon, who was chased, however, by the moon, and finally overcome by the triumphant sun when it broke through the darkening sand drift and brightened heaven and earth, "netting" the rebellious demon who desired to establish the rule of evil over gods and mankind.

In the "Legend of Etana" the Eagle, another demon which links with the Indian Garuda, slayer of serpents, devours the brood of the Mother Serpent. For this offence against divine law, Shamash, the sun god, pronounces the Eagle's doom. He instructs the Mother Serpent to slay a wild ox and conceal herself in its entrails. The Eagle comes to feed on the carcass, unheeding the warning of one of his children, who says, "The serpent lies in this wild ox":

> He swooped down and stood upon the wild ox,
> The Eagle ... examined the flesh;
> He looked about carefully before and behind him;
> He again examined the flesh;
> He looked about carefully before and behind him,
> Then, moving swiftly, he made for the hidden parts.
> When he entered into the midst,
> The serpent seized him by his wing.

In vain the Eagle appealed for mercy to the Mother Serpent, who was compelled to execute the decree of Shamash; she tore off the Eagle's pinions, wings, and claws, and threw him into a pit where he perished from hunger and thirst.[100] This myth may refer to the ravages of a winged demon of disease who was thwarted by the sacrifice of an ox. The Mother Serpent appears to be identical with an ancient goddess of maternity resembling the Egyptian Bast, the serpent mother of Bubastis. According to Sumerian belief, Nintu, "a form of the goddess Ma", was half a serpent. On her head there is a horn; she is "girt about the loins"; her left arm holds "a babe suckling her breast":

> From her head to her loins
> The body is that of a naked woman;
> From the loins to the sole of the foot
> Scales like those of a snake are visible.

R.C. Thompson's Translation.

The close association of gods and demons is illustrated in an obscure myth which may refer to an eclipse of the moon or a night storm at the beginning of the rainy season. The demons go to war against the high gods, and are assisted by Adad (Ramman) the thunderer, Shamash the sun, and Ishtar. They desire to wreck the heavens, the home of Anu:

> They clustered angrily round the crescent of the moon god,

And won over to their aid Shamash, the mighty, and Adad, the warrior,
And Ishtar, who with Anu, the King,
Hath founded a shining dwelling.

The moon god Sin, "the seed of mankind", was darkened by the demons who raged, "rushing loose over the land" like to the wind. Bel called upon his messenger, whom he sent to Ea in the ocean depths, saying: "My son Sin ... hath been grievously bedimmed". Ea lamented, and dispatched his son Merodach to net the demons by magic, using "a two-coloured cord from the hair of a virgin kid and from the wool of a virgin lamb".[101]

As in India, where Shitala, the Bengali goddess of smallpox, for instance, is worshipped when the dreaded disease she controls becomes epidemic, so in Babylonia the people sought to secure immunity from attack by worshipping spirits of disease. A tablet relates that Ura, a plague demon, once resolved to destroy all life, but ultimately consented to spare those who praised his name and exalted him in recognition of his bravery and power. This could be accomplished by reciting a formula. Indian serpent worshippers believe that their devotions "destroy all danger proceeding from snakes".[102]

Like the Ancient Egyptians, the Babylonians also had their kindly spirits who brought luck and the various enjoyments of life. A good "labartu" might attend on a human being like a household fairy of India or Europe: a friendly "shedu" could protect a household against the attacks of fierce demons and human enemies. Even the spirits of Fate who served Anu, god of the sky, and that "Norn" of the Underworld, Eresh-ki-gal, queen of Hades, might sometimes be propitious: if the deities were successfully invoked they could cause the Fates to smite spirits of disease and bringers of ill luck. Damu, a friendly fairy goddess, was well loved, because she inspired pleasant dreams, relieved the sufferings of the afflicted, and restored to good health those patients whom she selected to favour.

In the Egyptian *Book of the Dead* the kindly spirits are overshadowed by the evil ones, because the various magical spells which were put on record were directed against those supernatural beings who were enemies of mankind. Similarly in Babylonia the fragments of this class of literature which survive deal mainly with wicked and vengeful demons. It appears probable, however, that the highly emotional Sumerians and Akkadians were on occasion quite as cheerful a people as the inhabitants of ancient Egypt. Although they were surrounded by bloodthirsty furies who desired to shorten their days, and their nights were filled with vague lowering phantoms which inspired fear, they no doubt shared, in their charm-protected houses, a comfortable feeling of security after performing magical ceremonies, and were happy enough when they gathered round flickering lights to listen to ancient song and story and gossip about crops and traders, the members of the royal house, and the family affairs of their acquaintances.

The Babylonian spirit world, it will be seen, was of complex character. Its inhabitants were numberless, but often vaguely defined, and one class of demons linked with another. Like the European fairies of folk belief, the Babylonian spirits were extremely hostile and irresistible at certain seasonal periods; and they were fickle and perverse and difficult to please even when inclined to be friendly. They were also similarly manifested from time to time in various forms. Sometimes they were comely and beautiful; at other times they were apparitions of horror. The Jinn of present-day Arabians are of like character; these may be giants, cloudy shapes, comely women, serpents or cats, goats or pigs.

Some of the composite monsters of Babylonia may suggest the vague and exaggerated recollections of terror-stricken people who have had glimpses of unfamiliar wild beasts in the dusk or amidst reedy marshes. But they cannot be wholly accounted for in this way. While animals were often identified with supernatural beings, and foreigners were called "devils", it would be misleading to assert that the spirit world reflects confused folk memories of human and bestial enemies. Even when a demon was given concrete human form it remained essentially non-human: no ordinary weapon could inflict an injury, and it was never controlled by natural laws. The spirits of disease and tempest and darkness were creations of fancy: they symbolized moods; they were the causes which explained effects. A sculptor or storyteller who desired to convey an impression of a spirit of storm or pestilence created monstrous forms to inspire terror. Sudden and unexpected visits of fierce and devastating demons were accounted for by asserting that they had wings like eagles, were nimble-footed as gazelles, cunning and watchful as serpents; that they had claws to clutch, horns to gore, and powerful fore legs like a lion to smite down victims. Withal they drank blood like ravens and devoured corpses like hyaenas. Monsters were all the more repulsive when they were partly human. The human-headed snake or the snake-headed man and the man with the horns of a wild bull and the legs of a goat were horrible in the extreme. Evil spirits might sometimes achieve success by practising deception. They might appear as beautiful girls or handsome men and seize unsuspecting victims in deathly embrace or leave them demented and full of grief, or come as birds and suddenly assume awesome shapes.

Fairies and elves, and other half-human demons, are sometimes regarded as degenerate gods. It will be seen, however, that while certain spirits developed into deities, others remained something between these two classes of supernatural beings: they might attend upon gods and goddesses, or operate independently now against mankind and now against deities even. The "namtaru", for instance, was a spirit of fate, the son of Bel-Enlil and Eresh-ki-gal, queen of Hades. "Apparently", writes Professor Pinches, "he executed the instructions given him concerning the fate of men, and could also have power over certain of the gods."[103] To this middle class belong the evil gods who rebelled against the beneficent deities. According to Hebridean folk belief, the fallen angels are divided into three classes--the fairies, the "nimble men" (aurora borealis), and the "blue men of the Minch". In *Beowulf* the "brood of Cain" includes "monsters and elves and sea-devils--giants also, who long time fought with God, for which he gave them their reward".[104] Similarly the Babylonian spirit groups are liable to division and subdivision. The various classes may be regarded as relics of the various stages of development from crude animism to sublime monotheism: in the fragmentary legends we trace the floating material from which great mythologies have been framed.

[78] *The Acts*, xvii, 22-31.

[79] *Devils and Evil Spirits of Babylonia*, vol. ii, p. 149 *et seq.*

[80] *Egyptian Myth and Legend*, xxxix, *n.*

[81] *Development of Religion and Thought in Ancient Egypt*, J.H. Breasted, pp. 38, 74.

[82] *Custom and Myth*, p. 45 *et seq.*

[83] *The Religion of Babylonia and Assyria*, p. 108.

[84] Act iv, scene 1.

[85] *Paradise Lost*, book ix.

[86] Chapman's *Caesar and Pompey*.

[87] *Natural History*, 2nd book.

[88] *Indian Myth and Legend*, 70, n.

[89] *Indian Myth and Legend*, pp. 202-5, 400, 401.

[90] *Teutonic Myth and Legend*, p. 424 et seq.

[91] *Indian Myth and Legend*, p. 164 et seq.

[92] *Popular Religion and Folk Lore of Northern India*, W. Crooke, vol. i, p. 254.

[93] When a person, young or old, is dying, near relatives must not call out their names in case the soul may come back from the spirit world. A similar belief still lingers, especially among women, in the Lowlands. The writer was once present in a room when a child was supposed to be dying. Suddenly the mother called out the child's name in agonized voice. It revived soon afterwards. Two old women who had attempted to prevent "the calling" shook their heads and remarked: "She has done it! The child will never do any good in this world after being called back." In England and Ireland, as well as in Scotland, the belief also prevails in certain localities that if a dying person is "called back" the soul will tarry for another twenty-four hours, during which the individual will suffer great agony.

[94] *A Journey in Southern Siberia*, Jeremiah Curtin, pp. 103, 104.

[95] Vol. i, p. 305.

[96] *Adi Parva* section of *Mahàbhàrata*, Roy's trans., p. 635.

[97] Jastrow's *Aspects of Religious Belief in Babylonia*, &c., p. 312.

[98] R.C. Thompson's trans.

[99] *The Elder or Poetic Edda*, Olive Bray, part i, p. 53.

[100] *Babylonian Religion*, L.W. King, pp. 186-8.

[101] *The Devils and Evil Spirits of Babylonia*, R. Campbell Thompson, vol. i, p. 53 et seq.

[102] *Omens and Superstitions of Southern India*, E. Thurston, p. 124.

[103] *The Religion of Babylonia and Assyria*, p. 110.

[104] *Beowulf*, Clark Hall, p. 14.

Chapter V. Myths of Tammuz and Ishtar

Abstract

Forms of Tammuz--The Weeping Ceremony--Tammuz the Patriarch and the Dying God--Common Origin of Tammuz and other Deities from an Archaic God--The Mediterranean Racial Myth--Animal Forms of Gods of Fertility--Two Legends of the Death of Tammuz--Attis, Adonis, and Diarmid Slain by a Boar--Laments for Tammuz--His Soul in Underworld and the Deep--Myth of the Child God of Ocean--Sargon Myth Version--The Germanic Scyld of the Sheaf--Tammuz Links with Frey, Heimdal, Agni, &c.--Assyrian Legend of "Descent of Ishtar"--Sumerian Version--The Sister Belit-sheri and the Mother Ishtar--The

Egyptian Isis and Nepthys--Goddesses as Mothers, Sisters, and Wives--Great Mothers of Babylonia--Immortal Goddesses and Dying Gods--The Various Indras--Celtic Goddess with Seven Periods of Youth--Lovers of Germanic and Classic Goddesses--The Lovers of Ishtar--Racial Significance of Goddess Cult--The Great Fathers and their Worshippers--Process of Racial and Religious Fusion--Ishtar and Tiamat--Mother Worship in Palestine--Women among Goddess Worshippers.

Among the gods of Babylonia none achieved wider and more enduring fame than Tammuz, who was loved by Ishtar, the amorous Queen of Heaven--the beautiful youth who died and was mourned for and came to life again. He does not figure by his popular name in any of the city pantheons, but from the earliest times of which we have knowledge until the passing of Babylonian civilization, he played a prominent part in the religious life of the people.

Tammuz, like Osiris of Egypt, was an agricultural deity, and as the Babylonian harvest was the gift of the rivers, it is probable that one of his several forms was Dumu-zi-abzu, "Tammuz of the Abyss". He was also "the child", "the heroic lord", "the sentinel", "the healer", and the patriarch who reigned over the early Babylonians for a considerable period. "Tammuz of the Abyss" was one of the members of the family of Ea, god of the Deep, whose other sons, in addition to Merodach, were Nira, an obscure deity; Ki-gulla, "world destroyer", Burnunta-sa, "broad ear", and Bara and Baragulla, probably "revealers" or "oracles". In addition there was a daughter, Khi-dimme-azaga, "child of the renowned spirit". She may have been identical with Belit-sheri, who is referred to in the Sumerian hymns as the sister of Tammuz. This family group was probably formed by symbolizing the attributes of Ea and his spouse Damkina. Tammuz, in his character as a patriarch, may have been regarded as a hostage from the gods: the human form of Ea, who instructed mankind, like King Osiris, how to grow corn and cultivate fruit trees. As the youth who perished annually, he was the corn spirit. He is referred to in the Bible by his Babylonian name.

When Ezekiel detailed the various idolatrous practices of the Israelites, which included the worship of the sun and "every form of creeping things and abominable beasts"--a suggestion of the composite monsters of Babylonia --he was brought "to the door of the gate of the Lord's house, which was towards the north; and, behold, there sat women weeping for Tammuz".[105]

The weeping ceremony was connected with agricultural rites. Corn deities were weeping deities, they shed fertilizing tears; and the sowers simulated the sorrow of divine mourners when they cast seed in the soil "to die", so that it might spring up as corn. This ancient custom, like many others, contributed to the poetic imagery of the Bible. "They that sow in tears", David sang, "shall reap in joy. He that goeth forth and weepeth, bearing precious seed, shall doubtless come again with rejoicing, bringing his sheaves with him."[106] In Egypt the priestesses who acted the parts of Isis and Nepthys, mourned for the slain corn god Osiris.

Gods and men before the face of the gods are weeping for
thee at the same time, when they behold me!...
All thy sister goddesses are at thy side and behind thy couch,
Calling upon thee with weeping--yet thou are prostrate upon
thy bed!...
Live before us, desiring to behold thee.[107]

It was believed to be essential that human beings should share the universal sorrow caused by the death of a god. If they remained unsympathetic, the deities would punish them as enemies. Worshippers of nature gods, therefore, based their ceremonial practices on natural phenomena. "The dread of the worshippers that the neglect of the usual ritual would be followed by disaster, is particularly intelligible", writes Professor Robertson Smith, "if they regarded the necessary operations of agriculture as involving the violent extinction of a particle of divine life."[108] By observing their ritual, the worshippers won the sympathy and co-operation of deities, or exercised a magical control over nature.

The Babylonian myth of Tammuz, the dying god, bears a close resemblance to the Greek myth of Adonis. It also links with the myth of Osiris. According to Professor Sayce, Tammuz is identical with "Daonus or Daos, the shepherd of Pantibibla", referred to by Berosus as the ruler of one of the mythical ages of Babylonia. We have therefore to deal with Tammuz in his twofold character as a patriarch and a god of fertility.

The Adonis version of the myth may be summarized briefly. Ere the god was born, his mother, who was pursued by her angry sire, as the river goddesses of the folk tales are pursued by the well demons, transformed herself into a tree. Adonis sprang from the trunk of this tree, and Aphrodite, having placed the child in a chest, committed him to the care of Persephone, queen of Hades, who resembles the Babylonian Eresh-ki-gal. Persephone desired to retain the young god, and Aphrodite (Ishtar) appealed to Zeus (Anu), who decreed that Adonis should spend part of the year with one goddess and part of the year with the other.

It is suggested that the myth of Adonis was derived in post-Homeric times by the Greeks indirectly from Babylonia through the Western Semites, the Semitic title "Adon", meaning "lord", having been mistaken for a proper name. This theory, however, cannot be accepted without qualifications. It does not explain the existence of either the Phrygian myth of Attis, which was developed differently from the Tammuz myth, or the Celtic story of "Diarmid and the boar", which belongs to the archaeological "Hunting Period". There are traces in Greek mythology of pre-Hellenic myths about dying harvest deities, like Hyakinthos and Erigone, for instance, who appear to have been mourned for. There is every possibility, therefore, that the Tammuz ritual may have been attached to a harvest god of the pre-Hellenic Greeks, who received at the same time the new name of Adonis. Osiris of Egypt resembles Tammuz, but his Mesopotamian origin has not been proved. It would appear probable that Tammuz, Attis, Osiris, and the deities represented by Adonis and Diarmid were all developed from an archaic god of fertility and vegetation, the central figure of a myth which was not only as ancient as the knowledge and practice of agriculture, but had existence even in the "Hunting Period". Traces of the Tammuz-Osiris story in various forms are found all over the area occupied by the Mediterranean or Brown race from Sumeria to the British Isles. Apparently the original myth was connected with tree and water worship and the worship of animals. Adonis sprang from a tree; the body of Osiris was concealed in a tree which grew round the sea-drifted chest in which he was concealed. Diarmid concealed himself in a tree when pursued by Finn. The blood of Tammuz, Osiris, and Adonis reddened the swollen rivers which fertilized the soil. Various animals were associated with the harvest god, who appears to have been manifested from time to time in different forms, for his spirit pervaded all nature. In Egypt the soul of Osiris entered the Apis bull or the ram of Mendes.

Tammuz in the hymns is called "the pre-eminent steer of heaven", and a popular sacrifice was "a white kid of the god Tammuz", which, however, might be substituted by a sucking pig. Osiris had also associations with swine, and the Egyptians, according to Herodotus, sacrificed a pig to him annually. When Set at full moon hunted the boar in the Delta marshes, he probably hunted the boar form of Osiris, whose human body had been recovered from the sacred tree by Isis. As the soul of Bata, the hero of the Egyptian folk tale,[109] migrated from the blossom to the bull, and the bull to the tree, so apparently did the soul of Osiris pass from incarnation to incarnation. Set, the demon slayer of the harvest god, had also a boar form; he was the black pig who devoured the waning moon and blinded the Eye of Ra.

In his character as a long-lived patriarch, Tammuz, the King Daonus or Daos of Berosus, reigned in Babylonia for 36,000 years. When he died, he departed to Hades or the Abyss. Osiris, after reigning over the Egyptians, became Judge of the Dead.

Tammuz of the Sumerian hymns, however, is the Adonis-like god who lived on earth for a part of the year as the shepherd and agriculturist so dearly beloved by the goddess Ishtar. Then he died so that he might depart to the realm of Eresh-ki-gal (Persephone), queen of Hades. According to one account, his death was caused by the fickle Ishtar. When that goddess wooed Gilgamesh, the Babylonian Hercules, he upbraided her, saying:

On Tammuz, the spouse of thy youth,
Thou didst lay affliction every year.

King's Translation.

References in the Sumerian hymns suggest that there also existed a form of the legend which gave an account of the slaying of the young god by someone else than Ishtar. The slayer may have been a Set-like demon--perhaps Nin-shach, who appears to have symbolized the destroying influence of the sun. He was a war deity, and his name, Professor Pinches says, "is conjectured to mean 'lord of the wild boar'". There is no direct evidence, however, to connect Tammuz's slayer with the boar which killed Adonis. Ishtar's innocence is emphasized by the fact that she mourned for her youthful lover, crying:

Oh hero, my lord, ah me! I will say;
Food I eat not ... water I drink not ...
Because of the exalted one of the nether world, him of the
     radiant face, yea radiant,
Of the exalted one of the nether world, him of the dove-like
     voice, yea dove-like.[110]

The Phrygian Attis met his death, according to one legend, by self-mutilation under a sacred tree. Another account sets forth, however, that he was slain by a boar. The Greek Adonis was similarly killed by a boar. This animal was a form of Ares (Mars), god of war and tempest, who also loved Aphrodite (Ishtar). The Celtic Diarmid, in his character as a love god, with lunar attributes, was slain by "the green boar", which appears to have been one of the animals of a ferocious Hag, an earth and air "mother" with various names. In one of the many Fingalian stories the animal is

... That venomous boar, and he so fierce,
That Grey Eyebrows had with her herd of swine.[111]

Diarmid had eloped with the wife of Finn-mac-Coul (Fingal), who, like Ares, plotted to bring about his rival's death, and accordingly set the young hero to hunt the boar. As a thunder god Finn carried a hammer with which he smote his shield; the blows were heard in Lochlann (Scandinavia). Diarmid, like Tammuz, the "god of the tender voice and shining eyes", had much beauty. When he expired, Finn cried:

No maiden will raise her eye
Since the mould has gone over thy visage fair...
Blue without rashness in thine eye!
Passion and beauty behind thy curls!...
Oh, yesternight it was green the hillock,
Red is it this day with Diarmid's blood.[112]

Tammuz died with the dying vegetation, and Diarmid expired when the hills apparently were assuming their purple tints.[113] The month of Tammuz wailings was from 20th June till 20th July, when the heat and dryness brought forth the demons of pestilence. The mourners chanted:

He has gone, he has gone to the bosom of the earth,
And the dead are numerous in the land....
Men are filled with sorrow: they stagger by day in gloom ...
In the month of thy year which brings not peace hast thou gone.
Thou hast gone on a journey that makes an end of thy people.

The following extract contains a reference to the slaying of the god:

The holy one of Ishtar, in the middle of the year the fields languish...
The shepherd, the wise one, the man of sorrows, why have they slain?...
In his temple, in his inhabited domain,
The child, lord of knowledge, abides no more...
In the meadows, verily, verily, the soul of life perishes.

There is wailing for Tammuz "at the sacred cedar, where the mother bore thee", a reference which connects the god, like Adonis and Osiris, with tree worship:

The wailing is for the herbs: the first lament is, "they are not produced".
The wailing is for the grain, ears are not produced.
The wailing is for the habitations, for the flocks which bring forth no more.
The wailing is for the perishing wedded ones; for the perishing
children; the dark-headed people create no more.

The wailing is also for the shrunken river, the parched meadows, the fishpools, the cane brakes, the forests, the plains, the gardens, and the palace, which all suffer because the god of fertility has departed. The mourner cries:

How long shall the springing of verdure be restrained?
How long shall the putting forth of leaves be held back?

Whither went Tammuz? His destination has already been referred to as "the bosom of the earth", and in the Assyrian version of the "Descent of Ishtar" he dwells in "the house of darkness" among the dead, "where dust is their nourishment and their food mud", and "the light is never seen"--the gloomy Babylonian Hades. In one of the Sumerian hymns, however, it is stated that Tammuz "upon the flood was cast out". The reference may be to the submarine "house of Ea", or the Blessed Island to which the Babylonian Noah was carried. In this Hades bloomed the nether "garden of Adonis".

The following extract refers to the garden of Damu (Tammuz)[114]:--

Damu his youth therein slumbers ...
Among the garden flowers he slumbers; among the garden flowers
he is cast away ...
Among the tamarisks he slumbers, with woe he causes us to be
satiated.

Although Tammuz of the hymns was slain, he returned again from Hades. Apparently he came back as a child. He is wailed for as "child, Lord Gishzida", as well as "my hero Damu". In his lunar character the Egyptian Osiris appeared each month as "the child surpassingly beautiful"; the Osiris bull was also a child of the moon; "it was begotten", says

41

Plutarch, "by a ray of generative light falling from the moon". When the bull of Attis was sacrificed his worshippers were drenched with its blood, and were afterwards ceremonially fed with milk, as they were supposed to have "renewed their youth" and become children. The ancient Greek god Eros (Cupid) was represented as a wanton boy or handsome youth. Another god of fertility, the Irish Angus, who resembles Eros, is called "the ever young"; he slumbers like Tammuz and awakes in the Spring.

Apparently it was believed that the child god, Tammuz, returned from the earlier Sumerian Paradise of the Deep, and grew into full manhood in a comparatively brief period, like Vyasa and other super-men of Indian mythology. A couplet from a Tammuz hymn says tersely:

In his infancy in a sunken boat he lay.

In his manhood in the submerged grain he lay.[115]

The "boat" may be the "chest" in which Adonis was concealed by Aphrodite when she confided him to the care of Persephone, queen of Hades, who desired to retain the young god, but was compelled by Zeus to send him back to the goddess of love and vegetation. The fact that Ishtar descended to Hades in quest of Tammuz may perhaps explain the symbolic references in hymns to mother goddesses being in sunken boats also when their powers were in abeyance, as were those of the god for part of each year. It is possible, too, that the boat had a lunar and a solar significance. Khonsu, the Egyptian moon god, for instance, was associated with the Spring sun, being a deity of fertility and therefore a corn spirit; he was a form of Osiris, the Patriarch, who sojourned on earth to teach mankind how to grow corn and cultivate fruit trees. In the Egyptian legend Osiris received the corn seeds from Isis, which suggests that among Great-Mother-worshipping peoples, it was believed that agricultural civilization had a female origin. The same myths may have been attached to corn gods and corn goddesses, associated with water, sun, moon, and stars.

That there existed in Babylonia at an extremely remote period an agricultural myth regarding a Patriarch of divine origin who was rescued from a boat in his childhood, is suggested by the legend which was attached to the memory of the usurper King Sargon of Akkad. It runs as follows:

"I am Sargon, the mighty King of Akkad. My mother was a
vestal (priestess), my father an alien, whose brother inhabited the
mountain.... When my mother had conceived me, she bare
me in a hidden place. She laid me in a vessel of rushes, stopped
the door thereof with pitch, and cast me adrift on the river....
The river floated me to Akki, the water drawer, who, in drawing
water, drew me forth. Akki, the water drawer, educated me as
his son, and made me his gardener. As a gardener, I was beloved
by the goddess Ishtar."

It is unlikely that this story was invented by Sargon. Like the many variants of it found in other countries, it was probably founded on a form of the Tammuz-Adonis myth. Indeed, a new myth would not have suited Sargon's purpose so well as the adaptation of an old one, which was more likely to make popular appeal when connected with his name. The references to the goddess Ishtar, and Sargon's early life as a gardener, suggest that the king desired to be remembered as an agricultural Patriarch, if not of divine, at any rate of semi-divine origin.

What appears to be an early form of the widespread Tammuz myth is the Teutonic legend regarding the mysterious child who came over the sea to inaugurate a new era of civilization and instruct the people how to grow corn and become great warriors. The Northern peoples, as archaeological evidence suggests, derived their knowledge of agriculture, and therefore their agricultural myths, from the Neolithic representatives of the Mediterranean race with whom they came into contact. There can be no doubt but that the Teutonic legend refers to the introduction of agriculture. The child is called "Scef" or "Sceaf", which signifies "Sheaf", or "Scyld, the son of Sceaf". Scyld is the patriarch of the Scyldings, the Danes, a people of mixed origin. In the Anglo-Saxon *Beowulf* poem, the reference is to "Scyld", but Ethelweard, William of Malmesbury, and others adhered to "Sceaf" as the name of the Patriarch of the Western Saxons.

The legend runs that one day a boat was seen approaching the shore; it was not propelled by oars or sail. In it lay a child fast asleep, his head pillowed upon a sheaf of grain. He was surrounded by armour, treasure, and various implements, including the fire-borer. The child was reared by the people who found him, and he became a great instructor and warrior and ruled over the tribe as king. In *Beowulf* Scyld is the father of the elder Beowulf, whose grandson Hrothgar built the famous Hall. The poem opens with a reference to the patriarch "Scyld of the Sheaf". When he died, his body, according to the request he had made, was laid in a ship which was set adrift:

Upon his breast lay many treasures which were to travel with him into the power of the flood. Certainly they (the mourners) furnished him with no less of gifts, of tribal treasures, than those had done who, in his early days, started him over the sea alone, child as he was. Moreover, they set besides a gold-embroidered standard high above his head, and let the flood bear him--gave him to the sea. Their soul was sad, their spirit sorrowful. Who received that load, men, chiefs of council, heroes under heaven, cannot for certain tell.[116]

Sceaf or Scyld is identical with Yngve, the patriarch of the Ynglings; with Frey, the harvest and boar god, son of Njord,[117] the sea god; and with Hermod, referred to as follows in the Eddic "Lay of Hyndla":

> To some grants he wealth, to his children war fame,
> Word skill to many and wisdom to men,
> Fair winds to sea-farers, song craft to skalds,
> And might of manhood to many a warrior.

Tammuz is similarly "the heroic lord of the land", the "wise one", the "lord of knowledge", and "the sovereign, lord of invocation".

Heimdal, watchman of the Teutonic gods, also dwelt for a time among men as "Rig", and had human offspring, his son Thrall being the ancestor of the Thralls, his son Churl of churls, and Jarl of noblemen.

Tammuz, like Heimdal, is also a guardian. He watches the flocks and herds, whom he apparently guards against the Gallu demons as Heimdal guards the world and the heavens against attacks by giants and monsters. The flocks of Tammuz, Professor Pinches suggests, "recall the flocks of the Greek sun god Helios. These were the clouds illuminated by the sun, which were likened to sheep--indeed, one of the early Sumerian expressions for 'fleece' was 'sheep of the sky'. The name of Tammuz in Sumerian is Dumu-zi, or in its rare fullest form, Dumuzida, meaning 'true or faithful son'. There is probably some legend attached to this which is at present unknown."[118]

So the Sumerian hymn-chanters lamented:

> Like an herdsman the sentinel place of sheep and cattle he
> (Tammuz) has forsaken...
> From his home, from his inhabited domain, the son, he of wisdom,
> pre-eminent steer of heaven,
> The hero unto the nether herding place has taken his way.[119]

Agni, the Aryo-Indian god, who, as the sky sentinel, has points of resemblance to Heimdal, also links with Tammuz, especially in his Mitra character:

> Agni has been established among the tribes of men, the son of the waters, Mitra acting in the right way. *Rigveda*, iii, 5, 3.

> Agni, who has been looked and longed for in Heaven, who has been looked for on earth--he who has been looked for has entered all herbs. *Rigveda*, i, 98.[120]

Tammuz, like the Egyptian lunar and solar god Khonsu, is "the healer", and Agni "drives away all disease". Tammuz is the god "of sonorous voice"; Agni "roars like a bull"; and Heimdal blows a horn when the giants and demons threaten to attack the citadel of the gods. As the spring sun god, Tammuz is "a youthful warrior", says Jastrow, "triumphing over the storms of winter".[121] The storms, of course, were symbolized as demons. Tammuz, "the heroic lord", was therefore a demon slayer like Heimdal and Agni. Each of these gods appear to have been developed in isolation from an archaic spring god of fertility and corn whose attributes were symbolized. In Teutonic mythology, for instance, Heimdal was the warrior form of the patriarch Scef, while Frey was the deified agriculturist who came over the deep as a child. In Saxo's mythical history of Denmark, Frey as Frode is taken prisoner by a storm giant, Beli, "the howler", and is loved by his hag sister in the Teutonic Hades, as Tammuz is loved by Eresh-ki-gal, spouse of the storm god Nergal, in the Babylonian Hades. Frode returns to earth, like Tammuz, in due season.

It is evident that there were various versions of the Tammuz myth in Ancient Babylonia. In one the goddess Ishtar visited Hades to search for the lover of her youth. A part of this form of the legend survives in the famous Assyrian hymn known as "The Descent of Ishtar". It was first translated by the late Mr. George Smith, of the British Museum. A box containing inscribed tablets had been sent from Assyria to London, and Mr. Smith, with characteristic patience and skill, arranged and deciphered them, giving to the world a fragment of ancient literature infused with much sublimity and imaginative power. Ishtar is depicted descending to dismal Hades, where the souls of the dead exist in bird forms:

> I spread like a bird my hands.
> I descend, I descend to the house of darkness, the dwelling of the
> god Irkalla:

43

To the house out of which there is no exit,
To the road from which there is no return:
To the house from whose entrance the light is taken,
The place where dust is their nourishment and their food mud.
Its chiefs also are like birds covered with feathers;
The light is never seen, in darkness they dwell....
Over the door and bolts is scattered dust.
When the goddess reaches the gate of Hades she cries to the porter:
Keeper of the waters, open thy gate,
Open thy gate that I may enter.
If thou openest not the gate that I may enter
I will strike the door, the bolts I will shatter,
I will strike the threshold and will pass through the doors;
I will raise up the dead to devour the living,
Above the living the dead shall exceed in numbers.

The porter answers that he must first consult the Queen of Hades, here called Allatu, to whom he accordingly announces the arrival of the Queen of Heaven. Allatu's heart is filled with anger, and makes reference to those whom Ishtar caused to perish:

Let me weep over the strong who have left their wives,
Let me weep over the handmaidens who have lost the embraces of their husbands,
Over the only son let me mourn, who ere his days are come is taken away.
Then she issues abruptly the stern decree:
Go, keeper, open the gate to her,
Bewitch her according to the ancient rules;
that is, "Deal with her as you deal with others who come here".

As Ishtar enters through the various gates she is stripped of her ornaments and clothing. At the first gate her crown was taken off, at the second her ear-rings, at the third her necklace of precious stones, at the fourth the ornaments of her breast, at the fifth her gemmed waist-girdle,[122] at the sixth the bracelets of her hands and feet, and at the seventh the covering robe of her body. Ishtar asks at each gate why she is thus dealt with, and the porter answers, "Such is the command of Allatu."

After descending for a prolonged period the Queen of Heaven at length stands naked before the Queen of Hades. Ishtar is proud and arrogant, and Allatu, desiring to punish her rival whom she cannot humble,

commands the plague demon, Namtar, to strike her with disease in all parts of her body. The effect of Ishtar's fate was disastrous upon earth: growth and fertility came to an end.

Meanwhile Pap-sukal, messenger of the gods, hastened to Shamash, the sun deity, to relate what had occurred. The sun god immediately consulted his lunar father, Sin, and Ea, god of the deep. Ea then created a man lion, named Nadushu-namir, to rescue Ishtar, giving him power to pass through the seven gates of Hades. When this being delivered his message

Allatu ... struck her breast; she bit her thumb,
She turned again: a request she asked not.
In her anger she cursed the rescuer of the Queen of Heaven.
May I imprison thee in the great prison,
May the garbage of the foundations of the city be thy food,
May the drains of the city be thy drink,
May the darkness of the dungeon be thy dwelling,
May the stake be thy seat,
May hunger and thirst strike thy offspring.
She was compelled, however, to obey the high gods, and addressed Namtar,

saying:

Unto Ishtar give the waters of life and bring her before me.
Thereafter the Queen of Heaven was conducted through the various gates, and at each she received her robe and the ornaments which were taken from her on entering. Namtar says:

Since thou hast not paid a ransom for thy deliverance to her
(Allatu), so to her again turn back,
For Tammuz the husband of thy youth.
The glistening waters (of life) pour over him...
In splendid clothing dress him, with a ring of crystal adorn him.

Ishtar mourns for "the wound of Tammuz", smiting her breast, and she did not ask for "the precious eye-stones, her amulets", which were apparently to ransom Tammuz. The poem concludes with Ishtar's wail:

O my only brother (Tammuz) thou dost not lament for me.
In the day that Tammuz adorned me, with a ring of crystal,
With a bracelet of emeralds, together with himself, he adorned me,[123]
With himself he adorned me; may men mourners and women
   mourners
On a bier place him, and assemble the wake.[124]

A Sumerian hymn to Tammuz throws light on this narrative. It sets forth that Ishtar descended to Hades to entreat him to be glad and to resume care of his flocks, but Tammuz refused or was unable to return.

His spouse unto her abode he sent back.

She then instituted the wailing ceremony:

The amorous Queen of Heaven sits as one in darkness.[125]

Mr. Langdon also translates a hymn (Tammuz III) which appears to contain the narrative on which the Assyrian version was founded. The goddess who descends to Hades, however, is not Ishtar, but the "sister", Belit-sheri. She is accompanied by various demons-- the "gallu-demon", the "slayer", &c.--and holds a conversation with Tammuz which, however, is "unintelligible and badly broken". Apparently, however, he promises to return to earth.

... I will go up, as for me I will depart with thee ...
... I will return, unto my mother let us go back.

Probably two goddesses originally lamented for Tammuz, as the Egyptian sisters, Isis and Nepthys, lamented for Osiris, their brother. Ishtar is referred to as "my mother". Isis figures alternately in the Egyptian chants as mother, wife, sister, and daughter of Osiris. She cries, "Come thou to thy wife in peace; her heart fluttereth for thy love", ... "I am thy wife, made as thou art, the elder sister, soul of her brother".... "Come thou to us as a babe".... "Lo, thou art as the Bull of the two goddesses--come thou, child growing in peace, our lord!"... "Lo! the Bull, begotten of the two cows, Isis and Nepthys".... "Come thou to the two widowed goddesses".... "Oh child, lord, first maker of the body".... "Father Osiris."[126]

As Ishtar and Belit-sheri weep for Tammuz, so do Isis and Nepthys weep for Osiris.

Calling upon thee with weeping--yet thou art prostrate upon thy
   bed!
Gods and men ... are weeping for thee at the same time, when
   they behold me (Isis).
Lo! I invoke thee with wailing that reacheth high as heaven.

Isis is also identified with Hathor (Ishtar) the Cow.... "The cow weepeth for thee with her voice."[127]

There is another phase, however, to the character of the mother goddess which explains the references to the desertion and slaying of Tammuz by Ishtar. "She is", says Jastrow, "the goddess of the human instinct, or passion which accompanies human love. Gilgamesh ... reproaches her with abandoning the objects of her passion after a brief period of union." At Ishtar's temple "public maidens accepted temporary partners, assigned to them by Ishtar".[128] The worship of all mother goddesses in ancient times was accompanied by revolting unmoral rites which are referred to in condemnatory terms in various passages in the Old Testament, especially in connection with the worship of Ashtoreth, who was identical with Ishtar and the Egyptian Hathor.

Ishtar in the process of time overshadowed all the other female deities of Babylonia, as did Isis in Egypt. Her name, indeed, which is Semitic, became in the plural, Ishtaráte, a designation for goddesses in general. But although she was referred to as the daughter of the sky, Anu, or the daughter of the moon, Sin or Nannar, she still retained traces of her ancient character. Originally she was a great mother goddess, who was worshipped by those who believed that life and the universe had a female origin in contrast to those who believed in the theory of male origin. Ishtar is identical with Nina, the fish goddess, a creature who gave her name to the Sumerian city of Nina and the Assyrian city of Nineveh. Other forms of the Creatrix included Mama, or Mami, or Ama, "mother", Aruru, Bau, Gula, and Zerpanitum. These were all "Preservers" and healers. At the same time they were "Destroyers", like Nin-sun and the Queen of Hades, Eresh-ki-gal or Allatu. They were accompanied by shadowy male forms ere they became wives of strongly individualized gods, or by child gods, their sons, who might be regarded as "brothers" or "husbands of their mothers", to use the paradoxical Egyptian term. Similarly Great Father deities had vaguely defined wives. The "Semitic" Baal, "the lord", was accompanied by a female reflection of himself--Beltu, "the lady". Shamash, the sun god, had for wife the shadowy Aa.

As has been shown, Ishtar is referred to in a Tammuz hymn as the mother of the child god of fertility. In an Egyptian hymn the sky goddess Nut, "the mother" of Osiris, is stated to have "built up life from her own body".[129] Sri or Lakshmi, the Indian goddess, who became the wife of Vishnu, as the mother goddess Saraswati, a tribal deity, became the wife of Brahma, was, according to a Purana commentator, "the mother of the world ... eternal and undecaying".[130]

The gods, on the other hand, might die annually: the goddesses alone were immortal. Indra was supposed to perish of old age, but his wife, Indrani, remained ever young. There were fourteen Indras in every "day of Brahma", a reference apparently to the ancient conception of Indra among the Great-Mother-worshipping sections of the Aryo-Indians.[131] In the *Mahabharata* the god Shiva, as Mahadeva, commands Indra on "one of the peaks of Himavat", where they met, to lift up a stone and join the Indras who had been before him. "And Indra on removing that stone beheld a cave on the breast of that king of mountains in which were four others resembling himself." Indra exclaimed in his grief, "Shall I be even like these?" These five Indras, like the "Seven Sleepers", awaited the time when they would be called forth. They were ultimately reborn as the five Pandava warriors.[132]

The ferocious, black-faced Scottish mother goddess, Cailleach Bheur, who appears to be identical with Mala Lith, "Grey Eyebrows" of Fingalian story, and the English "Black Annis", figures in Irish song and legend as "The Old Woman of Beare". This "old woman" (Cailleach) "had", says Professor Kuno Meyer, "seven periods of youth one after another, so that every man who had lived with her came to die of old age, and her grandsons and great-grandsons were tribes and races". When old age at length came upon her she sang her "swan song", from which the following lines are extracted:

Ebb tide to me as of the sea!
Old age causes me reproach ...
It is riches
Ye love, it is not men:
In the time when *we* lived
It was men we loved ...
My arms when they are seen
Are bony and thin:
Once they would fondle,
They would be round glorious kings ...
I must take my garment even in the sun:
The time is at hand that shall renew me.[133]

Freyja, the Germanic mother goddess, whose car was drawn by cats, had similarly many lovers. In the Icelandic poem "Lokasenna", Loki taunts her, saying:

Silence, Freyja! Full well I know thee,
    And faultless art thou not found;
Of the gods and elves who here are gathered
    Each one hast thou made thy mate.

Idun, the keeper of the apples of immortal youth, which prevent the gods growing old, is similarly addressed:

Silence, Idun! I swear, of all women
    Thou the most wanton art;
Who couldst fling those fair-washed arms of thine
    About thy brother's slayer.

Frigg, wife of Odin, is satirized as well:

Silence, Frigg! Earth's spouse for a husband,
    And hast ever yearned after men![134]

The goddesses of classic mythology had similar reputations. Aphrodite (Venus) had many divine and mortal lovers. She links closely with Astarte and Ashtoreth (Ishtar), and reference has already been made to her relations with Adonis (Tammuz). These love deities were all as cruel as they were wayward. When Ishtar wooed the Babylonian hero, Gilgamesh, he spurned her advances, as has been indicated, saying:

On Tammuz, the spouse of thy youth,
Thou didst lay affliction every year.
Thou didst love the brilliant Allalu bird
But thou didst smite him and break his wing;
He stands in the woods and cries "O my wing".

46

He likewise charged her with deceiving the lion and the horse, making reference to obscure myths:

Thou didst also love a shepherd of the flock,
Who continually poured out for thee the libation,
And daily slaughtered kids for thee;
But thou didst smite him and didst change him into a leopard,
So that his own sheep boy hunted him,
And his own hounds tore him to pieces.[135]

These goddesses were ever prone to afflict human beings who might offend them or of whom they wearied. Demeter (Ceres) changed Ascalaphus into an owl and Stellio into a lizard. Rhea (Ops) resembled

The tow'red Cybele,
Mother of a hundred gods,

the wanton who loved Attis (Adonis). Artemis (Diana) slew her lover Orion, changed Actaeon into a stag, which was torn to pieces by his own dogs, and caused numerous deaths by sending a boar to ravage the fields of Oeneus, king of Calydon. Human sacrifices were frequently offered to the bloodthirsty "mothers". The most famous victim of Artemis was the daughter of Agamemnon, "divinely tall and most divinely fair".[136] Agamemnon had slain a sacred stag, and the goddess punished him by sending a calm when the war fleet was about to sail for Troy, with the result that his daughter had to be sacrificed. Artemis thus sold breezes like the northern wind hags and witches.

It used to be customary to account for the similarities manifested by the various mother goddesses by assuming that there was constant cultural contact between separate nationalities, and, as a result, a not inconsiderable amount of "religious borrowing". Greece was supposed to have received its great goddesses from the western Semites, who had come under the spell of Babylonian religion. Archaeological evidence, however, tends to disprove this theory. "The most recent researches into Mesopotamian history", writes Dr. Farnell, "establish with certainty the conclusion that there was no direct political contact possible between the powers in the valley of the Euphrates and the western shores of the Aegean in the second millennium B.C. In fact, between the nascent Hellas and the great world of Mesopotamia there were powerful and possibly independent strata of cultures interposing."[137]

The real connection appears to be the racial one. Among the Mediterranean Neolithic tribes of Sumeria, Arabia, and Europe, the goddess cult appears to have been influential. Mother worship was the predominant characteristic of their religious systems, so that the Greek goddesses were probably of pre-Hellenic origin, the Celtic of Iberian, the Egyptian of proto-Egyptian, and the Babylonian of Sumerian. The northern hillmen, on the other hand, who may be identified with the "Aryans" of the philologists, were father worshippers. The Vedic Aryo-Indians worshipped father gods,[138] as did also the Germanic peoples and certain tribes in the "Hittite confederacy". Earth spirits were males, like the Teutonic elves, the Aryo-Indian Ribhus, and the Burkans, "masters", of the present-day Buriats, a Mongolian people. When the father-worshipping peoples invaded the dominions of the mother-worshipping peoples, they introduced their strongly individualized gods, but they did not displace the mother goddesses. "The Aryan Hellenes", says Dr. Farnell, "were able to plant their Zeus and Poseidon on the high hill of Athens, but not to overthrow the supremacy of Athena in the central shrine and in the aboriginal soul of the Athenian people."[139] As in Egypt, the beliefs of the father worshippers, represented by the self-created Ptah, were fused with the beliefs of the mother worshippers, who adored Isis, Mut, Neith, and others. In Babylonia this process of racial and religious fusion was well advanced before the dawn of history. Ea, who had already assumed manifold forms, may have originally been the son or child lover of Damkina, "Lady of the Deep", as was Tammuz of Ishtar. As the fish, Ea was the offspring of the mother river.

The mother worshippers recognized male as well as female deities, but regarded the great goddess as the First Cause. Although the primeval spirits were grouped in four pairs in Egypt, and apparently in Babylonia also, the female in the first pair was more strongly individualized than the male. The Egyptian Nu is vaguer than his consort Nut, and the Babylonian Apsu than his consort Tiamat. Indeed, in the narrative of the Creation Tablets of Babylon, which will receive full treatment in a later chapter, Tiamat, the great mother, is the controlling spirit. She is more powerful and ferocious than Apsu, and lives longer. After Apsu's death she elevates one of her brood, named Kingu, to be her consort, a fact which suggests that in the Ishtar-Tammuz myth survives the influence of exceedingly ancient modes of thought. Like Tiamat, Ishtar is also a great battle heroine, and in this capacity she was addressed as "the lady of majestic rank exalted over all gods". This was no idle flattery on the part of worshippers, but a memory of her ancient supremacy.

Reference has been made to the introduction of Tammuz worship into Jerusalem. Ishtar, as Queen of Heaven, was also adored by the backsliding Israelites as a deity of battle and harvest. When Jeremiah censured the people for burning incense and serving gods "whom they knew not", he said, "neither they, ye, nor your fathers", they made answer: "Since we left off to burn incense to the queen of heaven, and to pour out drink offerings unto her, we have wanted all things, and have been consumed by the sword and the famine". The women took a leading part in these practices, but refused to accept all the blame, saying, "When we burned incense to the queen of heaven, and poured out drink offerings unto her, did we make our cakes and pour out drink offerings unto her without our men?"[140] That the husbands, and the children even, assisted at the ceremony is made evident in another reference to goddess worship: "The children gather wood, and the fathers kindle the fire, and the women knead the dough, to make cakes to the queen of heaven".[141]

Jastrow suggests that the women of Israel wept for Tammuz, offered cakes to the mother goddess, &c., because "in all religious bodies ... women represent the conservative element; among them religious customs continue in practice after they have been abandoned by men".[142] The evidence of Jeremiah, however, shows that the men certainly co-operated at the archaic ceremonials. In lighting the fires with the "vital spark", they apparently acted in imitation of the god of fertility. The women, on the other hand, represented the reproductive harvest goddess in providing the food supply. In recognition of her gift, they rewarded the goddess by offering her the cakes prepared from the newly ground wheat and barley--the "first fruits of the harvest". As the corn god came as a child, the children began the ceremony by gathering the wood for the sacred fire. When the women mourned for Tammuz, they did so evidently because the death of the god was lamented by the goddess Ishtar. It would appear, therefore, that the suggestion regarding the "conservative element" should really apply to the immemorial practices of folk religion. These differed from the refined ceremonies of the official cult in Babylonia, where there were suitable temples and organized bands of priests and priestesses. But the official cult received no recognition in Palestine; the cakes intended for a goddess were not offered up in the temple of Abraham's God, but "in the streets of Jerusalem" and those of other cities.[143]

The obvious deduction seems to be that in ancient times women everywhere played a prominent part in the ceremonial folk worship of the Great Mother goddess, while the men took the lesser part of the god whom she had brought into being and afterwards received as "husband of his mother". This may account for the high social status of women among goddess worshippers, like the representatives of the Mediterranean race, whose early religion was not confined to temples, but closely associated with the acts of everyday life.

[105] *Ezekiel*, viii.

[106] *Psalms*, cxxvi.

[107] *The Burden of Isis*, J.T. Dennis *(Wisdom of the East* series), pp. 21, 22.

[108] *Religion of the Semites*, pp. 412, 414.

[109] *Egyptian Myth and Legend*, pp. 45 et seq.

[110] Langdon's *Sumerian and Babylonian Psalms*, pp. 319-321.

[111] Campbell's *West Highland Tales*, vol. iii, p. 74.

[112] *West Highland Tales*, vol. iii, pp. 85, 86.

[113] If Finn and his band were really militiamen--the original Fenians--as is believed in Ireland, they may have had attached to their memories the legends of archaic Iberian deities who differed from the Celtic Danann deities. Theodoric the Goth, as Dietrich von Bern, was identified, for instance, with Donar or Thunor (Thor), the thunder god. In Scotland Finn and his followers are all giants. Diarmid is the patriarch of the Campbell clan, the MacDiarmids being "sons of Diarmid".

[114] Isaiah condemns a magical custom connected with the worship of Tammuz in the garden, *Isaiah*, xvii, 9, 11. This "Garden of Adonis" is dealt with in the next chapter.

[115] Quotations are from *Sumerian and Babylonian Psalms*, translated by Stephen Langdon, Ph.D. (Paris and London, 1909), pp. 299-341.

[116] *Beowulf*, translated by J.R. Clark Hall (London, 1911), pp. 9-11.

[117] For Frey's connection with the Ynglings see Morris and Magnusson's *Heimskringla* (*Saga Library*, vol. iii), pp. 23-71.

[118] *The Religion of Babylonia and Assyria*, p. 72.

[119] Langdon's *Sumerian and Babylonian Psalms*, pp. 325, 339.

[120] Professor Oldenberg's translation.

[121] Osiris is also invoked to "remove storms and rain and give fecundity in the nighttime". As a spring sun god he slays demons; as a lunar god he brings fertility.

[122] Like the love-compelling girdle of Aphrodite.

[123] A wedding bracelet of crystal is worn by Hindu women; they break it when the husband dies.

[124] Quotations from the translation in *The Chaldean Account of Genesis*, by George Smith.

[125] Langdon's *Sumerian and Babylonian Psalms*, p. 329 *et seq.*

[126] *The Burden of Isis*, translated by J.T. Dennis (*Wisdom of the East* series), pp. 24, 31, 32, 39, 45, 46, 49.

[127] *The Burden of Isis*, pp. 22, 46.

[128] *Aspects of Religious Belief and Practice in Babylonia and Assyria*, p. 137, and *Herodotus*, book i, 199.

[129] *The Burden of Isis*, p. 47.

[130] *Original Sanskrit Texts*, J. Muir, London, 1890, vol. i, p. 67.

[131] *Original Sanskrit Texts*, vol. i, p. 44.

[132] *Adi Parva* section of *Mahàbhàrata* (Roy's translation), pp. 553, 555.

[133] *Ancient Irish Poetry*, Kuno Meyer (London, 1911), pp. 88-90.

[134] Translations from *The Elder Edda*, by O. Bray (part i), London, 1908.

[135] *Babylonian Religion*, L.W. King, pp. 160, 161.

[136] Tennyson's *A Dream of Fair Women.*

[137] *Greece and Babylon*, L.R. Farnell (Edinburgh, 1911), p. 35.

[138] The goddesses did not become prominent until the "late invasion" of the post-Vedic Aryans.

[139] *Greece and Babylon*, p. 96.

[140] *Jeremiah*, xliv.

[141] *Jeremiah, vii, 18.*

[142] *Aspects of Religious Belief and Practice in Babylonia and Assyria*, pp. 348, 349.

[143] *Jeremiah, vii, 17.*

Chapter VI. Wars of the City States of Sumer and Akkad
Abstract

Civilization well advanced--The Patesi--Prominent City States--Surroundings of Babylonia--The Elamites--Biblical References to Susa--The Sumerian Temperament--Fragmentary Records--City States of Kish and Opis--A Shopkeeper who became a Queen--Goddess Worship--Tammuz as Nin-Girsu--Great Dynasty of Lagash--Ur-Nina and his Descendants--A Napoleonic Conqueror--Golden Age of Sumerian Art--The First Reformer in History--His Rise and Fall--The Dynasty of Erech--Sargon of Akkad--The Royal Gardener--Sargon Myth in India--A Great Empire--The King who Purchased Land--Naram Sin the Conqueror--Disastrous Foreign Raid--Lagash again Prominent--Gudea the Temple Builder--Dynasty of Ur--Dynasty of Isin--Another Gardener becomes King--Rise of Babylon--Humanized Deities--Why Sumerian Gods wore Beards.

When the curtain rises to reveal the drama of Babylonian civilization we find that we have missed the first act and its many fascinating scenes. Sumerians and Akkadians come and go, but it is not always possible to distinguish between them. Although most Semites are recognizable by their flowing beards, prominent noses, and long robes, some have so closely imitated the Sumerians as to suffer almost complete loss of identity. It is noticeable that in the north the Akkadians are more Semitic than their contemporaries in the south, but it is difficult at times to say whether a city is controlled by the descendants of the indigenous people or those of later settlers. Dynasties rise and fall, and, as in Egypt at times, the progress of the fragmentary narrative is interrupted by a sudden change of scene ere we have properly grasped a situation and realized its significance.

What we know for certain is that civilization is well advanced. Both in the north and the south there are many organized and independent city states, and not unfrequently these wage war one against another. Occasionally ambitious rulers tower among their fellows, conduct vigorous military campaigns, and become overlords of wide districts. As a rule, a subjugated monarch who has perforce to acknowledge the suzerainty of a powerful king is allowed to remain in a state of semi-independence on condition that he pays a heavy annual tribute of grain. His own laws continue in force, and the city deities remain supreme, although recognition may also be given to the deities of his conqueror. He styles himself a Patesi--a "priest king", or more literally, "servant of the chief deity". But as an independent monarch may also be a pious Patesi, it does not always follow when a ruler is referred to by that title he is necessarily less powerful than his neighbours.

When the historical narrative begins Akkad included the cities of Babylon, Cutha, Kish, Akkad, and Sippar, and north of Babylonia proper is Semitic Opis. Among the cities of

49

Sumer were Eridu, Ur, Lagash, Larsa, Erech, Shuruppak, and probably Nippur, which was situated on the "border". On the north Assyria was yet "in the making", and shrouded in obscurity. A vague but vast area above Hit on the Euphrates, and extending to the Syrian coast, was known as the "land of the Amorites". The fish-shaped Babylonian valley lying between the rivers, where walled towns were surrounded by green fields and numerous canals flashed in the sunshine, was bounded on the west by the bleak wastes of the Arabian desert, where during the dry season "the rocks branded the body" and occasional sandstorms swept in blinding folds towards the "plain of Shinar" (Sumer) like demon hosts who sought to destroy the world. To the east the skyline was fretted by the Persian Highlands, and amidst the southern mountains dwelt the fierce Elamites, the hereditary enemies of the Sumerians, although a people apparently of the same origin. Like the Nubians and the Libyans, who kept watchful eyes on Egypt, the Elamites seemed ever to be hovering on the eastern frontier of Sumeria, longing for an opportunity to raid and plunder.

The capital of the Elamites was the city of Susa, where excavations have revealed traces of an independent civilization which reaches back to an early period in the Late Stone Age. Susa is referred to in the Old Testament--"The words of Nehemiah.... I was in Shushan the palace".[144] An Assyrian plan of the city shows it occupying a strategic position at a bend of the Shawur river, which afforded protection against Sumerian attacks from the west, while a canal curved round its northern and eastern sides, so that Susa was completely surrounded by water. Fortifications had been erected on the river and canal banks, and between these and the high city walls were thick clumps of trees. That the kings of Elam imitated the splendours of Babylonian courts in the later days of Esther and Haman and Mordecai, is made evident by the Biblical references to the gorgeous palace, which had "white, green, and blue hangings, fastened with cords of fine linen and purple to silver rings and pillars of marble; the beds were of gold and silver, upon a pavement of red, and blue, and white, and black marble".[145] Beyond Elam were the plains, plateaus, and grassy steppes occupied by the Medes and other peoples of Aryan speech. Cultural influences came and went like spring winds between the various ancient communities.

For ten long centuries Sumer and Akkad flourished and prospered ere we meet with the great Hammurabi, whose name has now become almost as familiar as that of Julius Caesar. But our knowledge of the leading historical events of this vast period is exceedingly fragmentary. The Sumerians were not like the later Assyrians or their Egyptian contemporaries--a people with a passion for history. When inscriptions were composed and cut on stone, or impressed upon clay tablets and bricks, the kings selected as a general rule to record pious deeds rather than to celebrate their victories and conquests. Indeed, the average monarch had a temperament resembling that of Keats, who declared:

The silver flow
Of Hero's tears, the swoon of Imogen,
Fair Pastorella in the bandits' den,
Are things to brood on with more ardency
Than the death day of empires.

The Sumerian king was emotionally religious as the great English poet was emotionally poetical. The tears of Ishtar for Tammuz, and the afflictions endured by the goddess imprisoned in Hades, to which she had descended for love of her slain husband, seemed to have concerned the royal recorder to a greater degree than the memories of political upheavals and the social changes which passed over the land, like the seasons which alternately brought greenness and gold, barrenness and flood.

City chronicles, as a rule, are but indices of obscure events, to which meagre references were sometimes also made on mace heads, vases, tablets, stelae, and sculpturedmonoliths. Consequently, present-day excavators and students have often reason to be grateful that the habit likewise obtained of inscribing on bricks in buildings and the stone sockets of doors the names of kings and others. These records render obscure periods faintly articulate, and are indispensable for comparative purposes. Historical clues are also obtained from lists of year names. Each city king named a year in celebration of a great event--his own succession to the throne, the erection of a new temple or of a city wall, or, mayhap, the defeat of an invading army from a rival state. Sometimes, too, a monarch gave the name of his father in an official inscription, or happily mentioned several ancestors. Another may be found to have made an illuminating statement regarding a predecessor, who centuries previously erected the particular temple that he himself has piously restored. A reckoning of this kind, however, cannot always be regarded as absolutely correct. It must be compared with and tested by other records, for in these ancient days calculations were not unfrequently based on doubtful inscriptions, or mere oral traditions, perhaps. Nor can implicit trust be placed on every reference to historical events, for

50

the memoried deeds of great rulers were not always unassociated with persistent and cumulative myths. It must be recognized, therefore, that even portions of the data which had of late been sifted and systematized by Oriental scholars in Europe, may yet have to be subjected to revision. Many interesting and important discoveries, which will throw fresh light on this fascinating early period, remain to be made in that ancient and deserted land, which still lies under the curse of the Hebrew prophet, who exclaimed: "Babylon, the glory of kingdoms, the beauty of the Chaldees' excellency, shall be as when God overthrew Sodom and Gomorrah. It shall never be inhabited; neither shall the Arabian pitch tent there; neither shall the shepherds make their fold there. But wild beasts of the desert shall lie there; and their houses shall be full of doleful creatures; and owls shall dwell there, and satyrs shall dance there. And the wild beasts of the islands shall cry in their desolate houses and dragons in their pleasant palaces."[146]

The curtain rises, as has been indicated, after civilization had been well advanced. To begin with, our interests abide with Akkad, and during a period dated approximately between 3000 B.C. and 2800 B.C., when Egypt was already a united kingdom, and the Cretans were at the dawn of the first early Minoan period, and beginning to use bronze. In Kish Sumerian and Akkadian elements had apparently blended, and the city was the centre of a powerful and independent government. After years have fluttered past dimly, and with them the shadow-shapes of vigorous rulers, it is found that Kish came under the sway of the pronouncedly Semitic city of Opis, which was situated "farthest north" and on the western bank of the river Tigris. A century elapsed ere Kish again threw off the oppressor's yoke and renewed the strength of its youth.

The city of Kish was one of the many ancient centres of goddess worship. The Great Mother appears to have been the Sumerian Bau, whose chief seat was at Lagash. If tradition is to be relied upon, Kish owed its existence to that notable lady, Queen Azag-Bau. Although floating legends gathered round her memory as they have often gathered round the memories of famous men, like Sargon of Akkad, Alexander the Great, and Theodoric the Goth, who became Emperor of Rome, it is probable that the queen was a prominent historical personage. She was reputed to have been of humble origin, and to have first achieved popularity and influence as the keeper of a wine shop. Although no reference survives to indicate that she was believed to be of miraculous birth, the Chronicle of Kish gravely credits her with a prolonged and apparently prosperous reign of a hundred years. Her son, who succeeded her, sat on the throne for a quarter of a century. These calculations are certainly remarkable. If the Queen Azag-Bau founded Kish when she was only twenty, and gave birth to the future ruler in her fiftieth year, he must have been an elderly gentleman of seventy when he began to reign. When it is found, further, that the dynasty in which mother and son flourished was supposed to have lasted for 586 years, divided between eight rulers, one of whom reigned for only three years, two for six, and two for eleven, it becomes evident that the historian of Kish cannot be absolutely relied upon in detail. It seems evident that the memory of this lady of forceful character, who flourished about thirteen hundred years before the rise of Queen Hatshepsut of Egypt, has overshadowed the doubtful annals of ancient Kish at a period when Sumerian and Semite were striving in the various states to achieve political ascendancy.

Meanwhile the purely Sumerian city of Lagash had similarly grown powerful and aggressive. For a time it acknowledged the suzerainty of Kish, but ultimately it threw off the oppressor's yoke and asserted its independence. The cumulative efforts of a succession of energetic rulers elevated Lagash to the position of a metropolis in Ancient Babylonia.

The goddess Bau, "the mother of Lagash", was worshipped in conjunction with other deities, including the god Nin-Girsu, an agricultural deity, and therefore a deity of war, who had solar attributes. One of the titles of Nin-Girsu was En-Mersi, which, according to Assyrian evidence, was another name of Tammuz, the spring god who slew the storm and winter demons, and made the land fertile so that man might have food. Nin-Girsu was, it would seem, a developed form of Tammuz, like the Scandinavian Frey, god of harvest, or Heimdal, the celestial warrior. Bau was one of the several goddesses whose attributes were absorbed by the Semitic Ishtar. She was a "Great Mother", a creatrix, the source of all human and bestial life, and, of course, a harvest goddess. She was identified with Gula, "the great one", who cured diseases and prolonged life. Evidently the religion of Lagash was based on the popular worship of the "Queen of Heaven", and her son, the dying god who became "husband of his mother".

The first great and outstanding ruler of Lagash was Ur-Nina, who appears to have owed his power to the successful military operations of his predecessors. It is uncertain whether or not he himself engaged in any great war. His records are silent in that connection, but, judging from what we know of him, it may be taken for granted that he was able and fully prepared to give a good account of himself in battle. He certainly took steps to make secure his position, for he caused a strong wall to be erected round Lagash. His inscriptions are eloquent of his piety, which took practical shape, for he repaired and built temples, dedicated offerings to deities, and increased the wealth of religious bodies and the prosperity of the State by cutting canals and developing agriculture. In addition to serving local deities, he also gave practical recognition to Ea at Eridu and Enlil at Nippur. He, however, overlooked Anu at Erech, a fact which suggests that he held sway over Eridu and Nippur, but had to recognize Erech as an independent city state.

Among the deities of Lagash, Ur-Nina favoured most the goddess Nina, whose name he bore. As she was a water deity, and perhaps identical with Belit-sheri, sister of "Tammuz of the Abyss" and daughter of Ea, one of the canals was dedicated to her. She was also honoured with a new temple, in which was probably placed her great statue, constructed by special order of her royal worshipper. Like the Egyptian goddess, the "Mother of Mendes", Nina received offerings of fish, not only as a patroness of fishermen, but also as a corn spirit and a goddess of maternity. She was in time identified with Ishtar.

A famous limestone plaque, which is preserved in the Louvre, Paris, depicts on its upper half the pious King Ur-Nina engaged in the ceremony of laying the foundations of a temple dedicated either to the goddess Nina or to the god Nin-Girsu. His face and scalp are clean shaven, and he has a prominent nose and firm mouth, eloquent of decision. The folds of neck and jaw suggest Bismarckian traits. He is bare to the waist, and wears a pleated kilt, with three flounces, which reaches almost to his ankles. On his long head he has poised deftly a woven basket containing the clay with which he is to make the first brick. In front of him stand five figures. The foremost is honoured by being sculptured larger than the others, except the prominent monarch. Apparently this is a royal princess, for her head is unshaven, and her shoulder dress or long hair drops over one of her arms. Her name is Lida, and the conspicuous part she took in the ceremony suggests that she was the representative of the goddess Nina. She is accompanied by her brothers, and at least one official, Anita, the cup-bearer, or high priest. The concluding part of this ceremony, or another ceremonial act, is illustrated on the lower part of the plaque. Ur-Nina is seated on his throne, not, as would seem at first sight, raising the wine cup to his lips and toasting to the success of the work, but pouring out a libation upon the ground. The princess is not present; the place of honour next to the king is taken by the crown prince. Possibly in this case it is the god Nin-Girsu who is being honoured. Three male figures, perhaps royal sons, accompany the prominent crown prince. The cup-bearer is in attendance behind the throne.

The inscription on this plaque, which is pierced in the centre so as to be nailed to a sacred shrine, refers to the temples erected by Ur-Nina, including those of Nina and Nin-Girsu.

After Ur-Nina's prosperous reign came to a close, his son Akurgal ascended the throne. He had trouble with Umma, a powerful city, which lay to the north-west of Lagash, between the Shatt-el-Kai and Shatt-el-Hai canals. An army of raiders invaded his territory and had to be driven back.

The next king, whose name was Eannatum, had Napoleonic characteristics. He was a military genius with great ambitions, and was successful in establishing by conquest a small but brilliant empire. Like his grandfather, he strengthened the fortifications of Lagash; then he engaged in a series of successful campaigns. Umma had been causing anxiety in Lagash, but Eannatum stormed and captured that rival city, appropriated one of its fertile plains, and imposed an annual tribute to be paid in kind. An army of Elamites swept down from the hills, but Ur-Nina's grandson inflicted upon these bold foreigners a crushing defeat and pursued them over the frontier. Several cities were afterwards forced to come under the sway of triumphant Lagash, including Erech and Ur, and as his suzerainty was already acknowledged at Eridu, Eannatum's power in Sumeria became as supreme as it was firmly established.

Evidently Zuzu, king of the northern city of Opis, considered that the occasion was opportune to overcome the powerful Sumerian conqueror, and at the same time establish Semitic rule over the subdued and war-wasted cities. He marched south with a large army, but the tireless and ever-watchful Eannatum hastened to the fray, scattered the forces of Opis, and captured the foolhardy Zuzu.

Eannatum's activities, however, were not confined to battlefields. At Lagash he carried out great improvements in the interests of agriculture; he constructed a large reservoir and developed the canal system. He also extended and repaired existing temples in his native city and at Erech. Being a patron of the arts, he encouraged sculpture work, and the finest Sumerian examples belong to his reign.

Eannatum was succeeded by his brother, Enannatum I. Apparently the new monarch did not share the military qualities of his royal predecessor, for there were signs of unrest in the loose confederacy of states. Indeed, Umma revolted. From that city an army marched forth and took forcible possession of the plain which Eannatum had appropriated, removing and breaking the landmarks, and otherwise challenging the supremacy of the sovran state. A Lagash force defeated the men of Umma, but appears to have done little more than hold in check their aggressive tendencies.

No sooner had Entemena, the next king, ascended the throne than the flame of revolt burst forth again. The Patesi of Umma was evidently determined to free, once and for all, his native state from the yoke of Lagash. But he had gravely miscalculated the strength of the vigorous young ruler. Entemena inflicted upon the rebels a crushing defeat, and following up his success, entered the walled city and captured and slew the patesi. Then he took steps to stamp out the embers of revolt in Umma by appointing as its governor one of his own officials, named Ili, who was duly installed with great ceremony. Other military successes followed, including the sacking of Opis and Kish, which assured the supremacy of Lagash for many years. Entemena, with characteristic vigour, engaged himself during periods of peace in strengthening his city fortifications and in continuing the work of improving and developing the irrigation system. He lived in the golden age of Sumerian art, and to his reign belongs the exquisite silver vase of Lagash, which was taken from the Tello mound, and is now in the Louvre. This votive offering was placed by the king in the temple of Nin-Girsu. It is exquisitely shaped, and has a base of copper. The symbolic decorations include the lion-headed eagle, which was probably a form of the spring god of war and fertility, the lion, beloved by the Mother goddess, and deer and ibexes, which recall the mountain herds of Astarte. In the dedicatory inscription the king is referred to as a patesi, and the fact that the name of the high priest, Dudu, is given may be taken as an indication of the growing power of an aggressive priesthood. After a brilliant reign of twenty-nine years the king died, and was succeeded by his son, Enannatum II, who was the last ruler of Ur-Nina's line. An obscure period ensued. Apparently there had been a city revolt, which may have given the enemies of Lagash the desired opportunity to gather strength for the coming conflict. There is a reference to an Elamite raid which, although repulsed, may be regarded as proof of disturbed political conditions.

One or two priests sat on the throne of Lagash in brief succession, and then arose to power the famous Urukagina, the first reformer in history. He began to rule as patesi, but afterwards styled himself king. What appears certain is that he was the leader of a great social upheaval, which received the support of a section of the priesthood, for he recorded that his elevation was due to the intercession of the god Nin-Girsu. Other deities, who were sons and daughters of Nin-Girsu and Nina, had been given recognition by his predecessors, and it is possible that the orthodox section of Lagash, and especially the agricultural classes, supported the new ruler in sweeping away innovations to which they were hostile.

Like Khufu and his descendants, the Pyramid kings of Egypt's fourth dynasty, the vigorous and efficient monarchs of the Ur-Nina dynasty of Lagash were apparently remembered and execrated as tyrants and oppressors of the people. To maintain many endowed temples and a standing army the traders and agriculturists had been heavily taxed. Each successive monarch who undertook public works on a large scale for the purpose of extending and developing the area under cultivation, appears to have done so mainly to increase the revenue of the exchequer, so as to conserve the strength of the city and secure its pre-eminence as a metropolis. A leisured class had come into existence, with the result that culture was fostered and civilization advanced. Lagash seems to have been intensely modern in character prior to 2800 B.C., but with the passing of the old order of things there arose grave social problems which never appear to have been seriously dealt with. All indications of social unrest were, it would appear, severely repressed by the iron-gloved monarchs of Ur-Nina's dynasty.

The people as a whole groaned under an ever-increasing burden of taxation. Sumeria was overrun by an army of officials who were notoriously corrupt; they do not appear to have been held in check, as in Egypt, by royal auditors. "In the domain of Nin-Girsu", one of Urukagina's tablets sets forth, "there were tax gatherers down to the sea." They not only attended to the needs of the exchequer, but enriched themselves by sheer robbery, while the priests followed their example by doubling their fees and appropriating temple offerings to their own use. The splendid organization of Lagash was crippled by the dishonesty of those who should have been its main support.

Reforms were necessary and perhaps overdue, but, unfortunately for Lagash, Urukagina's zeal for the people's cause amounted to fanaticism. Instead of gradually readjusting the machinery of government so as to secure equality of treatment without impairing its efficiency as a defensive force in these perilous times, he inaugurated sweeping and revolutionary social changes of far-reaching character regardless of consequences. Taxes and temple fees were cut down, and the number of officials reduced to a minimum. Society was thoroughly disorganized. The army, which was recruited mainly from the leisured and official classes, went practically out of existence, so that traders and agriculturists obtained relief from taxation at the expense of their material security.

Urukagina's motives were undoubtedly above reproach, and he showed an example to all who occupied positions of trust by living an upright life and denying himself luxuries. He was disinterestedly pious, and built and restored temples, and acted as the steward of his god with desire to promote the welfare and comfort of all true worshippers. His laws were similar to those which over two centuries afterwards were codified by Hammurabi, and like that monarch he was professedly the guardian of the weak and the helper of the needy; he sought to establish justice and liberty in the kingdom. But his social Arcadia vanished like a dream because he failed to recognize that Right must be supported by Might.

In bringing about his sudden social revolution, Urukagina had at the same time unwittingly let loose the forces of disorder. Discontented and unemployed officials, and many representatives of the despoiled leisured and military classes of Lagash, no doubt sought refuge elsewhere, and fostered the spirit of revolt which ever smouldered in subject states. At any rate, Umma, remembering the oppressions of other days, was not slow to recognize that the iron hand of Lagash had become unnerved. The zealous and iconoclastic reformer had reigned but seven years when he was called upon to defend his people against the invader. He appears to have been utterly unprepared to do so. The victorious forces of Umma swept against the stately city of Lagash and shattered its power in a single day. Echoes of the great disaster which ensued rise from a pious tablet inscription left by a priest, who was convinced that the conquerors would be called to account for the sins they had committed against the great god Nin-Girsu. He lamented the butchery and robbery which had taken place. We gather from his composition that blood was shed by the raiders of Umma even in the sacred precincts of temples, that statues were shattered, that silver and precious stones were carried away, that granaries were plundered and standing crops destroyed, and that many buildings were set on fire. Amidst these horrors of savagery and vengeance, the now tragic figure of the great reformer suddenly vanishes from before our eyes. Perhaps he perished in a burning temple; perhaps he found a nameless grave with the thousands of his subjects whose bodies had lain scattered about the blood-stained streets. With Urukagina the glory of Lagash departed. Although the city was rebuilt in time, and was even made more stately than before, it never again became the metropolis of Sumeria.

The vengeful destroyer of Lagash was Lugal-zaggisi, Patesi of Umma, a masterful figure in early Sumerian history. We gather from the tablet of the unknown scribe, who regarded him as a sinner against the god Nin-Girsu, that his city goddess was named Nidaba. He appears also to have been a worshipper of Enlil of Nippur, to whose influence he credited his military successes. But Enlil was not his highest god, he was the interceder who carried the prayers of Lugal-zaggisi to the beloved father, Anu, god of the sky. No doubt Nin-Girsu represented a school of theology which was associated with unpleasant memories in Umma. The sacking and burning of the temples of Lagash suggests as much.

Having broken the power of Lagash, Lugal-zaggisi directed his attention to the rival city of Kish, where Semitic influence was predominating. When Nanizak, the last monarch of the line of the famous Queen Azag-Bau, had sat upon the throne for but three years, he perished by the sword of the Umma conqueror. Nippur likewise came under his sway, and he also subdued the southern cities.

Lugal-zaggisi chose for his capital ancient Erech, the city of Anu, and of his daughter, the goddess Nana, who afterwards was identified with Ishtar. Anu's spouse was Anatu, and the pair subsequently became abstract deities, like Anshar and Kishar, their parents, who figure in the Babylonian Creation story. Nana was worshipped as the goddess of vegetation, and her relation to Anu was similar to that of Belit-sheri to Ea at Eridu. Anu and Ea were originally identical, but it would appear that the one was differentiated as the god of the waters above the heaven and the other as god of the waters beneath the earth, both being forms of Anshar. Elsewhere the chief god of the spring sun or the moon, the lover of the goddess, became pre-eminent, displacing the elder god, like Nin-Girsu at Lagash. At Sippar the sun god, Babbar, whose Semitic name was Shamash, was exalted as the chief deity, while the moon god remained supreme at Ur. This specializing process, which was due to local theorizing and the influence of alien settlers, has been dealt with in a previous chapter.

In referring to himself as the favoured ruler of various city deities, Lugal-zaggisi appears as a ruler of all Sumeria. How far his empire extended it is impossible to determine with certainty. He appears to have overrun Akkad, and even penetrated to the Syrian coast, for in one inscription it is stated that he "made straight his path from the Lower Sea (the Persian Gulf) over the Euphrates and Tigris to the Upper Sea (the Mediterranean)". The allegiance of certain states, however, depended on the strength of the central power. One of his successors found it necessary to attack Kish, which was ever waiting for an opportunity to regain its independence.

According to the Chronicle of Kish, the next ruler of Sumer and Akkad after Lugal-zaggisi was the famous Sargon I. It would appear that he was an adventurer or usurper, and that he owed his throne indirectly to Lugal-zaggisi, who had dethroned the ruler of Akkad. Later traditions, which have been partly confirmed by contemporary inscriptions, agree that Sargon was of humble birth. In the previous chapter reference was made to the Tammuz-like myth attached to his memory. His mother was a vestal virgin dedicated to the sun god, Shamash, and his father an unknown stranger from the mountains--a suggestion of immediate Semitic affinities. Perhaps Sargon owed his rise to power to the assistance received by bands of settlers from the land of the Amorites, which Lugal-zaggisi had invaded.

According to the legend, Sargon's birth was concealed. He was placed in a vessel which was committed to the river. Brought up by a commoner, he lived in obscurity until the Semitic goddess, Ishtar, gave him her aid.

A similar myth was attached in India to the memory of Karna, the Hector of that great Sanskrit epic the *Mahabharata*. Karna's mother, the Princess Pritha, who afterwards became a queen, was loved by the sun god, Surya. When in secret she gave birth to her son she placed him in an ark of wickerwork, which was set adrift on a stream. Ultimately it reached the Ganges, and it was borne by that river to the country of Anga, where the child was rescued by a woman and afterwards reared by her and her husband, a charioteer. In time Karna became a great warrior, and was crowned King of Anga by the Kaurava warriors.[147]

Before he became king, Sargon of Akkad, the Sharrukin of the texts, was, according to tradition, a gardener and watchman attached to the temple of the war god Zamama of Kish. This deity was subsequently identified with Merodach, son of Ea; Ninip, son of Enlil; and Nin-Girsu of Lagash. He was therefore one of the many developed forms of Tammuz--a solar, corn, and military deity, and an interceder for mankind. The goddess of Kish appears to have been a form of Bau, as is testified by the name of Queen Azag-Bau, the legendary founder of the city.

Unfortunately our knowledge of Sargon's reign is of meagre character. It is undoubted that he was a distinguished general and able ruler. He built up an empire which included Sumer and Akkad, and also Amurru, "the western land", or "land of the Amorites". The Elamites gave him an opportunity to extend his conquests eastward. They appear to have attacked Opis, but he drove them back, and on more than one occasion penetrated their country, over the western part of which, known as Anshan, he ultimately imposed his rule. Thither went many Semitic settlers who had absorbed the culture of Sumeria.

During Sargon's reign Akkad attained to a splendour which surpassed that of Babylon. In an omen text the monarch is lauded as the "highly exalted one without a peer". Tradition relates that when he was an old man all the Babylonian states rose in revolt against him and besieged Akkad. But the old warrior led forth his army against the combined forces and achieved a shattering victory.

Manishtusu, who succeeded Sargon I, had similarly to subdue a great confederacy of thirty-two city states, and must therefore have been a distinguished general. But he is best known as the monarch who purchased several large estates adjoining subject cities, his aim having been probably to settle on these Semitic allies who would be less liable to rebel against him than the workers they displaced. For the latter, however, he found employment elsewhere. These transactions, which were recorded on a monument subsequently carried off with other spoils by the Elamites and discovered at Susa, show that at this early period (about 2600 B.C.) even a conquering monarch considered it advisable to observe existing land laws. Urumush,[148] the next ruler, also achieved successes in Elam and elsewhere, but his life was cut short by a palace revolution.

The prominent figure of Naram Sin, a later king of Akkad, bulks largely in history and tradition. According to the Chronicle of Kish, he was a son of Sargon. Whether he was or not, it is certain that he inherited the military and administrative genius of that famous ex-gardener. The arts flourished during his reign. One of the memorable products of the period was an exquisitely sculptured monument celebrating one of Naram Sin's victories, which was discovered at Susa. It is one of the most wonderful examples of Babylonian stone work which has come to light.

A successful campaign had been waged against a mountain people. The stele shows the warrior king leading his army up a steep incline and round the base of a great peak surmounted by stars. His enemies flee in confusion before him. One lies on the ground clutching a spear which has penetrated his throat, two are falling over a cliff, while others apparently sue for mercy. Trees have been depicted to show that part of the conquered territory is wooded. Naram Sin is armed with battleaxe and bow, and his helmet is decorated with horns. The whole composition is spirited and finely grouped; and the military bearing of the disciplined troops contrasts sharply with the despairing attitudes of the fleeing remnants of the defending army.

During this period the Semitized mountaineers to the north-east of Babylonia became the most aggressive opponents of the city states. The two most prominent were the Gutium, or men of Kutu, and the Lulubu. Naram Sin's great empire included the whole of Sumer and Akkad, Amurru and northern Palestine, and part of Elam, and the district to the north. He also penetrated Arabia, probably by way of the Persian Gulf, and caused diorite to be quarried there. One of his steles, which is now in the Imperial Ottoman Museum at Constantinople, depicts him as a fully bearded man with Semitic characteristics. During his lifetime he was deified--a clear indication of the introduction of foreign ideas, for the Sumerians were not worshippers of kings and ancestors.

Naram Sin was the last great king of his line. Soon after his death the power of Akkad went to pieces, and the Sumerian city of Erech again became the centre of empire. Its triumph, however, was shortlived. After a quarter of a century had elapsed, Akkad and Sumer were overswept by the fierce Gutium from the north-eastern mountains. They sacked and burned many cities, including Babylon, where the memory of the horrors perpetrated by these invaders endured until the Grecian Age. An obscure period, like the Egyptian Hyksos Age, ensued, but it was of comparatively brief duration.

When the mists cleared away, the city Lagash once more came to the front, having evidently successfully withstood the onslaughts of the Gutium, but it never recovered the place of eminence it occupied under the brilliant Ur-Nina dynasty. It is manifest that it must have enjoyed under the various overlords, during the interval, a considerable degree of independence, for its individuality remained unimpaired. Of all its energetic and capable patesis, the most celebrated was Gudea, who reigned sometime before 2400 B.C. In contrast to the Semitic Naram Sin, he was beardless and pronouncedly Sumerian in aspect. His favoured deity, the city god Nin-Girsu, again became prominent, having triumphed over his jealous rivals after remaining in obscurity for three or four centuries. Trade flourished, and the arts were fostered. Gudea had himself depicted, in one of the most characteristic sculptures of his age, as an architect, seated reverently with folded hands with a temple plan lying on his knees, and his head uplifted as if watching the builders engaged in materializing the dream of his life. The temple in which his interests were centred was erected in honour of Nin-Girsu. Its ruins suggest that it was of elaborate structure and great beauty. Like Solomon in later days, Gudea procured material for his temple from many distant parts--cedar from Lebanon, marble from Amurru, diorite from Arabia, copper from Elam, and so forth. Apparently the King of Lagash was strong enough or wealthy enough to command respect over a wide area.

Another city which also rose into prominence, amidst the shattered Sumerian states, was Ur, the centre of moon worship. After Gudea's death, its kings exercised sway over Lagash and Nippur, and, farther south, over Erech and Larsa as well. This dynasty endured for nearly a hundred and twenty years, during which Ur flourished like Thebes in Egypt. Its monarchs styled themselves as "Kings of the Four Regions". The worship of Nannar (Sin) became officially recognized at Nippur, the seat of Enlil, during the reign of King Dungi of Ur; while at Erech, the high priest of Anu, the sky god, became the high priest of the moon god. Apparently matriarchal ideas, associated with lunar worship, again came into prominence, for the king appointed two of his daughters to be rulers of conquered states in Elam and Syria. In the latter half of his reign, Dungi, the conqueror, was installed as high priest at Eridu. It would thus appear that there was a renascence of early Sumerian religious ideas. Ea, the god of the deep, had long been overshadowed, but a few years before Dungi's death a temple was erected to him at Nippur, where he was worshipped as Dagan. Until the very close of his reign, which lasted for fifty-eight years, this great monarch of tireless activity waged wars of conquest, built temples and palaces, and developed the natural resources of Sumer and Akkad. Among his many reforms was the introduction of standards of weights, which received divine sanction from the moon god, who, as in Egypt, was the measurer and regulator of human transactions and human life.

To this age also belongs many of the Sumerian business and legal records, which were ultimately carried off to Susa, where they have been recovered by French excavators.

About half a century after Dungi's death the Dynasty of Ur came to an end, its last king having been captured by an Elamite force.

At some time subsequent to this period, Abraham migrated from Ur to the northern city of Harran, where the moon god was also the chief city deity--the Baal, or "lord". It is believed by certain Egyptologists that Abraham sojourned in Egypt during its Twelfth Dynasty, which, according to the Berlin system of minimum dating, extended from about 2000 B.C. till 1780 B.C. The Hebrew patriarch may therefore have been a contemporary of Hammurabi's, who is identified with Amraphel, king of Shinar (Sumer) in the Bible.[149]

But after the decline of Ur's ascendancy, and long before Babylon's great monarch came to the throne, the centre of power in Sumeria was shifted to Isin, where sixteen kings

56

flourished for two and a quarter centuries. Among the royal names, recognition was given to Ea and Dagan, Sin, Enlil, and Ishtar, indicating that Sumerian religion in its Semitized form was receiving general recognition. The sun god was identical with Ninip and Nin-Girsu, a god of fertility, harvest, and war, but now more fully developed and resembling Babbar, "the shining one", the solar deity of Akkadian Sippar, whose Semitic name was Shamash. As Shamash was ultimately developed as the god of justice and righteousness, it would appear that his ascendancy occurred during the period when well-governed communities systematized their religious beliefs to reflect social conditions.

The first great monarch of the Isin dynasty was Ishbi-Urra, who reigned for thirty-two years. Like his successors, he called himself "King of Sumer and Akkad", and it appears that his sway extended to the city of Sippar, where solar worship prevailed. Traces of him have also been found at Eridu, Ur, Erech, and Nippur, so that he must have given recognition to Ea, Sin, Anu, and Enlil. In this period the early national pantheon may have taken shape, Bel Enlil being the chief deity. Enlil was afterwards displaced by Merodach of Babylon.

Before 2200 B.C. there occurred a break in the supremacy of Isin. Gungunu, King of Ur, combined with Larsa, whose sun temple he restored, and declared himself ruler of Sumer and Akkad. But Isin again gathered strength under Ur-Ninip, who was not related to his predecessor. Perhaps he came from Nippur, where the god Ninip was worshipped as the son of Bel Enlil.

According to a Babylonian document, a royal grandson of Ur-Ninip's, having no direct heir, selected as his successor his gardener, Enlil-bani. He placed the crown on the head of this obscure individual, abdicated in his favour, and then died a mysterious death within his palace.

It is highly probable that Enlil-bani, whose name signifies "Enlil is my creator", was a usurper like Sargon of Akkad, and he may have similarly circulated a myth regarding his miraculous origin to justify his sudden rise to power. The truth appears to be that he came to the throne as the leader of a palace revolution at a time of great unrest. But he was not allowed to remain in undisputed possession. A rival named Sin-ikisha, evidently a moon worshipper and perhaps connected with Ur, displaced the usurper, and proclaimed himself king. After a brief reign of six months he was overthrown, however, by Enlil-bani, who piously credited his triumph over his enemy to the chief god of Nippur, whose name he bore. Although he took steps to secure his position by strengthening the fortifications of Isin, and reigned for about a quarter of a century, he was not succeeded by his heir, if he had one. King Zambia, who was no relation, followed him, but his reign lasted for only three years. The names of the next two kings are unknown. Then came Sin-magir, who was succeeded by Damik-ilishu, the last King of Isin.

Towards the close of Damik-ilishu's reign of twenty-four years he came under the suzerainty of Larsa, whose ruler was Rim Sin. Then Isin was captured by Sin-muballit, King of Babylon, the father of the great Hammurabi. Rim Sin was an Elamite.

Afterwards the old order of things passed away. Babylon became the metropolis, the names of Sumer and Akkad dropped out of use, and the whole country between the rivers was called Babylonia.[150] The various systems of law which obtained in the different states were then codified by Hammurabi, who appointed governors in all the cities which came under his sway to displace the patesis and kings. A new national pantheon of representative character was also formed, over which Merodach (Marduk), the city god of Babylon, presided. How this younger deity was supposed to rise to power is related in the Babylonian legend of Creation, which is dealt with in the next chapter.[151] In framing this myth from the fragments of older myths, divine sanction was given to the supremacy achieved by Merodach's city. The allegiance of future generations was thus secured, not only by the strong arm of the law, but also by the combined influence of the reorganized priesthoods at the various centres of administration.

An interesting problem, which should be referred to here, arises in connection with the sculptured representations of deities before and after the rise of Akkad as a great Power. It is found, although the Sumerians shaved their scalps and faces at the dawn of the historical age, that they worshipped gods who had long hair and also beards, which were sometimes square and sometimes pointed.

At what period the Sumerian deities were given human shape it is impossible to determine. As has been shown (Chapters II and III) all the chief gods and goddesses had animal forms and composite monster forms before they became anthropomorphic deities. Ea had evidently a fish shape ere he was clad in the skin of a fish, as an Egyptian god was simply a bull before he was depicted in human shape wearing a bull's skin. The archaic Sumerian animal and composite monster gods of animistic and totemic origin survived after the anthropomorphic period as mythical figures, which were used for decorative or magical purposes and as symbols. A form of divine headdress was a cap enclosed in horns, between which appeared the soaring lion-headed eagle, which symbolized Nin-Girsu. This god had also lion and antelope forms, which probably figured in lost myths--perhaps they were like the animals loved by Ishtar and referred to in the Gilgamesh epic. Similarly the winged bull was associated with the moon god Nannar, or Sin, of Ur, who was "a horned steer". On various cylinder seals appear groups of composite monsters and rearing wild beasts, which were evidently representations of gods and demons in conflict.

Suggestive data for comparative study is afforded in this connection by ancient Egypt. Sokar, the primitive Memphite deity, retained until the end his animal and composite monster forms. Other gods were depicted with human bodies and the heads of birds, serpents, and crocodiles, thus forming links between the archaic demoniac and the later anthropomorphic deities. A Sumerian example is the deified Ea-bani, who, like Pan, has the legs and hoofs of a goat.

The earliest representations of Sumerian humanized deities appear on reliefs from Tello, the site of Lagash. These examples of archaic gods, however, are not bearded in Semitic fashion. On the contrary, their lips and cheeks are shaved, while an exaggerated chin tuft is retained. The explanation suggested is that the Sumerians gave their deities human shape before they themselves were clean shaven, and that the retention of the characteristic facial hair growth of the Mediterranean Race is another example of the conservatism of the religious instinct. In Egypt the clean-shaven Pharaohs, who represented gods, wore false chin-tuft beards; even Queen Hatshepsut considered it necessary to assume a beard on state occasions. Ptah-Osiris retained his archaic beard until the Ptolemaic period.

It seems highly probable that in similarly depicting their gods with beards, the early Sumerians were not influenced by the practices of any alien people or peoples. Not until the period of Gudea, the Patesi of Lagash, did they give their gods heavy moustaches, side whiskers, and flowing beards of Semitic type. It may be, however, that by then they had completely forgotten the significance of an ancient custom. Possibly, too, the sculptors of Lagash were working under the influence of the Akkadian school of art, which had produced the exquisite stele of victory for Naram-Sin, and consequently adopted the conventional Semitic treatment of bearded figures. At any rate, they were more likely to study and follow the artistic triumphs of Akkad than the crude productions of the archaic period. Besides, they lived in an age when Semitic kings were deified and the Semitic overlords had attained to great distinction and influence.

The Semitic folks were not so highly thought of in the early Sumerian period. It is not likely that the agricultural people regarded as models of gods the plunderers who descended from the hills, and, after achieving successes, returned home with their spoils. More probably they regarded them as "foreign devils". Other Semites, however, who came as traders, bringing wood, stone, and especially copper, and formed communities in cities, may well have influenced Sumerian religious thought. The god Ramman, for instance, who was given recognition all through Babylonia, was a god of hill folks as far north as Asia Minor and throughout Syria. He may have been introduced by settlers who adopted Sumerian habits of life and shaved scalp and face. But although the old cities could never have existed in a complete state of isolation from the outer world, it is unlikely that their inhabitants modelled their deities on those worshipped by groups of aliens. A severe strain is imposed on our credulity if we are expected to believe that it was due to the teachings and example of uncultured nomads that the highly civilized Sumerians developed their gods from composite monsters to anthropomorphic deities. Such a supposition, at any rate, is not supported by the evidence of Ancient Egypt.

[144] *Nehemiah*, i, 1.

[145] *Esther*, i, 6.

[146] *Isaiah*, xiii, 19-22.

[147] *Indian Myth and Legend*, pp. 173-175 and 192-194.

[148] Or Rimush.

[149] *Genesis*, xiv.

[150] That is, the equivalent of Babylonia. During the Kassite period the name was Karduniash.

[151] The narrative follows *The Seven Tablets of Creation* and other fragments, while the account given by Berosus is also drawn upon.

Chapter VII. Creation Legend: Merodach the Dragon Slayer

Abstract

Elder Spirits of the Primordial Deep--Apsu and the Tiamat Dragon--Plot to Destroy the Beneficent Gods--Ea overcomes Apsu and Muminu--The Vengeful Preparations of the Dragon--Anshar's Appeal to Merodach--The Festival of the High Gods--Merodach exalted as Ruler of the Universe--Dragon slain and Host taken captive--Merodach rearranges the Pantheon--Creation of Man--Merodach as Asari--The Babylonian Osiris--The Chief Purpose of Mankind--Tiamat as Source of Good and Evil--The Dragon as the Serpent or Worm--Folk Tale aspect of Creation Myth--British Neolithic Legends--German and Egyptian Contracts--Biblical references to Dragons--The Father and Son theme--Merodach and Tammuz--Monotheistic Tendency--Bisexual Deities.

In the beginning the whole universe was a sea. Heaven on high had not been named, nor the earth beneath. Their begetter was Apsu, the father of the primordial Deep, and their mother was Tiamat, the spirit of Chaos. No plain was yet formed, no marsh could be seen; the gods had no existence, nor had their fates been determined. Then there was a movement in the waters, and the deities issued forth. The first who had being were the god Lachmu and the goddess Lachamu. Long ages went past. Then were created the god Anshar and the goddess Kishar. When the days of these deities had increased and extended, they were followed by Anu, god of the sky, whose consort was Anatu; and Ea, most wise and all-powerful, who was without an equal. Now Ea, god of the deep, was also Enki, "lord of earth", and his eternal spouse, Damkina, was Gashan-ki, "lady of earth". The son of Ea and Damkina was Bel, the lord, who in time created mankind.[152] Thus were the high gods established in power and in glory.

Now Apsu and Tiamat remained amidst confusion in the deeps of chaos. They were troubled because their offspring, the high gods, aspired to control the universe and set it in order.[153] Apsu was still powerful and fierce, and Tiamat snarled and raised tempests, smiting herself. Their purpose was to work evil amidst eternal confusion.

Then Apsu called upon Mummu, his counsellor, the son who shared his desires, and said, "O Mummu, thou who art pleasing unto me, let us go forth together unto Tiamat and speak with her."

So the two went forth and prostrated themselves before the Chaos Mother to consult with her as to what should be done to prevent the accomplishment of the purpose of the high gods.

Apsu opened his mouth and spake, saying, "O Tiamat, thou gleaming one, the purpose of the gods troubles me. I cannot rest by day nor can I repose by night. I will thwart them and destroy their purpose. I will bring sorrow and mourning so that we may lie down undisturbed by them."

Tiamat heard these words and snarled. She raised angry and roaring tempests; in her furious grief she uttered a curse, and then spake to Apsu, saying, "What shall we do so that their purpose may be thwarted and we may lie down undisturbed again?"

Mummu, the counsellor, addressing Apsu, made answer, and said, "Although the gods are powerful, thou canst overcome them; although their purpose is strong, thou canst thwart it. Then thou shalt have rest by day and peace by night to lie down."

The face of Apsu grew bright when he heard these words spoken by Mummu, yet he trembled to think of the purpose of the high gods, to whom he was hostile. With Tiamat he lamented because the gods had changed all things; the plans of the gods filled their hearts with dread; they sorrowed and spake with Mummu, plotting evil.

Then Ea, who knoweth all, drew near; he beheld the evil ones conspiring and muttering together. He uttered a pure incantation and accomplished the downfall of Apsu and Mummu, who were taken captive.[154]

Kingu, who shared the desires of Tiamat, spake unto her words of counsel, saying, "Apsu and Mummu have been overcome and we cannot repose. Thou shalt be their Avenger, O Tempestuous One."

Tiamat heard the words of this bright and evil god, and made answer, saying, "On my strength thou canst trust. So let war be waged."

Then were the hosts of chaos and the deep gathered together. By day and by night they plotted against the high gods, raging furiously, making ready for battle, fuming and storming and taking no rest.

Mother Chuber,[155] the creator of all, provided irresistible weapons. She also brought into being eleven kinds of fierce monsters--giant serpents, sharp of tooth with unsparing fangs, whose bodies were filled with poison instead of blood; snarling dragons, clad with terror, and of such lofty stature that whoever saw them was overwhelmed with fear, nor could any escape their attack when they lifted themselves up; vipers and pythons, and the Lachamu, hurricane monsters, raging hounds, scorpion men, tempest furies, fish men, and mountain rams. These she armed with fierce weapons and they had no fear of war.

Then Tiamat, whose commands are unchangeable and mighty, exalted Kingu, who had come to her aid, above all the evil gods; she made him the leader to direct the army in battle, to go in front, to open the attack. Robing Kingu in splendour, she seated him on high and spoke, saying:

"I have established thy command over all the gods. Thou shalt rule over them. Be mighty, thou my chosen husband, and let thy name be exalted over all the spirits of heaven and spirits of earth."

Unto Kingu did Tiamat deliver the tablets of fate; she laid them in his bosom, and said, "Thy commands cannot be changed; thy words shall remain firm."

Thus was Kingu exalted; he was vested with the divine power of Anu to decree the fate of the gods, saying, "Let thy mouth open to thwart the fire god; be mighty in battle nor brook resistance."

Then had Ea knowledge of Tiamat's doings, how she had gathered her forces together, and how she had prepared to work evil against the high gods with purpose to avenge Apsu. The wise god was stricken with grief, and he moaned for many days. Thereafter he went and stood before his father, Anshar, and spake, saying, "Our mother, Tiamat, hath turned against us in her wrath. She hath gathered the gods about her, and those thou didst create are with her also."

When Anshar heard all that Ea revealed regarding the preparations made by Tiamat, he smote his loins and clenched his teeth, and was ill at ease. In sorrow and anger he spoke and said, "Thou didst go forth aforetime to battle; thou didst bind Mummu and smite Apsu. Now Kingu is exalted, and there is none who can oppose Tiamat."[156]

Anshar called his son, Anu, before him, and spoke, saying: "O mighty one without fear, whose attack is irresistible, go now before Tiamat and speak so that her anger may subside and her heart be made merciful. But if she will not hearken unto thee, speak thou for me, so that she may be reconciled."

Anu was obedient to the commands of Anshar. He departed, and descended by the path of Tiamat until he beheld her fuming and snarling, but he feared to approach her, and turned back.

Then Ea was sent forth, but he was stricken with terror and turned back also.[157]

Anshar then called upon Merodach, son of Ea, and addressed him, saying, "My son, who softeneth my heart, thou shalt go forth to battle and none shall stand against thee."

The heart of Merodach was made glad at these words. He stood before Anshar, who kissed him, because that he banished fear. Merodach spake, saying: "O lord of the gods, withdraw not thy words; let me go forth to do as is thy desire. What man hath challenged thee to battle?"

Anshar made answer and said: "No man hath challenged me. It is Tiamat, the woman, who hath resolved to wage war against us. But fear not and make merry, for thou shalt bruise the head of Tiamat. O wise god, thou shalt overcome her with thy pure incantation. Tarry not but hasten forth; she cannot wound thee; thou shalt come back again." The words of Anshar delighted the heart of Merodach, who spake, saying: "O lord of the gods, O fate of the high gods, if I, the avenger, am to subdue Tiamat and save all, then proclaim my greatness among the gods. Let all the high gods gather together joyfully in Upshukinaku (the Council Hall), so that my words like thine may remain unchanged, and what I do may never be altered. Instead of thee I will decree the fates of the gods."

Then Anshar called unto his counsellor, Gaga, and addressing him, said: "O thou who dost share my desires, thou who dost understand the purpose of my heart, go unto Lachmu and Lachamu and summon all the high gods to come before me to eat bread and drink wine. Repeat to them all I tell you of Tiamat's preparations for war, of my commands to Anu and Ea, who turned back, fearing the dragon, of my choice of Merodach to be our avenger, and his desire to be equipped with my power to decree fate, so that he may be made strong to combat against our enemy."

As Anshar commanded so did Gaga do. He went unto Lachmu and Lachamu and prostrated himself humbly before them. Then he rose and delivered the message of Anshar, their son, adding: "Hasten and speedily decide for Merodach your fate. Permit him to depart to meet your powerful foe."

When Lachmu and Lachamu heard all that Gaga revealed unto them they uttered lamentations, while the Igigi (heavenly spirits) sorrowed bitterly, and said: "What change hath happened that Tiamat hath become hostile to her own offspring? We cannot understand her deeds."

All the high gods then arose and went unto Anshar, They filled his council chamber and kissed one another. Then they sat down to eat bread and drink sesame wine. And when they were made drunk and were merry and at their ease, they decreed the fate for Merodach.

In the chamber of Anshar they honoured the Avenger. He was exalted as a prince over them all, and they said: "Among the high gods thou art the highest; thy command is the command of Anu. Henceforth thou wilt have power to raise up and to cast down. None of the gods will dispute thy authority. O Merodach, our avenger, we give thee sovereignty over the entire Universe. Thy weapon will ever be irresistible. Smite down the gods who have raised revolt, but spare the lives of those who repose their trust in thee."

Then the gods laid down a garment before Merodach, saying: "Open thy mouth and speak words of command, so that the garment may be destroyed; speak again and it will be brought back."

Merodach spake with his mouth and the garment vanished; he spake again and the garment was reproduced.

All the gods rejoiced, and they prostrated themselves and cried out, "Merodach is King!"

Thereafter they gave him the sceptre and the throne and the insignia of royalty, and also an irresistible weapon[158] with which to overcome his enemies, saying: "Now, O Merodach, hasten and slay Tiamat. Let the winds carry her blood to hidden places."

So was the fate of Merodach decreed by the gods; so was a path of prosperity and peace prepared for him. He made ready for battle; he strung his bow and hung his quiver; he slung a dart over his shoulder, and he grasped a club in his right hand; before him he set lightning, and with flaming fire he filled his body; Anu gave unto him a great net with which to snare his enemies and prevent their escape. Then Merodach created seven winds--the wind of evil, the uncontrollable wind, the sandstorm, and the whirlwind, the fourfold wind, the sevenfold wind, and the wind that has no equal--and they went after him. Next he seized his mighty weapon, the thunderstone, and leapt into his storm chariot, to which were yoked four rushing and destructive steeds of rapid flight, with foam-flecked mouths and teeth full of venom, trained for battle, to overthrow enemies and trample them underfoot. A light burned on the head of Merodach, and he was clad in a robe of terror. He drove forth, and the gods, his fathers, followed after him: the high gods clustered around and followed him, hastening to battle.

Merodach drove on, and at length he drew nigh to the secret lair of Tiamat, and he beheld her muttering with Kingu, her consort. For a moment he faltered, and when the gods who followed him beheld this, their eyes were troubled.

Tiamat snarled nor turned her head. She uttered curses, and said: "O Merodach, I fear not thy advance as chief of the gods. My allies are assembled here, and are more powerful than thou art."

Merodach uplifted his arm, grasping the dreaded thunderstone, and spake unto Tiamat, the rebellious one, saying: "Thou hast exalted thyself, and with wrathful heart hath prepared for war against the high gods and their fathers, whom thou dost hate in thy heart of evil. Unto Kingu thou hast given the power of Anu to decree fate, because thou art hostile to what is good and loveth what is sinful. Gather thy forces together, and arm thyself and come forth to battle."

When Tiamat heard these mighty words she raved and cried aloud like one who is possessed; all her limbs shook, and she muttered a spell. The gods seized their weapons.

Tiamat and Merodach advanced to combat against one another. They made ready for battle. The lord of the high gods spread out the net which Anu had given him. He snared the dragon and she could not escape. Tiamat opened her mouth which was seven miles wide, and Merodach called upon the evil wind to smite her; he caused the wind to keep her mouth agape so that she could not close it. All the tempests and the hurricanes entered in, filling her body, and her heart grew weak; she gasped, overpowered. Then the lord of the high gods seized his dart and cast it through the lower part of her body; it tore her inward parts and severed her heart. So was Tiamat slain.

Merodach overturned the body of the dead dragon and stood upon it. All the evil gods who had followed her were stricken with terror and broke into flight. But they were unable to escape. Merodach caught them in his great net, and they stumbled and fell uttering cries of distress, and the whole world resounded with their wailing and lamentations. The lord of the high gods broke the weapons of the evil gods and put them in bondage. Then he fell upon the monsters which Tiamat had created; he subdued them, divested them of their powers, and trampled them under his feet. Kingu he seized with the others. From this god great Merodach took the tablets of fate, and impressing upon them his own seal, placed them in his bosom.

So were the enemies of the high gods overthrown by the Avenger. Ansar's commands were fulfilled and the desires of Ea fully accomplished.

Merodach strengthened the bonds which he had laid upon the evil gods and then returned to Tiamat. He leapt upon the dragon's body; he clove her skull with his great club; he opened the channels of her blood which streamed forth, and caused the north to carry her blood to hidden places. The high gods, his fathers, clustered around; they raised shouts of triumph and made merry. Then they brought gifts and offerings to the great Avenger.

Merodach rested a while, gazing upon the dead body of the dragon. He divided the flesh of Ku-pu[159], and devised a cunning plan.

Then the lord of the high gods split the body of the dragon like that of a mashde fish into two halves. With one half he enveloped the firmament; he fixed it there and set a watchman to prevent the waters falling down[160]. With the other half he made the earth[161]. Then he made the abode of Ea in the deep, and the abode of Anu in high heaven. The abode of Enlil was in the air.

Merodach set all the great gods in their several stations. He also created their images, the stars of the Zodiac, and fixed them all. He measured the year and divided it into months; for twelve months he made three stars each. After he had given starry images of the gods separate control of each day of the year, he founded the station of Nibiru (Jupiter), his own star, to determine the limits of all stars, so that none might err or go astray. He placed beside his own the stations of Enlil and Ea, and on each side he opened mighty gates, fixing bolts on the left and on the right. He set the zenith in the centre.

Merodach decreed that the moon god should rule the night and measure the days, and each month he was given a crown. Its various phases the great lord determined, and he commanded that on the evening of its fullest brilliancy it should stand opposite the sun.[162]

He placed his bow in heaven (as a constellation) and his net also.

We have now reached the sixth tablet, which begins with a reference to words spoken to Merodach by the gods. Apparently Ea had conceived in his heart that mankind should be created. The lord of the gods read his thoughts and said: "I will shed my blood and fashion bone... I will create man to dwell on the earth so that the gods may be worshipped and shrines erected for them. I will change the pathways of the gods...."

The rest of the text is fragmentary, and many lines are missing. Berosus states, however, that Belus (Bel Merodach) severed his head from his shoulders. His blood flowed forth, and the gods mixed it with earth and formed the first man and various animals.

In another version of the creation of man, it is related that Merodach "laid a reed upon the face of the waters; he formed dust, and poured it out beside the reed.... That he might cause the gods to dwell in the habitation of their heart's desire, he formed mankind." The goddess Aruru, a deity of Sippar, and one of the forms of "the lady of the gods", is associated with Merodach as the creatrix of the seed of mankind. "The beasts of the field and living creatures in the field he formed." He also created the Tigris and Euphrates rivers, grass, reeds, herbs and trees, lands, marshes and swamps, cows, goats, &c.[163]

In the seventh tablet Merodach is praised by the gods--the Igigi (spirits of heaven). As he has absorbed all their attributes, he is addressed by his fifty-one names; henceforth each deity is a form of Merodach. Bel Enlil, for instance, is Merodach of lordship and domination; Sin, the moon god, is Merodach as ruler of night; Shamash is Merodach as god of law and holiness; Nergal is Merodach of war; and so on. The tendency to monotheism appears to have been most marked among the priestly theorists of Babylon.

Merodach is hailed to begin with as Asari, the introducer of agriculture and horticulture, the creator of grain and plants. He also directs the decrees of Anu, Bel, and Ea; but having rescued the gods from destruction at the hands of Kingu and Tiamat, he was greater than his "fathers", the elder gods. He set the Universe in order, and created all things anew. He is therefore Tutu, "the creator", a merciful and beneficent god. The following are renderings of lines 25 to 32:

> Tutu: Aga-azaga (the glorious crown) may he make the crowns glorious--
> The lord of the glorious incantation bringing the dead to life;
> He who had mercy on the gods who had been overpowered;
> Made heavy the yoke which he had laid on the gods who were his enemies,
> (And) to redeem (?) them created mankind.
> "The merciful one", "he with whom is salvation",
> May his word be established, and not forgotten,
> In the mouth of the black-headed ones whom his hands have made.

Pinches' Translation[164]

> Tutu as Aga-azag may mankind fourthly magnify!
> "The Lord of the Pure Incantation", "the Quickener of the Dead",

"Who had mercy upon the captive gods",
"Who removed the yoke from upon the gods his enemies".
"For their forgiveness did he create mankind",
"The Merciful One, with whom it is to bestow life!"
May his deeds endure, may they never be forgotten
In the mouth of mankind whom his hands have made.

King's Translation.[165]

Apparently the Babylonian doctrine set forth that mankind was created not only to worship the gods, but also to bring about the redemption of the fallen gods who followed Tiamat.

Those rebel angels *(ili*, gods) He prohibited return;
He stopped their service; He removed them unto the gods *(ili)* who were His enemies.

In their room he created mankind.[166]

Tiamat, the chaos dragon, is the Great Mother. She has a dual character. As the origin of good she is the creatrix of the gods. Her beneficent form survived as the Sumerian goddess Bau, who was obviously identical with the Phoenician Baau, mother of the first man. Another name of Bau was Ma, and Nintu, "a form of the goddess Ma", was half a woman and half a serpent, and was depicted with "a babe suckling her breast" (Chapter IV). The Egyptian goddesses Neheb-kau and Uazit were serpents, and the goddesses Isis and Nepthys had also serpent forms. The serpent was a symbol of fertility, and as a mother was a protector. Vishnu, the Preserver of the Hindu Trinity, sleeps on the world-serpent's body. Serpent charms are protective and fertility charms.

As the origin of evil Tiamat personified the deep and tempests. In this character she was the enemy of order and good, and strove to destroy the world.

I have seen
The ambitious ocean swell and rage and foam
To be exalted with the threatening clouds.[167]

Tiamat was the dragon of the sea, and therefore the serpent or leviathan. The word "dragon" is derived from the Greek "drakon", the serpent known as "the seeing one" or "looking one", whose glance was the lightning. The Anglo-Saxon "fire drake" ("draca", Latin "draco") is identical with the "flying dragon".

In various countries the serpent or worm is a destroyer which swallows the dead. "The worm shall eat them like wool", exclaimed Isaiah in symbolic language.[168] It lies in the ocean which surrounds the world in Egyptian, Babylonian, Greek, Teutonic, Indian, and other mythologies. The Irish call it "morúach", and give it a mermaid form like the Babylonian Nintu. In a Scottish Gaelic poem Tiamat figures as "The Yellow Muilearteach", who is slain by Finn-mac-Coul, assisted by his warrior band.

There was seen coming on the top of the waves
The crooked, clamouring, shivering brave ...
Her face was blue black of the lustre of coal,
And her bone-tufted tooth was like rusted bone.[169]

The serpent figures in folk tales. When Alexander the Great, according to Ethiopic legend, was lowered in a glass cage to the depths of the ocean, he saw a great monster going past, and sat for two days "watching for its tail and hinder parts to appear".[170] An Argyllshire Highlander had a similar experience. He went to fish one morning on a rock. "He was not long there when he saw the head of an eel pass. He continued fishing for an hour and the eel was still passing. He went home, worked in the field all day, and having returned to the same rock in the evening, the eel was still passing, and about dusk he saw her tail disappearing."[171] Tiamat's sea-brood is referred to in the Anglo-Saxon epic *Beowulf* as "nickers". The hero "slew by night sea monsters on the waves" (line 422).

The well dragon--the French "draco"--also recalls the Babylonian water monsters. There was a "dragon well" near Jerusalem.[172] From China to Ireland rivers are dragons, or goddesses who flee from the well dragons. The demon of the Rhone is called the "drac". Floods are also referred to as dragons, and the Hydra, or water serpent, slain by Hercules, belongs to this category. Water was the source of evil as well as good. To the Sumerians, the ocean especially was the abode of monsters. They looked upon it as did Shakespeare's Ferdinand, when, leaping into the sea, he cried: "Hell is empty and all the devils are here".[173]

There can be little doubt but that in this Babylonian story of Creation we have a glorified variation of the widespread Dragon myth. Unfortunately, however, no trace can be obtained of the pre-existing Sumerian oral version which the theorizing priests infused with such sublime symbolism. No doubt it enjoyed as great popularity as the immemorial legend of Perseus and Andromeda, which the sages of Greece attempted to rationalize, and parts of which the poets made use of and developed as these appealed to their imaginations.

The lost Sumerian story may be summarized as follows: There existed in the savage wilds, or the ocean, a family of monsters antagonistic to a group of warriors represented in the Creation legend by the gods. Ea, the heroic king, sets forth to combat with the enemies of man, and slays the monster father, Apsu, and his son, Mummu. But the most powerful demon remains to be dealt with. This is the mother Tiamat, who burns to avenge the deaths of her kindred. To wage war against her the hero makes elaborate preparations, and equips himself with special weapons. The queen of monsters cannot be overcome by ordinary means, for she has great cunning, and is less vulnerable than were her husband and son. Although Ea may work spells against her, she is able to thwart him by working counter spells. Only a hand-to-hand combat can decide the fray. Being strongly protected by her scaly hide, she must be wounded either on the under part of her body or through her mouth by a weapon which will pierce her liver, the seat of life. It will be noted in this connection that Merodach achieved success by causing the winds which followed him to distend the monster's jaws, so that he might be able to inflict the fatal blow and prevent her at the same time from uttering spells to weaken him.

This type of story, in which the mother monster is greater and more powerful than her husband or son, is exceedingly common in Scottish folklore. In the legend which relates the adventures of "Finn in the Kingdom of Big Men", the hero goes forth at night to protect his allies against the attacks of devastating sea monsters. Standing on the beach, "he saw the sea advancing in fiery kilns and as a darting serpent.... A huge monster came up, and looking down below where he (Finn) was, exclaimed, 'What little speck do I see here?'" Finn, aided by his fairy dog, slew the water monster. On Finn, aided by his fairy dog, slew the water monster. On the following night a bigger monster, "the father", came ashore, and he also was slain. But the most powerful enemy had yet to be dealt with. "The next night a Big Hag came ashore, and the tooth in the front of her mouth would make a distaff. 'You killed my husband and son,' she said." Finn acknowledged that he did, and they began to fight. After a prolonged struggle, in which Finn was almost overcome, the Hag fell and her head was cut off.[174]

The story of "Finlay the Changeling" has similar features. The hero slew first a giant and then the giant's father. Thereafter the Hag came against him and exclaimed, "Although with cunning and deceitfulness you killed my husband last night and my son on the night before last, I shall certainly kill you to-night." A fierce wrestling match ensued on the bare rock. The Hag was ultimately thrown down. She then offered treasures to ransom her life, including "a gold sword in my cave", regarding which she says, "never was it drawn to man or to beast whom it did not overcome".[175] In other Scottish stories of like character the hero climbs a tree, and says something to induce the hag to open her mouth, so that he may plunge his weapon down her throat.

The Grendel story in *Beowulf*,[176] the Anglo-Saxon epic, is of like character. A male water monster preys nightly upon the warriors who sleep in the great hall of King Hrothgar. Beowulf comes over the sea, as did Finn to the "Kingdom of Big Men", to sky Grendel. He wrestles with this man-eater and mortally wounds him. Great rejoicings ensue, but they have to be brought to an abrupt conclusion, because the mother of Grendel has meanwhile resolved "to go a sorry journey and avenge the death of her son".

The narrative sets forth that she enters the Hall in the darkness of night. "Quickly she grasped one of the nobles tight, and then she went towards the fen", towards her submarine cave. Beowulf follows in due course, and, fully armoured, dives through the waters and ultimately enters the monster's lair. In the combat the "water wife" proves to be a more terrible opponent than was her son. Indeed, Beowulf was unable to slay her until he possessed himself of a gigantic sword, "adorned with treasure", which was hanging in the cave. With this magic weapon he slays the mother monster, whose poisonous blood afterwards melts the "damasked blade". Like Finn, he subsequently returns with the head of one of the monsters.

An interesting point about this story is that it does not appear in any form in the North German cycle of Romance. Indeed, the poet who included in his epic the fiery dragon story, which links the hero Beowulf with Sigurd and Siegfried, appears to be doubtful about the mother monster's greatness, as if dealing with unfamiliar material, for he says: "The terror (caused by Grendel's mother) was less by just so much as woman's strength, woman's war terror, is (measured) by fighting men".[177] Yet, in the narrative which follows the Amazon is proved to be the stronger monster of the two. Traces of the mother monster survive in English folklore, especially in the traditions about the mythical "Long Meg of Westminster", referred to by Ben Jonson in his masque of the "Fortunate Isles":

Westminster Meg,

With her long leg,
As long as a crane;
And feet like a plane,
With a pair of heels
As broad as two wheels.

Meg has various graves. One is supposed to be marked by a huge stone in the south side of the cloisters of Westminster Abbey; it probably marks the trench in which some plague victims--regarded, perhaps, as victims of Meg--were interred. Meg was also reputed to have been petrified, like certain Greek and Irish giants and giantesses. At Little Salkeld, near Penrith, a stone circle is referred to as "Long Meg and her Daughters". Like "Long Tom", the famous giant, "Mons Meg" gave her name to big guns in early times, all hags and giants having been famous in floating folk tales as throwers of granite boulders, balls of hard clay, quoits, and other gigantic missiles.

The stories about Grendel's mother and Long Meg are similar to those still repeated in the Scottish Highlands. These contrast sharply with characteristic Germanic legends, in which the giant is greater than the giantess, and the dragon is a male, like Fafner, who is slain by Sigurd, and Regin whom Siegfried overcomes. It is probable, therefore, that the British stories of female monsters who were more powerful than their husbands and sons, are of Neolithic and Iberian origin--immemorial relics of the intellectual life of the western branch of the Mediterranean race.

In Egypt the dragon survives in the highly developed mythology of the sun cult of Heliopolis, and, as sun worship is believed to have been imported, and the sun deity is a male, it is not surprising to find that the night demon, Apep, was a personification of Set. This god, who is identical with Sutekh, a Syrian and Asia Minor deity, wasapparently worshipped by a tribe which was overcome in the course of early tribal struggles in pre-dynastic times. Being an old and discredited god, he became by a familiar process the demon of the conquerors. In the eighteenth dynasty, however, his ancient glory was revived, for the Sutekh of Rameses II figures as the "dragon slayer".[178] It is in accordance with Mediterranean modes of thought, however, to find that in Egypt there is a great celestial battle heroine. This is the goddess Hathor-Sekhet, the "Eye of Ra".[179] Similarly in India, the post-Vedic goddess Kali is a destroyer, while as Durga she is a guardian of heroes.[180] Kali, Durga, and Hathor-Sekhet link with the classical goddesses of war, and also with the Babylonian Ishtar, who, as has been shown, retained the outstanding characteristics of Tiamat, the fierce old "Great Mother" of primitive Sumerian folk religion.

It is possible that in the Babylonian dragon myth the original hero was Ea. As much may be inferred from the symbolic references in the Bible to Jah's victory over the monster of the deep: "Art thou not it that hath cut Rahab and wounded the dragon?"[181] "Thou brakest the heads of the dragons in the waters; thou brakest the heads of leviathan in pieces, and gavest him to be meat to the people inhabiting the wilderness";[182] "He divideth the sea with his power, and by his understanding he smiteth through the proud (Rahab). By his spirit he hath garnished the heavens: his hand hath formed (or pierced) the crooked serpent";[183] "Thou hast broken Rahab in pieces as one that is slain: thou hast scattered thine enemies with thy strong arm";[184] "In that day the Lord with his sore and great and strong sword shall punish leviathan the piercing (or stiff) serpent, even leviathan that crooked serpent; and he shall slay the dragon that is in the sea".[185]

In the Babylonian Creation legend Ea is supplanted as dragon slayer by his son Merodach. Similarly Ninip took the place of his father, Enlil, as the champion of the gods. "In other words," writes Dr. Langdon, "later theology evolved the notion of the son of the earth god, who acquires the attributes of the father, and becomes the god of war. It is he who stood forth against the rebellious monsters of darkness, who would wrest the dominion of the world from the gods who held their conclave on the mountain. The gods offer him the Tablets of Fate; the right to utter decrees is given unto him." This development is "of extreme importance for studying the growth of the idea of father and son, as creative and active principles of the world".[186] In Indian mythology Indra similarly takes the place of his bolt-throwing father Dyaus, the sky god, who so closely resembles Zeus. Andrew Lang has shown that this myth is of widespread character.[187] Were the Babylonian theorists guided by the folk-lore clue?

Now Merodach, as the son of Ea whom he consulted and received spells from, was a brother of "Tammuz of the Abyss". It seems that in the great god of Babylon we should recognize one of the many forms of the primeval corn spirit and patriarch--the shepherd youth who was beloved by Ishtar. As the deity of the spring sun, Tammuz slew the winter demons of rain and tempest, so that he was an appropriate spouse for the goddess of harvest and war. Merodach may have been a development of Tammuz in his character as a demon slayer. When he was raised to the position of Bel, "the Lord" by the Babylonian conquerors, Merodach

65

supplanted the older Bel--Enlil of Nippur. Now Enlil, who had absorbed all the attributes of rival deities, and become a world god, was the

Lord of the harvest lands ... lord of the grain fields,

being "lord of the anunnaki", or "earth spirits". As agriculturists in early times went to war so as to secure prisoners who could be sacrificed to feed the corn spirit, Enlil was a god of war and was adored as such:

The haughty, the hostile land thou dost humiliate ...
With thee who ventureth to make war?

He was also "the bull of goring horns ... Enlil the bull", the god of fertility as well as of battle.[188]

Asari, one of Merodach's names, links him with Osiris, the Egyptian Tammuz, who was supplanted by his son Horus. As the dragon slayer, he recalls, among others, Perseus, the Grecian hero, of whom it was prophesied that he would slay his grandfather. Perseus, like Tammuz and Osiris, was enclosed in a chest which was cast into the sea, to be rescued, however, by a fisherman on the island of Seriphos. This hero afterwards slew Medusa, one of the three terrible sisters, the Gorgons--a demon group which links with Tiamat. In time, Perseus returned home, and while an athletic contest was in progress, he killed his grandfather with a quoit. There is no evidence, however, to show that the displacement of Enlil by Merodach had any legendary sanction of like character. The god of Babylon absorbed all other deities, apparently for political purposes, and in accordance with the tendency of the thought of the times, when raised to supreme rank in the national pantheon; and he was depicted fighting the winged dragon, flapping his own storm wings, and carrying the thunder weapon associated with Ramman.

Merodach's spouse Zer-panitum was significantly called "the lady of the Abyss", a title which connects her with Damkina, the mother, and Belit-sheri, the sister of Tammuz. Damkina was also a sky goddess like Ishtar.

Zer-panitum was no pale reflection of her Celestial husband, but a goddess of sharply defined character with independent powers. Apparently she was identical with Aruru, creatrix of the seed of mankind, who was associated with Merodach when the first man and the first woman were brought into being. Originally she was one of the mothers in the primitive spirit group, and so identical with Ishtar and the other prominent goddesses.

As all goddesses became forms of Ishtar, so did all gods become forms of Merodach. Sin was "Merodach as illuminator of night", Nergal was "Merodach of war", Addu (Ramman) was "Merodach of rain", and so on. A colophon which contains a text in which these identifications are detailed, appears to be "a copy", says Professor Pinches, "of an old inscription", which, he thinks, "may go back as far as 2000 B.C. This is the period at which the name *Yaum-ilu*, 'Jah is god', is found, together with references to *ilu* as the name for the one great god, and is also, roughly, the date of Abraham, who, it may be noted, was a Babylonian of Ur of the Chaldees."[189]

In one of the hymns Merodach is addressed as follows:--
Who shall escape from before thy power?
Thy will is an eternal mystery!
Thou makest it plain in heaven
And in the earth,
Command the sea
And the sea obeyeth thee.
Command the tempest
And the tempest becometh a calm.
Command the winding course
Of the Euphrates,
And the will of Merodach
Shall arrest the floods.
Lord, thou art holy!
Who is like unto thee?
Merodach thou art honoured
Among the gods that bear a name.

The monotheistic tendency, which was a marked feature of Merodach worship, had previously become pronounced in the worship of Bel Enlil of Nippur. Although it did not affect the religion of the masses, it serves to show that among the ancient scholars and thinkers of Babylonia religious thought had, at an early period, risen far above the crude polytheism of those who bargained with their deities and propitiated them with offerings and extravagant flattery, or exercised over them a magical influence by the performance of seasonal ceremonies, like the backsliders in Jerusalem, censured so severely by Jeremiah, who baked cakes to reward the Queen of Heaven for an abundant harvest, and wept with her for the slain Tammuz when he departed to Hades.

Perhaps it was due to the monotheistic tendency, if not to the fusion of father-worshipping and mother-worshipping peoples, that bi-sexual deities were conceived of. Nannar, the moon god, was sometimes addressed as father and mother in one, and Ishtar as a god as well as a goddess. In Egypt Isis is referred to in a temple chant as "the woman who was made a male by her father Osiris", and the Nile god Hapi was depicted as a man with female breasts.

---

[152] The elder Bel was Enlil of Nippur and the younger Merodach of Babylon. According to Damascius the elder Bel came into existence before Ea, who as Enki shared his attributes.

[153] This is the inference drawn from fragmentary texts.

[154] A large portion of the narrative is awaiting here.

[155] A title of Tiamat; pron. *ch* guttural.

[156] There is another gap here which interrupts the narrative.

[157] This may refer to Ea's first visit when he overcame Kingu, but did not attack Tiamat.

[158] The lightning trident or thunderstone.

[159] The authorities are not agreed as to the meaning of "Ku-pu." Jensen suggests "trunk, body". In European dragon stories the heroes of the Siegfried order roast and eat the dragon's heart. Then they are inspired with the dragon's wisdom and cunning. Sigurd and Siegfried immediately acquire the language of birds. The birds are the "Fates", and direct the heroes what next they should do. Apparently Merodach's "cunning plan" was inspired after he had eaten a part of the body of Tiamat.

[160] The waters above the firmament.

[161] According to Berosus.

[162] This portion is fragmentary and seems to indicate that the Babylonians had made considerable progress in the science of astronomy. It is suggested that they knew that the moon derived its light from the sun.

[163] *The Seven Tablets of Creation*, L.W. King, pp. 134, 135.

[164] *The Religion of Babylonia and Assyria*, T.G. Pinches, p. 43.

[165] *The Seven Tablets of Creation*, L. W. King, vol. i, pp. 98, 99.

[166] *Trans. Soc. Bib. Arch.*, iv, 251-2.

[167] Shakespeare's *Julius Caesar*, i, 3, 8.

[168] *Isaiah*, li, 8.

[169] Campbell's *West Highland Tales*, pp. 136 *et seq*.

[170] *The Life and Exploits of Alexander the Great*, E. A. Wallis Budge, pp. 284, 285.

[171] Campbell's *West Highland Tales*.

[172] *Nehemiah*, ii, 13.

[173] *The Tempest*, i, 2, 212.

[174] *Waifs and Strays of Celtic Tradition*, vol. iv, p. 176 et seq.

[175] From unpublished folk tale.

[176] *Beowulf*, translated by Clark Hall, London, 1911, p. 18 et seq.

[177] *Beowulf*, translated by Clark Hall, London, 1911, p. 69, lines 1280-1287.

[178] *Egyptian Myth and Legend*, pp. 260, 261.

[179] *Egyptian Myth and Legend*, pp. 8, 9.

[180] *Indian Myth and Legend*, pp. xli, 149, 150.

[181] *Isaiah*, li, 9.

[182] *Psalms*, lxxiv, 13, 14. It will be noted that the Semitic dragon, like the Egyptian, is a male.

[183] *Job*, xxvi, 12, 13.

[184] *Psalms*, lxxxix, 10.

[185] *Isaiah*, xxvii, I.

[186] *Sumerian and Babylonian Psalms*, p. 204.

[187] *Custom and Myth*, pp. 45 et seq.

[188] Translation by Dr. Langdon, pp. 199 *et seq*.

[189] *The Religion of Babylonia and Assyria*, T.G. Pinches, pp. 118, 119.

Chapter VIII. Deified Heroes: Etana and Gilgamesh

Abstract

God and Heroes and the "Seven Sleepers"--Quests of Etana, Gilgamesh, Hercules, &c.--The Plant of Birth--Eagle carries Etana to Heaven--Indian Parallel--Flights of

Nimrod, Alexander the Great, and a Gaelic Hero--Eagle as a God--Indian Eagle identified with Gods of Creation, Fire, Fertility, and Death--Eagle carries Roman Emperor's Soul to Heaven--Fire and Agricultural Ceremonies--Nimrod of the *Koran* and John Barleycorn--Gilgamesh and the Eagle--Sargon-Tammuz Garden Myth--Ea-bani compared to Pan, Bast, and Nebuchadnezzar--Exploits of Gilgamesh and Ea-bani--Ishtar's Vengeance--Gilgamesh journeys to Otherworld--Song of Sea Maiden and "Lay of the Harper"--Babylonian Noah and the Plant of Life--Teutonic Parallels--Alexander the Great as Gilgamesh--Water of Life in the *Koran*--The Indian Gilgamesh and Hercules--The Mountain Tunnel in various Mythologies--Widespread Cultural Influences.

One of the oldest forms of folk stories relates to the wanderings of a hero in distant regions. He may set forth in search of a fair lady who has been taken captive, or to obtain a magic herb or stone to relieve a sufferer, to cure diseases, and to prolong life. Invariably he is a slayer of dragons and other monsters. A friendly spirit, or a group of spirits, may assist the hero, who acts according to the advice given him by a "wise woman", a magician, or a god. The spirits are usually wild beasts or birds--the "fates" of immemorial folk belief--and they may either carry the hero on their backs, instruct him from time to time, or come to his aid when called upon.

When a great national hero appealed by reason of his achievements to the imagination of a people, all the floating legends of antiquity were attached to his memory, and he became identified with gods and giants and knight-errants "old in story". In Scotland, for instance, the boulder-throwing giant of Eildon hills bears the name of Wallace, the Edinburgh giant of Arthur's Seat is called after an ancient Celtic king,[190] and Thomas the Rhymer takes the place, in an Inverness fairy mound called Tom-na-hurich, of Finn (Fingal) as chief of the "Seven Sleepers". Similarly Napoleon sleeps in France and Skobeleff in Russia, as do also other heroes elsewhere. In Germany the myths of Thunor (Thor) were mingled with hazy traditions of Theodoric the Goth (Dietrich), while in Greece, Egypt, and Arabia, Alexander the Great absorbed a mass of legendary matter of great antiquity, and displaced in the memories of the people the heroes of other Ages, as those heroes had previously displaced the humanized spirits of fertility and growth who alternately battled fiercely against the demons of spring, made love, gorged and drank deep and went to sleep--the sleep of winter. Certain folk tales, and the folk beliefs on which they were based, seem to have been of hoary antiquity before the close of the Late Stone Age.

There are two great heroes of Babylonian fame who link with Perseus and Hercules, Sigurd and Siegfried, Dietrich and Finn-mac-Coul. These are Etana and Gilgamesh, two legendary kings who resemble Tammuz the Patriarch referred to by Berosus, a form of Tammuz the Sleeper of the Sumerian psalms. One journeys to the Nether World to obtain the Plant of Birth and the other to obtain the Plant of Life. The floating legends with which they were associated were utilized and developed by the priests, when engaged in the process of systematizing and symbolizing religious beliefs, with purpose to unfold the secrets of creation and the Otherworld. Etana secures the assistance or a giant eagle who is an enemy of serpents like the Indian Garuda, half giant, half eagle. As Vishnu, the Indian god, rides on the back of Garuda, so does Etana ride on the back of the Babylonian Eagle. In one fragmentary legend which was preserved in the tablet-library of Ashur-banipal, the Assyrian monarch, Etana obtained the assistance of the Eagle to go in quest of the Plant of Birth. His wife was about to become a mother, and was accordingly in need of magical aid. A similar belief caused birth girdles of straw or serpent skins, and eagle stones found in eagles' nests, to be used in ancient Britain and elsewhere throughout Europe apparently from the earliest times.[191]

On this or another occasion Etana desired to ascend to highest heaven. He asked the Eagle to assist him, and the bird assented, saying: "Be glad, my friend. Let me bear thee to the highest heaven. Lay thy breast on mine and thine arms on my wings, and let my body be as thy body." Etana did as the great bird requested him, and together they ascended towards the firmament. After a flight which extended over two hours, the Eagle asked Etana to gaze downwards. He did so, and beheld the ocean surrounding the earth, and the earth seemed like a mountainous island. The Eagle resumed its flight, and when another two hours had elapsed, it again asked Etana to look downwards. Then the hero saw that the sea resembled a girdle which clasped the land. Two hours later Etana found that he had been raised to a height from which the sea appeared to be no larger than a pond. By this time he had reached the heaven of Anu, Bel, and Ea, and found there rest and shelter.

Here the text becomes fragmentary. Further on it is gathered from the narrative that Etana is being carried still higher by the Eagle towards the heaven of Ishtar, "Queen of Heaven", the supreme mother goddess. Three times, at intervals of two hours, the Eagle asks Etana to look downwards towards the shrinking earth. Then some disaster happens, for further onwards the broken tablet narrates that the Eagle is falling. Down and down eagle and man fall together until they strike the earth, and the Eagle's body is shattered.

The Indian Garuda eagle[192] never met with such a fate, but on one occasion Vishnu overpowered it with his right arm, which was heavier than the whole universe, and caused many feathers to fall *off*. In the story of Rama's wanderings, however, as told in the *Ramayana* and the *Mahabharata*, there are interesting references in this connection to Garuda's two "sons". One was mortally wounded by Ravana, the demon king of Ceylon. The other bird related to Rama, who found it disabled: "Once upon a time we two (brothers), with the desire of outstripping each other, flew towards the sun. My wings were burnt, but those of my brother were not.... I fell down on the top of this great mountain, where I still am."[193]

Another version of the Etana story survives among the Arabian Moslems. In the "Al Fatihat" chapter of the *Koran* it is related that a Babylonian king held a dispute with Abraham "concerning his Lord". Commentators identify the monarch with Nimrod, who afterwards caused the Hebrew patriarch to be cast into a fire from which he had miraculous deliverance. Nimrod then built a tower so as to ascend to heaven "to see Abraham's god", and make war against Him, but the tower was overthrown. He, however, persisted in his design. The narrative states that he was "carried to heaven in a chest borne by four monstrous birds; but after wandering for some time through the air, he fell down on a mountain with such a force that he made it shake". A reference in the *Koran* to "contrivances ... which make mountains tremble" is believed to allude to Nimrod's vain attempt.[194]

Alexander the Great was also reputed to have ascended on the back of an eagle. Among the myths attached to his memory in the Ethiopic "history" is one which explains how "he knew and comprehended the length and breadth of the earth", and how he obtained knowledge regarding the seas and mountains he would have to cross. "He made himself small and flew through the air on an eagle, and he arrived in the heights of the heavens and he explored them." Another Alexandrian version of the Etana myth resembles the Arabic legend of Nimrod. "In the Country of Darkness" Alexander fed and tamed great birds which were larger than eagles. Then he ordered four of his soldiers to mount them. The men were carried to the "Country of the Living", and when they returned they told Alexander "all that had happened and all that they had seen".[195]

In a Gaelic story a hero is carried off by a Cromhineach, "a vast bird like an eagle". He tells that it "sprang to the clouds with me, and I was a while that I did not know which was heaven or earth for me". The hero died, but, curiously enough, remained conscious of what was happening. Apparently exhausted, the eagle flew to an island in the midst of the ocean. It laid the hero on the sunny side. The hero proceeds: "Sleep came upon herself (the eagle) and she slept. The sun was enlivening me pretty well though I was dead." Afterwards the eagle bathed in a healing well, and as it splashed in the water, drops fell on the hero and he came to life. "I grew stronger and more active", he adds, "than I had ever been before."[196]

The eagle figures in various mythologies, and appears to have been at one time worshipped as the god or goddess of fertility, and storm and lightning, as the bringer of children, and the deity who carried souls to Hades. It was also the symbol of royalty, because the earthly ruler represented the controlling deity. Nin-Girsu, the god of Lagash, who was identified with Tammuz, was depicted as a lion-headed eagle. Zeus, the Greek sky and air god, was attended by an eagle, and may, at one time, have been simply an eagle. In Egypt the place of the eagle is taken by Nekhebit, the vulture goddess whom the Greeks identified with "Eileithyia, the goddess of birth; she was usually represented as a vulture hovering over the king".[197]

The double-headed eagle of the Hittites, which figures in the royal arms of Germany and Russia, appears to have symbolized the deity of whom the king was an incarnation or son. In Indian mythology Garuda, the eagle giant, which destroyed serpents like the Babylonian Etana eagle, issued from its egg like a flame of fire; its eyes flashed the lightning and its voice was the thunder. This bird is identified in a hymn with Agni, god of fire, who has the attributes of Tammuz and Mithra, with Brahma, the creator, with Indra, god of thunder and fertility, and with Yama, god of the dead, who carries off souls to Hades. It is also called "the steed-necked incarnation of Vishnu", the "Preserver" of the Hindu trinity who rode on its back. The hymn referred to lauds Garuda as "the bird of life, the presiding spirit of the animate and inanimate universe ... destroyer of all, creator of all". It burns all "as the sun in his anger burneth all creatures".[198]

Birds were not only fates, from whose movements in flight omens were drawn, but also spirits of fertility. When the childless Indian sage Mandapala of the *Mahabharata*was refused admittance to heaven until a son was born to him, he "pondered deeply" and "came to know that of all creatures birds alone were blest with fecundity"; so he became a bird.

It is of interest, therefore, to find the Etana eagle figuring as a symbol of royalty at Rome. The deified Roman Emperor's waxen image was burned on a pyre after his death, and an eagle was let loose from the great pile to carry his soul to heaven.[199] This custom was probably

69

a relic of seasonal fire worship, which may have been introduced into Northern and Western Syria and Asia Minor by the mysterious Mitanni rulers, if it was not an archaic Babylonian custom[200] associated with fire-and-water magical ceremonies, represented in the British Isles by May-Day and Midsummer fire-and-water festivals. Sandan, the mythical founder of Tarsus, was honouredeach year at that city by burning a great bonfire, and he was identified with Hercules. Probably he was a form of Moloch and Melkarth.[201] Doves were burned to Adonis. The burning of straw figures, representing gods of fertility, on May-Day bonfires may have been a fertility rite, and perhaps explains the use of straw birth-girdles.

According to the commentators of the *Koran*, Nimrod, the Babylonian king, who cast victims in his annual bonfires at Cuthah, died on the eighth day of the Tammuz month, which, according to the Syrian calendar, fell on 13th July.[202] It is related that gnats entered Nimrod's brain, causing the membrane to grow larger. He suffered great pain, and to relieve it had his head beaten with a mallet. Although he lived for several hundred years, like other agricultural patriarchs, including the Tammuz of Berosus, it is possible that he was ultimately sacrificed and burned. The beating of Nimrod recalls the beating of the corn spirit of the agricultural legend utilized by Burns in his ballad of "John Barleycorn", which gives a jocular account of widespread ancient customs that are not yet quite extinct even in Scotland:[203]

They laid him down upon his back
  And cudgelled him full sore;
They hung him up before a storm
  And turned him o'er and o'er.

They filled up a darksome pit
  With water to the brim,
They heaved in John Barleycorn--
  There let him sink or swim.

They wasted o'er a scorching flame
  The marrow of his bones,
But the miller used him worst of all,
  For he crushed him between two stones.

Hercules, after performing many mythical exploits, had himself burned alive on the pyre which he built upon Mount Oeta, and was borne to Olympus amidst peals of thunder.

Gilgamesh, the Babylonian Hercules, who links with Etana, Nimrod, and Sandan, is associated with the eagle, which in India, as has been shown, was identified with the gods of fertility, fire, and death. According to a legend related by Aelian,[204] "the guards of the citadel of Babylon threw down to the ground a child who had been conceived and brought forth in secret, and who afterwards became known as Gilgamos". This appears to be another version of the Sargon-Tammuz myth, and may also refer to the sacrifice of children to Melkarth and Moloch, who were burned or slain "in the valleys under the clefts of the rocks"[205] to ensure fertility and feed the corn god. Gilgamesh, however, did not perish. "A keen-eyed eagle saw the child falling, and before it touched the ground the bird flew under it and received it on its back, and carried it away to a garden and laid it down gently." Here we have, it would appear, Tammuz among the flowers, and Sargon, the gardener, in the "Garden of Adonis". Mimic Adonis gardens were cultivated by women. Corn, &c., was forced in pots and baskets, and thrown, with an image of the god, into streams. "Ignorant people", writes Professor Frazer, "suppose that by mimicking the effect which they desire to produce they actually help to produce it: thus by sprinkling water they make rain, by lighting a fire they make sunshine, and so on."[206] Evidently Gilgamesh was a heroic form of the god Tammuz, the slayer of the demons of winter and storm, who passed one part of the year in the world and another in Hades (Chapter VI).

Like Hercules, Gilgamesh figured chiefly in legendary narrative as a mighty hero. He was apparently of great antiquity, so that it is impossible to identify him with any forerunner of Sargon of Akkad, or Alexander the Great. His exploits were depicted on cylinder seals of the Sumerian period, and he is shown wrestling with a lion as Hercules wrestled with the monstrous lion in the valley of Nemea. The story of his adventures was narrated on twelve clay tablets, which were preserved in the library of Ashur-banipal, the Assyrian emperor. In the first tablet, which is badly mutilated, Gilgamesh is referred to as the man who beheld the world, and had great wisdom because he peered into the mysteries. He travelled to distant places, and was informed regarding the flood and the primitive race which the gods destroyed; he also obtained the plant of life, which his enemy, the earth-lion, in the form of a serpent or well demon, afterwards carried away.

70

Gilgamesh was associated with Erech, where he reigned as "the lord". There Ishtar had a great temple, but her worldly wealth had decreased. The fortifications of the city were crumbling, and for three years the Elamites besieged it. The gods had turned to flies and the winged bulls had become like mice. Men wailed like wild beasts and maidens moaned like doves. Ultimately the people prayed to the goddess Aruru to create a liberator. Bel, Shamash, and Ishtar also came to their aid.

Aruru heard the cries of her worshippers. She dipped her hands in water and then formed a warrior with clay. He was named Ea-bani, which signifies "Ea is my creator". It is possible, therefore, that an ancient myth of Eridu forms the basis of the narrative.

Ea-bani is depicted on the cylinder seals as a hairy man-monster resembling the god Pan. He ate grass with the gazelles and drank water with wild beasts, and he is compared to the corn god, which suggests that he was an early form of Tammuz, and of character somewhat resembling the Egyptian Bast, the half-bestial god of fertility. A hunter was sent out from Erech to search for the man-monster, and found him beside a stream in a savage place drinking with his associates, the wild animals. The description of Ea-bani recalls that of Nebuchadnezzar when he was stricken with madness. "He was driven from men, and did eat grass as oxen, and his body was wet with the dew of heaven, till his hairs were grown like eagles' feathers, and his nails like birds' claws."[207]

The hunter had no desire to combat with Ea-bani, so he had him lured from the wilds by a beautiful woman. Love broke the spell which kept Ea-bani in his savage state, and the wild beasts fled from him. Then the temptress pleaded with him to go with her to Erech, where Anu and Ishtar had their temples, and the mighty Gilgamesh lived in his palace. Ea-bani, deserted by his bestial companions, felt lonely and desired human friendship. So he consented to accompany his bride. Having heard of Gilgamesh from the hunter, he proposed to test his strength in single combat, but Shamash, god of the sun, warned Ea-bani that he was the protector of Gilgamesh, who had been endowed with great knowledge by Bel and Anu and Ea. Gilgamesh was also counselled in a vision of night to receive Ea-bani as an ally.

Ea-bani was not attracted by city life and desired to return to the wilds, but Shamash prevailed upon him to remain as the friend of Gilgamesh, promising that he would be greatly honoured and exalted to high rank.

The two heroes became close friends, and when the narrative becomes clear again, they are found to be setting forth to wage war against Chumbaba,[208] the King of Elam. Their journey was long and perilous. In time they entered a thick forest, and wondered greatly at the numerous and lofty cedars. They saw the great road which the king had caused to be made, the high mountain, and the temple of the god. Beautiful were the trees about the mountain, and there were many shady retreats that were fragrant and alluring.

At this point the narrative breaks off, for the tablet is mutilated. When it is resumed a reference is made to "the head of Chumbaba", who has apparently been slain by the heroes. Erech was thus freed from the oppression of its fierce enemy.

Gilgamesh and Ea-bani appear to have become prosperous and happy. But in the hour of triumph a shadow falls. Gilgamesh is robed in royal splendour and wears his dazzling crown. He is admired by all men, but suddenly it becomes known that the goddess Ishtar has been stricken with love for him. She "loved him with that love which was his doom". Those who are loved by celestials or demons become, in folk tales, melancholy wanderers and "night wailers". The "wretched wight" in Keats' "La Belle Dame Sans Merci" is a typical example.

> O what can ail thee, knight-at-arms,
> Alone and palely loitering?
> The sedge is withered from the lake
> And no birds sing.

*   *   *   *   *

> I met a lady in the meads,
> Full beautiful--a faery's child;
> Her hair was long, her foot was light,
> And her eyes were wild.

*   *   *   *   *

> She found me roots of relish sweet,
> And honey wild and manna dew;
> And sure in language strange she said,

71

"I love thee true".

Having kissed her lover to sleep, the fairy woman vanished. The "knight" then saw in a dream the ghosts of knights and warriors, her previous victims, who warned him of his fate.

I saw their starved lips in the gloam,
With horrid warning gaped wide;
And I awoke and found me here
On the cold hill's side.

The goddess Ishtar appeared as "La Belle Dame Sans Merci" before Gilgamesh and addressed him tenderly, saying: "Come, O Gilgamesh, and be my consort. Gift thy strength unto me. Be thou my husband and I will be thy bride. Thou shalt have a chariot of gold and lapis lazuli with golden wheels and gem-adorned. Thy steeds shall be fair and white and powerful. Into my dwelling thou shalt come amidst the fragrant cedars. Every king and every prince will bow down before thee, O Gilgamesh, to kiss thy feet, and all people will become subject unto thee."

Gilgamesh feared the fate which would attend him as the lover of Ishtar, and made answer saying: "To what husband hast thou ever remained faithful? Each year Tammuz, the lover of thy youth, is caused by thee to weep. Thou didst love the Allala bird and then broke his wings, and he moans in the woods crying, 'O my wings!' Thou didst love the lion and then snared him. Thou didst love the horse, and then laid harness on him and made him gallop half a hundred miles so that he suffered great distress, and thou didst oppress his mother Silili. Thou didst love a shepherd who sacrificed kids unto thee, and then thou didst smite him so that he became a jackal (or leopard); his own herd boy drove him away and his dogs rent him in pieces. Thou didst love Ishullanu, the gardener of Anu, who made offerings unto thee, and then smote him so that he was unable to move. Alas! if thou wouldst love me, my fate would be like unto the fates of those on whom thou hast laid affliction."

Ishtar's heart was filled with wrath when she heard the words which Gilgamesh had spoken, and she prevailed upon her father Anu to create a fierce bull which she sent against the lord of Erech.

This monster, however, was slain by Gilgamesh[209] and Ea-bani, but their triumph was shortlived. Ishtar cursed Gilgamesh. Ea-bani then defied her and threatened to deal with her as he had dealt with the bull, with the result that he was cursed by the goddess also.

Gilgamesh dedicated the horns of the bull to Shamash and returned with his friend to Erech, where they were received with great rejoicings. A festival was held, and afterwards the heroes lay down to sleep. Then Ea-bani dreamt a dream of ill omen. He met his death soon afterwards, apparently in a battle, and Gilgamesh lamented over him. From the surviving fragments of the narrative it would appear that Gilgamesh resolved to undertake a journey, for he had been stricken by disease. He wept and cried out, "Oh! let me not die like Ea-bani, for death is fearful. I will seek the aid of mine ancestor, Pir-napishtim"--the Babylonian Noah, who was believed to be dwelling on an island which corresponds to the Greek "Island of the Blessed". The Babylonian island lay in the ocean of the Nether World.

It seems that Gilgamesh not only hoped to obtain the Water of Life and the Plant of Life to cure his own disease, but also to restore to life his dead friend, Ea-bani, whom he loved.

Gilgamesh set out on his journey and in time reached a mountain chasm. Gazing on the rugged heights, he beheld fierce lions and his heart trembled. Then he cried upon the moon god, who took pity upon him, and under divine protection the hero pressed onward. He crossed the rocky range and then found himself confronted by the tremendous mountain of Mashi--"Sunset hill", which divided the land of the living from the western land of the dead. The mountain peak rose to heaven, and its foundations were in Aralu, the Underworld.[210] A dark tunnel pierced it and could be entered through a door, but the door was shut and on either side were two monsters of horrible aspect--the gigantic "scorpion man" and his wife, whose heads reached to the clouds. When Gilgamesh beheld them he swooned with terror. But they did him no harm, perceiving that he was a son of a god and had a body like a god.

When Gilgamesh revived, he realized that the monsters regarded him with eyes of sympathy. Addressing the scorpion giant, he told that he desired to visit his ancestor, Pir-napishtim, who sat in the council of the gods and had divine attributes. The giant warned him of the dangers which he would encounter, saying that the mountain passage was twelve miles long and beamless and black. Gilgamesh, however, resolved to encounter any peril, for he was no longer afraid, and he was allowed to go forward. So he entered through the monster-guarded mountain door and plunged into thick unbroken darkness. For twice twelve hours he groped blindly onward, until he saw a ray of light. Quickening his steps, he then escaped from the dreadful tunnel and once more rejoiced in the rays of the sun. He found himself in an enchanted garden, and in the midst of it he saw a divine and beautiful tree towards which he hastened. On

72

its gleaming branches hung clusters of precious stones and its leaves were of lapis lazuli. His eyes were dazzled, but he did not linger there. Passing many other wonderful trees, he came to a shoreland, and he knew that he was drawing nigh to the Sea of Death. The country which he entered was ruled over by the sea lady whose name was Sabitu. When she saw the pilgrim drawing nigh, she entered her palace and shut the door.

Gilgamesh called out requesting that he should be allowed to enter, and mingled his entreaties with threats to break open the door. In the end Sabitu appeared and spoke, saying:

Gilgamesh, whither hurriest thou?
The life that thou seekest thou wilt not find.
When the gods created man
They fixed death for mankind.
Life they took in their own hand.
Thou, O Gilgamesh, let thy belly be filled!
Day and night be merry,
Daily celebrate a feast,
Day and night dance and make merry!
Clean be thy clothes,
Thy head be washed, bathe in water!
Look joyfully on the child that grasps thy hand,
Be happy with the wife in thine arms![211]

This is the philosophy of the Egyptian "Lay of the Harper". The following quotations are from two separate versions:--

How rests this just prince!
The goodly destiny befalls,
The bodies pass away
Since the time of the god,
And generations come into their places.

*   *   *   *   *

(Make) it pleasant for thee to follow thy desire
While thou livest.
Put myrrh upon thy head,
And garments on thee of fine linen....
Celebrate the glad day,
Be not weary therein....
Thy sister (wife) who dwells in thy heart.
She sits at thy side.
Put song and music before thee,
Behind thee all evil things,
And remember thou (only) joy.[212]

Jastrow contrasts the Babylonian poem with the following quotation from Ecclesiastes:--

Go thy way, eat thy bread with joy, and drink thy wine with
a merry heart.... Let thy garments be always white; and
let thy head lack no ointment. Live joyfully with the wife whom
thou lovest all the days of the life of thy vanity, which he [God]
hath given thee under the sun, all the days of thy vanity: for that
is thy portion in this life, and in thy labour which thou takest
under the sun.[213]

"The pious Hebrew mind", Jastrow adds, "found the corrective to this view of life in the conception of a stern but just God, acting according to self-imposed standards of right and wrong, whose rule extends beyond the grave." The final words of the Preacher are, "Fear God and keep his commandments".[214]

Gilgamesh did not accept the counsel of the fatalistic sea lady. He asked her how he could reach Pir-napishtim, his ancestor, saying he was prepared to cross the Sea of Death: if he could not cross it he would die of grief.

Sabitu answered him, saying: "O Gilgamesh, no mortal is ferried over this great sea. Who can pass over it save Shamash alone? The way is full of peril. O Gilgamesh, how canst thou battle against the billows of death?"

At length, however, the sea lady revealed to the pilgrim that he might obtain the aid of the sailor, Arad Ea, who served his ancestor Pir-napishtim.

73

Gilgamesh soon found where Arad Ea dwelt, and after a time prevailed upon him to act as ferryman. Arad Ea required a helm for his boat, and Gilgamesh hastened to fashion one from a tree. When it was fixed on, the boat was launched and the voyage began. Terrible experiences were passed through as they crossed the Sea of Death, but at length they drew nigh to the "Island of the Blessed" on which dwelt Pir-napishtim and his wife. Wearied by his exertions and wasted by disease, Gilgamesh sat resting in the boat. He did not go ashore.

Pir-napishtim had perceived the vessel crossing the Sea of Death and marvelled greatly.

The story is unfortunately interrupted again, but it appears that Gilgamesh poured into the ears of his ancestor the tale of his sufferings, adding that he feared death and desired to escape his fate.

Pir-napishtim made answer, reminding the pilgrim that all men must die. Men built houses, sealed contracts, disputed one with another, and sowed seeds in the earth, but as long as they did so and the rivers rose in flood, so long would their fate endure. Nor could any man tell when his hour would come. The god of destiny measured out the span of life: he fixed the day of death, but never revealed his secrets.

Gilgamesh then asked Pir-napishtim how it chanced that he was still alive. "Thou hast suffered no change," he said, "thou art even as I am. Harden not thy heart against me, but reveal how thou hast obtained divine life in the company of the gods."

Pir-napishtim thereupon related to his descendant the story of the deluge, which is dealt with fully in the next chapter. The gods had resolved to destroy the world, and Ea in a dream revealed unto Pir-napishtim how he could escape. He built a ship which was tossed about on the waters, and when the world had been destroyed, Bel discovered him and transported him to that island in the midst of the Sea of Death.

Gilgamesh sat in the boat listening to the words of his ancestor. When the narrative was ended, Pir-napishtim spoke sympathetically and said: "Who among the gods will restore thee to health, O Gilgamesh? Thou hast knowledge of my life, and thou shalt be given the life thou dost strive after. Take heed, therefore, to what I say unto thee. For six days and seven nights shalt thou not lie down, but remain sitting like one in the midst of grief."[215]

Gilgamesh sat in the ship, and sleep enveloped him like to a black storm cloud.

Pir-napishtim spoke to his wife and said: "Behold the hero who desireth to have life. Sleep envelops him like to a black storm cloud."

To that lone man his wife made answer: "Lay thine hand upon him so that he may have perfect health and be enabled to return to his own land. Give him power to pass through the mighty door by which he entered."

Then Pir-napishtim addressed his wife, saying: "His sufferings make me sad. Prepare thou for him the magic food, and place it near his head."

On the day when Gilgamesh lay down, the food was prepared by seven magic processes, and the woman administered it while yet he slept. Then Pir-napishtim touched him, and he awoke full of life.

Gilgamesh spake unto Pir-napishtim and said: "I was suddenly overcome by sleep.... But thou didst awaken me by touching me, even thou.... Lo! I am bewitched. What hast thou done unto thy servant?"

Then Pir-napishtim told Gilgamesh that he had been given to eat of the magic food. Afterwards he caused Arad Ea to carry Gilgamesh to a fountain of healing, where his disease-stricken body was cleansed. The blemished skin fell from him, and he was made whole.

Thereafter Gilgamesh prepared to return to his own land. Ere he bade farewell, however, Pir-napishtim revealed unto him the secret of a magic plant which had power to renew life and give youth and strength unto those who were old.

Arad Ea conducted the hero to the island where the plant grew, and when Gilgamesh found it he rejoiced, and said that he would carry it to Erech, his own city, where he would partake of it and restore his youth.

So Gilgamesh and Arad Ea went on their way together, nor paused until they came to a well of pure water. The hero stooped down to draw water.[216] But while he was thus engaged that demon, the Earth Lion, crept forth as a serpent, and, seizing the magic plant of life, carried it away. Stricken with terror, Gilgamesh uttered a curse. Then he sat down and wept bitterly, and the tears streamed over his face. To Arad Ea he spake, saying: "Why has my health been restored to me? Why should I rejoice because that I live? The benefit which I should have derived for myself has now fallen to the Earth Lion."

The two travellers then resumed their journey, performing religious acts from time to time; chanting dirges and holding feasts for the dead, and at length Gilgamesh returned to

Erech. He found that the city walls were crumbling, and he spake regarding the ceremonies which had been performed while yet he was in a far-distant country.

During the days which followed Gilgamesh sorrowed for his lost friend Ea-bani, whose spirit was in the Underworld, the captive of the spirits of death. "Thou canst not draw thy bow now," he cried, "nor raise the battle shout. Thou canst not kiss the woman thou hast loved; thou canst not kiss the child thou hast loved, nor canst thou smite those whom thou hast hated."

In vain Gilgamesh appealed to his mother goddess to restore Ea-bani to him. Then he turned to the gods, and Ea heard him. Thereafter Nergal, god of death, caused the grave to yawn, and the spirit of Ea-bani arose like a wind gust.

Gilgamesh, still dreading death, spoke to the ghost of his friend, saying: "Tell me, my friend, O tell me regarding the land in which thou dost dwell."

Ea-bani made answer sorrowfully: "Alas! I cannot tell thee, my friend. If I were to tell thee all, thou wouldst sit down and weep."

Said Gilgamesh: "Let me sit down and weep, but tell me regarding the land of spirits."

The text is mutilated here, but it can be gathered that Ea-bani described the land where ill-doers were punished, where the young were like the old, where the worm devoured, and dust covered all. But the state of the warrior who had been given burial was better than that of the man who had not been buried, and had no one to lament or care for him. "He who hath been slain in battle," the ghost said, "reposeth on a couch drinking pure water--one slain in battle as thou hast seen and I have seen. His head is supported by his parents: beside him sits his wife. His spirit doth not haunt the earth. But the spirit of that man whose corpse has been left unburied and uncared for, rests not, but prowls through the streets eating scraps of food, the leavings of the feast, and drinking the dregs of vessels."

So ends the story of Gilgamesh in the form which survives to us.

The journey of Gilgamesh to the Island of the Blessed recalls the journeys made by Odin, Hermod, Svipdag, Hotherus and others to the Germanic Hela. When Hermod went to search for Balder, as the Prose Edda relates, he rode through thick darkness for nine days and nine nights ere he crossed the mountains. As Gilgamesh met Sabitu, Hermod met Modgudur, "the maiden who kept the bridge" over the river Gjöll. Svipdag, according to a Norse poem, was guided like the Babylonian hero by the moon god, Gevar, who instructed him what way he should take to find the irresistible sword. Saxo's Hother, who is instructed by "King Gewar", crosses dismal mountains "beset with extraordinary cold".[217] Thorkill crosses a stormy ocean to the region of perpetual darkness, where the ghosts of the dead are confined in loathsome and dusty caves. At the main entrance "the door posts were begrimed with the soot of ages".[218] In the *Elder Edda* Svipdag is charmed against the perils he will be confronted by as he fares "o'er seas mightier than men do know", or is overtaken by night "wandering on the misty way".[219] When Odin "downward rode into Misty Hel" he sang spells at a "witch's grave", and the ghost rose up to answer his questions regarding Balder. "Tell me tidings of Hel", he addressed her, as Gilgamesh addressed the ghost of Ea-bani.

In the mythical histories of Alexander the Great, the hero searches for the Water of Life, and is confronted by a great mountain called Musas (Mashti). A demon stops him and says; "O king, thou art not able to march through this mountain, for in it dwelleth a mighty god who is like unto a monster serpent, and he preventeth everyone who would go unto him." In another part of the narrative Alexander and his army arrive at a place of darkness "where the blackness is not like the darkness of night, but is like unto the mists and clouds which descend at the break of day". A servant uses a shining jewel stone, which Adam had brought from Paradise, to guide him, and found the well. He drank of the "waters of life" and bathed in them, with the result that he was strengthened and felt neither hunger nor thirst. When he came out of the well "all the flesh of his body became bluish-green and his garments likewise bluish-green". Apparently he assumed the colour of supernatural beings. Rama of India was blue, and certain of his monkey allies were green, like the fairies of England and Scotland. This fortunate man kept his secret. His name was Matun, but he was afterwards nicknamed "'El-Khidr', that is to say, 'Green'". What explanation he offered for his sudden change of appearance has not been recorded.[220] It is related that when Matun reached the Well of Life a dried fish which he dipped in the water was restored to life and swam away. In the *Koran* a similar story is told regarding Moses and Joshua, who travelled "for a long space of time" to a place where two seas met. "They forgot their fish which they had taken with them, and the fish took its way freely to the sea." The Arabian commentators explain that Moses once agreed to the suggestion that he was the wisest of men. In a dream he was directed to visit Al Khedr, who was "more knowing than he", and to take a fish with him in a basket. On the seashore Moses fell asleep, and the fish, which had been roasted, leapt out of the basket into the sea. Another version sets forth that

Joshua, "making the ablution at the fountain of life", some of the water happened to be sprinkled on the fish, which immediately leapt up.[221]

The Well of Life is found in Fingalian legends. When Diarmid was mortally wounded by the boar, he called upon Finn to carry water to him from the well:

Give me a draught from thy palms, O Finn,
Son of my king for my succour,
For my life and my dwelling.

Campbell's West Highland Tales, vol. iii, 80.

The quest of the plant, flower, or fruit of life is referred to in many folk tales. In the *Mahabharata*, Bhima, the Indian Gilgamesh or Hercules, journeys to north-eastern Celestial regions to find the lake of the god Kuvera (Kubera), on which grow the "most beautiful and unearthly lotuses", which restore health and give strength to the weary. As Gilgamesh meets with Pir-napishtim, who relates the story of the Deluge which destroyed the "elder race", Bhima meets with Hanuman, who informs him regarding the Ages of the Universe and the races which were periodically destroyed by deluges. When Bhima reaches the lotus lake he fights with demons. To heal his wounds and recover strength he plunges into the lake. "As he drank of the waters, like unto nectar, his energy and strength were again fully restored."[222]

Hercules similarly sets out to search for the golden apples which grow in
  those Hesperian gardens famed of old,
Fortunate fields, and groves and flowery vales.

As Bhima slew Yakshas which guarded the lotuses, Hercules slew Ladon, the guardian of the apples. Other heroes kill treasure-protecting dragons of various kinds.

There is a remarkable resemblance between the Babylonian account of Gilgamesh's journey through the mountain tunnel to the garden and seashore, and the Indian story of the demigod Hanuman passing through the long cavern to the shoreland palace of the female ascetic, when he was engaged searching for Sita, the wife of Rama, who had been carried away by Ravana, the demon king of Ceylon. In the version of the latter narrative which is given in the *Mahabharata*, Hanuman says: "I bring thee good news, O Rama; for Janaka's daughter hath been seen by me. Having searched the southern region with all its hills, forests, and mines for some time, we became very weary. At length we beheld a great cavern. And having beheld it, we entered that cavern which extended over many *yojanas*. It was dark and deep, and overgrown with trees and infested by worms. And having gone a great way through it, we came upon sunshine and beheld a beautiful palace. It was the abode of the Daitya (sea demon) Maya. And there we beheld a female ascetic named Parbhàvati engaged in ascetic austerities. And she gave us food and drink of various kinds. And having refreshed ourselves therewith and regained our strength, we proceeded along the way shown by her. At last we came out of the cavern and beheld the briny sea, and on its shores, the *Sahya*, the *Malaya*, and the great *Dardura* mountains. And ascending the mountains of *Malaya*, we beheld before us the vast ocean (or, "the abode of Varuna"). And beholding it, we felt sorely grieved in mind.... We despaired of returning with our lives.... We then sat together, resolved to die there of starvation."

Hanuman and his friends, having had, so far, experiences similar to those of Gilgamesh, next discovered the eagle giant which had burned its wings when endeavouring to soar to the sun. This great bird, which resembles the Etana eagle, expressed the opinion that Sita was in Lanka (Ceylon), whither she must have been carried by Ravana. But no one dared to cross the dangerous ocean. Hanuman at length, however, obtained the assistance of Vayu, the wind god, his divine father, and leapt over the sea, slaying monsters as he went. He discovered where the fair lady was concealed by the king of demons.[223]

The dark tunnel is met with in many British stories of daring heroes who set out to explore it, but never return. In the Scottish versions the adventurers are invariably pipers who are accompanied by dogs. The sound of the pipes is heard for a time; then the music ceases suddenly, and shortly afterwards the dog returns without a hair upon its body. It has evidently been in conflict with demons.

The tunnel may run from a castle to the seashore, from a cave on one side of a hill to a cave on the other, or from a seashore cave to a distant island.

It is possible that these widespread tunnel stories had origin among the cave dwellers of the Palaeolithic Age, who believed that deep caverns were the doors of the underground retreats of dragons and giants and other supernatural enemies of mankind.

In Babylonia, as elsewhere, the priests utilized the floating material from which all mythologies were framed, and impressed upon it the stamp of their doctrines. The symbolized stories were afterwards distributed far and wide, as were those attached to the memory of Alexander the Great at a later period. Thus in many countries may be found at the present day different versions of immemorial folk tales, which represent various stages of culture, and direct and indirect contact at different periods with civilizations that have stirred the ocean of human thought, and sent their ideas rippling in widening circles to far-distant shores.

[190] It is suggested that Arthur is derived from the Celtic word for "bear". If so, the bear may have been the "totem" of the Arthur tribe represented by the Scottish clan of MacArthurs.

[191] See "Lady in the Straw" beliefs in *Brand's Popular Antiquities*, vol. ii, 66 *et seq.* 1899 ed.).

[192] Like the Etana "mother eagle" Garuda was a slayer of serpents (Chapter III).

[193] *Vana Parva* section of the *Mahábhárata* (Roy's trans.), p. 818 *et seq.*, and *Indian Myth and Legend*, p. 413.

[194] *The Koran* (with notes from approved commentators), trans. by George Sale, P-246, *n.*

[195] *The Life and Exploits of Alexander the Great*, E. Wallis Budge (London, 1896), pp. 277-8, 474-5.

[196] Campbell's *West Highland Tales*, vol. iii, pp. 251-4 (1892 ed.).

[197] *Religion of the Ancient Egyptians*, A. Wiedemann, p. 141.

[198] *Adi Parva* section of the *Mahábhárata* (Hymn to Garuda), Roy's trans., p. 88, 89.

[199] Herodian, iv, 2.

[200] The image made by Nebuchadnezzar is of interest in this connection. He decreed that "whoso falleth not down and worshippeth" should be burned in the "fiery furnace". The Hebrews, Shadrach, Meshach, and Abed-nego, were accordingly thrown into the fire, but were delivered by God. *Daniel*, iii, 1-30.

[201] The Assyrian and Phoenician Hercules is discussed by Raoul Rochette in *Mémoires de l'Académie des Inscriptions et Belles Lettres* (Paris, 1848), pp. 178 et seq.

[202] G. Sale's *Koran*, p. 246, n.

[203] In the Eddic poem "Lokasenna" the god Byggvir (Barley) is addressed by Loki, "Silence, Barleycorn!" *The Elder Edda*, translation by Olive Bray, pp. 262, 263.

[204] *De Nat. Animal.*, xii, 21, ed. Didot, p. 210, quoted by Professor Budge in *The Life and Exploits of Alexander the Great*, p. 278, n.

[205] *Isaiah*, lvii, 4 and 5.

[206] *The Golden Bough* (*Adonis, Attis, Osiris* vol.), "The Gardens of Adonis", pp. 194 *et seq.* (3rd ed.).

[207] *Daniel*, iv, 33. It is possible that Nebuchadnezzar, as the human representative of the god of corn and fertility, imitated the god by living a time in the wilds like Ea-bani.

[208] Pronounce *ch* guttural.

[209] On a cylinder seal the heroes each wrestle with a bull.

[210] Alexander the Great in the course of his mythical travels reached a mountain at the world-end. "Its peak reached to the first heaven and its base to the seventh earth."--*Budge*.

[211] Jastrow's trans., *Aspects of Religious Belief and Practice in Babylonia and Assyria*, p. 374.

[212] *Development of Religion and Thought in Ancient Egypt* (1912), J.H. Breasted, pp. 183-5.

[213] *Ecclesiastes*, ix, 7-9.

[214] Ibid., xii, 13.

[215] Perhaps brooding and undergoing penance like an Indian Rishi with purpose to obtain spiritual power.

[216] Probably to perform the ceremony of pouring out a libation.

[217] *Saxo*, iii, 71.

[218] Ibid., viii, 291.

[219] *The Elder Edda*, O. Bray, pp. 157 et seq. See also *Teutonic Myth and Legend*.

[220] *The Life and Exploits of Alexander the Great*, E. Wallis Budge, pp. xl et seq., 167 et seq.

[221] *The Koran*, trans, by G. Sale, pp. 222, 223 (chap. xviii).

[222] *Vana Parva* section of the *Mahábhárata* (Roy's trans.), pp. 435-60, and *Indian Myth and Legend*, pp. 105-9.

[223] *Vana Parva* section of the *Mahábhárata* (Roy's translation), pp. 832, 833.

Chapter IX. Deluge Legend, the Island of the Blessed, and Hades

Abstract

Babylonian Story of the Flood--The Two Immortals on the Island of the Blessed--Deluge Legends in the Old and New Worlds--How Babylonian Culture reached India--Theory of Cosmic Periods--Gilgamesh resembles the Indian Yama and Persian Yimeh--Links with Varuna and Mitra--The Great Winter in Persian and Teutonic Mythologies--Babylonian Hades compared with the Egyptian, Greek, Indian, Teutonic, and Celtic Otherworlds--Legend of Nergal and the Queen of Death--Underworld originally the Grave--Why Weapons, &c., were Buried with the Dead--Japanese and Roman Beliefs--Palaeolithic Burial Customs--"Our Graves are our Houses"--Importance of Babylonian Funerary Ceremonies--Doctrine of Eternal Bliss in Egypt and India--Why Suppressed in Babylonia--Heavy Burial Fees--Various Burial Customs.

The story of the Deluge which was related to Gilgamesh by Pir-napishtim runs as follows:--

"Hear me, O Gilgamesh, and I will make revelation regarding the hidden doings of the high gods. As thou knowest, the city of Shurippak is situated upon the bank of the Euphrates. The gods were within it: there they assembled together in council. Anu, the father, was there, and Bel the counsellor and warrior, Ninip the messenger, and Ennugi the governor. Ea, the wise lord, sat also with them. In their hearts the gods agreed together to send a great deluge.

"Thereafter Ea made known the purpose of the divine rulers in the hut of reeds, saying:[224] 'O hut of reeds, hear; O wall, understand ... O man of Shurippak, son of Umbara Tutu, tear down thy house and build a ship; leave all thou dost possess and save thy life, and preserve in the ship the living seed of every kind. The ship that thou wilt build must be of goodly proportions in length and height. It must be floated on the great deep.'

"I heard the command of Ea and understood, and I made answer, saying, 'O wise lord, as thou hast said so will I do, for thy counsel is most excellent. But how shall I give reason for my doings to the young men and the elders?'

"Ea opened his mouth and said unto me, his servant: 'What thou shalt say unto them is this.... *It hath been revealed unto me that Bel doth hate me, therefore I cannot remain any longer in his domain, this city of Shurippak, so I must depart unto the domain of Ea and dwell with him.... Unto you will Bel send abundance of rain, so that you may obtain birds and fishes in plenty and have a rich harvest. But Shamash hath appointed a time for Ramman to pour down destruction from the heavens.*'[225]

Ea then gave instructions to Pir-napishtim how to build the ship in which he should find refuge. So far as can be gathered from the fragmentary text, it appears that this vessel was to have a deck house six stories high, with nine apartments in each story. According to another account, Ea drew a plan of the great ship upon the sand.

Pir-napishtim set to work and made a flat-bottomed vessel, which was 120 cubits wide and 120 cubits in height. He smeared it with bitumen inside and pitch outside; and on the seventh day it was ready. Then he carried out Ea's further instructions. Continuing his narrative to Gilgamesh, he said:

"I gathered together all that I possessed, my silver and gold and seeds of every kind, and my goods also. These I placed in the ship. Then I caused to go aboard all my family and house servants, the animals of the field and the beasts of the field and the workers--every one of them I sent up.

"The god Shamash appointed the time, saying: 'I will cause the Night Lord to send much rain and bring destruction. Then enter thou the ship and shut thy door.'

"At the appointed time the Night Lord sent at even-time much rain. I saw the beginning of the deluge and I was afraid to look up. I entered the ship and shut the door. I appointed Buzur-Kurgala, the sailor, to be captain, and put under his command the great vessel and all that it contained.

"At the dawn of day I saw rising athwart the heavens a dark cloud, and in the midst of it Ramman thundered. Nebo and Merodach went in front, speeding like emissaries over hills and plains. The cables of the ship were let loose.

"Then Ninip, the tempest god, came nigh, and the storm broke in fury before him. All the earth spirits leapt up with flaming torches and the whole land was aflare. The thunder god swept over the heavens, blotting out the sunlight and bringing thick darkness. Rain poured down the whole day long, and the earth was covered with water; the rivers were swollen; the land was in confusion; men stumbled about in the darkness, battling with the elements. Brothers were unable to see brothers; no man could recognize his friends.... The spirits above looked down and beheld the rising flood and were afraid: they fled away, and in the heaven of Anu they crouched like to hounds in the protecting enclosures.

"In time Ishtar, the lady of the gods, cried out distressfully, saying: 'The elder race hath perished and turned to clay because that I have consented to evil counsel in the assembly of the gods. Alas! I have allowed my people to be destroyed. I gave being to man, but where is he? Like the offspring of fish he cumbers the deep.'

"The earth spirits were weeping with Ishtar: they sat down cowering with tightened lips and spake not; they mourned in silence.

"Six days and six nights went past, and the tempest raged over the waters which gradually covered the land. But when the seventh day came, the wind fell, the whirling waters grew peaceful, and the sea retreated. The storm was over and the rain of destruction had ceased. I looked forth. I called aloud over the waters. But all mankind had perished and turned to clay. Where fields had been I saw marshes only.

"Then I opened wide the window of the ship, and the sunlight suffused my countenance. I was dazzled and sank down weeping and the tears streamed over my face. Everywhere I looked I saw water.

"At length, land began to appear. The ship drifted towards the country of Nitsir, and then it was held fast by the mountain of Nitsir. Six days went past and the ship remained stedfast. On the seventh day I sent forth a dove, and she flew away and searched this way and that, but found no resting place, so she returned. I then sent forth a swallow, and she returned likewise. Next I sent forth a raven, and she flew away. She saw that the waters were shrinking, and gorged and croaked and waded, but did not come back. Then I brought forth all the animals into the air of heaven.

"An offering I made on the mountain. I poured out a libation. I set up incense vessels seven by seven on heaped-up reeds and used cedar wood with incense. The gods smelt the sweet savour, and they clustered like flies about the sacrificer.

"Thereafter Ishtar (Sirtu) drew nigh. Lifting up the jewels, which the god Anu had fashioned for her according to her desire, she spake, saying: 'Oh! these gods! I vow by the lapis lazuli gems upon my neck that I will never forget! I will remember these days for ever and ever. Let all the gods come hither to the offering, save Bel (Enlil) alone, because that he ignored my counsel, and sent a great deluge which destroyed my people.'

"But Bel Enlil came also, and when he beheld the ship he paused. His heart was filled with wrath against the gods and the spirits of heaven. Angrily he spake and said: 'Hath one escaped? It was decreed that no human being should survive the deluge.'

"Ninip, son of Bel, spoke, saying: 'Who hath done this save Ea alone? He knoweth all things.'

"Ea, god of the deep, opened his mouth and said unto the warrior Bel: 'Thou art the lord of the gods, O warrior. But thou wouldst not hearken to my counsel and caused the deluge to be. Now punish the sinner for his sins and the evil doer for his evil deed, but be merciful and do not destroy all mankind. May there never again be a flood. Let the lion come and men will decrease. May there never again be a flood. Let the leopard come and men will decrease. May there never again be a flood. Let famine come upon the land; let Ura, god of pestilence, come and snatch off mankind.... I did not reveal the secret purpose of the mighty gods, but I caused Atra-chasis (Pir-napishtim) to dream a dream in which he had knowledge of what the gods had decreed.'

"Having pondered a time over these words, Bel entered the ship alone. He grasped my hand and led me forth, even me, and he led forth my wife also, and caused her to kneel down beside me. Then he stood between us and gave his blessing. He spoke, saying: 'In time past Pir-napishtim was a man. Henceforth Pir-napishtim and his wife will be like unto deities, even us. Let them dwell apart beyond the river mouths.'

"Thereafter Bel carried me hither beyond the mouths of rivers."

Flood myths are found in many mythologies both in the Old World and the New.

The violent and deceitful men of the mythical Bronze Age of Greece were destroyed by a flood. It is related that Zeus said on one occasion to Hermes: "I will send a great rain, such as hath not been since the making of the world, and the whole race of men shall perish. I am weary of their iniquity."

For receiving with hospitable warmth these two gods in human guise, Deucalion, an old man, and his wife Pyrrha were spared, however. Zeus instructed his host to build an ark of oak, and store it well with food. When this was done, the couple entered the vessel and shut the door. Then Zeus "broke up all the fountains of the deep, and opened the well springs of heaven, and it rained for forty days and forty nights continually". The Bronze folk perished: not even those who fled to the hilltops could escape. The ark rested on Parnassus, and when the waters ebbed the old couple descended the mountain and took up their abode in a cave.[226]

79

In Indian mythology the world is destroyed by a flood at the end of each Age of the Universe. There are four ages: the Krita or Perfect Age, the Treta Age, the Dwapara Age, and the Kali or Wicked Age. These correspond closely to the Greek and Celtic ages.[227] There are also references in Sanskrit literature to the destruction of the world because too many human beings lived upon it. "When the increase of population had been so frightful," a sage related, "the Earth, oppressed with the excessive burden, sank down for a hundred Yojanas. Suffering pain in all her limbs, and being deprived of her senses by excessive pressure, the Earth in distress sought the protection of Narayana, the foremost of the gods."[228]

Manu's account of the flood has been already referred to (Chapter II). The god in fish shape informed him: "The time is ripe for purging the world.... Build a strong and massive ark, and furnish it with a long rope...." When the waters rose the horned fish towed the ark over the roaring sea, until it grounded on the highest peak of the Himavat, which is still called Naubandha (the harbour). Manu was accompanied by seven rishis.[229]

In the Celtic (Irish) account of the flood, Cessair, granddaughter of Noah, was refused a chamber for herself in the ark, and fled to the western borders of the world as advised by her idol.[230] Her fleet consisted of three ships, but two foundered before Ireland was reached. The survivors in addition to Cessair were, her father Bith, two other men, Fintan and Ladru, and fifty women. All of these perished on the hills except Fintan, who slept on the crest of a great billow, and lived to see Partholon, the giant, arriving from Greece.

There is a deluge also in Egyptian mythology. When Ra, the sun god, grew old as an earthly king, men began to mutter words against him. He called the gods together and said: "I will not slay them (his subjects) until I have heard what ye say concerning them." Nu, his father, who was the god of primeval waters, advised the wholesale destruction of mankind.

Said Ra: "Behold men flee unto the hills; their heart is full of fear because of that which they said."

The goddess Hathor-Sekhet, the Eye of Ra, then went forth and slew mankind on the hills. Thereafter Ra, desiring to protect the remnant of humanity, caused a great offering to be made to the goddess, consisting of corn beer mixed with herbs and human blood. This drink was poured out during the night. "And the goddess came in the morning; she found the fields inundated, she rejoiced thereat, she drank thereof, her heart was rejoiced, she went about drunken and took no more cognizance of men."[231]

It is obvious that the Egyptian myth refers to the annual inundation of the Nile, the "human blood" in the "beer" being the blood of the slain corn god, or of his earthly representative. It is probable that the flood legends of North and South America similarly reflected local phenomena, although the possibility that they were of Asiatic origin, like the American Mongoloid tribes, cannot be overlooked. Whether or not Mexican civilization, which was flourishing about the time of the battle of Hastings, received any cultural stimulus from Asia is a question regarding which it would be unsafe to dogmatize, owing to the meagre character of the available data.

The Mexican deluge was caused by the "water sun", which suddenly discharged the moisture it had been drawing from the earth in the form of vapour through long ages. All life was destroyed.

A flood legend among the Nahua tribes resembles closely the Babylonian story as told by Pir-napishtim. The god Titlacahuan instructed a man named Nata to make a boat by hollowing out a cypress tree, so as to escape the coming deluge with his wife Nena. This pair escaped destruction. They offered up a fish sacrifice in the boat and enraged the deity who visited them, displaying as much indignation as did Bel when he discovered that Pir-napishtim had survived the great disaster. Nata and Nena had been instructed to take with them one ear of maize only, which suggests that they were harvest spirits.

In Brazil, Monan, the chief god, sent a great fire to burn up the world and its wicked inhabitants. To extinguish the flames a magician caused so much rain to fall that the earth was flooded.

The Californian Indians had a flood legend, and believed that the early race was diminutive; and the Athapascan Indians of the north-west professed to be descendants of a family who escaped the deluge. Indeed, deluge myths were widespread in the "New World".

The American belief that the first beings who were created were unable to live on earth was shared by the Babylonians. According to Berosus the first creation was a failure, because the animals could not bear the light and they all died.[232] Here we meet with the germs of the Doctrine of the World's Ages, which reached its highest development in Indian, Greek, and Celtic (Irish) mythologies.

The Biblical account of the flood is familiar to readers. "It forms", says Professor Pinches, "a good subject for comparison with the Babylonian account, with which it agrees so closely in all the main points, and from which it differs so much in many essential details."[233]

The drift of Babylonian culture was not only directed westward towards the coast of Palestine, and from thence to Greece during the Phoenician period, but also eastward through Elam to the Iranian plateau and India. Reference has already been made to the resemblances between early Vedic and Sumerian mythologies. When the "new songs" of the Aryan invaders of India were being composed, the sky and ocean god, Varuna, who resembles Ea-Oannes, and Mitra, who links with Shamash, were already declining in splendour. Other cultural influences were at work. Certain of the Aryan tribes, for instance, buried their dead in Varuna's "house of clay", while a growing proportion cremated their dead and worshipped Agni, the fire god. At the close of the Vedic period there were fresh invasions into middle India, and the "late comers" introduced new beliefs, including the doctrines of the Transmigration of Souls and of the Ages of the Universe. Goddesses also rose into prominence, and the Vedic gods became minor deities, and subject to Brahma, Vishnu, and Shiva. These "late comers" had undoubtedly been influenced by Babylonian ideas before they entered India. In their Doctrine of the World's Ages or Yugas, for instance, we are forcibly reminded of the Euphratean ideas regarding space and time. Mr. Robert Brown, junr., who is an authority in this connection, shows that the system by which the "Day of Brahma" was calculated in India resembles closely an astronomical system which obtained in Babylonia, where apparently the theory of cosmic periods had origin.[234]

The various alien peoples, however, who came under the spell of Babylonian modes of thought did not remain in a state of intellectual bondage. Thought was stimulated rather than arrested by religious borrowing, and the development of ideas regarding the mysteries of life and death proceeded apace in areas over which the ritualistic and restraining priesthood of Babylonia exercised no sway. As much may be inferred from the contrasting conceptions of the Patriarchs of Vedic and Sumerian mythologies. Pir-napishtim, the Babylonian Noah, and the semi-divine Gilgamesh appear to be represented in Vedic mythology by Yama, god of the dead. Yama was "the first man", and, like Gilgamesh, he set out on a journey over mountains and across water to discover Paradise. He is lauded in the Vedic hymns as the explorer of "the path" or "way" to the "Land of the Pitris" (Fathers), the Paradise to which the Indian uncremated dead walked on foot. Yama never lost his original character. He is a traveller in the Epics as in the Vedas.[235]

Him who along the mighty heights departed, Him who searched and spied the path for many, Son of Vivasvat, gatherer of the people, Yama, the King, with sacrifices worship. *Rigveda*, x, 14, 1.[236] To Yama, mighty King, be gifts and homage paid, He was the first of men that died, the first to brave Death's rapid rushing stream, the first to point the road To heaven, and welcome others to that bright abode. *Sir M. Monier Williams' Translation.*[237]

Yama and his sister Yami were the first human pair. They are identical with the Persian Celestial twins, Yima and Yimeh. Yima resembles Mitra (Mithra); Varuna, the twin brother of Mitra, in fact, carries the noose associated with the god of death.[238]

The Indian Yama, who was also called Pitripati, "lord of the fathers", takes Mitra's place in the Paradise of Ancestors beside Varuna, god of the sky and the deep. He sits below a tree, playing on a flute and drinking the Soma drink which gives immortality. When the descendants of Yama reached Paradise they assumed shining forms "refined and from all taint set free".[239]

In Persian mythology "Yima", says Professor Moulton, "reigns over a community which may well have been composed of his own descendants, for he lived yet longer than Adam. To render them immortal, he gives them to eat forbidden food, being deceived by the Daevas (demons). What was this forbidden food? May we connect it with another legend whereby, at the Regeneration, Mithra is to make men immortal by giving them to eat the fat of the *Ur-Kuh*, the primeval cow from whose slain body, according to the Aryan legends adopted by Mithraism, mankind was first created?"

Yima is punished for "presumptuously grasping at immortality for himself and mankind, on the suggestion of an evil power, instead of waiting Ahura's good time". Professor Moulton wonders if this story, which he endeavours to reconstruct, "owed anything to Babylon?"

Yima, like the Babylonian Pir-napishtim, is also a revealer of the secrets of creation. He was appointed to be "Guardian, Overseer, Watcher over my Creation" by Ahura, the supreme god. Three hundred years went past--

Then the earth became abounding,
Full of flocks and full of cattle,
Full of men, of birds, dogs likewise,
Full of fires all bright and blazing,

Nor did men, flocks, herds of cattle,
Longer find them places in it.

Jackson's Translation.

The earth was thereafter cloven with a golden arrow. Yima then built a refuge in which mankind and the domesticated animals might find shelter during a terrible winter. "The picture", says Professor Moulton, "strongly tempts us to recognize the influence of the Babylonian Flood-Legend."[240] The "Fimbul winter" of Germanic mythology is also recalled. Odin asks in one of the Icelandic Eddie poems:

What beings shall live when the long dread winter
  Comes o'er the people of earth?[241]

In another Eddie poem, the Voluspa, the Vala tells of a Sword Age, an Axe Age, a Wind Age, and a Wolf Age which is to come "ere the world sinks". After the battle of the gods and demons,

The sun is darkened, earth sinks in the sea.
In time, however, a new world appears.
I see uprising a second time
Earth from the Ocean, green anew;
The waters fall, on high the eagle
Flies o'er the fell and catches fish.

When the surviving gods return, they will talk, according to the Vala (prophetess), of "the great world serpent" (Tiamat). The fields will be sown and "Balder will come"[242]-- apparently as Tammuz came. The association of Balder with corn suggests that, like Nata of the Nahua tribes, he was a harvest spirit, among other things.

Leaving, meantime, the many problems which arise from consideration of the Deluge legends and their connection with primitive agricultural myths, the attention of readers may be directed to the Babylonian conception of the Otherworld.

Pir-napishtim, who escaped destruction at the Flood, resides in an Island Paradise, which resembles the Greek "Islands of the Blessed", and the Irish "Tir nan og" or "Land of the Young", situated in the western ocean, and identical with the British[243]

island-valley of Avilion,
Where falls not hail, or rain, or any snow,
Nor ever wind blows loudly, but it lies
Deep meadow'd, happy, fair with orchard lawns
And bowery hollows crowned with summer sea.[244]

Only two human beings were permitted to reside on the Babylonian island paradise, however. These were Pir-napishtim and his wife. Apparently Gilgamesh could not join them there. His gods did not transport heroes and other favoured individuals to a happy isle or isles like those of the Greeks and Celts and Aryo-Indians. There was no Heaven for the Babylonian dead. All mankind were doomed to enter the gloomy Hades of the Underworld, "the land of darkness and the shadow of death; a land of darkness, as darkness itself; and of the shadow of death, without any order, and where the light is darkness", as Job exclaimed in the hour of despair, lamenting his fate.[245]

This gloomy habitation of the dead resembles the Greek Hades, the Teutonic Nifelhel, and the Indian "Put". No detailed description of it has been found. The references, however, in the "Descent of Ishtar" and the Gilgamesh epic suggest that it resembled the hidden regions of the Egyptians, in which souls were tortured by demons who stabbed them, plunged them in pools of fire, and thrust them into cold outer darkness where they gnashed their teeth, or into places of horror swarming with poisonous reptiles.

Ishtar was similarly tortured by the plague demon, Namtar, when she boldly entered the Babylonian Underworld to search for Tammuz. Other sufferings were, no doubt, in store for her, resembling those, perhaps, with which the giant maid in the Eddic poem "Skirnismal" was threatened when she refused to marry Frey, the god of fertility and harvest:

Trolls shall torment thee from morn till eve
  In the realms of the Jotun race,
Each day to the dwellings of Frost giants must thou
  Creep helpless, creep hopeless of love;
Thou shalt weeping have in the stead of joy,
  And sore burden bear with tears....
May madness and shrieking, bondage and yearning
  Burden thee with bondage and tears.[246]

In like manner, too, the inhabitants of the Indian Hell suffered endless and complicated tortures.[247]

The Persephone of the Babylonian Underworld was Eresh-ki-gal, who was also called Allatu. A myth, which was found among the Egyptian Tel-el-Amarna "Letters", sets forth that on one occasion the Babylonian gods held a feast. All the deities attended it, except Eresh-ki-gal. She was unable to leave her gloomy Underworld, and sent her messenger, the plague demon Namtar, to obtain her share. The various deities honoured Namtar, except Nergal, by standing up to receive him. When Eresh-ki-gal was informed of this slight she became very angry, and demanded that Nergal should be delivered up to her so that he might be put to death. The storm god at once hastened to the Underworld, accompanied by his own group of fierce demons, whom he placed as guardians at the various doors so as to prevent the escape of Eresh-ki-gal. Then he went boldly towards the goddess, clutched her by the hair, and dragged her from her throne. After a brief struggle, she found herself overpowered. Nergal made ready to cut off her head, but she cried for mercy and said: "Do not kill me, my brother! Let me speak to thee."

This appeal indicated that she desired to ransom her life--like the hags in the European folk tales--so Nergal unloosed his hold.

Then Eresh-ki-gal continued: "Be thou my husband and I will be thy wife. On thee I confer sovereignty over the wide earth, giving thee the tablet of wisdom. Thou shalt be my lord and I will be thy lady."

Nergal accepted these terms by kissing the goddess. Affectionately drying her tears, he spoke, saying: "Thou shalt now have from me what thou hast demanded during these past months."

In other words, Nergal promises to honour her as she desired, after becoming her husband and equal.

In the "Descent of Ishtar" the Babylonian Underworld is called Cuthah. This city had a famous cemetery, like Abydos in Egypt, where many pious and orthodox worshippers sought sepulture. The local god was Nergal, who symbolized the destructive power of the sun and the sand storm; he was a gloomy, vengeful deity, attended by the spirits of tempest, weariness, pestilence, and disease, and was propitiated because he was dreaded.

In Nether Cuthah, as Ea-bani informed Gilgamesh, the worm devoured the dead amidst the dust and thick darkness.

It is evident that this Underworld was modelled on the grave. In early times men believed that the spirits of the dead hovered in or about the place of sepulture. They were therefore provided with "houses" to protect them, in the same manner as the living were protected in their houses above the ground.

The enemies of the human ghosts were the earth spirits. Weapons were laid beside the dead in their graves so that they might wage war against demons when necessary. The corpse was also charmed, against attack, by the magical and protecting ornaments which were worn by the living--necklaces, armlets, ear-rings, &c. Even face paint was provided, probably as a charm against the evil eye and other subtle influences.

So long as corpses were left in their graves, the spirits of the dead were, it would appear, believed to be safe. But they required food and refreshment. Food vessels and drinking urns were therefore included in the funerary furniture, and the dead were given food offerings at regular intervals. Once a year the living held feasts in the burial ground, and invited the ghosts to share in the repast. This custom was observed in Babylonia, and is not yet obsolete in Egypt; Moslems and Coptic Christians alike hold annual all-night feasts in their cemeteries.

The Japanese "Land of Yomi" is similarly an underworld, or great grave, where ghosts mingle with the demons of disease and destruction. Souls reach it by "the pass of Yomi". The Mikado, however, may be privileged to ascend to heaven and join the gods in the "Eternal Land".

Among the ancient Romans the primitive belief survived that the spirit of the dead "just sank into the earth where it rested, and returned from time to time to the upper world through certain openings in the ground (mundi), whose solemn uncovering was one of the regular observances of the festal calendar".[248]

According to Babylonian belief, the dead who were not properly buried roamed through the streets searching for food, eating refuse and drinking impure water.

Prior to the period of ceremonial burials, the dead were interred in the houses in which they had lived--a custom which has made it possible for present-day scientists to accumulate much valuable data regarding primitive races and their habits of life. The Palaeolithic cave-dwellers of Europe were buried in their caves. These were then deserted and became the haunts of wild animals. After a long interval a deserted cave was occupied by strangers. In certain characteristic caves the various layers containing human remains represent distinct periods of the vast Pleistocene Age.

When Mediterranean man moved northward through Europe, he utilized some of these caves, and constructed in them well-built graves for his dead, digging down through older layers. In thus making a "house" within a "house", he has provided us with a link between an old custom and a new. Apparently he was influenced by local practices and beliefs, for he met and mingled in certain localities with the men of the Late Palaeolithic Age.

The primitive house-burial rite is referred to in the Ethiopic version of the life of Alexander the Great. The "Two-horned", as the hero was called, conversed with Brahmans when he reached India. He spoke to one of them, "saying: 'Have ye no tombs wherein to bury any man among ye who may die?' And an interpreter made answer to him, saying: 'Man and woman and child grow up, and arrive at maturity, and become old, and when any one of them dieth we bury him in the place wherein he lived; thus our graves are our houses. And our God knoweth that we desire this more than the lust for food and meat which all men have: this is our life and manner of living in the darkness of our tombs.'" When Alexander desired to make a gift to these Brahmans, and asked them what they desired most, their answer was, "Give us immortality".[249]

In the Gilgamesh epic the only ray of hope which relieves the gloomy closing passages is Ea-bani's suggestion that the sufferings endured by the dead may be alleviated by the performance of strict burial rites. Commenting on this point Professor Jastrow says: "A proper burial with an affectionate care of the corpse ensures at least a quiet repose.

Such a one rests on a couch and drinks pure water;
But he whose shade has no rest in the earth, as I have seen and you will see,
His shade has no rest in the earth
Whose shade no one cares for ...
What is left over in the pot, remains of food
That are thrown in the street, he eats."[250]

Gilgamesh Epic.

By disseminating the belief that the dead must be buried with much ceremony, the priests secured great power over the people, and extracted large fees.

In Egypt, on the other hand, the teachers of the sun cult sold charms and received rewards to perform ceremonies so that chosen worshippers might enter the sun-barque of Ra; while the Osirian priests promised the just and righteous that they would reach an agricultural Paradise where they could live and work as on earth, but receive a greater return for their labour, the harvests of the Otherworld being of unequalled abundance.

In the sacred books of India a number of Paradises are referred to. No human beings, however, entered the Paradise of Varuna, who resembles the Sumerian Ea-Oannes. The souls of the dead found rest and enjoyment in the Paradise of Yama, while "those kings that yield up their lives, without turning their backs on the field of battle, attain", as the sage told a hero, "to the mansion of Indra", which recalls the Valhal of Odin. It will thus be seen that belief in immortality was a tenet of the Indian cults of Indra and Yama.

It is possible that the Gilgamesh epic in one of its forms concluded when the hero reached the island of Pir-napishtim, like the Indian Yama who "searched and spied the path for many". The Indian "Land of the Pitris" (Ancestors), over which Yama presided, may be compared to the Egyptian heaven of Osiris. It contains, we are told, "all kinds of enjoyable articles", and also "sweet, juicy, agreeable and delicious edibles ... floral wreaths of the most delicious fragrance, and trees that yield fruits that are desired of them". Thither go "all sinners among human beings, as also (those) that have died during the winter solstice"[251]--a suggestion that this Paradise was not unconnected with the Tammuz-like deity who took up his abode in the spirit land during the barren season.

The view may be urged that in the Gilgamesh epic we have a development of the Tammuz legend in its heroic form. Like Ishtar, when she descended to Hades, the King of Erech could not return to earth until he had been sprinkled by the water of life. No doubt, an incident of this character occurred also in the original Tammuz legend. The life of the god had to be renewed before he could return. Did he slumber, like one of the Seven Sleepers, in Ea's house, and not awake again until he arrived as a child in his crescent moon boat--"the sunken boat" of the hymns--like Scef, who came over the waves to the land of the Scyldings?

It seems remarkable that the doctrine of Eternal Bliss, which obtained in Egypt on the one hand and in India on the other, should never have been developed among the Babylonians. Of course, our knowledge in this connection is derived from the orthodox religious texts. Perhaps the great thinkers, whose influence can be traced in the tendencies towards monotheism which became marked at various periods, believed in a Heaven for the just and good. If they did, their teachings must have been suppressed by the mercenary priests. It was extremely profitable for these priests to perpetuate the belief that the spirits of the dead were consigned to a gloomy Hades, where the degree of suffering which they endured depended on the manner in which their bodies were disposed of upon earth. An orthodox funeral ceremony was costly at all times. This is made evident by the inscriptions which record the social reforms of Urukagina, the ill-fated patesi of Lagash. When he came to the throne he cut down the burial fees by more than a half. "In the case of an ordinary burial," writes Mr. King, "when a corpse was laid in a grave, it had been the custom for the presiding priest to demand as a fee for himself seven urns of wine or strong drink, four hundred and twenty loaves of bread, one hundred and twenty measures of corn, a garment, a kid, a bed, and a seat." The reformer reduced the perquisites to "three urns of wine, eighty loaves of bread, a bed, and a kid, while the fee of his (the priest's) assistant was cut down from sixty to thirty measures of corn".[252]

The conservative element in Babylonian religion is reflected by the burial customs. These did not change greatly after the Neolithic period. Prehistoric Sumerian graves resemble closely those of pre-Dynastic Egypt. The bodies of the dead were laid on their sides in crouching posture, with a "beaker", or "drinking cup" urn, beside the right hand. Other vessels were placed near the head. In this connection it may be noted that the magic food prepared for Gilgamesh by Pir-napishtim's wife, when he lay asleep, was also placed near his head.

The corpse was always decked with various ornaments, including rings, necklaces, and armlets. As has been indicated, these were worn by the living as charms, and, no doubt, they served the same purpose for the dead. This charm-wearing custom was condemned by the Hebrew teachers. On one occasion Jacob commanded his household to "put away the strange gods which were in their hand, and all the ear-rings which were in their ears; and Jacob buried them under the oak which was by Shechem".[253]To Jacob, personal ornaments had quite evidently an idolatrous significance.

"A very typical class of grave furniture", writes Mr. King, "consisted of palettes, or colour dishes, made of alabaster, often of graceful shape, and sometimes standing on four feet.... There is no doubt as to their use, for colour still remains in many of them, generally black and yellow, but sometimes a light rose and light green." Palettes for face paint have also been found in many early Egyptian graves.

The gods had their faces painted like the living and the dead and were similarly adorned with charms. In the course of the daily service in the Egyptian temples an important ceremony was "dressing the god with white, green, bright-red, and dark-red sashes, and supplying two kinds of ointment and black and green eye paint".[254] In the word-picture of the Aryo-Indian Varuna's heaven in the *Mahabharata* the deity is depicted "attired in celestial robes and decked with celestial ornaments and jewels". His attendants, the Adityas, appear "adorned with celestial garlands and perfumed with celestial scents and besmeared with paste of celestial fragrance".[255] Apparently the "paste", like the face paint of the Babylonians and Egyptians, had protective qualities. The Picts of Scotland may have similarly painted themselves to charm their bodies against magical influences and the weapons of their enemies. A painted man was probably regarded as one who was likely to have good luck, being guarded against bad luck.

Weapons and implements were also laid in the Sumerian graves, indicating a belief that the spirits of the dead could not only protect themselves against their enemies but also provide themselves with food. The funerary gifts of fish-hooks suggests that spirits were expected to catch fish and thus obtain clean food, instead of returning to disturb the living as they searched for the remnants of the feast, like the Scottish Gunna,

> perched alone
> On a chilly old grey stone,
> Nibbling, nibbling at a bone
> That we'll maybe throw away.

Some bodies which were laid in Sumerian graves were wrapped up in reed matting, a custom which suggests that the reeds afforded protection or imparted magical powers. Magical ceremonies were performed in Babylonian reed huts. As we have seen, Ea revealed the "purpose" of the gods, when they resolved to send a flood, by addressing the reed hut in which Pir-napishtim lay asleep. Possibly it was believed that the dead might also have visions in their dreams which would reveal the "purpose" of demons who were preparing to attack them. In Syria it was customary to wrap the dead in a sheep skin.[256] As priests and gods were clad in the skins of animals from which their powers were derived, it is probable that the dead were similarly supposed to receive inspiration in their skin coverings. The Highland seer was wrapped in a bull's skin and left all night beside a stream so as to obtain knowledge of the future. This was a form of the Taghairm ceremony, which is referred to by Scott in his "Lady of the Lake".[257] The belief in the magical influence of sacred clothing gave origin to the priestly robes. When David desired to ascertain what Saul intended to do he said, "Bring hither the ephod". Then he came to know that his enemy had resolved to attack Keilah.[258] Elisha became a prophet when he received Elijah's mantle.[259]

Sometimes the bodies of the Sumerians were placed in sarcophagi of clay. The earlier type was of "bath-tub" shape, round and flat-bottomed, with a rounded lid, while the later was the "slipper-shaped coffin", which was ornamented with charms. There is a close resemblance between the "bath-tub" coffins of Sumeria and the Egyptian pottery coffins of oval shape found in Third and Fourth Dynasty tombs in rock chambers near Nuerat. Certain designs on wooden coffins, and tombs as early as the First Dynasty, have direct analogies in Babylonia.[260]

No great tombs were erected in Sumeria. The coffins were usually laid in brick vaults below dwellings, or below temples, or in trenches outside the city walls. On the "stele of victory", which belongs to the period of Eannatum, patesi of Lagash, the dead bodies on the battlefield are piled up in pairs quite naked, and earth is being heaped over them; this is a specimen of mound burial.

According to Herodotus the Babylonians "buried their dead in honey, and had funeral lamentations like the Egyptians".[261] The custom of preserving the body in this manner does not appear to have been an ancient one, and may have resulted from cultural contact with the Nile valley during the late Assyrian period. So long as the bones were undisturbed, the spirit was supposed to be assured of rest in the Underworld. This archaic belief was widespread, and finds an echo in the quaint lines over Shakespeare's grave in Stratford church:--

Good friend, for Jesus' sake forbeare
To dig the dust enclosed heare;
Blest be the man that spares these stones,
And curst be he that moves my bones.

In Babylonia the return of the spirits of the dead was greatly dreaded. Ishtar once uttered the terrible threat: "I will cause the dead to rise; they will then eat and live. The dead will be more numerous than the living." When a foreign country was invaded, it was a common custom to break open the tombs and scatter the bones they contained. Probably it was believed, when such acts of vandalism were committed, that the offended spirits would plague their kinsfolk. Ghosts always haunted the homes they once lived in, and were as malignant as demons. It is significant to find in this connection that the bodies of enemies who were slain in battle were not given decent burial, but mutilated and left for birds and beasts of prey to devour.

The demons that plagued the dead might also attack the living. A fragmentary narrative, which used to be referred to as the "Cuthean Legend of Creation",[262] and has been shown by Mr. L.W. King to have no connection with the struggle between Merodach and the dragon,[263] deals with a war waged by an ancient king against a horde of evil spirits, led by "the lord of heights, lord of the Anunaki (earth spirits)". Some of the supernatural warriors had bodies like birds; others had "raven faces", and all had been "suckled by Tiamat".

For three years the king sent out great armies to attack the demons, but "none returned alive". Then he decided to go forth himself to save his country from destruction. So he prepared for the conflict, and took the precaution of performing elaborate and therefore costly religious rites so as to secure the co-operation of the gods. His expedition was successful, for he routed the supernatural army. On his return home, he recorded his great victory on tablets which were placed in the shrine of Nergal at Cuthah.

This myth may be an echo of Nergal's raid against Eresh-ki-gal. Or, being associated with Cuthah, it may have been composed to encourage burial in that city's sacred cemetery, which had been cleared by the famous old king of the evil demons which tormented the dead and made seasonal attacks against the living.

---

[224] Ea addresses the hut in which his human favourite, Pir-napishtim, slept. His message was conveyed to this man in a dream.

[225] The second sentence of Ea's speech is conjectural, as the lines are mutilated.

[226] *The Muses' Pageant*, W.M.L. Hutchinson, pp. 5 *et seq.*

[227] *Indian Myth and Legend*, pp. 107 *et seq.*

[228] *Vana Parva* section of the *Mahábhárata* (Roy's trans.), p. 425.

[229] *Indian Myth and Legend*, p. 141.

[230] *Book of Leinster*, and Keating's *History of Ireland*, p. 150 (1811 ed.).

[231] *Religion of the Ancient Egyptians*, A. Wiedemann, pp. 58 *et seq.*

[232] Pinches' *The Religion of Babylonia and Assyria*, p. 42.

[233] The problems involved are discussed from different points of view by Mr. L.W. King in *Babylonian Religion* (Books on Egypt and Chaldaea, vol. iv), Professor Pinches in *The Old Testament in the Light of the Historical Records and Legends of Assyria and Babylonia*, and other vols.

[234] *Primitive Constellations*, vol. i, pp. 334-5.

[235] *Indian Myth and Legend*, chap. iii.

[236] Professor Macdonell's translation.

[237] *Indian Wisdom*.

[238] "Varuna, the deity bearing the noose as his weapon", *Sabha Parva* section of the *Mahábhárata* (Roy's trans.), p. 29.

[239] *Indian Myth and Legend*, pp. 38-42.

[240] *Early Religious Poetry of Persia*, J.H. Moulton, pp. 41 *et seq.* and 154 *et seq.*

[241] *The Elder Edda*, O. Bray, p. 55.

[242] *The Elder Edda*, O. Bray, pp. 291 *et seq.*

[243] *Celtic Myth and Legend*, pp. 133 *et seq.*

[244] Tennyson's *The Passing of Arthur*.

[245] *Job*, x, 1-22.

[246] *The Elder Edda*, O. Bray, pp. 150-1.

[247] *Indian Myth and Legend*, p. 326.

[248] *The Religion of Ancient Rome*, Cyril Bailey, p. 50.

[249] *The Life and Exploits of Alexander the Great (Ethiopic version of the Pseudo Callisthenes)*, pp. 133-4. The conversation possibly never took place, but it is of interest in so far as it reflects beliefs which were familiar to the author of this ancient work. His Brahmans evidently believed that immortality was denied to ordinary men, and reserved only for the king, who was the representative of the deity, of course.

[250] *Aspects of Religious Belief and Practice in Babylonia and Assyria*, Morris Jastrow, pp. 358-9.

[251] The *Mahàbhàrata (Sabha Parva* section), Roy's translation, pp. 25-7.

[252] *A History of Sumer and Akkad*, L.W. King, pp. 181-2.

[253] *Genesis*, xxxv, 2-4.

[254] *The Religion of Ancient Egypt*, W.M. Flinders Petrie, p. 72.

[255] *Sabha Parva* section of the *Mahàbhàrata* (Roy's trans.), p. 29.

[256] *Egyptian Myth and Legend*, p. 214.

[257] Canto iv:--

Last eventide

Brian an augury hath tried....

The Taghairm called; by which afar

Our sires foresaw the events of war.

Duncraggan's milk-white bull they slew....

[258] *1 Samuel*, xxiii, 9-11.

[259] *1 Kings*, xix, 19 and *2 Kings*, ii, 13-15.

[260] *The Burial Customs of Ancient Egypt*, John Garstang, pp. 28, 29 (London, 1907).

[261] *Herod.*, book i, 198.

[262] *Records of the Past* (old series), xi, pp. 109 et seq., and (new series), vol. i, pp. 149 et seq.

[263] L.W. King's *The Seven Tablets of Creation*.

Chapter X. Buildings and Laws and Customs of Babylon

Abstract

Decline and Fall of Sumerian Kingdoms--Elamites and Semites strive for Supremacy--Babylon's Walls, Gates, Streets, and Canals--The Hanging Gardens--Merodach's Great Temple--The Legal Code of Hammurabi--The Marriage Market--Position of Women--Marriage brought Freedom--Vestal Virgins--Breach of Promise and Divorce--Rights of Children--Female Publicans--The Land Laws--Doctors legislated out of Existence--Folk Cures--Spirits of Disease expelled by Magical Charms--The Legend of the Worm--"Touch Iron"--Curative Water--Magical Origin of Poetry and Music.

The rise of Babylon inaugurated a new era in the history of Western Asia. Coincidentally the political power of the Sumerians came to an end. It had been paralysed by the Elamites, who, towards the close of the Dynasty of Isin, successfully overran the southern district and endeavoured to extend their sway over the whole valley. Two Elamite kings, Warad-Sin and his brother Rim-Sin, struggled with the rulers of Babylon for supremacy, and for a time it appeared as if the intruders from the East were to establish themselves permanently as a military aristocracy over Sumer and Akkad. But the Semites were strongly reinforced by new settlers of the same blended stock who swarmed from the land of the Amorites. Once again Arabia was pouring into Syria vast hordes of its surplus population, with the result that ethnic disturbances were constant and widespread. This migration is termed the Canaanitic or Amorite: it flowed into Mesopotamia and across Assyria, while it supplied the "driving power" which secured the ascendancy of the Hammurabi Dynasty at Babylon. Indeed, the ruling family which came into prominence there is believed to have been of Canaanitic origin.

Once Babylon became the metropolis it retained its pre-eminence until the end. Many political changes took place during its long and chequered history, but no rival city in the south ever attained to its splendour and greatness. Whether its throne was occupied by Amorite or Kassite, Assyrian or Chaldean, it was invariably found to be the most effective centre of administration for the lower Tigro-Euphrates valley. Some of the Kassite monarchs, however, showed a preference for Nippur.

Of its early history little is known. It was overshadowed in turn by Kish and Umma, Lagash and Erech, and may have been little better than a great village when Akkad rose into prominence. Sargon I, the royal gardener, appears to have interested himself in its development, for it was recorded that he cleared its trenches and strengthened its fortifications. The city occupied a strategic position, and probably assumed importance on that account as well as a trading and industrial centre. Considerable wealth had accumulated at Babylon when the Dynasty of Ur reached the zenith of its power. It is recorded that King Dungi plundered its famous "Temple of the High Head", E-sagila, which some identify with the Tower of Babel, so as to secure treasure for Ea's temple at Eridu, which he specially favoured. His vandalistic raid, like that of the Gutium, or men of Kutu, was remembered for long centuries afterwards, and the city god was invoked at the time to cut short his days.

No doubt, Hammurabi's Babylon closely resembled the later city so vividly described by Greek writers, although it was probably not of such great dimensions. According to Herodotus, it occupied an exact square on the broad plain, and had a circumference of sixty of our miles. "While such is its size," the historian wrote, "in magnificence there is no other city that approaches to it." Its walls were eighty-seven feet thick and three hundred and fifty feet high, and each side of the square was fifteen miles in length. The whole city was surrounded by a deep, broad canal or moat, and the river Euphrates ran through it.

"Here", continued Herodotus, "I may not omit to tell the use to which the mould dug out of the great moat was turned, nor the manner in which the wall was wrought. As fast as they dug the moat the soil which they got from the cutting was made into bricks, and when a sufficient number were completed they baked the bricks in kilns. Then they set to building, and began with bricking the borders of the moat, after which they proceeded to construct the wall itself, using throughout for their cement hot bitumen, and interposing a layer of wattled reeds at every thirtieth course of the bricks. On the top, along the edges of the wall, they constructed buildings of a single chamber facing one another, leaving between them room for a four-horse chariot to turn. In the circuit of the wall are a hundred gates, all of brass, with brazen lintels and side posts."[264] These were the gates referred to by Isaiah when God called Cyrus:

I will loose the loins of kings, to open before him the two
leaved gates; and the gates shall not be shut: I will go before
thee, and make the crooked places straight; I will break in pieces
the gates of brass, and cut in sunder the bars of iron.[265]

The outer wall was the main defence of the city, but there was also an inner wall less thick but not much inferior in strength. In addition, a fortress stood in each division of the city. The king's palace and the temple of Bel Merodach were surrounded by walls.

All the main streets were perfectly straight, and each crossed the city from gate to gate, a distance of fifteen miles, half of them being interrupted by the river, which had to be ferried. As there were twenty-five gates on each side of the outer wall, the great thoroughfares numbered fifty in all, and there were six hundred and seventy-six squares, each over two miles in circumference. From Herodotus we gather that the houses were three or four stories high, suggesting that the tenement system was not unknown, and according to Q. Curtius, nearly half of the area occupied by the city was taken up by gardens within the squares.

In Greek times Babylon was famous for the hanging or terraced gardens of the "new palace", which had been erected by Nebuchadnezzar II. These occupied a square which was more than a quarter of a mile in circumference. Great stone terraces, resting on arches, rose up like a giant stairway to a height of about three hundred and fifty feet, and the whole structure was strengthened by a surrounding wall over twenty feet in thickness. So deep were the layers of mould on each terrace that fruit trees were grown amidst the plants of luxuriant foliage and the brilliant Asian flowers. Water for irrigating the gardens was raised from the river by a mechanical contrivance to a great cistern situated on the highest terrace, and it was prevented from leaking out of the soil by layers of reeds and bitumen and sheets of lead. Spacious apartments, luxuriously furnished and decorated, were constructed in the spaces between the arches and were festooned by flowering creepers. A broad stairway ascended from terrace to terrace.

The old palace stood in a square nearly four miles in circumference, and was strongly protected by three walls, which were decorated by sculptures in low relief, representing battle scenes and scenes of the chase and royal ceremonies. Winged bulls with human heads guarded the main entrance.

Another architectural feature of the city was E-sagila, the temple of Bel Merodach, known to the Greeks as "Jupiter-Belus". The high wall which enclosed it had gates of solid brass. "In the middle of the precinct", wrote Herodotus, "there was a tower of solid masonry, a furlong in length and breadth, upon which was raised a second tower, and on that a third, and so on up to eight. The ascent to the top is on the outside, by a path which winds round all the towers. When one is about halfway up, one finds a resting-place and seats, where persons are wont to sit some time on their way to the summit. On the topmost tower there is a spacious temple, and inside the temple stands a couch of unusual size, richly adorned, with a golden table by its side. There is no statue of any kind set up in the place, nor is the chamber occupied of nights by anyone but a single native woman, who, as the Chaldaeans, the priests of this god, affirm, is chosen for himself by the deity out of all the women of the land."

A woman who was the "wife of Amon" also slept in that god's temple at Thebes in Egypt. A similar custom was observed in Lycia.

"Below, in the same precinct," continued Herodotus, "there is a second temple, in which is a sitting figure of Jupiter, all of gold. Before the figure stands a large golden table, and the throne whereon it sits, and the base on which the throne is placed, are likewise of pure gold.... Outside the temple are two altars, one of solid gold, on which it is only lawful to offer sucklings; the other, a common altar, but of great size, on which the full-grown animals are sacrificed. It is also on the great altar that the Chaldaeans burn the frankincense, which is offered to the amount of a thousand talents' weight, every year, at the festival of the god. In the time of Cyrus there was likewise in this temple a figure of a man, twelve cubits high, entirely of solid gold.... Besides the ornaments which I have mentioned, there are a large number of private offerings in this holy precinct."[266]

The city wall and river gates were closed every night, and when Babylon was besieged the people were able to feed themselves. The gardens and small farms were irrigated by canals, and canals also controlled the flow of the river Euphrates. A great dam had been formed above the town to store the surplus water during inundation and increase the supply when the river sank to its lowest.

In Hammurabi's time the river was crossed by ferry boats, but long ere the Greeks visited the city a great bridge had been constructed. So completely did the fierce Sennacherib destroy the city, that most of the existing ruins date from the period of Nebuchadnezzar II.[267]

Our knowledge of the social life of Babylon and the territory under its control is derived chiefly from the Hammurabi Code of laws, of which an almost complete copy was discovered at Susa, towards the end of 1901, by the De Morgan expedition. The laws were inscribed on a stele of black diorite 7 ft. 3 in. high, with a circumference at the base of 6 ft. 2 in. and at the top of 5 ft. 4 in. This important relic of an ancient law-abiding people had been broken in three pieces, but when these were joined together it was found that the text was not much impaired. On one side are twenty-eight columns and on the other sixteen. Originally there were in all nearly 4000 lines of inscriptions, but five columns, comprising about 300 lines, had been erased to give space, it is conjectured, for the name of the invader who carried the stele away, but unfortunately the record was never made.

On the upper part of the stele, which is now one of the treasures of the Louvre, Paris, King Hammurabi salutes, with his right hand reverently upraised, the sun god Shamash, seated on his throne, at the summit of E-sagila, by whom he is being presented with the stylus with which to inscribe the legal code. Both figures are heavily bearded, but have shaven lips and chins. The god wears a conical headdress and a flounced robe suspended from his left shoulder, while the king has assumed a round dome-shaped hat and a flowing garment which almost sweeps the ground.

It is gathered from the Code that there were three chief social grades--the aristocracy, which included landowners, high officials and administrators; the freemen, who might be wealthy merchants or small landholders; and the slaves. The fines imposed for a given offence upon wealthy men were much heavier than those imposed upon the poor. Lawsuits were heard in courts. Witnesses were required to tell the truth, "affirming before the god what they knew", and perjurers were severely dealt with; a man who gave false evidence in connection with a capital charge was put to death. A strict watch was also kept over the judges, and if one was found to have willingly convicted a prisoner on insufficient evidence he was fined and degraded.

Theft was regarded as a heinous crime, and was invariably punished by death. Thieves included those who made purchases from minors or slaves without the sanction of elders or trustees. Sometimes the accused was given the alternative of paying a fine, which might exceed by ten or even thirty fold the value of the article or animal he had appropriated. It was imperative that lost property should be restored. If the owner of an article of which he had been wrongfully deprived found it in possession of a man who declared that he had purchased it from another, evidence was taken in court. When it happened that the seller was proved to have been the thief, the capital penalty was imposed. On the other hand, the alleged purchaser was dealt with in like manner if he failed to prove his case. Compensation for property stolen by a brigand was paid by the temple, and the heirs of a man slain by a brigand within the city had to be compensated by the local authority.

Of special interest are the laws which relate to the position of women. In this connection reference may first be made to the marriage-by-auction custom, which Herodotus described as follows: "Once a year in each village the maidens of age to marry were collected all together into one place, while the men stood round them in a circle. Then a herald called up the damsels one by one, and offered them for sale. He began with the most beautiful. When she was sold for no small sum of money, he offered for sale the one who came next to her in beauty. All of them were sold to be wives. The richest of the Babylonians who wished to wed bid against each other for the loveliest maidens, while the humbler wife-seekers, who were indifferent about beauty, took the more homely damsels with marriage portions. For the custom was that when the herald had gone through the whole number of the beautiful damsels, he should then call up the ugliest--a cripple, if there chanced to be one--and offer her to the men, asking who would agree to take her with the smallest marriage portion. And the man who offered to take the smallest sum had her assigned to him. The marriage portions were furnished by the money paid for the beautiful damsels, and thus the fairer maidens portioned out the uglier. No one was allowed to give his daughter in marriage to the man of his choice, nor might anyone carry away the damsel whom he had purchased without finding bail really and truly to make her his wife; if, however, it turned out that they did not agree, the money might be paid back. All who liked might come, even from distant villages, and bid for the women."[268]

This custom is mentioned by other writers, but it is impossible to ascertain at what period it became prevalent in Babylonia and by whom it was introduced. Herodotus understood that it obtained also in "the Illyrian tribe of the Eneti", which was reputed to have entered Italy with Antenor after the fall of Troy, and has been identified with the Venetians of later times. But the ethnic clue thus afforded is exceedingly vague. There is no direct reference to the custom in the Hammurabi Code, which reveals a curious blending of the principles of "Father right" and "Mother right". A girl was subject to her father's will; he could dispose of her as he thought best, and she always remained a member of his family; after marriage she was known as the daughter of so and so rather than the wife of so and so. But marriage brought her freedom and the rights of citizenship. The power vested in her father was never transferred to her husband.

A father had the right to select a suitable spouse for his daughter, and she could not marry without his consent. That this law did not prevent "love matches" is made evident by the fact that provision was made in the Code for the marriage of a free woman with a male slave, part of whose estate in the event of his wife's death could be claimed by his master.

When a betrothal was arranged, the father fixed the "bride price", which was paid over before the contract could be concluded, and he also provided a dowry. The amount of the "bride price" might, however, be refunded to the young couple to give them a start in life. If, during the interval between betrothal and marriage, the man "looked upon another woman", and said to his father-in-law, "I will not marry your daughter", he forfeited the "bride price" for breach of promise of marriage.

A girl might also obtain a limited degree of freedom by taking vows of celibacy and becoming one of the vestal virgins, or nuns, who were attached to the temple of the sun god. She did not, however, live a life of entire seclusion. If she received her due proportion of her father's estate, she could make business investments within certain limits. She was not, for instance, allowed to own a wineshop, and if she even entered one she was burned at the stake. Once she took these vows she had to observe them until the end of her days. If she married, as she might do to obtain the legal status of a married woman and enjoy the privileges of that position, she denied her husband conjugal rites, but provided him with a concubine who might bear him children, as Sarah did to Abraham. These nuns must not be confused with the unmoral women who were associated with the temples of Ishtar and other love goddesses of shady repute.

The freedom secured by a married woman had its legal limitations. If she became a widow, for instance, she could not remarry without the consent of a judge, to whom she was expected to show good cause for the step she proposed to take. Punishments for breaches of the marriage law were severe. Adultery was a capital crime; the guilty parties were bound together and thrown into the river. If it happened, however, that the wife of a prisoner went to reside with another man on account of poverty, she was acquitted and allowed to return to her husband after his release. In cases where no plea of poverty could be urged the erring women were drowned. The wife of a soldier who had been taken prisoner by an enemy was entitled to a third part of her husband's estate if her son was a minor, the remainder was held in trust. The husband could enter into possession of all his property again if he happened to return home.

Divorce was easily obtained. A husband might send his wife away either because she was childless or because he fell in love with another woman. Incompatibility of temperament was also recognized as sufficient reason for separation. A woman might hate her husband and wish to leave him. "If", the Code sets forth, "she is careful and is without blame, and is neglected by her husband who has deserted her", she can claim release from the marriage contract. But if she is found to have another lover, and is guilty of neglecting her duties, she is liable to be put to death.

A married woman possessed her own property. Indeed, the value of her marriage dowry was always vested in her. When, therefore, she divorced her husband, or was divorced by him, she was entitled to have her dowry refunded and to return to her father's house. Apparently she could claim maintenance from her father.

A woman could have only one husband, but a man could have more than one wife. He might marry a secondary wife, or concubine, because he was without offspring, but "the concubine", the Code lays down, "shall not rank with the wife". Another reason for second marriage recognized by law was a wife's state of health. In such circumstances a man could not divorce his sickly wife. He had to support her in his house as long as she lived.

Children were the heirs of their parents, but if a man during his lifetime gifted his property to his wife, and confirmed it on "a sealed tablet", the children could have no claim, and the widow was entitled to leave her estate to those of her children she preferred; but she could not will any portion of it to her brothers. In ordinary cases the children of a first marriage shared equally the estate of a father with those of a second marriage. If a slave bore children to her employer, their right to inheritance depended on whether or not the father had recognized them as his offspring during his lifetime. A father might legally disown his son if the young man was guilty of criminal practices.

The legal rights of a vestal virgin were set forth in detail. If she had received no dowry from her father when she took vows of celibacy, she could claim after his death one-third of the portion of a son. She could will her estate to anyone she favoured, but if she died intestate her brothers were her heirs. When, however, her estate consisted of fields or gardens allotted to her by her father, she could not disinherit her legal heirs. The fields or gardens might be worked during her lifetime by her brothers if they paid rent, or she might employ a manager on the "share system".

Vestal virgins and married women were protected against the slanderer. Any man who "pointed the finger" against them unjustifiably was charged with the offence before a judge, who could sentence him to have his forehead branded. It was not difficult, therefore, in ancient Babylonia to discover the men who made malicious and unfounded statements regarding an innocent woman. Assaults on women were punished according to the victim's rank; even slaves were protected.

Women appear to have monopolized the drink traffic. At any rate, there is no reference to male wine sellers. A female publican had to conduct her business honestly, and was bound to accept a legal tender. If she refused corn and demanded silver, when the value of the silver by "grand weight" was below the price of corn, she was prosecuted and punished by being thrown into the water. Perhaps she was simply ducked. As much may be inferred from the fact that when she was found guilty of allowing rebels to meet in her house, she was put to death.

The land laws were strict and exacting. A tenant could be penalized for not cultivating his holding properly. The rent paid was a proportion of the crop, but the proportion could be fixed according to the average yield of a district, so that a careless or inefficient tenant had to bear the brunt of his neglect or want of skill. The punishment for allowing a field to lie fallow was to make a man hoe and sow it and then hand it over to his landlord, and this applied even to a man who leased unreclaimed land which he had contracted to cultivate. Damage done to fields by floods after the rent was paid was borne by the cultivator; but if it occurred before the corn was reaped the landlord's share was calculated in proportion to the amount of the yield which was recovered. Allowance was also made for poor harvests, when the shortage was not due to the neglect of the tenant, but to other causes, and no interest was paid for borrowed money even if the farm suffered from the depredations of the tempest god; the moneylender had to share risks with borrowers. Tenants who neglected their dykes, however, were not exempted from their legal liabilities, and their whole estates could be sold to reimburse their creditors.

The industrious were protected against the careless. Men who were negligent about controlling the water supply, and caused floods by opening irrigation ditches which damaged the crops of their neighbours, had to pay for the losses sustained, the damages being estimated according to the average yield of a district. A tenant who allowed his sheep to stray on to a neighbour's pasture had to pay a heavy fine in corn at the harvest season, much in excess of the value of the grass cropped by his sheep. Gardeners were similarly subject to strict laws. All business contracts had to be conducted according to the provisions of the Code, and in every case it was necessary that a proper record should be made on clay tablets. As a rule a dishonest tenant or trader had to pay sixfold the value of the sum under dispute if the judge decided in court against his claim.

The law of an eye for an eye and a tooth for a tooth was strictly observed in Babylonia. A freeman who destroyed an eye of a freeman had one of his own destroyed; if he broke a bone, he had a bone broken. Fines were imposed, however, when a slave was injured. For striking a gentleman, a commoner received sixty lashes, and the son who smote his father had his hands cut off. A slave might have his ears cut off for assaulting his master's son.

Doctors must have found their profession an extremely risky one. No allowance was made for what is nowadays known as a "professional error". A doctor's hands were cut off if he opened a wound with a metal knife and his patient afterwards died, or if a man lost his eye as the result of an operation. A slave who died under a doctor's hands had to be replaced by a slave, and if a slave lost his eye, the doctor had to pay half the man's market value to the owner. Professional fees were fixed according to a patient's rank. Gentlemen had to pay five shekels of silver to a doctor who set a bone or restored diseased flesh, commoners three shekels, and masters for their slaves two shekels. There was also a scale of fees for treating domesticated animals, and it was not over-generous. An unfortunate surgeon who undertook to treat an ox or ass suffering from a severe wound had to pay a quarter of its price to its owner if it happened to die. A shrewd farmer who was threatened with the loss of an animal must have been extremely anxious to engage the services of a surgeon.

It is not surprising, after reviewing this part of the Hammurabi Code, to find Herodotus stating bluntly that the Babylonians had no physicians. "When a man is ill", he wrote, "they lay him in the public square, and the passers-by come up to him, and if they have ever had his disease themselves, or have known anyone who has suffered from it, they give him advice, recommending him to do whatever they found good in their own case, or in the case known to them; and no one is allowed to pass the sick man in silence without asking him what his ailment is." One might imagine that Hammurabi had legislated the medical profession out of existence, were it not that letters have been found in the Assyrian library of Ashur-banipal which indicate that skilled physicians were held in high repute. It is improbable, however, that they were numerous. The risks they ran in Babylonia may account for their ultimate disappearance in that country.

No doubt patients received some benefit from exposure in the streets in the sunlight and fresh air, and perhaps, too, from some of the old wives' remedies which were gratuitously prescribed by passers-by. In Egypt, where certain of the folk cures were recorded on papyri, quite effective treatment was occasionally given, although the "medicines" were exceedingly repugnant as a rule; ammonia, for instance, was taken with the organic substances found in farmyards. Elsewhere some wonderful instances of excellent folk cures have come to light, especially among isolated peoples, who have received them interwoven in their immemorial traditions. A medical man who has investigated this interesting subject in the Scottish Highlands has shown that "the simple observation of the people was the starting-point of our fuller knowledge, however complete we may esteem it to be". For dropsy and heart troubles, foxglove, broom tops, and juniper berries, which have reputations "as old as the hills", are "the most reliable medicines in our scientific armoury at the present time". These discoveries of the ancient folks have been "merely elaborated in later days". Ancient cures for indigestion are still in use. "Tar water, which was a remedy for chest troubles, especially for those of a consumptive nature, has endless imitations in our day"; it was also "the favourite remedy for skin diseases". No doubt the present inhabitants of Babylonia, who utilize bitumen as a germicide, are perpetuating an ancient folk custom.

This medical man who is being quoted adds: "The whole matter may be summed up, that we owe infinitely more to the simple nature study of our people in the great affair of health than we owe to all the later science."[269]

Herodotus, commenting on the custom of patients taking a census of folk cures in the streets, said it was one of the wisest institutions of the Babylonian people. It is to be regretted that he did not enter into details regarding the remedies which were in greatest favour in his day. His data would have been useful for comparative purposes.

So far as can be gathered from the clay tablets, faith cures were not unknown, and there was a good deal of quackery. If surgery declined, as a result of the severe restrictions which hampered progress in an honourable profession, magic flourished like tropical fungi. Indeed, the worker of spells was held in high repute, and his operations were in most cases allowed free play. There are only two paragraphs in the Hammurabi Code which deal with magical practices. It is set forth that if one man cursed another and the curse could not be justified, the perpetrator of it must suffer the death penalty. Provision was also made for discovering whether a spell had been legally imposed or not. The victim was expected to plunge himself in a holy river. If the river carried him away it was held as proved that he deserved his punishment, and "the layer of the spell" was given possession of the victim's house. A man who could swim was deemed to be innocent; he claimed the residence of "the layer of the spell", who was promptly put to death. With this interesting glimpse of ancient superstition the famous Code opens, and then strikes a modern note by detailing the punishments for perjury and the unjust administration of law in the courts.

The poor sufferers who gathered at street corners in Babylon to make mute appeal for cures believed that they were possessed by evil spirits. Germs of disease were depicted by lively imaginations as invisible demons, who derived nourishment from the human body. When a patient was wasted with disease, growing thinner and weaker and more bloodless day by day, it was believed that a merciless vampire was sucking his veins and devouring his flesh. It had therefore to be expelled by performing a magical ceremony and repeating a magical formula. The demon was either driven or enticed away.

A magician had to decide in the first place what particular demon was working evil. He then compelled its attention and obedience by detailing its attributes and methods of attack, and perhaps by naming it. Thereafter he suggested how it should next act by releasing a raven, so that it might soar towards the clouds like that bird, or by offering up a sacrifice which it received for nourishment and as compensation. Another popular method was to fashion a waxen figure of the patient and prevail upon the disease demon to enter it. The figure was then carried away to be thrown in the river or burned in a fire.

Occasionally a quite effective cure was included in the ceremony. As much is suggested by the magical treatment of toothache. First of all the magician identified the toothache demon as "the worm". Then he recited its history, which is as follows: After Anu created the heavens, the heavens created the earth, the earth created the rivers, the rivers created the canals, the canals created the marshes, and last of all the marshes created "the worm".

This display of knowledge compelled the worm to listen, and no doubt the patient was able to indicate to what degree it gave evidence of its agitated mind. The magician continued:
Came the worm and wept before Shamash,
Before Ea came her tears:
"What wilt thou give me for my food,
What wilt thou give me to devour?"
One of the deities answered: "I will give thee dried bones and scented ... wood"; but the hungry worm protested:
"Nay, what are these dried bones of thine to me?
Let me drink among the teeth;
And set me on the gums
That I may devour the blood of the teeth,
And of their gums destroy their strength--
Then shall I hold the bolt of the door."
The magician provided food for "the worm", and the following is his recipe: "Mix beer, the plant sa-kil-bir, and oil together; put it on the tooth and repeat Incantation." No doubt this mixture soothed the pain, and the sufferer must have smiled gladly when the magician finished his incantation by exclaiming:
"So must thou say this, O Worm!
May Ea smite thee with the might of his fist."[270]
Headaches were no doubt much relieved when damp cloths were wrapped round a patient's head and scented wood was burned beside him, while the magician, in whom so much faith was reposed, droned out a mystical incantation. The curative water was drawn from the confluence of two streams and was sprinkled with much ceremony. In like manner the evil-eye curers, who still operate in isolated districts in these islands, draw water from under bridges "over which the dead and the living pass",[271] and mutter charms and lustrate victims.

Headaches were much dreaded by the Babylonians. They were usually the first symptoms of fevers, and the demons who caused them were supposed to be bloodthirsty and exceedingly awesome. According to the charms, these invisible enemies of man were of the brood of Nergal. No house could be protected against them. They entered through keyholes and chinks of doors and windows; they crept like serpents and stank like mice; they had lolling tongues like hungry dogs.

Magicians baffled the demons by providing a charm. If a patient "touched iron"--meteoric iron, which was the "metal of heaven"--relief could be obtained. Or, perhaps, the sacred water would dispel the evil one; as the drops trickled from the patient's face, so would the fever spirit trickle away. When a pig was offered up in sacrifice as a substitute for a patient, the wicked spirit was commanded to depart and allow a kindly spirit to take its place--an indication that the Babylonians, like the Germanic peoples, believed that they were guarded by spirits who brought good luck.

The numerous incantations which were inscribed on clay tablets and treasured in libraries, do not throw much light on the progress of medical knowledge, for the genuine folk cures were regarded as of secondary importance, and were not as a rule recorded. But these metrical compositions are of special interest, in so far as they indicate how poetry originated and achieved widespread popularity among ancient peoples. Like the religious dance, the earliest poems were used for magical purposes. They were composed in the first place by men and women who were supposed to be inspired in the literal sense; that is, possessed by spirits. Primitive man associated "spirit" with "breath", which was the "air of life", and identical with wind. The poetical magician drew in a "spirit", and thus received inspiration, as he stood on some sacred spot on the mountain summit, amidst forest solitudes, beside a' whispering stream, or on the sounding shore. As Burns has sung:

The muse, nae poet ever fand her,
Till by himsel' he learn'd to wander,
Adown some trottin' burn's meander,
    An' no think lang:
O sweet to stray, an' pensive ponder
    A heart-felt sang!

Or, perhaps, the bard received inspiration by drinking magic water from the fountain called Hippocrene, or the skaldic mead which dripped from the moon.

The ancient poet did not sing for the mere love of singing: he knew nothing about "Art for Art's sake". His object in singing appears to have been intensely practical. The world was inhabited by countless hordes of spirits, which were believed to be ever exercising themselves to influence mankind. The spirits caused suffering; they slew victims; they brought misfortune; they were also the source of good or "luck". Man regarded spirits emotionally; he conjured them with emotion; he warded off their attacks with emotion; and his emotions were given rhythmical expression by means of metrical magical charms.

Poetic imagery had originally a magical significance; if the ocean was compared to a dragon, it was because it was supposed to be inhabited by a storm-causing dragon; the wind whispered because a spirit whispered in it. Love lyrics were charms to compel the love god to wound or possess a maiden's heart--to fill it, as an Indian charm sets forth, with "the yearning of the Apsaras (fairies)"; satires conjured up evil spirits to injure a victim; and heroic narratives chanted at graves were statements made to the god of battle, so that he might award the mighty dead by transporting him to the Valhal of Odin or Swarga of Indra.

Similarly, music had magical origin as an imitation of the voices of spirits--of the piping birds who were "Fates", of the wind high and low, of the thunder roll, or the bellowing sea. So the god Pan piped on his reed bird-like notes, Indra blew his thunder horn, Thor used his hammer like a drumstick, Neptune imitated on his "wreathed horn" the voice of the deep, the Celtic oak god Dagda twanged his windy wooden harp, and Angus, the Celtic god of spring and love, came through budding forest ways with a silvern harp which had strings of gold, echoing the tuneful birds, the purling streams, the whispering winds, and the rustling of scented fir and blossoming thorn.

Modern-day poets and singers, who voice their moods and cast the spell of their moods over readers and audiences, are the representatives of ancient magicians who believed that moods were caused by the spirits which possessed them--the rhythmical wind spirits, those harpers of the forest and songsters of ocean.

The following quotations from Mr. R.C. Thompson's translations of Babylonian charms will serve to illustrate their poetic qualities:--

Fever like frost hath come upon the land.

Fever hath blown upon the man as the wind blast,
It hath smitten the man and humbled his pride.

Headache lieth like the stars of heaven in the desert and hath no praise;
Pain in the head and shivering like a scudding cloud turn unto the form of man.

Headache whose course like the dread windstorm none knoweth.

Headache roareth over the desert, blowing like the wind,
Flashing like lightning, it is loosed above and below,
It cutteth off him, who feareth not his god, like a reed ...
From amid mountains it hath descended upon the land.

Headache ... a rushing hag-demon,
Granting no rest, nor giving kindly sleep ...
Whose shape is as the whirlwind.
Its appearance is as the darkening heavens,
And its face as the deep shadow of the forest.

Sickness ... breaking the fingers as a rope of wind ...
Flashing like a heavenly star, it cometh like the dew.

These early poets had no canons of Art, and there were no critics to disturb their meditations. Many singers had to sing and die ere a critic could find much to say. In ancient times, therefore, poets had their Golden Age-- they were a law unto themselves. Even the "minors" were influential members of society.

---

[264] *Herodotus*, book i, 179 (Rawlinson's translation).

[265] *Isaiah*, xlv, 1, 2.

[266] *Herodotus*, book i, 181-3 (Rawlinson's translation).

[267] *History of Sumer and Akkad*, L.W. King, p. 37.

[268] *Herodotus*, book i, 196 (Rawlinson's translation).

[269] *Home Life of the Highlanders* (Dr. Cameron Gillies on *Medical Knowledge*,) pp. 85 *et seq.* Glasgow, 1911.

[270] Translations by R.C. Thompson in *The Devils and Spirits of Babylon*, vol. i, pp. lxiii *et seq.*

[271] Bridges which lead to graveyards.

Chapter XI. The Golden Age of Babylonia
Abstract

Rise of the Sun God--Amorites and Elamites struggle for Ascendancy--The Conquering Ancestors of Hammurabi--Sumerian Cities Destroyed--Widespread Race Movements--Phoenician Migration from Persian Gulf--Wanderings of Abraham and Lot--Biblical References to Hittites and Amorites--Battles of Four Kings with Five--Amraphel, Arioch, and Tidal--Hammurabi's Brilliant Reign--Elamite Power Stamped Out--Babylon's Great General and Statesman--The Growth of Commerce, Agriculture, and Education--An Ancient School--Business and Private Correspondence--A Love Letter--Postal System--Hammurabi's Successors--The Earliest Kassites--The Sealand Dynasty--Hittite Raid on Babylon and Hyksos Invasion of Egypt.

Sun worship came into prominence in its most fully developed form during the obscure period which followed the decline of the Dynasty of Isin. This was probably due to the changed political conditions which brought about the ascendancy for a time of Larsa, the seat of the Sumerian sun cult, and of Sippar, the seat of the Akkadian sun cult. Larsa was selected as the capital of the Elamite conquerors, while their rivals, the Amorites, appear to have first established their power at Sippar.

Babbar, the sun god of Sippar, whose Semitic name was Shamash, must have been credited with the early successes of the Amorites, who became domiciled under his care, and it was possibly on that account that the ruling family subsequently devoted so much attention to his worship in Merodach's city of Babylon, where a sun temple was erected, and Shamash received devout recognition as an abstract deity of righteousness and law, who reflected the ideals of well organized and firmly governed communities.

The first Amoritic king was Sumu-abum, but little is known regarding him except that he reigned at Sippar. He was succeeded by Sumu-la-ilu, a deified monarch, who moved from

95

Sippar to Babylon, the great wall of which he either repaired or entirely reconstructed in his fifth year. With these two monarchs began the brilliant Hammurabi, or First Dynasty of Babylonia, which endured for three centuries. Except Sumu-abum, who seems to stand alone, all its kings belonged to the same family, and son succeeded father in unbroken succession.

Sumu-la-ilu was evidently a great general and conqueror of the type of Thothmes III of Egypt. His empire, it is believed, included the rising city states of Assyria, and extended southward as far as ancient Lagash.

Of special interest on religious as well as political grounds was his association with Kish. That city had become the stronghold of a rival family of Amoritic kings, some of whom were powerful enough to assert their independence. They formed the Third Dynasty of Kish. The local god was Zamama, the Tammuz-like deity, who, like Nin-Girsu of Lagash, was subsequently identified with Merodach of Babylon. But prominence was also given to the moon god Nannar, to whom a temple had been erected, a fact which suggests that sun worship was not more pronounced among the Semites than the Arabians, and may not, indeed, have been of Semitic origin at all. Perhaps the lunar temple was a relic of the influential Dynasty of Ur.

Sumu-la-ilu attacked and captured Kish, but did not slay Bunutakhtunila, its king, who became his vassal. Under the overlordship of Sumu-la-ilu, the next ruler of Kish, whose name was Immerum, gave prominence to the public worship of Shamash. Politics and religion went evidently hand in hand.

Sumu-la-ilu strengthened the defences of Sippar, restored the wall and temple of Cuthah, and promoted the worship of Merodach and his consort Zerpanitum at Babylon. He was undoubtedly one of the forceful personalities of his dynasty. His son, Zabium, had a short but successful reign, and appears to have continued the policy of his father in consolidating the power of Babylon and securing the allegiance of subject cities. He enlarged Merodach's temple, E-sagila, restored the Kish temple of Zamama, and placed a golden image of himself in the temple of the sun god at Sippar. Apil-Sin, his son, surrounded Babylon with a new wall, erected a temple to Ishtar, and presented a throne of gold and silver to Shamash in that city, while he also strengthened Borsippa, renewed Nergal's temple at Cuthah, and dug canals.

The next monarch was Sin-muballit, son of Apil-Sin and father of Hammurabi. He engaged himself in extending and strengthening the area controlled by Babylon by building city fortifications and improving the irrigation system. It is recorded that he honoured Shamash with the gift of a shrine and a golden altar adorned with jewels. Like Sumu-la-ilu, he was a great battle lord, and was specially concerned in challenging the supremacy of Elam in Sumeria and in the western land of the Amorites.

For a brief period a great conqueror, named Rim-Anum, had established an empire which extended from Kish to Larsa, but little is known regarding him. Then several kings flourished at Larsa who claimed to have ruled over Ur. The first monarch with an Elamite name who became connected with Larsa was Kudur-Mabug, son of Shimti-Shilkhak, the father of Warad-Sin and Rim-Sin.

It was from one of these Elamite monarchs that Sin-muballit captured Isin, and probably the Elamites were also the leaders of the army of Ur which he had routed before that event took place. He was not successful, however, in driving the Elamites from the land, and possibly he arranged with them a treaty of peace or perhaps of alliance.

Much controversy has been waged over the historical problems connected with this disturbed age. The records are exceedingly scanty, because the kings were not in the habit of commemorating battles which proved disastrous to them, and their fragmentary references to successes are not sufficient to indicate what permanent results accrued from their various campaigns. All we know for certain is that for a considerable period, extending perhaps over a century, a tremendous and disastrous struggle was waged at intervals, which desolated middle Babylonia. At least five great cities were destroyed by fire, as is testified by the evidence accumulated by excavators. These were Lagash, Umma, Shurruppak, Kisurra, and Adab. The ancient metropolis of Lagash, whose glory had been revived by Gudea and his kinsmen, fell soon after the rise of Larsa, and lay in ruins until the second century B.C., when, during the Seleucid Period, it was again occupied for a time. From its mound at Tello, and the buried ruins of the other cities, most of the relics of ancient Sumerian civilization have been recovered.

It was probably during one of the intervals of this stormy period that the rival kings in Babylonia joined forces against a common enemy and invaded the Western Land. Probably there was much unrest there. Great ethnic disturbances were in progress which were changing the political complexion of Western Asia. In addition to the outpourings of Arabian peoples into Palestine and Syria, which propelled other tribes to invade Mesopotamia, northern Babylonia, and Assyria, there was also much unrest all over the wide area to north and west of

Elam. Indeed, the Elamite migration into southern Babylonia may not have been unconnected with the southward drift of roving bands from Media and the Iranian plateau.

It is believed that these migrations were primarily due to changing climatic conditions, a prolonged "Dry Cycle" having caused a shortage of herbage, with the result that pastoral peoples were compelled to go farther and farther afield in quest of "fresh woods and pastures new". Innumerable currents and cross currents were set in motion once these race movements swept towards settled districts either to flood them with human waves, or surround them like islands in the midst of tempest-lashed seas, fretting the frontiers with restless fury, and ever groping for an inlet through which to flow with irresistible force.

The Elamite occupation of Southern Babylonia appears to have propelled migrations of not inconsiderable numbers of its inhabitants. No doubt the various sections moved towards districts which were suitable for their habits of life. Agriculturists, for instance, must have shown preference for those areas which were capable of agricultural development, while pastoral folks sought grassy steppes and valleys, and seafarers the shores of alien seas.

Northern Babylonia and Assyria probably attracted the tillers of the soil. But the movements of seafarers must have followed a different route. It is possible that about this time the Phoenicians began to migrate towards the "Upper Sea". According to their own traditions their racial cradle was on the northern shore of the Persian Gulf. So far as we know, they first made their appearance on the Mediterranean coast about 2000 B.C., where they subsequently entered into competition as sea traders with the mariners of ancient Crete. Apparently the pastoral nomads pressed northward through Mesopotamia and towards Canaan. As much is suggested by the Biblical narrative which deals with the wanderings of Terah, Abraham, and Lot. Taking with them their "flocks and herds and tents", and accompanied by wives, and families, and servants, they migrated, it is stated, from the Sumerian city of Ur northwards to Haran "and dwelt there". After Terah's death the tribe wandered through Canaan and kept moving southward, unable, it would seem, to settle permanently in any particular district. At length "there was a famine in the land"--an interesting reference to the "Dry Cycle"--and the wanderers found it necessary to take refuge for a time in Egypt. There they appear to have prospered. Indeed, so greatly did their flocks and herds increase that when they returned to Canaan they found that "the land was not able to bear them", although the conditions had improved somewhat during the interval. "There was", as a result, "strife between the herdmen of Abram's cattle and the herdmen of Lot's cattle."

It is evident that the area which these pastoral flocks were allowed to occupy must have been strictly circumscribed, for more than once it is stated significantly that "the Canaanite and the Perizzite dwelled in the land". The two kinsmen found it necessary, therefore, to part company. Lot elected to go towards Sodom in the plain of Jordan, and Abraham then moved towards the plain of Mamre, the Amorite, in the Hebron district.[272] With Mamre, and his brothers, Eshcol and Aner, the Hebrew patriarch formed a confederacy for mutual protection.[273]

Other tribes which were in Palestine at this period included the Horites, the Rephaims, the Zuzims, the Zamzummims, and the Emims. These were probably representatives of the older stocks. Like the Amorites, the Hittites or "children of Heth" were evidently "late comers", and conquerors. When Abraham purchased the burial cave at Hebron, the landowner with whom he had to deal was one Ephron, son of Zohar, the Hittite.[274] This illuminating statement agrees with what we know regarding Hittite expansion about 2000 B.C. The "Hatti" or "Khatti" had constituted military aristocracies throughout Syria and extended their influence by forming alliances. Many of their settlers were owners of estates, and traders who intermarried with the indigenous peoples and the Arabian invaders. As has been indicated (Chapter I), the large-nosed Armenoid section of the Hittite confederacy appear to have contributed to the racial blend known vaguely as the Semitic. Probably the particular group of Amorites with whom Abraham became associated had those pronounced Armenoid traits which can still be traced in representatives of the Hebrew people. Of special interest in this connection is Ezekiel's declaration regarding the ethnics of Jerusalem: "Thy birth and thy nativity", he said, "is of the land of Canaan; thy father was an Amorite, and thy mother an Hittite."[275]

It was during Abraham's residence in Hebron that the Western Land was raided by a confederacy of Babylonian and Elamite battle lords. The Biblical narrative which deals with this episode is of particular interest and has long engaged the attention of European scholars:

"And it came to pass in the days of Amraphel (Hammurabi) king of Shinar (Sumer), Arioch (Eri-aku or Warad-Sin) king of Ellasar (Larsa), Chedor-laomer (Kudur-Mabug) king of Elam, and Tidal (Tudhula) king of nations; that these made war with Bera king of Sodom, and with Birsha king of Gomorrah, Shinab king of Admah, and Shemeber king of Zeboiim, and the king of Bela, which is Zoar. All these joined together in the vale of Siddim, which is the salt sea. Twelve years they served Chedor-laomer, and in the thirteenth year they rebelled."[276] Apparently the Elamites had conquered part of Syria after entering southern Babylonia.

Chedor-laomer and his allies routed the Rephaims, the Zuzims, the Emims, the Horites and others, and having sacked Sodom and Gomorrah, carried away Lot and "his goods". On hearing of this disaster, Abraham collected a force of three hundred and eighteen men, all of whom were no doubt accustomed to guerrilla warfare, and delivered a night attack on the tail of the victorious army which was withdrawing through the area afterwards allotted to the Hebrew tribe of Dan. The surprise was complete; Abraham "smote" the enemy and "pursued them unto Hobah, which is on the left hand of Damascus. And he brought back all the goods, and also brought again his brother Lot, and his goods, and the women also, and the people."[277]

The identification of Hammurabi with Amraphel is now generally accepted. At first the guttural "h", which gives the English rendering "Khammurabi", presented a serious difficulty, but in time the form "Ammurapi" which appears on a tablet became known, and the conclusion was reached that the softer "h" sound was used and not the guttural. The "l" in the Biblical Amraphel has suggested "Ammurapi-ilu", "Hammurabi, the god", but it has been argued, on the other hand, that the change may have been due to western habitual phonetic conditions, or perhaps the slight alteration of an alphabetical sign. Chedor-laomer, identified with Kudur-Mabug, may have had several local names. One of his sons, either Warad-Sin or Rim-Sin, but probably the former, had his name Semitized as Eri-Aku, and this variant appears in inscriptions. "Tidal, king of nations", has not been identified. The suggestion that he was "King of the Gutium" remains in the realm of suggestion. Two late tablets have fragmentary inscriptions which read like legends with some historical basis. One mentions Kudur-lahmal (?Chedor-laomer) and the other gives the form "Kudur-lahgumal", and calls him "King of the land of Elam". Eri-Eaku (?Eri-aku) and Tudhula (?Tidal) are also mentioned. Attacks had been delivered on Babylon, and the city and its great temple E-sagila were flooded. It is asserted that the Elamites "exercised sovereignty in Babylon" for a period. These interesting tablets have been published by Professor Pinches.

The fact that the four leaders of the expedition to Canaan are all referred to as "kings" in the Biblical narrative need not present any difficulty. Princes and other subject rulers who governed under an overlord might be and, as a matter of fact, were referred to as kings. "I am a king, son of a king", an unidentified monarch recorded on one of the two tablets just referred to. Kudur-Mabug, King of Elam, during his lifetime called his son Warad-Sin (Eri-Aku = Arioch) "King of Larsa". It is of interest to note, too, in connection with the Biblical narrative regarding the invasion of Syria and Palestine, that he styled himself "overseer of the Amurru (Amorites)".

No traces have yet been found in Palestine of its conquest by the Elamites, nor have the excavators been able to substantiate the claim of Lugal-zaggizi of a previous age to have extended his empire to the shores of the Mediterranean. Any relics which these and other eastern conquerors may have left were possibly destroyed by the Egyptians and Hittites.

When Hammurabi came to the throne he had apparently to recognize the overlordship of the Elamite king or his royal son at Larsa. Although Sin-muballit had captured Isin, it was retaken, probably after the death of the Babylonian war-lord, by Rim-Sin, who succeeded his brother Warad-Sin, and for a time held sway in Lagash, Nippur, and Erech, as well as Larsa.

It was not until the thirty-first year of his reign that Hammurabi achieved ascendancy over his powerful rival. Having repulsed an Elamite raid, which was probably intended to destroy the growing power of Babylon, he "smote down Rim-Sin", whose power he reduced almost to vanishing point. For about twenty years afterwards that subdued monarch lived in comparative obscurity; then he led a force of allies against Hammurabi's son and successor, Samsu-iluna, who defeated him and put him to death, capturing, in the course of his campaign, the revolting cities of Emutbalum, Erech, and Isin. So was the last smouldering ember of Elamite power stamped out in Babylonia.

Hammurabi, statesman and general, is one of the great personalities of the ancient world. No more celebrated monarch ever held sway in Western Asia. He was proud of his military achievements, but preferred to be remembered as a servant of the gods, a just ruler, a father of his people, and "the shepherd that gives peace". In the epilogue to his code of laws he refers to "the burden of royalty", and declares that he "cut off the enemy" and "lorded it over the conquered" so that his subjects might have security. Indeed, his anxiety for their welfare was the most pronounced feature of his character. "I carried all the people of Sumer and Akkad in my bosom", he declared in his epilogue. "By my protection, I guided in peace its brothers. By my wisdom I provided for them." He set up his stele, on which the legal code was inscribed, so "that the great should not oppress the weak" and "to counsel the widow and orphan", and "to succour the injured.... The king that is gentle, king of the city, exalted am I."[278]

Hammurabi was no mere framer of laws but a practical administrator as well. He acted as supreme judge, and his subjects could appeal to him as the Romans could to Caesar. Nor was any case too trivial for his attention. The humblest man was assured that justice would be done if his grievance were laid before the king. Hammurabi was no respecter of persons, and treated alike all his subjects high and low. He punished corrupt judges, protected citizens against unjust governors, reviewed the transactions of moneylenders with determination to curb extortionate demands, and kept a watchful eye on the operations of taxgatherers.

There can be little doubt but that he won the hearts of his subjects, who enjoyed the blessings of just administration under a well-ordained political system. He must also have endeared himself to them as an exemplary exponent of religious tolerance. He respected the various deities in whom the various groups of people reposed their faith, restored despoiled temples, and re-endowed them with characteristic generosity. By so doing he not only afforded the pious full freedom and opportunity to perform their religious ordinances, but also promoted the material welfare of his subjects, for the temples were centres of culture and the priests were the teachers of the young. Excavators have discovered at Sippar traces of a school which dates from the Hammurabi Dynasty. Pupils learned to read and write, and received instruction in arithmetic and mensuration. They copied historical tablets, practised the art of composition, and studied geography.

Although there were many professional scribes, a not inconsiderable proportion of the people of both sexes were able to write private and business letters. Sons wrote from a distance to their fathers when in need of money then as now, and with the same air of undeserved martyrdom and subdued but confident appeal. One son indited a long complaint regarding the quality of the food he was given in his lodgings. Lovers appealed to forgetful ladies, showing great concern regarding their health. "Inform me how it fares with thee," one wrote four thousand years ago. "I went up to Babylon so that I might meet thee, but did not, and was much depressed. Let me know why thou didst go away so that I may be made glad. And do come hither. Ever have care of thy health, remembering me." Even begging-letter writers were not unknown. An ancient representative of this class once wrote to his employer from prison. He expressed astonishment that he had been arrested, and, having protested his innocence, he made touching appeal for little luxuries which were denied to him, adding that the last consignment which had been forwarded had never reached him.

Letters were often sent by messengers who were named, but there also appears to have been some sort of postal system. Letter carriers, however, could not have performed their duties without the assistance of beasts of burden. Papyri were not used as in Egypt. Nor was ink required. Babylonian letters were shapely little bricks resembling cushions. The angular alphabetical characters, bristling with thorn-like projections, were impressed with a wedge-shaped stylus on tablets of soft clay which were afterwards carefully baked in an oven. Then the letters were placed in baked clay envelopes, sealed and addressed, or wrapped in pieces of sacking transfixed by seals. If the ancient people had a festive season which was regarded, like the European Yuletide or the Indian Durga fortnight, as an occasion suitable for the general exchange of expressions of goodwill, the Babylonian streets and highways must have been greatly congested by the postal traffic, while muscular postmen worked overtime distributing the contents of heavy and bulky letter sacks. Door to door deliveries would certainly have presented difficulties. Wood being dear, everyone could not afford doors, and some houses were entered by stairways leading to the flat and partly open roofs.

King Hammurabi had to deal daily with a voluminous correspondence. He received reports from governors in all parts of his realm, legal documents containing appeals, and private communications from relatives and others. He paid minute attention to details, and was probably one of the busiest men in Babylonia. Every day while at home, after worshipping Merodach at E-sagila, he dictated letters to his scribes, gave audiences to officials, heard legal appeals and issued interlocutors, and dealt with the reports regarding his private estates. He looks a typical man of affairs in sculptured representations-- shrewd, resolute, and unassuming, feeling "the burden of royalty", but ever ready and well qualified to discharge his duties with thoroughness and insight. His grasp of detail was equalled only by his power to conceive of great enterprises which appealed to his imagination. It was a work of genius on his part to weld together that great empire of miscellaneous states extending from southern Babylonia to Assyria, and from the borders of Elam to the Mediterranean coast, by a universal legal Code which secured tranquillity and equal rights to all, promoted business, and set before his subjects the ideals of right thinking and right living.

Hammurabi recognized that conquest was of little avail unless followed by the establishment of a just and well-arranged political system, and the inauguration of practical measures to secure the domestic, industrial, and commercial welfare of the people as a whole. He engaged himself greatly, therefore, in developing the natural resources of each particular district. The network of irrigating canals was extended in the homeland so that agriculture might prosper: these canals also promoted trade, for they were utilized for travelling by boat and for the distribution of commodities. As a result of his activities Babylon became not only the administrative, but also the commercial centre of his Empire--the London of Western Asia--and it enjoyed a spell of prosperity which was never surpassed in subsequent times. Yet it never lost its pre-eminent position despite the attempts of rival states, jealous of its glory and influence, to suspend its activities. It had been too firmly established during the Hammurabi Age, which was the Golden Age of Babylonia, as the heartlike distributor and controller of business life through a vast network of veins and arteries, to be displaced by any other Mesopotamian city to pleasure even a mighty monarch. For two thousand years, from the time of Hammurabi until the dawn of the Christian era, the city of Babylon remained amidst many political changes the metropolis of Western Asiatic commerce and culture, and none was more eloquent in its praises than the scholarly pilgrim from Greece who wondered at its magnificence and reverenced its antiquities.

Hammurabi's reign was long as it was prosperous. There is no general agreement as to when he ascended the throne--some say in 2123 B.C., others hold that it was after 2000 B.C.--but it is certain that he presided over the destinies of Babylon for the long period of forty-three years.

There are interesting references to the military successes of his reign in the prologue to the legal Code. It is related that when he "avenged Larsa", the seat of Rim-Sin, he restored there the temple of the sun god. Other temples were built up at various ancient centres, so that these cultural organizations might contribute to the welfare of the localities over which they held sway. At Nippur he thus honoured Enlil, at Eridu the god Ea, at Ur the god Sin, at Erech the god Anu and the goddess Nana (Ishtar), at Kish the god Zamama and the goddess Ma-ma, at Cuthah the god Nergal, at Lagash the god Nin-Girsu, while at Adab and Akkad, "celebrated for its wide squares", and other centres he carried out religious and public works. In Assyria he restored the colossus of Ashur, which had evidently been carried away by a conqueror, and he developed the canal system of Nineveh.

Apparently Lagash and Adab had not been completely deserted during his reign, although their ruins have not yielded evidence that they flourished after their fall during the long struggle with the aggressive and plundering Elamites.

Hammurabi referred to himself in the Prologue as "a king who commanded obedience in all the four quarters". He was the sort of benevolent despot whom Carlyle on one occasion clamoured vainly for--not an Oriental despot in the commonly accepted sense of the term. As a German writer puts it, his despotism was a form of Patriarchal Absolutism. "When Marduk (Merodach)", as the great king recorded, "brought me to direct all people, and commissioned me to give judgment, I laid down justice and right in the provinces, I made all flesh to prosper."[279] That was the keynote of his long life; he regarded himself as the earthly representative of the Ruler of all--Merodach, "the lord god of right", who carried out the decrees of Anu, the sky god of Destiny.

The next king, Samsu-iluna, reigned nearly as long as his illustrious father, and similarly lived a strenuous and pious life. Soon after he came to the throne the forces of disorder were let loose, but, as has been stated, he crushed and slew his most formidable opponent, Rim-Sin, the Elamite king, who had gathered together an army of allies. During his reign a Kassite invasion was repulsed. The earliest Kassites, a people of uncertain racial affinities, began to settle in the land during Hammurabi's lifetime. Some writers connect them with the Hittites, and others with the Iranians, vaguely termed as Indo-European or Indo-Germanic folk. Ethnologists as a rule regard them as identical with the Cossaei, whom the Greeks found settled between Babylon and Media, east of the Tigris and north of Elam. The Hittites came south as raiders about a century later. It is possible that the invading Kassites had overrun Elam and composed part of Rim-Sin's army. After settled conditions were secured many of them remained in Babylonia, where they engaged like their pioneers in agricultural pursuits. No doubt they were welcomed in that capacity, for owing to the continuous spread of culture and the development of commerce, rural labour had become scarce and dear. Farmers had a long-standing complaint, "The harvest truly is plenteous, but the labourers are few".[280] "Despite the existence of slaves, who were for the most part domestic servants, there was", writes Mr. Johns, "considerable demand for free labour in ancient Babylonia. This is clear from the large number of contracts relating to hire which have come down to us.... As a rule, the man was hired for the harvest and was free directly after. But there are many examples in which the term of service was different--one month, half a year, or a whole year.... Harvest labour was probably far dearer than any other, because of its importance, the skill and exertion demanded, and the fact that so many were seeking for it at once." When a farm worker was engaged he received a shekel for "earnest money" or arles, and was penalized for non-appearance or late arrival.[281]

So great was the political upheaval caused by Rim-Sin and his allies and imitators in southern Babylonia, that it was not until the seventeenth year of his reign that Samsu-iluna had recaptured Erech and Ur and restored their walls. Among other cities which had to be chastised was ancient Akkad, where a rival monarch endeavoured to establish himself. Several years were afterwards spent in building new fortifications, setting up memorials in temples, and cutting and clearing canals. On more than one occasion during the latter part of his reign he had to deal with aggressive bands of Amorites.

The greatest danger to the Empire, however, was threatened by a new kingdom which had been formed in Bit-Jakin, a part of Sealand which was afterwards controlled by the mysterious Chaldeans. Here may have collected evicted and rebel bands of Elamites and Sumerians and various "gentlemen of fortune" who were opposed to the Hammurabi regime. After the fall of Rim-Sin it became powerful under a king called Ilu-ma-ilu. Samsu-iluna conducted at least two campaigns against his rival, but without much success. Indeed, he was in the end compelled to retreat with considerable loss owing to the difficult character of that marshy country.

Abeshu, the next Babylonian king, endeavoured to shatter the cause of the Sealanders, and made it possible for himself to strike at them by damming up the Tigris canal. He achieved a victory, but the wily Ilu-ma-ilu eluded him, and after a reign of sixty years was succeeded by his son, Kiannib. The Sealand Dynasty, of which little is known, lasted for over three and a half centuries, and certain of its later monarchs were able to extend their sway over part of Babylonia, but its power was strictly circumscribed so long as Hammurabi's descendants held sway.

During Abeshu's reign of twenty-eight years, of which but scanty records survive, he appears to have proved an able statesman and general. He founded a new city called Lukhaia, and appears to have repulsed a Kassite raid.

His son, Ammiditana, who succeeded him, apparently inherited a prosperous and well-organized Empire, for during the first fifteen years of his reign he attended chiefly to the adornment of temples and other pious undertakings. He was a patron of the arts with archaeological leanings, and displayed traits which suggest that he inclined, like Sumu-la-ilu, to ancestor worship. Entemena, the pious patesi of Lagash, whose memory is associated with the famous silver vase decorated with the lion-headed eagle form of Nin-Girsu, had been raised to the dignity of a god, and Ammiditana caused his statue to be erected so that offerings might be made to it. He set up several images of himself also, and celebrated the centenary of the accession to the throne of his grandfather, Samsu-iluna, "the warrior lord", by unveiling his statue with much ceremony at Kish. About the middle of his reign he put down a Sumerian rising, and towards its close had to capture a city which is believed to be Isin, but the reference is too obscure to indicate what political significance attached to this incident. His son, Ammizaduga, reigned for over twenty years quite peacefully so far as is known, and was succeeded by Samsuditana, whose rule extended over a quarter of a century. Like Ammiditana, these two monarchs set up images of themselves as well as of the gods, so that they might be worshipped, no doubt. They also promoted the interests of agriculture and commerce, and incidentally increased the revenue from taxation by paying much attention to the canals and extending the cultivatable areas.

But the days of the brilliant Hammurabi Dynasty were drawing to a close. It endured for about a century longer than the Twelfth Dynasty of Egypt, which came to an end, according to the Berlin calculations, in 1788 B.C. Apparently some of the Hammurabi and Amenemhet kings were contemporaries, but there is no evidence that they came into direct touch with one another. It was not until at about two centuries after Hammurabi's day that Egypt first invaded Syria, with which, however, it had for a long period previously conducted a brisk trade. Evidently the influence of the Hittites and their Amoritic allies predominated between Mesopotamia and the Delta frontier of Egypt, and it is significant to find in this connection that the "Khatti" or "Hatti" were referred to for the first time in Egypt during the Twelfth Dynasty, and in Babylonia during the Hammurabi Dynasty, sometime shortly before or after 2000 B.C. About 1800 B.C. a Hittite raid resulted in the overthrow of the last king of the Hammurabi family at Babylon. The Hyksos invasion of Egypt took place after 1788 B.C.

[272] *Genesis*, xii and xiii.

[273] *Genesis,* xiv, 13.

[274] *Ibid.,* xxiii.

[275] *Ezekiel,* xvi, 3.

[276] *Genesis,* xiv, 1-4.

[277] *Ibid.,* 5-24.

[278] *Babylonian and Assyrian Laws, Contracts, and Letters,* C.H.W. Johns, pp. 392 *et seq.*

[279] Translation by Johns in *Babylonian and Assyrian Laws, Contracts, and Letters,* pp. 390 *et seq.*

[280] *Matthew,* ix, 37.

[281] Johns's *Babylonian and Assyrian Laws, &c.,* pp. 371-2.

Chapter XII. Rise of the Hittites, Mitannians, Kassites, Hyksos, and Assyrians

Abstract

The War God of Mountaineers--Antiquity of Hittite Civilization--Prehistoric Movements of "Broad Heads"--Evidence of Babylon and Egypt--Hittites and Mongolians--Biblical References to Hittites in Canaan--Jacob's Mother and her Daughters-in-law--Great Father and Great Mother Cults--History in Mythology--The Kingdom of Mitanni--Its Aryan Aristocracy--The Hyksos Problem--The Horse in Warfare--Hittites and Mitannians--Kassites and Mitannians--Hyksos Empire in Asia--Kassites overthrow Sealand Dynasty--Egyptian Campaigns in Syria--Assyria in the Making--Ethnics of Genesis--Nimrod as Merodach--Early Conquerors of Assyria--Mitannian Overlords--Tell-el-Amarna Letters--Fall of Mitanni--Rise of Hittite and Assyrian Empires--Egypt in Eclipse--Assyrian and Babylonian Rivalries.

When the Hammurabi Dynasty, like the Twelfth Dynasty of Egypt, is found to be suffering languid decline, the gaps in the dulled historical records are filled with the echoes of the thunder god, whose hammer beating resounds among the northern mountains. As this deity comes each year in Western Asia when vegetation has withered and after fruits have dropped from trees, bringing tempests and black rainclouds to issue in a new season of growth and fresh activity, so he descended from the hills in the second millennium before the Christian era as the battle lord of invaders and the stormy herald of a new age which was to dawn upon the ancient world.

He was the war god of the Hittites as well as of the northern Amorites, the Mitannians, and the Kassites; and he led the Aryans from the Iranian steppes towards the verdurous valley of the Punjab. His worshippers engraved his image with grateful hands on the beetling cliffs of Cappadocian chasms in Asia Minor, where his sway was steadfast and pre-eminent for long centuries. In one locality he appears mounted on a bull wearing a fringed and belted tunic with short sleeves, a conical helmet, and upturned shoes, while he grasps in one hand the lightning symbol, and in the other a triangular bow resting on his right shoulder. In another locality he is the bringer of grapes and barley sheaves. But his most familiar form is the bearded and thick-set mountaineer, armed with a ponderous thunder hammer, a flashing trident, and a long two-edged sword with a hemispherical knob on the hilt, which dangles from his belt, while an antelope or goat wearing a pointed tiara prances beside him. This deity is identical with bluff, impetuous Thor of northern Europe, Indra of the Himalayas, Tarku of Phrygia, and Teshup or Teshub of Armenia and northern Mesopotamia, Sandan, the Hercules of Cilicia, Adad or Hadad of Amurru and Assyria, and Ramman, who at an early period penetrated Akkad and Sumer in various forms. His Hittite name is uncertain, but in the time of Rameses II he was identified with Sutekh (Set). He passed into southern Europe as Zeus, and became "the lord" of the deities of the Aegean and Crete.

The Hittites who entered Babylon about 1800 B.C., and overthrew the last king of the Hammurabi Dynasty, may have been plundering raiders, like the European Gauls of a later age, or a well-organized force of a strong, consolidated power, which endured for a period of uncertain duration. They were probably the latter, for although they carried off Merodach and Zerpanitum, these idols were not thrust into the melting pot, but retained apparently for political reasons.

These early Hittites are "a people of the mist". More than once in ancient history casual reference is made to them; but on most of these occasions they soon vanish suddenly behind their northern mountains. The explanation appears to be that at various periods great leaders arose who were able to weld together the various tribes, and make their presence felt in Western Asia. But when once the organization broke down, either on account of internal rivalries or the influence of an outside power, they lapsed back again into a state of political insignificance in the affairs of the ancient world. It is possible that about 1800 B.C. the Hittite confederacy was controlled by an ambitious king who had dreams of a great empire, and was accordingly pursuing a career of conquest.

Judging from what we know of the northern worshippers of the hammer god in later times, it would appear that when they were referred to as the Hatti or Khatti, the tribe of that name was the dominating power in Asia Minor and north Syria. The Hatti are usually identified with the broad-headed mountaineers of Alpine or Armenoid type--the ancestors of the modern Armenians. Their ancient capital was at Boghaz-Köi, the site of Pteria, which was destroyed, according to the Greeks, by Croesus, the last King of Lydia, in the sixth century B.C. It was strongly situated in an excellent pastoral district on the high, breezy plateau of Cappadocia, surrounded by high mountains, and approached through narrow river gorges, which in winter were blocked with snow.

Hittite civilization was of great antiquity. Excavations which have been conducted at an undisturbed artificial mound at Sakje-Geuzi have revealed evidences of a continuous culture which began to flourish before 3000 B.C.[282] In one of the lower layers occurred that particular type of Neolithic yellow-painted pottery, with black geometric designs, which resembles other specimens of painted fabrics found in Turkestan by the Pumpelly expedition; in Susa, the capital of Elam, and its vicinity, by De Morgan; in the Balkan peninsula by Schliemann; in a First Dynasty tomb at Abydos in Egypt by Petrie; and in the late Neolithic and early Bronze Age (Minoan) strata of Crete by Evans. It may be that these interesting relics were connected with the prehistoric drift westward of the broad-headed pastoral peoples who ultimately formed the Hittite military aristocracy.

According to Professor Elliot Smith, broad-headed aliens from Asia Minor first reached Egypt at the dawn of history. There they blended with the indigenous tribes of the Mediterranean or Brown Race. A mesocephalic skull then became common. It is referred to as the Giza type, and has been traced by Professor Elliot Smith from Egypt to the Punjab, but not farther into India.[283]

During the early dynasties this skull with alien traits was confined chiefly to the Delta region and the vicinity of Memphis, the city of the pyramid builders. It is not improbable that the Memphite god Ptah may have been introduced into Egypt by the invading broad heads. This deity is a world artisan like Indra, and is similarly associated with dwarfish artisans; he hammers out the copper sky, and therefore links with the various thunder gods--Tarku, Teshup, Adad, Ramman, &c, of the Asian mountaineers. Thunderstorms were of too rare occurrence in Egypt to be connected with the food supply, which has always depended on the river Nile. Ptah's purely Egyptian characteristics appear to have been acquired after fusion with Osiris-Seb, the Nilotic gods of inundation, earth, and vegetation. The ancient god Set (Sutekh), who became a demon, and was ultimately re-exalted as a great deity during the Nineteenth Dynasty, may also have had some connection with the prehistoric Hatti.

Professor Elliot Smith, who has found alien traits in the mummies of the Rameses kings, is convinced that the broad-headed folks who entered Europe by way of Asia Minor, and Egypt through the Delta, at the close of the Neolithic Age, represent "two streams of the same Asiatic folk".[284] The opinion of such an authority cannot be lightly set aside.

The earliest Egyptian reference to the Kheta, as the Hittites were called, was made in the reign of the first Amenemhet of the Twelfth Dynasty, who began to reign about 2000 B.C. Some authorities, including Maspero,[285] are of opinion that the allusion to the Hatti which is found in the Babylonian *Book of Omens* belongs to the earlier age of Sargon of Akkad and Naram-Sin, but Sayce favours the age of Hammurabi. Others would connect the Gutium, or men of Kutu, with the Kheta or Hatti. Sayce has expressed the opinion that the Biblical Tidal, identified with Tudkhul or Tudhula, "king of nations", the ally of Arioch, Amraphel, and Chedor-laomer, was a Hittite king, the "nations" being the confederacy of Asia Minor tribes controlled by the Hatti. "In the fragments of the Babylonian story of Chedor-laomer published by Dr. Pinches", says Professor Sayce, "the name of Tid^{c}al is written Tudkhul, and he is described as King of the *Umman Manda*, or Nations of the North, of which the Hebrew *Goyyim* is a literal translation. Now the name is Hittite. In the account of the campaign of Rameses II against the Hittites it appears as Tid^{c}al, and one of the Hittite kings of Boghaz-Köi bears the same name, which is written as Dud-khaliya in cuneiform.[286]

One of the racial types among the Hittites wore pigtails. These head adornments appear on figures in certain Cappadocian sculptures and on Hittite warriors in the pictorial records of a north Syrian campaign of Rameses II at Thebes. It is suggestive, therefore, to find that on the stele of Naram-Sin of Akkad, the mountaineers who are conquered by that battle lord wear pigtails also. Their split robes are unlike the short fringed tunics of the Hittite gods, but resemble the long split mantles worn over their tunics by high dignitaries like King Tarku-dimme, who figures on a famous silver boss of an ancient Hittite dagger. Naram-Sin inherited the Empire of Sargon of Akkad, which extended to the Mediterranean Sea. If his enemies were not natives of Cappadocia, they may have been the congeners of the Hittite pigtailed type in another wooded and mountainous country.

It has been suggested that these wearers of pigtails were Mongolians. But although high cheek bones and oblique eyes occurred in ancient times, and still occur, in parts of Asia Minor, suggesting occasional Mongolian admixture with Ural-Altaic broad heads, the Hittite pigtailed warriors must not be confused with the true small-nosed Mongols of north-eastern Asia. The Egyptian sculptors depicted them with long and prominent noses, which emphasize their strong Armenoid affinities.

Other tribes in the Hittite confederacy included the representatives of the earliest settlers from North Africa of Mediterranean racial stock. These have been identified with the Canaanites, and especially the agriculturists among them, for the Palestinian Hittites are also referred to as Canaanites in the Bible, and in one particular connection under circumstances which afford an interesting glimpse of domestic life in those far-off times. When Esau, Isaac's eldest son, was forty years of age, "he took to wife Judith the daughter of Beeri the Hittite, and Bashemath the daughter of Elon the Hittite"[287]. Apparently the Hittite ladies considered themselves to be of higher caste than the indigenous peoples and the settlers from other countries, for when Ezekiel declared that the mother of Jerusalem was a Hittite he said: "Thou art thy mother's daughter, that lotheth her husband and her children."[288] Esau's marriage was "a grief of mind unto Isaac and to Rebekah".[287] The Hebrew mother seems to have entertained fears that her favourite son Jacob would fall a victim to the allurements of other representatives of the same stock as her superior and troublesome daughters-in-law, for she said to Isaac: "I am weary of my life because of the daughters of Heth; if Jacob take a wife of the daughters of Heth, such as these which are of the daughters of the land, what good shall my life do me?"[289] Isaac sent for Jacob, "and charged him, and said unto him, Thou shalt not take a wife of the daughters of Canaan. Arise, go to Padan-aram, to the house of Bethuel, thy mother's father; and take thee a wife from thence of the daughters of Laban, thy mother's brother."[290] From these quotations two obvious deductions may be drawn: the Hebrews regarded the Hittites "of the land" as one with the Canaanites, the stocks having probably been so well fused, and the worried Rebekah had the choosing of Jacob's wife or wives from among her own relations in Mesopotamia who were of Sumerian stock and kindred of Abraham.[291] It is not surprising to find traces of Sumerian pride among the descendants of the evicted citizens of ancient Ur, especially when brought into association with the pretentious Hittites.

Evidence of racial blending in Asia Minor is also afforded by Hittite mythology. In the fertile agricultural valleys and round the shores of that great Eur-Asian "land bridge" the indigenous stock was also of the Mediterranean race, as Sergi and other ethnologists have demonstrated. The Great Mother goddess was worshipped from the earliest times, and she bore various local names. At Comana in Pontus she was known to the Greeks as Ma, a name which may have been as old as that of the Sumerian Mama (the creatrix), or Mamitum (goddess of destiny); in Armenia she was Anaitis; in Cilicia she was Ate ('Atheh of Tarsus); while in Phrygia she was best known as Cybele, mother of Attis, who links with Ishtar as mother and wife of Tammuz, Aphrodite as mother and wife of Adonis, and Isis as mother and wife of Osiris. The Great Mother was in Phoenicia called Astarte; she was a form of Ishtar, and identical with the Biblical Ashtoreth. In the Syrian city of Hierapolis she bore the name of Atargatis, which Meyer, with whom Frazer agrees, considers to be the Greek rendering of the Aramaic 'Athar-'Atheh--the god 'Athar and the goddess 'Atheh. Like the "bearded Aphrodite", Atargatis may have been regarded as a bisexual deity. Some of the specialized mother goddesses, whose outstanding attributes reflected the history and politics of the states they represented, were imported into Egypt--the land of ancient mother deities--during the Empire period, by the half-foreign Rameses kings; these included the voluptuous Kadesh and the warlike Anthat. In every district colonized by the early representatives of the Mediterranean race, the goddess cult came into prominence, and the gods and the people were reputed to be descendants of the great Creatrix. This rule obtained as far distant as Ireland, where the Danann folk and the Danann gods were the children of the goddess Danu.

Among the Hatti proper--that is, the broad-headed military aristocracy--the chief deity of the pantheon was the Great Father, the creator, "the lord of Heaven", the Baal. As Sutekh, Tarku, Adad, or Ramman, he was the god of thunder, rain, fertility, and war, and he ultimately acquired solar attributes. A famous rock sculpture at Boghaz-Köi depicts a mythological scene which is believed to represent the Spring marriage of the Great Father and the Great Mother, suggesting a local fusion of beliefs which resulted from the union of tribes of the god cult with tribes of the goddess cult. So long as the Hatti tribe remained the predominant partner in the Hittite confederacy, the supremacy was assured of the Great Father who symbolized their sway. But when, in the process of time, the power of the Hatti declined, their chief god "fell... from his predominant place in the religion of the interior", writes Dr. Garstang. "But the Great Mother lived on, being the goddess of the land."[292]

In addition to the Hittite confederacy of Asia Minor and North Syria, another great power arose in northern Mesopotamia. This was the Mitanni Kingdom. Little is known regarding it, except what is derived from indirect sources. Winckler believes that it was first established by early "waves" of Hatti people who migrated from the east.

The Hittite connection is based chiefly on the following evidence. One of the gods of the Mitanni rulers was Teshup, who is identical with Tarku, the Thor of Asia Minor. The raiders who in 1800 B.C. entered Babylon, set fire to E-sagila, and carried off Merodach and his consort Zerpanitum, were called the Hatti. The images of these deities were afterwards obtained from Khani (Mitanni).

At a later period, when we come to know more about Mitanni from the letters of one of its kings to two Egyptian Pharaohs, and the Winckler tablets from Bog-haz-Köi, it is found that its military aristocracy spoke an Indo-European language, as is shown by the names of their kings--Saushatar, Artatama, Sutarna, Artashshumara, Tushratta, and Mattiuza. They worshipped the following deities:

Mi-it-ra, Uru-w-na, In-da-ra, and Na-sa-at-ti-ia--

Mitra, Varuna, Indra, and Nasatyau (the "Twin Aswins" = Castor and Pollux)-- whose names have been deciphered by Winckler. These gods were also imported into India by the Vedic Aryans. The Mitanni tribe (the military aristocracy probably) was called "Kharri", and some philologists are of opinion that it is identical with "Arya", which was "the normal designation in Vedic literature from the Rigveda onwards of an Aryan of the three upper classes".[293] Mitanni signifies "the river lands", and the descendants of its inhabitants, who lived in Cappadocia, were called by the Greeks "Mattienoi". "They are possibly", says Dr. Haddon, "the ancestors of the modern Kurds",[294] a conspicuously long-headed people, proverbial, like the ancient Aryo-Indians and the Gauls, for their hospitality and their raiding propensities.

It would appear that the Mitannian invasion of northern Mesopotamia and the Aryan invasion of India represented two streams of diverging migrations from a common cultural centre, and that the separate groups of wanderers mingled with other stocks with whom they came into contact. Tribes of Aryan speech were associated with the Kassite invaders of Babylon, who took possession of northern Babylonia soon after the disastrous Hittite raid. It is believed that they came from the east through the highlands of Elam.

For a period, the dating of which is uncertain, the Mitannians were overlords of part of Assyria, including Nineveh and even Asshur, as well as the district called "Musri" by the Assyrians, and part of Cappadocia. They also occupied the cities of Harran and Kadesh. Probably they owed their great military successes to their cavalry. The horse became common in Babylon during the Kassite Dynasty, which followed the Hammurabi, and was there called "the ass of the east", a name which suggests whence the Kassites and Mitannians came.

The westward movement of the Mitannians in the second millennium B.C. may have been in progress prior to the Kassite conquest of Babylon and the Hyksos invasion of Egypt. Their relations in Mesopotamia and Syria with the Hittites and the Amorites are obscure. Perhaps they were for a time the overlords of the Hittites. At any rate it is of interest to note that when Thothmes III struck at the last Hyksos stronghold during his long Syrian campaign of about twenty years' duration, his operations were directly against Kadesh on the Orontes, which was then held by his fierce enemies the Mitannians of Naharina.[295]

During the Hyksos Age the horse was introduced into Egypt. Indeed the Hyksos conquest was probably due to the use of the horse, which was domesticated, as the Pumpelly expedition has ascertained, at a remote period in Turkestan, whence it may have been obtained by the horse-sacrificing Aryo-Indians and the horse-sacrificing ancestors of the Siberian Buriats.

If the Mitanni rulers were not overlords of the Hittites about 1800 B.C., the two peoples may have been military allies of the Kassites. Some writers suggest, indeed, that the Kassites came from Mitanni. Another view is that the Mitannians were the Aryan allies of the Kassites who entered Babylon from the Elamite highlands, and that they afterwards conquered Mesopotamia and part of Cappadocia prior to the Hyksos conquest of Egypt. A third solution of the problem is that the Aryan rulers of the Mitannian Hittites were the overlords of northern Babylonia, which they included in their Mesopotamian empire for a century before the Kassites achieved political supremacy in the Tigro-Euphrates valley, and that they were also the leaders of the Hyksos invasion of Egypt, which they accomplished with the assistance of their Hittite and Amoritic allies.

The first Kassite king of Babylonia of whom we have knowledge was Gandash. He adopted the old Akkadian title, "king of the four quarters", as well as the title "king of Sumer and Akkad", first used by the rulers of the Dynasty of Ur. Nippur appears to have been selected by Gandash as his capital, which suggests that his war and storm god, Shuqamuna, was identified with Bel Enlil, who as a "world giant" has much in common with the northern hammer gods. After reigning for sixteen years, Gandash was succeeded by his son, Agum the Great, who sat on the throne for twenty-two years. The great-grandson of Agum the Great was Agum II, and not until his reign were the statues of Merodach and his consort Zerpanitum brought back to the city of Babylon. This monarch recorded that, in response to the oracle of Shamash, the sun god, he sent to the distant land of Khani (Mitanni) for the great deity and his consort. Babylon would therefore appear to have been deprived of Merodach for about two centuries. The Hittite-Mitanni raid is dated about 1800 B.C., and the rise of Gandash, the Kassite, about 1700 B.C. At least a century elapsed between the reigns of Gandash and Agum II. These calculations do not coincide, it will be noted, with the statement in a Babylonian hymn, that Merodach remained in the land of the Hatti for twenty-four years, which, however, may be either a priestly fiction or a reference to a later conquest. The period which followed the fall of the Hammurabi Dynasty of Babylonia is as obscure as the Hyksos Age of Egypt.

Agum II, the Kassite king, does not state whether or not he waged war against Mitanni to recover Babylon's god Merodach. If, however, he was an ally of the Mitanni ruler, the transference of the deity may have been an ordinary diplomatic transaction. The possibility may also be suggested that the Hittites of Mitanni were not displaced by the Aryan military aristocracy until after the Kassites were firmly established in northern Babylonia between 1700 B.C. and 1600 B.C. This may account for the statements that Merodach was carried off by the Hatti and returned from the land of Khani.

The evidence afforded by Egypt is suggestive in this connection. There was a second Hyksos Dynasty in that country. The later rulers became "Egyptianized" as the Kassites became "Babylonianized", but they were all referred to by the exclusive and sullen-Egyptians as "barbarians" and "Asiatics". They recognized the sun god of Heliopolis, but were also concerned in promoting the worship of Sutekh, a deity of sky and thunder, with solar attributes, whom Rameses II identified with the "Baal" of the Hittites. The Mitannians, as has been stated, recognized a Baal called Teshup, who was identical with Tarku of the Western Hittites and with their own tribal Indra also. One of the Hyksos kings, named Ian or Khian, the Ianias of Manetho, was either an overlord or the ally of an overlord, who swayed a great empire in Asia. His name has been deciphered on relics found as far apart as Knossos in Crete and Baghdad on the Tigris, which at the time was situated within the area of Kassite control. Apparently peaceful conditions prevailed during his reign over a wide extent of Asia and trade was brisk between far-distant centres of civilization. The very term Hyksos is suggestive in this connection. According to Breasted it signifies "rulers of countries", which compares with the Biblical "Tidal king of nations", whom Sayce, as has been indicated, regards as a Hittite monarch. When the Hittite hieroglyphics have been read and Mesopotamia thoroughly explored, light may be thrown on the relations of the Mitannians, the Hittites, the Hyksos, and the Kassites between 1800 B.C. and 1500 B.C. It is evident that a fascinating volume of ancient history has yet to be written.

The Kassites formed the military aristocracy of Babylonia, which was called Karduniash, for nearly six centuries. Agum II was the first of their kings who became thoroughly Babylonianized, and although he still gave recognition to Shuqamuna, the Kassite god of battle, he re-exalted Merodach, whose statue he had taken back from "Khani", and decorated E-sagila with gifts of gold, jewels, rare woods, frescoes, and pictorial tiles; he also re-endowed the priesthood. During the reign of his successor, Burnaburiash I, the Dynasty of Sealand came to an end.

Little is known regarding the relations between Elam and Babylonia during the Kassite period. If the Kassite invaders crossed the Tigris soon after the raid of the Mitannian Hittites they must have previously overrun a great part of Elam, but strongly situated Susa may have for a time withstood their attacks. At first the Kassites held northern Babylonia only, while the ancient Sumerian area was dominated by the Sealand power, which had gradually regained strength during the closing years of the Hammurabi Dynasty. No doubt many northern Babylonian refugees reinforced its army.

The Elamites, or perhaps the Kassites of Elam, appear to have made frequent attacks on southern Babylonia. At length Ea-gamil, king of Sealand, invaded Elam with purpose, no doubt, to shatter the power of his restless enemies. He was either met there, however, by an army from Babylon, or his country was invaded during his absence. Prince Ulamburiash, son of Burnaburiash I, defeated Ea-gamil and brought to an end the Sealand Dynasty which had been founded by Ilu-ma-ilu, the contemporary and enemy of Samsu-la-ilu, son of Hammurabi. Ulamburiash is referred to on a mace-head which was discovered at Babylon as "king of

Sealand", and he probably succeeded his father at the capital. The whole of Babylonia thus came under Kassite sway.

Agum III, a grandson of Ulamburiash, found it necessary, however, to invade Sealand, which must therefore have revolted. It was probably a centre of discontent during the whole period of Kassite ascendancy.

After a long obscure interval we reach the period when the Hyksos power was broken in Egypt, that is, after 1580 B.C. The great Western Asiatic kingdoms at the time were the Hittite, the Mitannian, the Assyrian, and the Babylonian (Kassite). Between 1557 B.C. and 1501 B.C. Thothmes I of Egypt was asserting his sway over part of Syria. Many years elapsed, however, before Thothmes III, who died in 1447 B.C., established firmly, after waging a long war of conquest, the supremacy of Egypt between the Euphrates and the Mediterranean coast as far north as the borders of Asia Minor.

"At this period", as Professor Flinders Petrie emphasizes, "the civilization of Syria was equal or superior to that of Egypt." Not only was there in the cities "luxury beyond that of the Egyptians", but also "technical work which could teach them". The Syrian soldiers had suits of scale armour, which afterwards were manufactured in Egypt, and they had chariots adorned with gold and silver and highly decorated, which were greatly prized by the Egyptians when they captured them, and reserved for royalty. "In the rich wealth of gold and silver vases", obtained from captured cities by the Nilotic warriors, "we see also", adds Petrie, "the sign of a people who were their (the Egyptians') equals, if not their superiors in taste and skill."[296] It is not to be wondered at, therefore, when the Pharaohs received tribute from Syria that they preferred it to be carried into Egypt by skilled workmen. "The keenness with which the Egyptians record all the beautiful and luxurious products of the Syrians shows that the workmen would probably be more in demand than other kinds or slave tribute."[297]

One of the monarchs with whom Thothmes III corresponded was the king of Assyria. The enemies of Egypt in northern Mesopotamia were the Hittites and Mitannians, and their allies, and these were also the enemies of Assyria. But to enable us to deal with the new situation which was created by Egypt in Mesopotamia, it is necessary in the first place to trace the rise of Assyria, which was destined to become for a period the dominating power in Western Asia, and ultimately in the Nile valley also.

The Assyrian group of cities grew up on the banks of the Tigris to the north of Babylonia, the mother country. The following Biblical references regarding the origins of the two states are of special interest:--

Now these are the generations of the sons of Noah: Shem, Ham, and Japheth.... The sons of Ham: Cush, and Mizraim, and Phut, and Canaan.... And Cush begat Nimrod; he began to be a mighty one in the earth. He was a mighty hunter before the Lord; wherefore it is said, Even as Nimrod the mighty hunter before the Lord. And the beginning of his kingdom was Babel, and Erech, and Accad, and Calneh, in the land of Shinar. Out of that land went forth Asshur and builded Nineveh, and the city Rehoboth, and Calah, and Resen between Nineveh and Calah: the same is a great city. The children of Shem: Elam and Asshur ... (*Genesis*, x, 1-22). The land of Assyria ... and the land of Nimrod in the entrances thereof (*Micah*, v, 6).

It will be observed that the Sumero-Babylonians are Cushites or Hamites, and therefore regarded as racially akin to the proto-Egyptians of the Mediterranean race--an interesting confirmation of recent ethnological conclusions.

Nimrod, the king of Babel (Babylon), in Shinar (Sumer), was, it would appear, a deified monarch who became ultimately identified with the national god of Babylonia. Professor Pinches has shown[298] that his name is a rendering of that of Merodach. In Sumerian Merodach was called Amaruduk or Amarudu, and in the Assyro-Babylonian language Marduk. By a process familiar to philologists the suffix "uk" was dropped and the rendering became Marad. The Hebrews added "ni" = "ni-marad", assimilating the name "to a certain extent to the 'niphal forms' of the Hebrew verbs and making a change", says Pinches, "in conformity with the genius of the Hebrew language".

Asshur, who went out of Nimrod's country to build Nineveh, was a son of Shem-- a Semite, and so far as is known it was after the Semites achieved political supremacy in Akkad that the Assyrian colonies were formed. Asshur may have been a subject ruler who was deified and became the god of the city of Asshur, which probably gave its name to Assyria.

According to Herodotus, Nineveh was founded by King Ninus and Queen Semiramis. This lady was reputed to be the daughter of Derceto, the fish goddess, whom Pliny identified with Atargatis. Semiramis was actually an Assyrian queen of revered memory. She was deified and took the place of a goddess, apparently Nina, the prototype of Derceto. This Nina, perhaps a form of Damkina, wife of Ea, was the great mother of the Sumerian city of Nina, and there, and also at Lagash, received offerings of fish. She was one of the many goddesses of maternity absorbed by Ishtar. The Greek Ninus is regarded as a male form of her name; like Atargatis, she may have become a bisexual deity, if she was not always accompanied by a shadowy male form. Nineveh (Ninua) was probably founded or conquered by colonists from Nina or Lagash, and called after the fish goddess.

All the deities of Assyria were imported from Babylonia except, as some hold, Ashur, the national god.[299] The theory that Ashur was identical with the Aryo-Indian Asura and the Persian Ahura is not generally accepted. One theory is that he was an eponymous hero who became the city god of Asshur, although the early form of his name, Ashir, presents a difficulty in this connection. Asshur was the first capital of Assyria. Its city god may have become the national god on that account.

At an early period, perhaps a thousand years before Thothmes III battled with the Mitannians in northern Syria, an early wave of one of the peoples of Aryan speech may have occupied the Assyrian cities. Mr. Johns points out in this connection that the names of Ushpia, Kikia, and Adasi, who, according to Assyrian records, were early rulers in Asshur, "are neither Semitic nor Sumerian". An ancient name of the goddess of Nineveh was Shaushka, which compares with Shaushkash, the consort of Teshup, the Hittite-Mitanni hammer god. As many of the Mitannian names "are", according to Mr. Johns, "really Elamitic", he suggests an ethnic connection between the early conquerors of Assyria and the people of Elam.[300] Were the pre-Semitic Elamites originally speakers of an agglutinative language, like the Sumerians and present-day Basques, who were conquered in prehistoric times by a people of Aryan speech?

The possibility is urged by Mr. Johns's suggestion that Assyria may have been dominated in pre-Semitic times by the congeners of the Aryan military aristocracy of Mitanni. As has been shown, it was Semitized by the Amoritic migration which, about 2000 B.C., brought into prominence the Hammurabi Dynasty of Babylon.

A long list of kings with Semitic names held sway in the Assyrian cities during and after the Hammurabi Age. But not until well on in the Kassite period did any of them attain prominence in Western Asia. Then Ashur-bel-nish-eshu, King of Asshur, was strong enough to deal on equal terms with the Kassite ruler Kara-indash I, with whom he arranged a boundary treaty. He was a contemporary of Thothmes III of Egypt.

After Thothmes III had secured the predominance of Egypt in Syria and Palestine he recognized Assyria as an independent power, and supplied its king with Egyptian gold to assist him, no doubt, in strengthening his territory against their common enemy. Gifts were also sent from Assyria to Egypt to fan the flame of cordial relations.

The situation was full of peril for Saushatar, king of Mitanni. Deprived by Egypt of tribute-paying cities in Syria, his exchequer must have been sadly depleted. A standing army had to be maintained, for although Egypt made no attempt to encroach further on his territory, the Hittites were ever hovering on his north-western frontier, ready when opportunity offered to win back Cappadocia. Eastward, Assyria was threatening to become a dangerous rival. He had himself to pay tribute to Egypt, and Egypt was subsidizing his enemy. It was imperative on his part, therefore, to take action without delay. The power of Assyria had to be crippled; its revenues were required for the Mitannian exchequer. So Saushatar raided Assyria during the closing years of the reign of Thothmes III, or soon after his successor, Amenhotep II, ascended the Egyptian throne.

Nothing is known from contemporary records regarding this campaign; but it can be gathered from the references of a later period that the city of Asshur was captured and plundered; its king, Ashur-nadin-akhe, ceased corresponding and exchanging gifts with Egypt. That Nineveh also fell is made clear by the fact that a descendant of Saushatar (Tushratta) was able to send to a descendant of Thothmes III at Thebes (Amenhotep III) the image of Ishtar (Shaushka) of Nineveh. Apparently five successive Mitannian kings were overlords of Assyria during a period which cannot be estimated at much less than a hundred years.

Our knowledge regarding these events is derived chiefly from the Tell-el-Amarna letters, and the tablets found by Professor Hugo Winckler at Boghaz-Köi in Cappadocia, Asia Minor.

The Tell-el-Amarna letters were discovered among the ruins of the palace of the famous Egyptian Pharaoh, Akhenaton, of the Eighteenth Dynasty, who died about 1358 B.C. During the winter of 1887-8 an Egyptian woman was excavating soil for her garden, when she happened upon the cellar of Akhenaton's foreign office in which the official correspondence had been stored. The "letters" were baked clay tablets inscribed with cuneiform alphabetical signs in the Babylonian-Assyrian language, which, like French in modern times, was the language of international diplomacy for many centuries in Western Asia after the Hyksos period.

The Egyptian natives, ever so eager to sell antiquities so as to make a fortune and retire for life, offered some specimens of the tablets for sale. One or two were sent to Paris, where they were promptly declared to be forgeries, with the result that for a time the inscribed bricks were not a marketable commodity. Ere their value was discovered, the natives had packed them into sacks, with the result that many were damaged and some completely destroyed. At length, however, the majority of them reached the British Museum and the Berlin Museum, while others drifted into the museums at Cairo, St. Petersburg, and Paris. When they were deciphered, Mitanni was discovered, and a flood of light thrown on the internal affairs of Egypt and its relations with various kingdoms in Asia, while glimpses were also afforded of the life and manners of the times.

The letters covered the reigns of Amenhotep III, the great-grandson of Thothmes III, and of his son Akhenaton, "the dreamer king", and included communications from the kings of Babylonia, Assyria, Mitanni, Cyprus, the Hittites, and the princes of Phoenicia and Canaan. The copies of two letters from Amenhotep III to Kallima-Sin, King of Babylonia, had also been preserved. One deals with statements made by Babylonian ambassadors, whom the Pharaoh stigmatizes as liars. Kallima-Sin had sent his daughter to the royal harem of Egypt, and desired to know if she was alive and well. He also asked for "much gold" to enable him to carry on the work of extending his temple. When twenty minas of gold was sent to him, he complained in due course that the quantity received was not only short but that the gold was not pure; it had been melted in the furnace, and less than five minas came out. In return he sent to Akhenaton two minas of enamel, and some jewels for his daughter, who was in the Egyptian royal harem.

Ashur-uballit, king of Ashur, once wrote intimating to Akhenaton that he was gifting him horses and chariots and a jewel seal. He asked for gold to assist in building his palace. "In your country", he added, "gold is as plentiful as dust." He also made an illuminating statement to the effect that no ambassador had gone from Assyria to Egypt since the days of his ancestor Ashur-nadin-akhe. It would therefore appear that Ashur-uballit had freed part of Assyria from the yoke of Mitanni.

The contemporary king of Mitanni was Tushratta. He corresponded both with his cousin Amenhotep III and his son-in-law Akhenaton. In his correspondence with Amenhotep III Tushratta tells that his kingdom had been invaded by the Hittites, but his god Teshup had delivered them into his hand, and he destroyed them; "not one of them", he declared, "returned to his own country". Out of the booty captured he sent Amenhotep several chariots and horses, and a boy and a girl. To his sister Gilu-khipa, who was one of the Egyptian Pharaoh's wives, he gifted golden ornaments and a jar of oil. In another letter Tushratta asked for a large quantity of gold "without measure". He complained that he did not receive enough on previous occasions, and hinted that some of the Egyptian gold looked as if it were alloyed with copper. Like the Assyrian king, he hinted that gold was as plentiful as dust in Egypt. His own presents to the Pharaoh included precious stones, gold ornaments, chariots and horses, and women (probably slaves). This may have been tribute. It was during the third Amenhotep's illness that Tushratta forwarded the Nineveh image of Ishtar to Egypt, and he made reference to its having been previously sent thither by his father, Sutarna.

When Akhenaton came to the throne Tushratta wrote to him, desiring to continue the friendship which had existed for two or three generations between the kings of Mitanni and Egypt, and made complimentary references to "the distinguished Queen Tiy", Akhenaton's mother, who evidently exercised considerable influence in shaping Egypt's foreign policy. In the course of his long correspondence with the Pharaohs, Tushratta made those statements regarding his ancestors which have provided so much important data for modern historians of his kingdom.

During the early part of the Tell-el-Amarna period, Mitanni was the most powerful kingdom in Western Asia. It was chiefly on that account that the daughters of its rulers were selected to be the wives and mothers of great Egyptian Pharaohs. But its numerous enemies were ever plotting to accomplish its downfall. Among these the foremost and most dangerous were the Hittites and the Assyrians.

The ascendancy of the Hittites was achieved in northern Syria with dramatic suddenness. There arose in Asia Minor a great conqueror, named Subbi-luliuma, the successor of Hattusil I, who established a strong Hittite empire which endured for about two centuries. His capital was at Boghaz-Köi. Sweeping through Cappadocia, at the head of a finely organized army, remarkable for its mobility, he attacked the buffer states which owed allegiance to Mitanni and Egypt. City after city fell before him, until at length he invaded Mitanni; but it is uncertain whether or not Tushratta met him in battle. Large numbers of the Mitannians were, however, evicted and transferred to the land of the Hittites, where the Greeks subsequently found them, and where they are believed to be represented by the modern Kurds, the hereditary enemies of the Armenians.

In the confusion which ensued, Tushratta was murdered by Sutarna II, who was recognized by Subbi-luliuma. The crown prince, Mattiuza, fled to Babylon, where he found protection, but was unable to receive any assistance. Ultimately, when the Hittite emperor had secured his sway over northern Syria, he deposed Sutarna II and set Mattiuza as his vassal on the throne of the shrunken Mitanni kingdom.

Meanwhile the Egyptian empire in Asia had gone to pieces. When Akhenaton, the dreamer king, died in his palace at Tell-el-Amarna, the Khabiri were conquering the Canaanite cities which had paid him tribute, and the Hittite ruler was the acknowledged overlord of the Amorites.

The star of Assyria was also in the ascendant. Its king, Ashur-uballit, who had corresponded with Akhenaton, was, like the Hittite king, Subbi-luliuma, a distinguished statesman and general, and similarly laid the foundations of a great empire. Before or after Subbi-luliuma invaded Tushratta's domains, he drove the Mitannians out of Nineveh, and afterwards overcame the Shubari tribes of Mitanni on the north-west, with the result that he added a wide extent of territory to his growing empire.

He had previously thrust southward the Assyro-Babylonian frontier. In fact, he had become so formidable an opponent of Babylonia that his daughter had been accepted as the wife of Karakhardash, the Kassite king of that country. In time his grandson, Kadashman-Kharbe, ascended the Babylonian throne. This young monarch co-operated with his grandfather in suppressing the Suti, who infested the trade routes towards the west, and plundered the caravans of merchants and the messengers of great monarchs with persistent impunity.

A reference to these bandits appears in one of the Tell-el-Amarna letters. Writing to Akhenaton, Ashur-uballit said: "The lands (of Assyria and Egypt) are remote, therefore let our messengers come and go. That your messengers were late in reaching you, (the reason is that) if the Suti had waylaid them, they would have been dead men. For if I had sent them, the Suti would have sent bands to waylay them; therefore I have retained them. My messengers (however), may they not (for this reason) be delayed."[301]

Ashur-uballit's grandson extended his Babylonian frontier into Amurru, where he dug wells and erected forts to protect traders. The Kassite aristocracy, however, appear to have entertained towards him a strong dislike, perhaps because he was so closely associated with their hereditary enemies the Assyrians. He had not reigned for long when the embers of rebellion burst into flame and he was murdered in his palace. The Kassites then selected as their king a man of humble origin, named Nazibugash, who was afterwards referred to as "the son of nobody". Ashur-uballit deemed the occasion a fitting one to interfere in the affairs of Babylonia. He suddenly appeared at the capital with a strong army, overawed the Kassites, and seized and slew Nazibugash. Then he set on the throne his great grandson the infant Kurigalzu II, who lived to reign for fifty-five years.

Ashur-uballit appears to have died soon after this event. He was succeeded by his son Bel-nirari, who carried on the policy of strengthening and extending the Assyrian empire. For many years he maintained excellent relations with his kinsman Kurigalzu II, but ultimately they came into conflict apparently over disputed territory. A sanguinary battle was fought, in which the Babylonians suffered heavily and were put to rout. A treaty of peace was afterwards arranged, which secured for the Assyrians a further extension of their frontier "from the borders of Mitanni as far as Babylonia". The struggle of the future was to be for the possession of Mesopotamia, so as to secure control over the trade routes.

Thus Assyria rose from a petty state in a comparatively brief period to become the rival of Babylonia, at a time when Egypt at the beginning of its Nineteenth Dynasty was endeavouring to win back its lost empire in Syria, and the Hittite empire was being consolidated in the north.

[282] *The Land of the Hittites*, John Garstang, pp. 312 *et seq.* and 315 *et seq.*

[283] *The Ancient Egyptian*, pp. 106 *et seq.*

[284] *The Ancient Egyptians*, p. 130.

[285] *Struggle of the Nations* (1896), p. 19.

[286] Note contributed to *The Land of the Hittites*, J. Garstang, p. 324.

[287] *Genesis*, xxvi, 34, 35.

[288] *Ezekiel*, xvi, 45.

[289] *Genesis*, xxvii, 46.

[290] *Genesis*, xxviii, 1, 2.

[291] *Genesis*, xxiv.

[292] *The Syrian Goddess*, John Garstang (London, 1913), pp. 17-8.

[293] *Vedic Index of Names and Subjects*, Macdonald & Keith, vol. i, pp. 64-5 (London, 1912).

[294] *The Wanderings of Peoples*, p. 21.

[295] Breasted's *History of Egypt*, pp. 219-20.

[296] *A History of Egypt*, W.M. Flinders Petrie, vol. ii, p. 146 *et seq.* (1904 ed.).

[297] *A History of Egypt*, W.M. Flinders Petrie, vol. ii, p. 147 (1904 ed.).

[298] *The Old Testament in the Light of the Historical Records and Legends of Assyria and Babylonia*, pp. 126 *et seq.*

[299] His connection with Anu is discussed in chapter xiv.

[300] *Ancient Assyria*, C.H.W. Johns, p. 11 (London, 1912).

[301] *The Tell-el-Amarna Letters*, Hugo Winckler, p. 31.

Chapter XIII. Astrology and Astronomy

Abstract

Culture and Superstition--Primitive Star Myths--Naturalism, Totemism, and Animism--Stars as Ghosts of Men, Giants, and Wild Animals--Gods as Constellations and Planets--Babylonian and Egyptian Mysticism--Osiris, Tammuz, and Merodach--Ishtar and Isis as Bisexual Deities--The Babylonian Planetary Deities--Planets as Forms of Tammuz and Ghosts of Gods--The Signs of the Zodiac--The "Four Quarters"--Cosmic Periods in Babylonia, India, Greece, and Ireland--Babylonian System of Calculation--Traced in Indian Yuga System--Astrology--Beliefs of the Masses--Rise of Astronomy--Conflicting Views of Authorities--Greece and Babylonia--Eclipses Foretold--The Dial of Ahaz--Omens of Heaven and Air--Biblical References to Constellations--The Past in the Present.

The empire builders of old who enriched themselves with the spoils of war and the tribute of subject States, not only satisfied personal ambition and afforded protection for industrious traders and workers, but also incidentally promoted culture and endowed research. When a conqueror returned to his capital laden with treasure, he made generous gifts to the temples. He believed that his successes were rewards for his piety, that his battles were won for him by his god or goddess of war. It was necessary, therefore, that he should continue to find favour in the eyes of the deity who had been proved to be more powerful than the god of his enemies. Besides, he had to make provision during his absence on long campaigns, or while absorbed in administrative work, for the constant performance of religious rites, so that the various deities of water, earth, weather, and corn might be sustained or propitiated with sacrificial offerings, or held in magical control by the performance of ceremonial rites. Consequently an endowed priesthood became a necessity in all powerful and well-organized states.

Thus came into existence in Babylonia, as elsewhere, as a result of the accumulation of wealth, a leisured official class, whose duties tended to promote intellectual activity, although they were primarily directed to perpetuate gross superstitious practices. Culture was really a by-product of temple activities; it flowed forth like pure gold from furnaces of thought which were walled up by the crude ores of magic and immemorial tradition.

No doubt in ancient Babylonia, as in Europe during the Middle Ages, the men of refinement and intellect among the upper classes were attracted to the temples, while the more robust types preferred the outdoor life, and especially the life of the soldier.[302] The permanent triumphs of Babylonian civilization were achieved either by the priests, or in consequence of the influence they exercised. They were the grammarians and the scribes, the mathematicians and the philosophers of that ancient country, the teachers of the young, and the patrons of the arts and crafts. It was because the temples were centres of intellectual activity that the Sumerian language remained the language of culture for long centuries after it ceased to be the everyday speech of the people.

Reference has already been made to the growth of art, and the probability that all the arts had their origin in magical practices, and to the growth of popular education necessitated by the centralization of business in the temples. It remains with us to deal now with priestly contributions to the more abstruse sciences. In India the ritualists among the Brahmans, who concerned themselves greatly regarding the exact construction and measurements of altars, gave the world algebra; the pyramid builders of Egypt, who erected vast tombs to protect royal mummies, had perforce to lay the groundwork of the science of geometry; and the Babylonian priests who elaborated the study of astrology became great astronomers because they found it necessary to observe and record accurately the movements of the heavenly bodies.

From the earliest times of which we have knowledge, the religious beliefs of the Sumerians had vague stellar associations. But it does not follow that their myths were star myths to begin with. A people who called constellations "the ram", "the bull", "the lion", or "the scorpion", did not do so because astral groups suggested the forms of animals, but rather because the animals had an earlier connection with their religious life.

111

At the same time it should be recognized that the mystery of the stars must ever have haunted the minds of primitive men. Night with all its terrors appealed more strongly to their imaginations than refulgent day when they felt more secure; they were concerned most regarding what they feared most. Brooding in darkness regarding their fate, they evidently associated the stars with the forces which influenced their lives--the ghosts of ancestors, of totems, the spirits that brought food or famine and controlled the seasons. As children see images in a fire, so they saw human life reflected in the starry sky. To the simple minds of early folks the great moon seemed to be the parent of the numerous twinkling and moving orbs. In Babylon, indeed, the moon was regarded as the father not only of the stars but of the sun also; there, as elsewhere, lunar worship was older than solar worship.

Primitive beliefs regarding the stars were of similar character in various parts of the world. But the importance which they assumed in local mythologies depended in the first place on local phenomena. On the northern Eur-Asian steppes, for instance, where stars vanished during summer's blue nights, and were often obscured by clouds in winter, they did not impress men's minds so persistently and deeply as in Babylonia, where for the greater part of the year they gleamed in darkness through a dry transparent atmosphere with awesome intensity. The development of an elaborate system of astral myths, besides, was only possible in a country where the people had attained to a high degree of civilization, and men enjoyed leisure and security to make observations and compile records. It is not surprising, therefore, to find that Babylonia was the cradle of astronomy. But before this science had destroyed the theory which it was fostered to prove, it lay smothered for long ages in the debris of immemorial beliefs. It is necessary, therefore, in dealing with Babylonian astral myths to endeavour to approach within reasonable distance of the point of view, or points of view, of the people who framed them.

Babylonian religious thought was of highly complex character. Its progress was ever hampered by blended traditions. The earliest settlers in the Tigro-Euphrates valley no doubt imported many crude beliefs which they had inherited from their Palaeolithic ancestors--the modes of thought which were the moulds of new theories arising from new experiences. When consideration is given to the existing religious beliefs of various peoples throughout the world, in low stages of culture, it is found that the highly developed creeds of Babylonia, Egypt and other countries where civilization flourished were never divested wholly of their primitive traits.

Among savage peoples two grades of religious ideas have been identified, and classified as Naturalism and Animism. In the plane of Naturalism the belief obtains that a vague impersonal force, which may have more than one manifestation and is yet manifested in everything, controls the world and the lives of human beings. An illustration of this stage of religious consciousness is afforded by Mr. Risley, who, in dealing with the religion of the jungle dwellers of Chota Nagpur, India, says that "in most cases the indefinite something which they fear and attempt to propitiate is not a person at all in any sense of the word; if one must state the case in positive terms, I should say that the idea which lies at the root of their religion is that of a power rather than many powers".[303]

Traces of Naturalism appear to have survived in Sumeria in the belief that "the spiritual, the Zi, was that which manifested life.... The test of the manifestation of life was movement."[304] All things that moved, it was conceived in the plane of Naturalism, possessed "self power"; the river was a living thing, as was also the fountain; a stone that fell from a hill fell of its own accord; a tree groaned because the wind caused it to suffer pain. This idea that inanimate objects had conscious existence survived in the religion of the Aryo-Indians. In the Nala story of the Indian epic, the *Mahabharata*, the disconsolate wife Damayanti addresses a mountain when searching for her lost husband:

"This, the monarch of all mountains, ask I of the king of men;
O all-honoured Prince of Mountains, with thy heavenward soaring peaks ...
Hast thou seen the kingly Nala in this dark and awful wood....
Why repliest thou not, O Mountain?"
She similarly addresses the Asoka tree:
"Hast thou seen Nishadha's monarch, hast thou seen my only love?...
That I may depart ungrieving, fair Asoka, answer me...."
Many a tree she stood and gazed on....[305]

It will be recognized that when primitive men gave names to mountains, rivers, or the ocean, these possessed for them a deeper significance than they do for us at the present day. The earliest peoples of Indo-European speech who called the sky "dyeus", and those of Sumerian speech who called it "ana", regarded it not as the sky "and nothing more", but as something which had conscious existence and "self power". Our remote ancestors resembled, in this respect, those imaginative children who hold conversations with articles of furniture, and administer punishment to stones which, they believe, have tripped them up voluntarily and with desire to commit an offence.

In this early stage of development the widespread totemic beliefs appear to have had origin. Families or tribes believed that they were descended from mountains, trees, or wild animals.

Aesop's fable about the mountain which gave birth to a mouse may be a relic of Totemism; so also may be the mountain symbols on the standards of Egyptian ships which appear on pre-dynastic pottery; the black dwarfs of Teutonic mythology were earth children.[306]

Adonis sprang from a tree; his mother may have, according to primitive belief, been simply a tree; Dagda, the patriarchal Irish corn god, was an oak; indeed, the idea of a "world tree", which occurs in Sumerian, Vedic-Indian, Teutonic, and other mythologies, was probably a product of Totemism.

Wild animals were considered to be other forms of human beings who could marry princes and princesses as they do in so many fairy tales. Damayanti addressed the tiger, as well as the mountain and tree, saying:

I approach him without fear.
"Of the beasts art thou the monarch, all this forest thy domain;...
Thou, O king of beasts, console me, if my Nala thou hast seen."[307]

A tribal totem exercised sway over a tribal district. In Egypt, as Herodotus recorded, the crocodile was worshipped in one district and hunted down in another. Tribes fought against tribes when totemic animals were slain. The Babylonian and Indian myths about the conflicts between eagles and serpents may have originated as records of battles between eagle clans and serpent clans. Totemic animals were tabooed. The Set pig of Egypt and the devil pig of Ireland, Scotland, and Wales were not eaten except sacrificially. Families were supposed to be descended from swans and were named Swans, or from seals and were named Seals, like the Gaelic "Mac Codrums", whose surname signifies "son of the seal"; the nickname of the Campbells, "sons of the pig", may refer to their totemic boar's head crest, which commemorated the slaying, perhaps the sacrificial slaying, of the boar by their ancestor Diarmid. Mr. Garstang, in *The Syrian Goddess*, thinks it possible that the boar which killed Adonis was of totemic origin. So may have been the fish form of the Sumerian god Ea. When an animal totem was sacrificed once a year, and eaten sacrificially so that the strength of the clan might be maintained, the priest who wrapped himself in its skin was supposed to have transmitted to him certain magical powers; he became identified with the totem and prophesied and gave instruction as the totem. Ea was depicted clad in the fish's skin.

Animism, the other early stage of human development, also produced distinctive modes of thought. Men conceived that the world swarmed with spirits, that a spirit groaned in the wind-shaken tree, that the howling wind was an invisible spirit, that there were spirits in fountains, rivers, valleys, hills, and in ocean, and in all animals; and that a hostile spirit might possess an individual and change his nature. The sun and the moon were the abodes of spirits, or the vessels in which great spirits sailed over the sea of the sky; the stars were all spirits, the "host of heaven". These spirits existed in groups of seven, or groups of three, and the multiple of three, or in pairs, or operated as single individuals.

Although certain spirits might confer gifts upon mankind, they were at certain seasons and in certain localities hostile and vengeful, like the grass-green fairies in winter, or the earth-black elves when their gold was sought for in forbidden and secret places. These spirits were the artisans of creation and vegetation, like the Egyptian Khnumu and the Indian Rhibus; they fashioned the grass blades and the stalks of corn, but at times of seasonal change they might ride on their tempest steeds, or issue forth from flooding rivers and lakes. Man was greatly concerned about striking bargains with them to secure their services, and about propitiating them, or warding off their attacks with protective charms, and by performing "ceremonies of riddance". The ghosts of the dead, being spirits, were similarly propitious or harmful on occasion; as emissaries of Fate they could injure the living.

Ancestor worship, the worship of ghosts, had origin in the stage of Animism. But ancestor worship was not developed in Babylonia as in China, for instance, although traces of it survived in the worship of stars as ghosts, in the deification of kings, and the worship of patriarchs, who might be exalted as gods or identified with a supreme god. The Egyptian Pharaoh Unas became the sun god and the constellation of Orion by devouring his predecessors[308]. He ate his god as a tribe ate its animal totem; he became the "bull of heaven".

There were star totems as well as mountain totems. A St. Andrew's cross sign, on one of the Egyptian ship standards referred to, may represent a star. The Babylonian goddess Ishtar was symbolized as a star, and she was the "world mother". Many primitive currents of thought shaped the fretted rocks of ancient mythologies.

In various countries all round the globe the belief prevailed that the stars were ghosts of the mighty dead--of giants, kings, or princes, or princesses, or of pious people whom the gods loved, or of animals which were worshipped. A few instances may be selected at random. When the Teutonic gods slew the giant Thjasse, he appeared in the heavens as Sirius. In India the ghosts of the "seven Rishis", who were semi-divine Patriarchs, formed the constellation of the Great Bear, which in Vedic times was called the "seven bears". The wives of the seven Rishis were the stars of the Pleiades. In Greece the Pleiades were the ghosts of the seven daughters of Atlas and Pleione, and in Australia they were and are a queen and six handmaidens. In these countries, as elsewhere, stories were told to account for the "lost Pleiad", a fact which suggests that primitive men were more constant observers of the heavenly bodies than might otherwise be supposed. The Arcadians believed that they were descended, as Hesiod recorded, from a princess who was transformed by Zeus into a bear; in this form Artemis slew her and she became the "Great Bear" of the sky. The Egyptian Isis was the star Sirius, whose rising coincided with the beginning of the Nile inundation. Her first tear for the dead Osiris fell into the river on "the night of the drop". The flood which ensued brought the food supply. Thus the star was not only the Great Mother of all, but the sustainer of all.

The brightest stars were regarded as being the greatest and most influential. In Babylonia all the planets were identified with great deities. Jupiter, for instance, was Merodach, and one of the astral forms of Ishtar was Venus. Merodach was also connected with "the fish of Ea" (Pisces), so that it is not improbable that Ea worship had stellar associations. Constellations were given recognition before the planets were identified.

A strange blending of primitive beliefs occurred when the deities were given astral forms. As has been shown (Chapter III) gods were supposed to die annually. The Egyptian priests pointed out to Herodotus the grave of Osiris and also his star. There are "giants' graves" also in those countries in which the gods were simply ferocious giants. A god might assume various forms; he might take the form of an insect, like Indra, and hide in a plant, or become a mouse, or a serpent, like the gods of Erech in the Gilgamesh epic. The further theory that a god could exist in various forms at one and the same time suggests that it had its origin among a people who accepted the idea of a personal god while yet in the stage of Naturalism. In Egypt Osiris, for instance, was the moon, which came as a beautiful child each month and was devoured as the wasting "old moon" by the demon Set; he was the young god who was slain in his prime each year; he was at once the father, husband, and son of Isis; he was the Patriarch who reigned over men and became the Judge of the Dead; he was the earth spirit, he was the bisexual Nile spirit, he was the spring sun; he was the Apis bull of Memphis, and the ram of Mendes; he was the reigning Pharaoh. In his fusion with Ra, who was threefold--Khepera, Ra, and Tum--he died each day as an old man; he appeared in heaven at night as the constellation Orion, which was his ghost, or was, perhaps, rather the Sumerian Zi, the spiritual essence of life. Osiris, who resembled Tammuz, a god of many forms also, was addressed as follows in one of the Isis chants:

There proceedeth from thee the strong Orion in heaven at evening, at the resting of every day!

Lo it is I (Isis), at the approach of the Sothis (Sirius) period, who doth watch for him (the child Osiris),

Nor will I leave off watching for him; for that which proceedeth from thee (the living Osiris) is revered.

An emanation from thee causeth life to gods and men, reptiles and animals, and they live by means thereof.

Come thou to us from thy chamber, in the day when thy soul begetteth emanations,--

The day when offerings upon offerings are made to thy spirit, which causeth the gods and men likewise to live.[309]

This extract emphasizes how unsafe it is to confine certain deities within narrow limits by terming them simply "solar gods", "lunar gods", "astral gods", or "earth gods". One deity may have been simultaneously a sun god and moon god, an air god and an earth god, one who was dead and also alive, unborn and also old. The priests of Babylonia and Egypt were less accustomed to concrete and logical definitions than their critics and expositors of the twentieth century. Simple explanations of ancient beliefs are often by reason of their very simplicity highly improbable. Recognition must ever be given to the puzzling complexity of religious thought in Babylonia and Egypt, and to the possibility that even to the priests the doctrines of a particular cult, which embraced the accumulated ideas of centuries, were invariably confusing and vague, and full of inconsistencies; they were mystical in the sense that the understanding could not grasp them although it permitted their acceptance. A god, for instance, might be addressed at once in

114

the singular and plural, perhaps because he had developed from an animistic group of spirits, or, perhaps, for reasons we cannot discover. This is shown clearly by the following pregnant extract from a Babylonian tablet: "*Powerful, O Sevenfold, one are ye*". Mr. L.W. King, the translator, comments upon it as follows: "There is no doubt that the name was applied to a group of gods who were so closely connected that, though addressed in the plural, they could in the same sentence be regarded as forming a single personality".[310]

Like the Egyptian Osiris, the Babylonian Merodach was a highly complex deity. He was the son of Ea, god of the deep; he died to give origin to human life when he commanded that his head should be cut off so that the first human beings might be fashioned by mixing his blood with the earth; he was the wind god, who gave "the air of life"; he was the deity of thunder and the sky; he was the sun of spring in his Tammuz character; he was the daily sun, and the planets Jupiter and Mercury as well as Sharru (Regulus); he had various astral associations at various seasons. Ishtar, the goddess, was Iku (Capella), the water channel star, in January-February, and Merodach was Iku in May-June. This strange system of identifying the chief deity with different stars at different periods, or simultaneously, must not be confused with the monotheistic identification of him with other gods. Merodach changed his forms with Ishtar, and had similarly many forms. This goddess, for instance, was, even when connected with one particular heavenly body, liable to change. According to a tablet fragment she was, as the planet Venus, "a female at sunset and a male at sunrise[311]"--that is, a bisexual deity like Nannar of Ur, the father and mother deity combined, and Isis of Egypt. Nannar is addressed in a famous hymn:

Father Nannar, Lord, God Sin, ruler among the gods....

Mother body which produceth all things....

Merciful, gracious Father, in whose hand the life of the whole land is contained.

One of the Isis chants of Egypt sets forth, addressing Osiris:

There cometh unto thee Isis, lady of the horizon, who hath begotten herself alone in the image of the gods....

She hath taken vengeance before Horus, *the woman who was made a male by her father Osiris.*[312]

Merodach, like Osiris-Sokar, was a "lord of many existences", and likewise "the mysterious one, he who is unknown to mankind[313]". It was impossible for the human mind "a greater than itself to know".

Evidence has not yet been forthcoming to enable us to determine the period at which the chief Babylonian deities were identified with the planets, but it is clear that Merodach's ascendancy in astral form could not have occurred prior to the rise of that city god of Babylon as chief of the pantheon by displacing Enlil. At the same time it must be recognized that long before the Hammurabi age the star-gazers of the Tigro-Euphrates valley must have been acquainted with the movements of the chief planets and stars, and, no doubt, they connected them with seasonal changes as in Egypt, where Isis was identified with Sirius long before the Ptolemaic age, when Babylonian astronomy was imported. Horus was identified not only with the sun but also with Saturn, Jupiter, and Mars.[314] Even the primitive Australians, as has been indicated, have their star myths; they refer to the stars Castor and Pollux as two young men, like the ancient Greeks, while the African Bushmen assert that these stars are two girls. It would be a mistake, however, to assume that the prehistoric Sumerians were exact astronomers. Probably they were, like the Aryo-Indians of the Vedic period, "not very accurate observers".[315]

It is of special interest to find that the stars were grouped by the Babylonians at the earliest period in companies of seven. The importance of this magical number is emphasized by the group of seven demons which rose from the deep to rage over the land (p. 71). Perhaps the sanctity of Seven was suggested by Orion, the Bears, and the Pleiad, one of which constellations may have been the "Sevenfold" deity addressed as "one". At any rate arbitrary groupings of other stars into companies of seven took place, for references are made to the seven Tikshi, the seven Lumashi, and the seven Mashi, which are older than the signs of the Zodiac; so far as can be ascertained these groups were selected from various constellations. When the five planets were identified, they were associated with the sun and moon and connected with the chief gods of the Hammurabi pantheon. A bilingual list in the British Museum arranges the sevenfold planetary group in the following order:--

The moon, Sin.
The sun, Shamash.
Jupiter, Merodach.
Venus, Ishtar.
Saturn, Ninip (Nirig).
Mercury, Nebo.
Mars, Nergal.

115

An ancient name of the moon was Aa, Â, or Ai, which recalls the Egyptian Aâh or Ah. The Sumerian moon was Aku, "the measurer", like Thoth of Egypt, who in his lunar character as a Fate measured out the lives of men, and was a god of architects, mathematicians, and scribes. The moon was the parent of the sun or its spouse; and might be male, or female, or both as a bisexual deity.

As the "bull of light" Jupiter had solar associations; he was also the shepherd of the stars, a title shared by Tammuz as Orion; Nin-Girsu, a developed form of Tammuz, was identified with both Orion and Jupiter.

Ishtar's identification with Venus is of special interest. When that planet was at its brightest phase, its rays were referred to as "the beard" of the goddess; she was the "bearded Aphrodite"--a bisexual deity evidently. The astrologers regarded the bright Venus as lucky and the rayless Venus as unlucky.

Saturn was Nirig, who is best known as Ninip, a deity who was displaced by Enlil, the elder Bel, and afterwards regarded as his son. His story has not been recovered, but from the references made to it there is little doubt that it was a version of the widespread myth about the elder deity who was slain by his son, as Saturn was by Jupiter and Dyaus by Indra. It may have resembled the lost Egyptian myth which explained the existence of the two Horuses--Horus the elder, and Horus, the posthumous son of Osiris. At any rate, it is of interest to find in this connection that in Egypt the planet Saturn was Her-Ka, "Horus the Bull". Ninip was also identified with the bull. Both deities were also connected with the spring sun, like Tammuz, and were terrible slayers of their enemies. Ninip raged through Babylonia like a storm flood, and Horus swept down the Nile, slaying the followers of Set. As the divine sower of seed, Ninip may have developed from Tammuz as Horus did from Osiris. Each were at once the father and the son, different forms of the same deity at various seasons of the year. The elder god was displaced by the son (spring), and when the son grew old his son slew him in turn. As the planet Saturn, Ninip was the ghost of the elder god, and as the son of Bel he was the solar war god of spring, the great wild bull, the god of fertility. He was also as Ber "lord of the wild boar", an animal associated with Rimmon[316].

Nebo (Nabu), who was identified with Mercury, was a god of Borsippa. He was a messenger and "announcer" of the gods, as the Egyptian Horus in his connection with Jupiter was Her-ap-sheta, "Horus the opener of that which is secret[317]". Nebo's original character is obscure. He appears to have been a highly developed deity of a people well advanced in civilization when he was exalted as the divine patron of Borsippa. Although Hammurabi ignored him, he was subsequently invoked with Merodach, and had probably much in common with Merodach. Indeed, Merodach was also identified with the planet Mercury. Like the Greek Hermes, Nebo was a messenger of the gods and an instructor of mankind. Jastrow regards him as "a counterpart of Ea", and says: "Like Ea, he is the embodiment and source of wisdom. The art of writing--and therefore of all literature--is more particularly associated with him. A common form of his name designates him as the 'god of the stylus'."[318] He appears also to have been a developed form of Tammuz, who was an incarnation of Ea. Professor Pinches shows that one of his names, Mermer, was also a non-Semitic name of Ramman.[319]Tammuz resembled Ramman in his character as a spring god of war. It would seem that Merodach as Jupiter displaced at Babylon Nebo as Saturn, the elder god, as Bel Enlil displaced the elder Ninip at Nippur.

The god of Mars was Nergal, the patron deity of Cuthah,[320] who descended into the Underworld and forced into submission Eresh-ki-gal (Persephone), with whom he was afterwards associated. His "name", says Professor Pinches, "is supposed to mean 'lord of the great habitation', which would be a parallel to that of his spouse, Eresh-ki-gal".[321] At Erech he symbolized the destroying influence of the sun, and was accompanied by the demons of pestilence. Mars was a planet of evil, plague, and death; its animal form was the wolf. In Egypt it was called Herdesher, "the Red Horus", and in Greece it was associated with Ares (the Roman Mars), the war god, who assumed his boar form to slay Adonis (Tammuz).

Nergal was also a fire god like the Aryo-Indian Agni, who, as has been shown, links with Tammuz as a demon slayer and a god of fertility. It may be that Nergal was a specialized form of Tammuz, who, in a version of the myth, was reputed to have entered the Underworld as a conqueror when claimed by Eresh-ki-gal, and to have become, like Osiris, the lord of the dead. If so, Nergal was at once the slayer and the slain.

The various Babylonian deities who were identified with the planets had their characters sharply defined as members of an organized pantheon. But before this development took place certain of the prominent heavenly bodies, perhaps all the planets, were evidently regarded as manifestations of one deity, the primeval Tammuz, who was a form of Ea, or of the twin deities Ea and Anu. Tammuz may have been the "sevenfold one" of the hymns. At a still earlier period the stars were manifestations of the Power whom the jungle dwellers of Chota

116

Nagpur attempt to propitiate--the "world soul" of the cultured Brahmans of the post-Vedic Indian Age. As much is suggested by the resemblances which the conventionalized planetary deities bear to Tammuz, whose attributes they symbolized, and by the Egyptian conception that the sun, Jupiter, Saturn, and Mars were manifestations of Horus. Tammuz and Horus may have been personifications of the Power or World Soul vaguely recognized in the stage of Naturalism.

The influence of animistic modes of thought may be traced in the idea that the planets and stars were the ghosts of gods who were superseded by their sons. These sons were identical with their fathers; they became, as in Egypt, "husbands of their mothers". This idea was perpetuated in the Aryo-Indian *Laws of Manu*, in which it is set forth that "the husband, after conception by his wife, becomes an embryo and is born again of her[322]". The deities died every year, but death was simply change. Yet they remained in the separate forms they assumed in their progress round "the wide circle of necessity". Horus was remembered as various planets--as the falcon, as the elder sun god, and as the son of Osiris; and Tammuz was the spring sun, the child, youth, warrior, the deity of fertility, and the lord of death (Orion-Nergal), and, as has been suggested, all the planets.

The stars were also the ghosts of deities who died daily. When the sun perished as an old man at evening, it rose in the heavens as Orion, or went out and in among the stars as the shepherd of the flock, Jupiter, the planet of Merodach in Babylonia, and Attis in Asia Minor. The flock was the group of heavenly spirits invisible by day, the "host of heaven"--manifestations or ghosts of the emissaries of the controlling power or powers.

The planets presided over various months of the year. Sin (the moon) was associated with the third month; it also controlled the calendar; Ninip (Saturn) was associated with the fourth month, Ishtar (Venus) with the sixth, Shamash (the sun) with the seventh, Merodach (Jupiter) with the eighth, Nergal (Mars) with the ninth, and a messenger of the gods, probably Nebo (Mercury), with the tenth.

Each month was also controlled by a zodiacal constellation. In the Creation myth of Babylon it is stated that when Merodach engaged in the work of setting the Universe in order he "set all the great gods in their several stations", and "also created their images, the stars of the Zodiac,[323] and fixed them all" (p. 147).

Our signs of the Zodiac are of Babylonian origin. They were passed on to the Greeks by the Phoenicians and Hittites. "There was a time", says Professor Sayce, "when the Hittites were profoundly affected by Babylonian civilization, religion, and art...." They "carried the time-worn civilizations of Babylonia and Egypt to the furthest boundary of Egypt, and there handed them over to the West in the grey dawn of European history.... Greek traditions affirmed that the rulers of Mykenae had come from Lydia, bringing with them the civilization and treasures of Asia Minor. The tradition has been confirmed by modern research. While certain elements belonging to the prehistoric culture of Greece, as revealed at Mykenae and elsewhere, were derived from Egypt and Phoenicia, there are others which point to Asia Minor as their source. And the culture of Asia Minor was Hittite."[324]

The early Babylonian astronomers did not know, of course, that the earth revolved round the sun. They believed that the sun travelled across the heavens flying like a bird or sailing like a boat.[325] In studying its movements they observed that it always travelled from west to east along a broad path, swinging from side to side of it in the course of the year. This path is the Zodiac--the celestial "circle of necessity". The middle line of the sun's path is the Ecliptic. The Babylonian scientists divided the Ecliptic into twelve equal parts, and grouped in each part the stars which formed their constellations; these are also called "Signs of the Zodiac". Each month had thus its sign or constellation.

The names borne at the present day by the signs of the Zodiac are easily remembered even by children, who are encouraged to repeat the following familiar lines:

The *Ram*, the *Bull*, the heavenly *Twins*,
And next the *Crab*, the *Lion* shines.
  The *Virgin* and the *Scales*,
The *Scorpion*, *Archer*, and *Sea goat*,
The man that holds the *water pot*,
  And *Fish* with glitt'ring[326] tails.

The table on p. 308 shows that our signs are derived from ancient Babylonia.

The celestial regions were also divided into three or more parts. Three "fields" were allotted to the ancient triad formed by Ea, Anu, and Bel. The zodiacal "path" ran through these "fields". Ea's field was in the west, and was associated with Amurru, the land of the Amorites; Anu's field was in the south, and was associated with Elam; and Bel's central "field" was associated with the land of Akkad. When the rulers of Akkad called themselves "kings of the four quarters", the reference was to the countries associated with the three divine fields and to

Gutium[327](east = our north-east). Was Gutium associated with demons, as in Scandinavia the north-east was associated with the giants against whom Thor waged war?

Table XIII.1.

Const ellations.	Date of Sun's Entry (Babylonian Month in brackets).	Babylonian Equivalent.
Aries (the Ram).	20th March (Nisan = March-April)	The Labourer or Messenger.
Tauru s (the Bull).	20th April (Iyyar = April-May)	A divine figure and the "bull of heaven".
Gemi ni (the Twins).	21st May (Sivan = May-June).	The Faithful Shepherd and Twins side by side, or head to head and feet to teet.
Cance r (the Crab).	21st June (Tammuz = June-July).	Crab or Scorpion.
Leo (the Lion).	22nd July (Ab = July-August).	The big dog (Lion).
Virgo (the Virgin).	23rd August (Elul = August-Sept.).	Ishtar, the Virgin's ear of corn.
Libra (the Balance).	23rd September (Tisri = Sept.-Oct.).	The Balance.
Scorpi o (the Scorpion).	23rd October (Marcheswan = Oct.-Nov.).	Scorpion of darkness.
Sagitta rius (the Archer).	22nd November (Chisleu = Nov.-Dec.).	Man or man-horse with bow, or an arrow symbol.
Capric ornus (the Goat).	21st December (Tebet = Dec.-Jan.).	Ea's goat-fish.
Aquari us (the Water Carrier).	19th January (Sebat = Jan.-Feb.).	God with water urn.
Pisces (the Fishes).	18th February (Adar = Feb.-March).	Fish tails in canal.

The Babylonian Creation myth states that Merodach, having fixed the stars of the Zodiac, made three stars for each month (p. 147). Mr. Robert Brown, jun., who has dealt as exhaustively with the astronomical problems of Babylonia as the available data permitted him, is of opinion that the leading stars of three constellations are referredto, viz.: (1) the central or zodiacal constellations, (2) the northern constellations, and (3) the southern constellations. We have thus a scheme of thirty-six constellations. The "twelve zodiacal stars were flanked on either side by twelve non-zodiacal stars". Mr. Brown quotes Diodorus, who gave a résumé of Babylonian astronomico-astrology, in this connection. He said that "the five planets were called 'Interpreters'; and in subjection to these were marshalled 'Thirty Stars', which were styled 'Divinities of the Council'.... The chiefs of the Divinities are twelve in number, to each of whom they assign a month and one of the twelve signs of the Zodiac." Through these twelve signs sun, moon, and planets run their courses. "And with the zodiacal circle they mark out twenty-four stars, half of which they say are arranged in the north and half in the south."[328] Mr. Brown shows that the thirty stars referred to "constituted the original Euphratean Lunar Zodiac, the parent of the seven ancient lunar zodiacs which have come down to us, namely, the Persian, Sogdian, Khorasmian, Chinese, Indian, Arab, and Coptic schemes".

The three constellations associated with each month had each a symbolic significance: they reflected the characters of their months. At the height of the rainy season, for instance, the month of Ramman, the thunder god, was presided over by the zodiacal constellation of the water urn, the northern constellation "Fish of the Canal", and the southern "the Horse". In India the black horse was sacrificed at rain-getting and fertility ceremonies. The months of growth, pestilence, and scorching sun heat were in turn symbolized. The "Great Bear" was the "chariot" = "Charles's Wain", and the "Milky Way" the "river of the high cloud", the Celestial Euphrates, as in Egypt it was the Celestial Nile.

118

Of special interest among the many problems presented by Babylonian astronomical lore is the theory of Cosmic periods or Ages of the Universe. In the Indian, Greek, and Irish mythologies there are four Ages--the Silvern (white), Golden (yellow), the Bronze (red), and the Iron (black). As has been already indicated, Mr. R. Brown, jun., shows that "the Indian system of Yugas, or ages of the world, presents many features which forcibly remind us of the Euphratean scheme". The Babylonians had ten antediluvian kings, who were reputed to have reigned for vast periods, the total of which amounted to 120 saroi, or 432,000 years. These figures at once recall the Indian Maha-yuga of 4,320,000 years = 432,000 x 10. Apparently the Babylonian and Indian systems of calculation were of common origin. In both countries the measurements of time and space were arrived at by utilizing the numerals 10 and 6.

When primitive man began to count he adopted a method which comes naturally to every schoolboy; he utilized his fingers. Twice five gave him ten, and from ten he progressed to twenty, and then on to a hundred and beyond. In making measurements his hands, arms, and feet were at his service. We are still measuring by feet and yards (standardized strides) in this country, while those who engage in the immemorial art of knitting, and, in doing so, repeat designs found on neolithic pottery, continue to measure in finger breadths, finger lengths, and hand breadths as did the ancient folks who called an arm length a cubit. Nor has the span been forgotten, especially by boys in their games with marbles; the space from the end of the thumb to the end of the little finger when the hand is extended must have been an important measurement from the earliest times.

As he made progress in calculations, the primitive Babylonian appears to have been struck by other details in his anatomy besides his sets of five fingers and five toes. He observed, for instance, that his fingers were divided into three parts and his thumb into two parts only;[329] four fingers multiplied by three gave him twelve, and multiplying 12 by 3 he reached 36. Apparently the figure 6 attracted him. His body was divided into 6 parts--2 arms, 2 legs, the head, and the trunk; his 2 ears, 2 eyes, and mouth, and nose also gave him 6. The basal 6, multiplied by his 10 fingers, gave him 60, and 60 x 2 (for his 2 hands) gave him 120. In Babylonian arithmetic 6 and 60 are important numbers, and it is not surprising to find that in the system of numerals the signs for 1 and 10 combined represent 60.

In fixing the length of a mythical period his first great calculation of 120 came naturally to the Babylonian, and when he undertook to measure the Zodiac he equated time and space by fixing on 120 degrees. His first zodiac was the Sumerian lunar zodiac, which contained thirty moon chambers associated with the "Thirty Stars" of the tablets, and referred to by Diodorus as "Divinities of the Council". The chiefs of the Thirty numbered twelve. In this system the year began in the winter solstice. Mr. Hewitt has shown that the chief annual festival of the Indian Dravidians begins with the first full moon after the winter festival, and Mr. Brown emphasizes the fact that the list of Tamil (Dravidian) lunar and solar months are named like the Babylonian constellations.[330] "Lunar chronology", wrote Professor Max Mailer, "seems everywhere to have preceded solar chronology."[331] The later Semitic Babylonian system had twelve solar chambers and the thirty-six constellations.

Each degree was divided into sixty minutes, and each minute into sixty seconds. The hours of the day and night each numbered twelve.

Multiplying 6 by 10 (pur), the Babylonian arrived at 60 (soss); 60x10 gave him 600 (ner), and 600x6, 3600 (sar), while 3600x10 gave him 36,000, and 36,000x12, 432,000 years, or 120 saroi, which is equal to the "sar" multiplied by the "soss"x2. "Pur" signifies "heap"--the ten fingers closed after being counted; and "ner" signifies "foot". Mr. George Bertin suggests that when 6x10 fingers gave 60 this number was multiplied by the ten toes, with the result that 600 was afterwards associated with the feet (ner). The Babylonian sign for 10 resembles the impression of two feet with heels closed and toes apart. This suggests a primitive record of the first round of finger counting.

In India this Babylonian system of calculation was developed during the Brahmanical period. The four Yugas or Ages, representing the four fingers used by the primitive mathematicians, totalled 12,000 divine years, a period which was called a Maha-yuga; it equalled the Babylonian 120 saroi, multiplied by 100. Ten times a hundred of these periods gave a "Day of Brahma".

Each day of the gods, it was explained by the Brahmans, was a year to mortals. Multiplied by 360 days, 12,000 divine years equalled 4,320,000 human years. This Maha-yuga, multiplied by 1000, gave the "Day of Brahma" as 4,320,000,000 human years.

The shortest Indian Yuga is the Babylonian 120 saroi multiplied by 10=1200 divine years for the Kali Yuga; twice that number gives the Dvapara Yuga of 2400 divine years; then the Treta Yuga is 2400 + 1200 = 3600 divine years, and Krita Yuga 3600 + 1200 = 4800 divine years.

The influence of Babylonia is apparent in these calculations. During the Vedic period "Yuga" usually signified a "generation", and there are no certain references to the four Ages as such. The names "Kali", "Dvapara", "Treta", and "Krita" "occur as the designations of throws of dice".[332] It was after the arrival of the "late comers", the post-Vedic Aryans, that the Yuga system was developed in India.[333]

In *Indian Myth and Legend[334]* it is shown that the Indian and Irish Ages have the same colour sequence: (1) White or Silvern, (2) Red or Bronze, (3) Yellow or Golden, and (4) Black or Iron. The Greek order is: (1) Golden, (2) Silvern, (3) Bronze, and (4) Iron.

The Babylonians coloured the seven planets as follows: the moon, silvern; the sun, golden; Mars, red; Saturn, black; Jupiter, orange; Venus, yellow; and Mercury, blue.

As the ten antediluvian kings who reigned for 120 saroi had an astral significance, their long reigns corresponding "with the distances separating certain of the principal stars in or near the ecliptic",[335]) it seems highly probable that the planets were similarly connected with mythical ages which were equated with the "four quarters" of the celestial regions and the four regions of the earth, which in Gaelic story are called "the four red divisions of the world".

Three of the planets may have been heralds of change. Venus, as "Dilbat", was the "Proclaimer", and both Jupiter and Mercury were called "Face voices of light", and "Heroes of the rising sun" among other names. Jupiter may have been the herald of the "Golden Age" as a morning star. This planet was also associated with bronze, as "Kakkub Urud", "the star of bronze", while Mars was "Kakkub Aban Kha-urud," "the star of the bronze fish stone". Mercury, the lapis lazuli planet, may have been connected with the black Saturn, the ghost of the dead sun, the demoniac elder god; in Egypt lapis lazuli was the hair colour of Ra when he grew old, and Egyptologists translate it as black.[336] The rare and regular appearances of Mercury may have suggested the planet's connection with a recurring Age. Venus as an evening star might be regarded as the herald of the lunar or silver age; she was propitious as a bearded deity and interchanged with Merodach as a seasonal herald.

Connecting Jupiter with the sun as a propitious planet, and with Mars as a destroying planet, Venus with the moon, and Mercury with Saturn, we have left four colour schemes which suggest the Golden, Silvern, Bronze, and Iron Ages. The Greek order of mythical ages may have had a solar significance, beginning as it does with the "golden" period. On the other hand the Indian and Irish systems begin with the Silvern or white lunar period. In India the White Age (Treta Yuga) was the age of perfect men, and in Greece the Golden Age was the age of men who lived like gods. Thus the first ages in both cases were "Perfect" Ages. The Bronze Age of Greece was the age of notorious fighters and takers of life; in Babylonia the bronze planet Mars was the symbol of the destroying Nergal, god of war and pestilence, while Jupiter was also a destroyer as Merodach, the slayer of Tiamat. In India the Black Age is the age of wickedness. The Babylonian Saturn, as we have seen, is black, and its god, Ninip, was the destroying boar, which recalls the black boar of the Egyptian demon (or elder god) Set. The Greek Cronos was a destroyer even of his own children. All the elder gods had demoniac traits like the ghosts of human beings.

As the Babylonian lunar zodiac was imported into India before solar worship and the solar zodiac were developed, so too may have been the germs of the Yuga doctrine, which appears to have a long history. Greece, on the other hand, came under the influence of Babylon at a much later period. In Egypt Ra, the sun god, was an antediluvian king, and he was followed by Osiris. Osiris was slain by Set, who was depicted sometimes red and sometimes black. There was also a Horus Age.

The Irish system of ages suggests an early cultural drift into Europe, through Asia Minor, and along the uplands occupied by the representatives of the Alpine or Armenoid peoples who have been traced from Hindu Kush to Brittany. The culture of Gaul resembles that of India in certain particulars; both the Gauls and the post-Vedic Aryans, for instance, believed in the doctrine of Transmigration of Souls, and practised "suttee". After the Roman occupation of Gaul, Ireland appears to have been the refuge of Gaulish scholars, who imported their beliefs and traditions and laid the foundations of that brilliant culture which shed lustre on the Green Isle in late Pagan and early Christian times.

The part played by the Mitanni people of Aryan speech in distributing Asiatic culture throughout Europe may have been considerable, but we know little or nothing regarding their movements and influence, nor has sufficient evidence been forthcoming to connect them with the cremating invaders of the Bronze Age, who penetrated as far as northern Scotland and Scandinavia. On the other hand it is certain that the Hittites adopted the planetary system of Babylonia and passed it on to Europeans, including the Greeks. The five planets Ninip, Merodach, Nergal, Ishtar, and Nebo were called by the Greeks after their gods Kronos, Zeus, Ares, Aphrodite, and Hermes, and by the Romans Saturnus, Jupiter, Mars, Venus, and Mercurius.

120

It must be recognized, however, that these equations were somewhat arbitrary. Ninip resembled Kronos and Saturnus as a father, but he was also at the same time a son; he was the Egyptian Horus the elder and Horus the younger in one. Merodach was similarly of complex character--a combination of Ea, Anu, Enlil, and Tammuz, who acquired, when exalted by the Amoritic Dynasty of Babylon, the attributes of the thunder god Adad-Ramman in the form of Amurru, "lord of the mountains". During the Hammurabi Age Amurru was significantly popular in personal names. It is as Amurru-Ramman that Merodach bears comparison with Zeus. He also links with Hercules. Too much must not be made, therefore, of the Greek and Roman identifications of alien deities with their own. Mulla, the Gaulish mule god, may have resembled Mars somewhat, but it is a "far cry" from Mars-Mulla to Mars-Nergal, as it is also from the Gaulish Moccus, the boar, called "Mercury", to Nebo, the god of culture, who was the "Mercury" of the Tigro-Euphrates valley. Similarly the differences between "Jupiter-Amon" of Egypt and "Jupiter-Merodach" of Babylon were more pronounced than the resemblances.

The basal idea in Babylonian astrology appears to be the recognition of the astral bodies as spirits or fates, who exercised an influence over the gods, the world, and mankind. These were worshipped in groups when they were yet nameless. The group addressed, "Powerful, O sevenfold, one are ye", may have been a constellation consisting of seven stars.[337] The worship of stars and planets, which were identified and named, "seems never to have spread", says Professor Sayce, "beyond the learned classes, and to have remained to the last an artificial system. The mass of the people worshipped the stars as a whole, but it was only as a whole and not individually."[338]The masses perpetuated ancient animistic beliefs, like the pre-Hellenic inhabitants of Greece. "The Pelasgians, as I was informed at Dodona," wrote Herodotus, "formerly offered all things indiscriminately to the gods. They distinguished them by no name or surname, for they were hitherto unacquainted with either; but they called them gods, which by its etymology means disposers, from observing the orderly disposition and distribution of the various parts of the universe."[339] The oldest deities are those which bore no individual names. They were simply "Fates" or groups called "Sevenfold". The crude giant gods of Scotland are "Fomhairean" (Fomorians), and do not have individual names as in Ireland. Families and tribes were controlled by the Fates or nameless gods, which might appear as beasts or birds, or be heard knocking or screaming.

In the Babylonian astral hymns, the star spirits are associated with the gods, and are revealers of the decrees of Fate. "Ye brilliant stars... ye bright ones... to destroy evil did Anu create you.... At thy command mankind was named (created)! Give thou the Word, and with thee let the great gods stand! Give thou my judgment, make my decision!"[340]

The Indian evidence shows that the constellations, and especially the bright stars, were identified before the planets. Indeed, in Vedic literature there is no certain reference to a single planet, although constellations are named. It seems highly probable that before the Babylonian gods were associated with the astral bodies, the belief obtained that the stars exercised an influence over human lives. In one of the Indian "Forest Books", for instance, reference is made to a man who was "born under the Nakshatra Rohini".[341] "Nakshatras" are stars in the *Rigveda* and later, and "lunar mansions" in Brahmanical compositions.[342] "Rohini, 'ruddy', is the name of a conspicuously reddish star, a Tauri or Aldebaran, and denotes the group of the Hyades."[343] This reference may be dated before 600 B.C., perhaps 800 B.C.

From Greece comes the evidence of Plutarch regarding the principles of Babylonian astrology. "Respecting the planets, which they call *the birth-ruling divinities*, the Chaldeans", he wrote, "lay down that two (Venus and Jupiter) are propitious, and two (Mars and Saturn) malign, and three (Sun, Moon, and Mercury) of a middle nature, and one common." "That is," Mr. Brown comments, "an astrologer would say, these three are propitious with the good, and may be malign with the bad."[344]

Jastrow's views in this connection seem highly controversial. He holds that Babylonian astrology dealt simply with national affairs, and had no concern with "the conditions under which the individual was born"; it did not predict "the fate in store for him". He believes that the Greeks transformed Babylonian astrology and infused it with the spirit of individualism which is a characteristic of their religion, and that they were the first to give astrology a personal significance.

Jastrow also perpetuates the idea that astronomy began with the Greeks. "Several centuries before the days of Alexander the Great," he says, "the Greeks had begun to cultivate the study of the heavens, not for purposes of divination, but prompted by a scientific spirit as an intellectual discipline that might help them to solve the mysteries of the universe." It is possible, however, to overrate the "scientific spirit" of the Greeks, who, like the Japanese in our own day, were accomplished borrowers from other civilizations. That astronomy had humble beginnings in Greece as elsewhere is highly probable. The late Mr. Andrew Lang wrote in this connection: "The very oddest example of the survival of the notion that the stars are men and women is found in the *Pax* of Aristophanes. Trygaeus in that comedy has just made an expedition to heaven. A slave meets him, and asks him: 'Is not the story true, then, that we become stars when we die?' The answer is, 'Certainly'; and Trygaeus points out the star into which Ion of Chios has just been metamorphosed." Mr. Lang added: "Aristophanes is making fun of some popular Greek superstition". The Eskimos, Persians, Aryo-Indians, Germans, New Zealanders, and others had a similar superstition.[345]

Jastrow goes on to say that the Greeks "imparted their scientific view of the Universe to the East. They became the teachers of the East in astronomy as in medicine and other sciences, and the credit of having discovered the law of the precession of the equinoxes belongs to Hipparchus, the Greek astronomer, who announced this important theory about the year 130 B.C."[346] Undoubtedly the Greeks contributed to the advancement of the science of astronomy, with which, as other authorities believe, they became acquainted after it had become well developed as a science by the Assyrians and Babylonians.

"In return for improved methods of astronomical calculation which," Jastrow says, "*it may be assumed* (the italics are ours), contact with Greek science gave to the Babylonian astronomers, the Greeks accepted from the Babylonians the names of the constellations of the ecliptic."[347] This is a grudging admission; they evidently accepted more than the mere names.

Jastrow's hypothesis is certainly interesting, especially as he is an Oriental linguist of high repute. But it is not generally accepted. The sudden advance made by the Tigro-Euphratean astronomers when Assyria was at the height of its glory, may have been due to the discoveries made by great native scientists, the Newtons and the Herschels of past ages, who had studied the data accumulated by generations of astrologers, the earliest recorders of the movements of the heavenly bodies. It is hard to believe that the Greeks made much progress as scientists before they had identified the planets, and become familiar with the Babylonian constellations through the medium of the Hittites or the Phoenicians. What is known for certain is that long centuries before Greek science was heard of, there were scientists in Babylonia. During the Sumerian period "the forms and relations of geometry", says Professor Goodspeed, "were employed for purposes of augury. The heavens were mapped out, and the courses of the heavenly bodies traced to determine the bearing of their movements upon human destinies."[348]

Several centuries before Hipparchus was born, the Assyrian kings had in their palaces official astronomers who were able to foretell, with varying degrees of accuracy, when eclipses would take place. Instructions were sent to various observatories, in the king's name, to send in reports of forthcoming eclipses. A translation of one of these official documents sent from the observatory of Babylon to Nineveh, has been published by Professor Harper. The following are extracts from it: "As for the eclipse of the moon about which the king my lord has written to me, a watch was kept for it in the cities of Akkad, Borsippa, and Nippur. We observed it ourselves in the city of Akkad.... And whereas the king my lord ordered me to observe also the eclipse of the sun, I watched to see whether it took place or not, and what passed before my eyes I now report to the king my lord. It was an eclipse of the moon that took place.... It was total over Syria, and the shadow fell on the land of the Amorites, the land of the Hittites, and in part on the land of the Chaldees." Professor Sayce comments: "We gather from this letter that there were no less than three observatories in Northern Babylonia: one at Akkad, near Sippara; one at Nippur, now Niffer; and one at Borsippa, within sight of Babylon. As Borsippa possessed a university, it was natural that one of the three observatories should be established there."[349]

It is evident that before the astronomers at Nineveh could foretell eclipses, they had achieved considerable progress as scientists. The data at their disposal probably covered nearly two thousand years. Mr. Brown, junior, calculates that the signs of the Zodiac were fixed in the year 2084 B.C.[350] These star groups do not now occupy the positions in which they were observed by the early astronomers, because the revolving earth is rocking like a top, with the result that the pole does not always keep pointing at the same spot in the heavens. Each year the meeting-place of the imaginary lines of the ecliptic and equator is moving westward at the rate of about fifty seconds. In time--ages hence--the pole will circle round to the point it spun at when the constellations were named by the Babylonians. It is by calculating the period occupied by this world-curve that the date 2084 B.C. has been arrived at.

As a result of the world-rocking process, the present-day "signs of the Zodiac" do not correspond with the constellations. In March, for instance, when the sun crosses the equator it enters the sign of the Ram (Aries), but does not reach the constellation till the 20th, as the comparative table shows on p. 308.

When "the ecliptic was marked off into the twelve regions" and the signs of the Zodiac were designated, "the year of three hundred sixty-five and one-fourth days was known", says Goodspeed, "though the common year was reckoned according to twelve months of thirty days each[351], and equated with the solar year by intercalating a month at the proper times.... The month was divided into weeks of seven days.... The clepsydra and the sundial were Babylonian inventions for measuring time."[352]

The sundial of Ahaz was probably of Babylonian design. When the shadow went "ten degrees backward" (2 Kings, xx, II) ambassadors were sent from Babylon "to enquire of the wonder that was done in the land" (2 Chron. xxxii, 31). It was believed that the king's illness was connected with the incident. According to astronomical calculation there was a partial eclipse of the sun which was visible at Jerusalem on 11th January, 689 B.C., about 11.30 a.m. When the upper part of the solar disc was obscured, the shadow on the dial was strangely affected.

The Babylonian astrologers in their official documents were more concerned regarding international omens than those which affected individuals. They made observations not only of the stars, but also the moon, which, as has been shown, was one of their planets, and took note of the clouds and the wind likewise.

As portions of the heavens were assigned to various countries, so was the moon divided into four quarters for the same purpose--the upper part for the north, Gutium, the lower for the south, Akkad or Babylonia, the eastern part for Elam, and the western for Amurru. The crescent was also divided in like manner; looking southward the astrologers assigned the right horn to the west and the left to the east. In addition, certain days and certain months were connected with the different regions. Lunar astrology was therefore of complicated character. When the moon was dim at the particular phase which was connected with Amurru, it was believed that the fortunes of that region were in decline, and if it happened to shine brightly in the Babylonian phase the time was considered auspicious to wage war in the west. Great importance was attached to eclipses, which were fortunately recorded, with the result that the ancient astronomers were ultimately enabled to forecast them.

The destinies of the various states in the four quarters were similarly influenced by the planets. When Venus, for instance, rose brightly in the field of Anu, it was a "prosperor" for Elam; if it were dim it foretold misfortune. Much importance was also attached to the positions occupied by the constellations when the planets were propitious or otherwise; no king would venture forth on an expedition under a "yoke of inauspicious stars".

Biblical references to the stars make mention of well-known Babylonian constellations:

Canst thou bind the sweet influences of Pleiades, or loose the bands of Orion? Canst thou bring forth Mazzaroth (? the Zodiac) in his season? or canst thou guide Arcturus with his sons? Knowest thou the ordinances of heaven? canst thou set the dominion thereof in the earth? Job, xxxviii, 31-33. Which maketh Arcturus, Orion, and Pleiades, and the chambers of the south. Job, ix, 9. Seek him that maketh the seven stars and Orion, and turneth the shadow of death into the morning, and maketh the day dark with night. Amos, v, 8.

The so-called science of astrology, which had origin in ancient Babylonia and spread eastward and west, is not yet extinct, and has its believers even in our own country at the present day, although they are not nearly so numerous as when Shakespeare made Malvolio read:

In my stars I am above thee; but be not afraid of greatness: some are born great, some achieve greatness, and some have greatness thrust upon 'em. Thy Fates open their hands....[353]

or when Byron wrote:
Ye stars! which are the poetry of heaven!
If in your bright leaves we would read the fate
Of men and empires--'t is to be forgiven
That in our aspirations to be great,
Our destinies o'erleap their mortal state
And claim a kindred with you....[354]

Our grave astronomers are no longer astrologers, but they still call certain constellations by the names given them in Babylonia. Every time we look at our watches we are reminded of the ancient mathematicians who counted on their fingers and multiplied 10 by 6, to give us minutes and seconds, and divided the day and the night into twelve hours by multiplying six by the two leaden feet of Time. The past lives in the present.

---

[302] "It may be worth while to note again", says Beddoe, "how often finely developed skulls are discovered in the graveyards of old monasteries, and how likely seems Galton's conjecture, that progress was arrested in the Middle Ages, because the celibacy of the clergy brought about the extinction of the best strains of blood." The Anthropological History of Europe, p. 161 (1912).

[303] *Census of India*, vol. I, part i, pp. 352 et seq.

[304] *Hibbert Lectures*, Professor Sayce, p. 328.

[305] *The Story of Nala*, Monier Williams, pp. 68-9 and 77.

[306] "In Ymer's flesh (the earth) the dwarfs were engendered and began to move and live.... The dwarfs had been bred in the mould of the earth, just as worms are in a dead body." *The Prose Edda*. "The gods ... took counsel whom they should make the lord of dwarfs out of Ymer's blood (the sea) and his swarthy limbs (the earth)." *The Elder Edda (Voluspa*, stanza 9).

[307] *The Story of Nala*, Monier Williams, p. 67.

[308] *Egyptian Myth and Legend*, pp. 168 it seq.

[309] *The Burden of Isis*, Dennis, p. 24.

[310] *Babylonian Magic and Sorcery*, p. 117.

[311] *Babylonian and Assyrian Religion*, T.G. Pinches, p. l00.

[312] *The Burden of Isis*, J.T. Dennis, p. 49.

[313] *Ibid.*, p. 52.

[314] *Religion of the Ancient Egyptians*, A. Wiedemann, p. 30.

[315] *Vedic Index*, Macdonell & Keith, vol. i, pp. 423 *et seq.*

[316] *Religion of the Ancient Babylonians*, Sayce, p. 153, n. 6.

[317] *Religion of the Ancient Egyptians*, A. Wiedemann, p. 30.

[318] *Aspects of Religious Belief and Practice in Babylonia and Assyria*, p. 95.

[319] *Babylonian and Assyrian Religion*, pp. 63 and 83.

[320] When the King of Assyria transported the Babylonians, &c., to Samaria "the men of Cuth made Nergal", *2 Kings*, xvii, 30.

[321] *Babylonian and Assyrian Religion*, p. 80.

[322] *Indian Myth and Legend*, p. 13.

[323] Derived from the Greek zōon, an animal.

[324] *The Hittites*, pp. 116, 119, 120, 272.

[325] "The sun... is as a bridegroom coming out of his chamber, and rejoiceth as a strong man to run a race." (*Psalm* xix, 4 *et seq.*) The marriage of the sun bridegroom with the moon bride appears to occur in Hittite mythology. In Aryo-Indian Vedic mythology the bride of the sun (Surya) is Ushas, the Dawn. The sun maiden also married the moon god. The Vedic gods ran a race and Indra and Agni were the winners. The sun was "of the nature of Agni". *Indian Myth and Legend*, pp. 14, 36, 37.

[326] Or golden.

[327] The later reference is to Assyria. There was no Assyrian kingdom when these early beliefs were developed.

[328] *Primitive Constellations*, R. Brown, jun., vol. ii, p. 1 *et seq.*

[329] In India "finger counting" (Kaur guna) is associated with prayer or the repeating of mantras. The counting is performed by the thumb, which, when the hand is drawn up, touches the upper part of the third finger. The two upper "chambers" of the third finger are counted, then the two upper "chambers" of the little finger; the thumb then touches the tip of each finger from the little finger to the first; when it comes down into the upper chamber of the first finger 9 is counted. By a similar process each round of 9 on the right hand is recorded by the left up to 12; 12 X 9 = 108 repetitions of a mantra. The upper "chambers" of the fingers are the "best" or "highest" (uttama), the lower (adhama) chambers are not utilized in the prayer-counting process. When Hindus sit cross-legged at prayers, with closed eyes, the right hand is raised from the elbow in front of the body, and the thumb moves each time a mantra is repeated; the left hand lies palm upward on the left knee, and the thumb moves each time nine mantras have been counted.

[330] *Primitive Constellations*, R. Brown, jun., vol. ii, p. 61; and *Early History of Northern India*, J.F. Hewitt, pp. 551-2.

[331] *Rigveda-Samhita*, vol. iv (1892), p. 67.

[332] *Vedic Index*, Macdonell & Keith, vol. ii, pp. 192 *el seq.*

[333] *Indian Myth and Legend*

[334] Pp. 107 *et seq.*

[335] *Primitive Constellation*, R. Brown, jun., vol. i, 1. 333. A table is given showing how 120 saroi equals 360 degrees, each king being identified with a star.

[336] "Behold, his majesty the god Ra is grown old; his bones are become silver, his limbs gold, and his hair pure lapis lazuli." *Religion of the Ancient Egyptians*, A. Wiedemann, p. 58. Ra became a destroyer after completing his reign as an earthly king.

[337] As Nin-Girau, Tammuz was associated with "sevenfold" Orion.

[338] *Babylonian and Assyrian Life*, pp. 61, 62.

[339] Herodotus (ii, 52) as quoted in *Egypt and Scythia* (London, 1886), p. 49.

[340] *Babylonian Magic and Sorcery*, L.W. King (London, 1896), pp. 43 and 115.

[341] *Vedic Index*, Macdonell & Keith, vol. ii, p. 229.

[342] *Ibid* vol. i, pp. 409, 410.

[343] *Ibid* vol. i, p. 415.

[344] *Primitive Constellations*, vol. i, p. 343.

[345] *Custom and Myth*, pp. 133 *et seq.*

[346] Dr. Alfred Jeremias gives very forcible reasons for believing that the ancient Babylonians were acquainted with the precession of the equinoxes. *Das Alter der Babylonischen Astronomie* (Hinrichs, Leipzig, 1908), pp. 47 *et seq.*

[347] *Aspects of Religious Belief and Practice in Babylonia and Assyria*, pp. 207 *et seq.*

[348] *A History of the Babylonians and Assyrians*, p. 93.

[349] *Babylonians and Assyrians: Life and Customs*, pp. 219, 220.

[350] *Primitive Constellations*, vol. ii, pp. 147 et seq.

[351] The Aryo-Indians had a lunar year of 360 days (*Vedic Index*, ii, 158).

[352] *A History of the Babylonians and Assyrians*, p. 94.

[353] *Twelfth Night*, act ii, scene 5.

[354] *Childe Harold*, canto iii, v, 88.

Chapter XIV. Ashur the National God of Assyria

Abstract

Derivation of Ashur--Ashur as Anshar and Anu--Animal forms of Sky God--Anshar as Star God on the Celestial Mount--Isaiah's Parable--Symbols of World God and World Hill--Dance of the Constellations and Dance of Satyrs--Goat Gods and Bull Gods--Symbols of Gods as "High Heads"--The Winged Disc--Human Figure as Soul of the Sun--Ashur as Hercules and Gilgamesh--Gods differentiated by Cults--Fertility Gods as War Gods--Ashur's Tree and Animal forms--Ashur as Nisroch--Lightning Symbol in Disc--Ezekiel's Reference to Life Wheel--Indian Wheel and Discus--Wheels of Shamash and Ahura-Mazda--Hittite Winged Disc--Solar Wheel causes Seasonal Changes--Bonfires to stimulate Solar Deity--Burning of Gods and Kings--Magical Ring and other Symbols of Scotland--Ashur's Wheel of Life and Eagle Wings--King and Ashur associated with Lunar, Fire, and Star Gods--The Osirian Clue--Hittite and Persian Influences.

The rise of Assyria brings into prominence the national god Ashur, who had been the city god of Asshur, the ancient capital. When first met with, he is found to be a complex and mystical deity, and the problem of his origin is consequently rendered exceedingly difficult. Philologists are not agreed as to the derivation of his name, and present as varied views as they do when dealing with the name of Osiris. Some give Ashur a geographical significance, urging that its original form was Aushar, "water field"; others prefer the renderings "Holy", "the Beneficent One", or "the Merciful One"; while not a few regard Ashur as simply a dialectic form of the name of Anshar, the god who, in the Assyrian version, or copy, of the Babylonian Creation myth, is chief of the "host of heaven", and the father of Anu, Ea, and Enlil.

If Ashur is to be regarded as an abstract solar deity, who was developed from a descriptive place name, it follows that he had a history, like Anu or Ea, rooted in Naturalism or Animism. We cannot assume that his strictly local character was produced by modes of thought which did not obtain elsewhere. The colonists who settled at Asshur no doubt imported beliefs from some cultural area; they must have either given recognition to a god, or group of gods, or regarded the trees, hills, rivers, sun, moon, and stars, and the animals as manifestations of the "self power" of the Universe, before they undertook the work of draining and cultivating the "water field" and erecting permanent homes. Those who settled at Nineveh, for instance, believed that they were protected by the goddess Nina, the patron deity of the Sumerian city of Nina. As this goddess was also worshipped at Lagash, and was one of the many forms of the Great Mother, it would appear that in ancient times deities had a tribal rather than a geographical significance.

If the view is accepted that Ashur is Anshar, it can be urged that he was imported from Sumeria. "Out of that land (Shinar)", according to the Biblical reference, "went forth Asshur, and builded Nineveh."[355] Asshur, or Ashur (identical, Delitzsch and Jastrow believe, with Ashir),[356] may have been an eponymous hero--a deified king like Etana, or Gilgamesh, who was regarded as an incarnation of an ancient god. As Anshar was an astral or early form of Anu, the Sumerian city of origin may have been Erech, where the worship of the mother goddess was also given prominence.

Damascius rendered Anshar's name as "Assōros", a fact usually cited to establish Ashur's connection with that deity. This writer stated that the Babylonians passed over "Sige,[357] the mother, that has begotten heaven and earth", and made two--Apason (Apsu), the husband, and Tauthe (Tiawath or Tiamat), whose son was Moymis (Mummu). From these another progeny came forth--Lache and Lachos (Lachmu and Lachamu). These were followed by the progeny Kissare and Assōros (Kishar and Anshar), "from which were produced Anos (Anu), Illillos (Enlil) and Aos (Ea). And of Aos and Dauke (Dawkina or Damkina) was born Belos (Bel Merodach), whom they say is the Demiurge"[358] (the world artisan who carried out the decrees of a higher being).

Lachmu and Lachamu, like the second pair of the ancient group of Egyptian deities, probably symbolized darkness as a reproducing and sustaining power. Anshar was apparently an impersonation of the night sky, as his son Anu was of the day sky. It may have been believed that the soul of Anshar was in the moon as Nannar (Sin), or in a star, or that the moon and the stars were manifestations of him, and that the soul of Anu was in the sun or the firmament, or that the sun, firmament, and the wind were forms of this "self power".

If Ashur combined the attributes of Anshar and Anu, his early mystical character may be accounted for. Like the Indian Brahma, he may have been in his highest form an impersonation, or symbol, of the "self power" or "world soul" of developed Naturalism--the "creator", "preserver", and "destroyer" in one, a god of water, earth, air, and sky, of sun, moon, and stars, fire and lightning, a god of the grove, whose essence was in the fig, or the fir cone, as it was in all animals. The Egyptian god Amon of Thebes, who was associated with water, earth, air, sky, sun and moon, had a ram form, and was "the hidden one", was developed from one of the elder eight gods; in the Pyramid Texts he and his consort are the fourth pair. When Amon was fused with the specialized sun god Ra, he was placed at the head of the Ennead as the Creator. "We have traces", says Jastrow, "of an Assyrian myth of Creation in which the sphere of creator is given to Ashur."[359]

Before a single act of creation was conceived of, however, the early peoples recognized the eternity of matter, which was permeated by the "self power" of which the elder deities were vague phases. These were too vague, indeed, to be worshipped individually. The forms of the "self power" which were propitiated were trees, rivers, hills, or animals. As indicated in the previous chapter, a tribe worshipped an animal or natural object which dominated its environment. The animal might be the source of the food supply, or might have to be propitiated to ensure the food supply. Consequently they identified the self power of the Universe with the particular animal with which they were most concerned. One section identified the spirit of the heavens with the bull and another with the goat. In India Dyaus was a bull, and his spouse, the earth mother, Prithivi, was a cow. The Egyptian sky goddess Hathor was a cow, and other goddesses were identified with the hippopotamus, the serpent, the cat, or the vulture. Ra, the sun god, was identified in turn with the cat, the ass, the bull, the ram, and the crocodile, the various animal forms of the local deities he had absorbed. The eagle inBabylonia and India, and the vulture, falcon, and mysterious Phoenix in Egypt, were identified with the sun, fire, wind, and lightning. The animals associated with the god Ashur were the bull, the eagle, and the lion. He either absorbed the attributes of other gods, or symbolized the "Self Power" of which the animals were manifestations.

The earliest germ of the Creation myth was the idea that night was the parent of day, and water of the earth. Out of darkness and death came light and life. Life was also motion. When the primordial waters became troubled, life began to be. Out of the confusion came order and organization. This process involved the idea of a stable and controlling power, and the succession of a group of deities--passive deities and active deities. When the Babylonian astrologers assisted in developing the Creation myth, they appear to have identified with the stable and controlling spirit of the night heaven that steadfast orb the Polar Star. Anshar, like Shakespeare's Caesar, seemed to say:

I am constant as the northern star, Of whose true-fixed and resting quality There is no fellow in the firmament. The skies are painted with unnumbered sparks; They are all fire, and every one doth shine; But there's but one in all doth hold his place.[360]

Associated with the Polar Star was the constellation Ursa Minor, "the Little Bear", called by the Babylonian astronomers, "the Lesser Chariot". There were chariots before horses were introduced. A patesi of Lagash had a chariot which was drawn by asses.

The seemingly steadfast Polar Star was called "Ilu Sar", "the god Shar", or Anshar, "star of the height", or "Shar the most high". It seemed to be situated at the summit of the vault of heaven. The god Shar, therefore, stood upon the Celestial mountain, the Babylonian Olympus. He was the ghost of the elder god, who in Babylonia was displaced by the younger god, Merodach, as Mercury, the morning star, or as the sun, the planet of day; and in Assyria by Ashur, as the sun, or Regulus, or Arcturus, or Orion. Yet father and son were identical. They were phases of the One, the "self power".

A deified reigning king was an incarnation of the god; after death he merged in the god, as did the Egyptian Unas. The eponymous hero Asshur may have similarly merged in the universal Ashur, who, like Horus, an incarnation of Osiris, had many phases or forms.

Isaiah appears to have been familiar with the Tigro-Euphratean myths about the divinity of kings and the displacement of the elder god by the younger god, of whom the ruling monarch was an incarnation, and with the idea that the summit of the Celestial mountain was crowned by the "north star", the symbol of Anshar. "Thou shalt take up this parable", he exclaimed, making use of Babylonian symbolism, "against the king of Babylon and say, How hath the oppressor ceased! the golden city ceased!... How art thou fallen from heaven, O Lucifer, son of the morning! how art thou cut down to the ground, which didst weaken the nations! For thou hast said in thine heart, I will ascend unto heaven, I will exalt my throne above the stars of God; I will sit also upon the mount of the congregation, *in the sides of the north*, I will ascend above the heights of the clouds; I will be like the most High."[361] The king is identified with Lucifer as the deity of fire and the morning star; he is the younger god who aspired to occupy the mountain throne of his father, the god Shar--the Polar or North Star.

It is possible that the Babylonian idea of a Celestial mountain gave origin to the belief that the earth was a mountain surrounded by the outer ocean, beheld by Etana when he flew towards heaven on the eagle's back. In India this hill is Mount Meru, the "world spine", which "sustains the earth"; it is surmounted by Indra's Valhal, or "the great city of Brahma". In Teutonic mythology the heavens revolve round the Polar Star, which is called "Veraldar nagli",[362] the "world spike"; while the earth is sustained by the "world tree". The "ded" amulet of Egypt symbolized the backbone of Osiris as a world god: "ded" means "firm", "established";[363] while at burial ceremonies the coffin was set up on end, inside the tomb, "on a small sandhill intended to represent the Mountain of the West--the realm of the dead".[364] The Babylonian temple towers were apparently symbols of the "world hill". At Babylon, the Du-azaga, "holy mound", was Merodach's temple E-sagila, "the Temple of the High Head". E-kur, rendered "the house or temple of the Mountain", was the temple of Bel Enlil at Nippur. At Erech, the temple of the goddess Ishtar was E-anna, which connects her, as Nina or Ninni, with Anu, derived from "ana", "heaven". Ishtar was "Queen of heaven".

Now Polaris, situated at the summit of the celestial mountain, was identified with the sacred goat, "the highest of the flock of night".[365] Ursa Minor (the "Little Bear" constellation) may have been "the goat with six heads", referred to by Professor Sayce.[366] The six astral goats or goat-men were supposed to be dancing round the chief goat-man or Satyr (Anshar). Even in the dialogues of Plato the immemorial belief was perpetuated that the constellations were "moving as in a dance". Dancing began as a magical or religious practice, and the earliest astronomers saw their dancing customs reflected in the heavens by the constellations, whose movements were rhythmical. No doubt, Isaiah had in mind the belief of the Babylonians regarding the dance of their goat-gods when he foretold: "Their houses shall be full of doleful creatures; and owls (ghosts) shall dwell there, and *satyrs shall dance there*".[367] In other words, there would be no people left to perform religious dances beside the "desolate houses"; the stars only would be seen dancing round Polaris.

Tammuz, like Anshar, as sentinel of the night heaven, was a goat, as was also Nin-Girsu of Lagash. A Sumerian reference to "a white kid of En Mersi (Nin-Girsu)" was translated into Semitic, "a white kid of Tammuz". The goat was also associated with Merodach. Babylonians, having prayed to that god to take away their diseases or their sins, released a goat, which was driven into the desert. The present Polar Star, which was not, of course, the Polar star of the earliest astronomers, the world having rocked westward, is called in Arabic Al-Jedy, "the kid". In India, the goat was connected with Agni and Varuna; it was slain at funeral ceremonies to inform the gods that a soul was about to enter heaven. Ea, the Sumerian lord of water, earth, and heaven, was symbolized as a "goat fish". Thor, the Teutonic fertility and thunder god, had a chariot drawn by goats. It is of interest to note that the sacred Sumerian goat bore on its forehead the same triangular symbol as the Apis bull of Egypt.

Ashur was not a "goat of heaven", but a "bull of heaven", like the Sumerian Nannar (Sin), the moon god of Ur, Ninip of Saturn, and Bel Enlil. As the bull, however, he was, like Anshar, the ruling animal of the heavens; and like Anshar he had associated with him "six divinities of council".

Other deities who were similarly exalted as "high heads" at various centres and at various periods, included Anu, Bel Enlil, and Ea, Merodach, Nergal, and Shamash. A symbol of the first three was a turban on a seat, or altar, which may have represented the "world mountain". Ea, as "the world spine", was symbolized as a column, with ram's head, standing on a throne, beside which crouched a "goat fish". Merodach's column terminated in a lance head, and the head of a lion crowned that of Nergal. These columns were probably connected with pillar

127

worship, and therefore with tree worship, the pillar being the trunk of the "world tree". The symbol of the sun god Shamash was a disc, from which flowed streams of water; his rays apparently were "fertilizing tears", like the rays of the Egyptian sun god Ra. Horus, the Egyptian falcon god, was symbolized as the winged solar disc.

It is necessary to accumulate these details regarding other deities and their symbols before dealing with Ashur. The symbols of Ashur must be studied, because they are one of the sources of our knowledge regarding the god's origin and character. These include (1) a winged disc with horns, enclosing four circles revolving round a middle circle; rippling rays fall down from either side of the disc; (2) a circle or wheel, suspended from wings, and enclosing a warrior drawing his bow to discharge an arrow; and (3) the same circle; the warrior's bow, however, is carried in his left hand, while the right hand is uplifted as if to bless his worshippers. These symbols are taken from seal cylinders.

An Assyrian standard, which probably represented the "world column", has the disc mounted on a bull's head with horns. The upper part of the disc is occupied by a warrior, whose head, part of his bow, and the point of his arrow protrude from the circle. The rippling water rays are **V**-shaped, and two bulls, treading river-like rays, occupy the divisions thus formed. There are also two heads--a lion's and a man's--with gaping mouths, which may symbolize tempests, the destroying power of the sun, or the sources of the Tigris and Euphrates.

Jastrow regards the winged disc as "the purer and more genuine symbol of Ashur as a solar deity". He calls it "a sun disc with protruding rays", and says: "To this symbol the warrior with the bow and arrow was added--a despiritualization that reflects the martial spirit of the Assyrian empire".[368]

The sun symbol on the sun boat of Ra encloses similarly a human figure, which was apparently regarded as the soul of the sun: the life of the god was in the "sun egg". In an Indian prose treatise it is set forth: "Now that man in yonder orb (the sun) and that man in the right eye truly are no other than Death (the soul). His feet have stuck fast in the heart, and having pulled them out he comes forth; and when he comes forth then that man dies; whence they say of him who has passed away, 'he has been cut off (his life or life string has been severed)'."[369] The human figure did not indicate a process of "despiritualization" either in Egypt or in India. The Horus "winged disc" was besides a symbol of destruction and battle, as well as of light and fertility. Horus assumed that form in one legend to destroy Set and his followers.[370] But, of course, the same symbols may not have conveyed the same ideas to all peoples. As Blake put it:

What to others a trifle appears Fills me full of smiles and tears.... With my inward Eye, 't is an old Man grey, With my outward, a Thistle across my way.

Indeed, it is possible that the winged disc meant one thing to an Assyrian priest, and another thing to a man not gifted with what Blake called "double vision".

What seems certain, however, is that the archer was as truly solar as the "wings" or "rays". In Babylonia and Assyria the sun was, among other things, a destroyer from the earliest times. It is not surprising, therefore, to find that Ashur, like Merodach, resembled, in one of his phases, Hercules, or rather his prototype Gilgamesh. One of Gilgamesh's mythical feats was the slaying of three demon birds. These may be identical with the birds of prey which Hercules, in performing his sixth labour, hunted out of Stymphalus.[371] In the Greek Hipparcho-Ptolemy star list Hercules was the constellation of the "Kneeler", and in Babylonian-Assyrian astronomy he was (as Gilgamesh or Merodach) "Sarru", "the king". The astral "Arrow" (constellation of Sagitta) was pointed against the constellations of the "Eagle", "Vulture", and "Swan". In Phoenician astronomy the Vulture was "Zither" (Lyra), a weapon with which Hercules (identified with Melkarth) slew Linos, the musician. Hercules used a solar arrow, which he received from Apollo. In various mythologies the arrow is associated with the sun, the moon, and the atmospheric deities, and is a symbol of lightning, rain, and fertility, as well as of famine, disease, war, and death. The green-faced goddess Neith of Libya, compared by the Greeks to Minerva, carries in one hand two arrows and a bow.[372] If we knew as little of Athena (Minerva), who was armed with a lance, a breastplate made of the skin of a goat, a shield, and helmet, as we do of Ashur, it might be held that she was simply a goddess of war. The archer in the sun disc of the Assyrian standard probably represented Ashur as the god of the people--a deity closely akin to Merodach, with pronounced Tammuz traits, and therefore linking with other local deities like Ninip, Nergal, and Shamash, and partaking also like these of the attributes of the elder gods Anu, Bel Enlil, and Ea.

All the other deities worshipped by the Assyrians were of Babylonian origin. Ashur appears to have differed from them just as one local Babylonian deity differed from another. He reflected Assyrian experiences and aspirations, but it is difficult to decide whether the sublime spiritual aspect of his character was due to the beliefs of alien peoples, by whom the early Assyrians were influenced, or to the teachings of advanced Babylonian thinkers, whose doctrines found readier acceptance in a "new country" than among the conservative ritualists of ancient Sumerian and Akkadian cities. New cults were formed from time to time in Babylonia, and when they achieved political power they gave a distinctive character to the religion of their city states. Others which did not find political support and remained in obscurity at home, may have yet extended their influence far and wide. Buddhism, for instance, originated in India, but now flourishes in other countries, to which it was introduced by missionaries. In the homeland it was submerged by the revival of Brahmanism, from which it sprung, and which it was intended permanently to displace. An instance of an advanced cult suddenly achieving prominence as a result of political influence is afforded by Egypt, where the fully developed Aton religion was embraced and established as a national religion by Akhenaton, the so-called "dreamer". That migrations were sometimes propelled by cults, which sought new areas in which to exercise religious freedom and propagate their beliefs, is suggested by the invasion of India at the close of the Vedic period by the "later comers", who laid the foundations of Brahmanism. They established themselves in Madhyadesa, "the Middle Country", "the land where the Brahmanas and the later Samhitas were produced". From this centre went forth missionaries, who accomplished the Brahmanization of the rest of India.[373]

It may be, therefore, that the cult of Ashur was influenced in its development by the doctrines of advanced teachers from Babylonia, and that Persian Mithraism was also the product of missionary efforts extended from that great and ancient cultural area. Mitra, as has been stated, was one of the names of the Babylonian sun god, who was also a god of fertility. But Ashur could not have been to begin with merely a battle and solar deity. As the god of a city state he must have been worshipped by agriculturists, artisans, and traders; he must have been recognized as a deity of fertility, culture, commerce, and law. Even as a national god he must have made wider appeal than to the cultured and ruling classes. Bel Enlil of Nippur was a "world god" and war god, but still remained a local corn god.

Assyria's greatness was reflected by Ashur, but he also reflected the origin and growth of that greatness. The civilization of which he was a product had an agricultural basis. It began with the development of the natural resources of Assyria, as was recognized by the Hebrew prophet, who said: "Behold, the Assyrian was a cedar in Lebanon with fair branches.... The waters made him great, the deep set him up on high with her rivers running round about his plants, and sent out her little rivers unto all the trees of the field. Therefore his height was exalted above all the trees of the field, and his boughs were multiplied, and his branches became long because of the multitude of waters when he shot forth. All the fowls of heaven made their nests in his boughs, and under his branches did all the beasts of the field bring forth their young, and under his shadow dwelt all great nations. Thus was he fair in his greatness, in the length of his branches; for his root was by great waters. The cedars in the garden of God could not hide him: the fir trees were not like his boughs, and the chestnut trees were not like his branches; nor any tree in the garden of God was like unto him in his beauty."[374]

Asshur, the ancient capital, was famous for its merchants. It is referred to in the Bible as one of the cities which traded with Tyre "in all sorts of things, in blue clothes, and broidered work, and in chests of rich apparel, bound with cords, and made of cedar".[375]

As a military power, Assyria's name was dreaded. "Behold," Isaiah said, addressing King Hezekiah, "thou hast heard what the kings of Assyria have done to all lands by destroying them utterly."[376] The same prophet, when foretelling how Israel would suffer, exclaimed: "O Assyrian, the rod of mine anger, and the staff in their hand is mine indignation. I will send him against an hypocritical nation, and against the people of my wrath will I give him a charge, to take the spoil, and to take the prey, and to tread them down like the mire of the streets."[377]

We expect to find Ashur reflected in these three phases of Assyrian civilization. If we recognize him in the first place as a god of fertility, his other attributes are at once included. A god of fertility is a corn god and a water god. The river as a river was a "creator" (p. 29), and Ashur was therefore closely associated with the "watery place", with the canals or "rivers running round about his plants". The rippling water-rays, or fertilizing tears, appear on the solar discs. As a corn god, he was a god of war. Tammuz's first act was to slay the demons of winter and storm, as Indra's in India was to slay the demons of drought, and Thor's in Scandinavia was to exterminate the frost giants. The corn god had to be fed with human sacrifices, and the people therefore waged war against foreigners to obtain victims. As the god made a contract with his people, he was a deity of commerce; he provided them with food and they in turn fed him with offerings.

In Ezekiel's comparison of Assyria to a mighty tree, there is no doubt a mythological reference. The Hebrew prophets invariably utilized for their poetic imagery the characteristic beliefs of the peoples to whom they made direct reference. The "owls", "satyrs", and "dragons" of Babylon, mentioned by Isaiah, were taken from Babylonian mythology, as has been indicated. When, therefore, Assyria is compared to a cedar, which is greater than fir or chestnut, and it is stated that there are nesting birds in the branches, and under them reproducing beasts of the field, and that the greatness of the tree is due to "the multitude of waters", the conclusion is suggested that Assyrian religion, which Ashur's symbols reflect, included the worship of trees, birds, beasts, and water. The symbol of the Assyrian tree--probably the "world tree" of its religion--appears to be "the rod of mine anger ... the staff in their hand"; that is, the battle standard which was a symbol of Ashur. Tammuz and Osiris were tree gods as well as corn gods.

Now, as Ashur was evidently a complex deity, it is futile to attempt to read his symbols without giving consideration to the remnants of Assyrian mythology which are found in the ruins of the ancient cities. These either reflect the attributes of Ashur, or constitute the material from which he evolved.

As Layard pointed out many years ago, the Assyrians had a sacred tree which became conventionalized. It was "an elegant device, in which curved branches, springing from a kind of scroll work, terminated in flowers of graceful form. As one of the figures last described[378] was turned, as if in act of adoration, towards this device, it was evidently a sacred emblem; and I recognized in it the holy tree, or tree of life, so universally adored at the remotest period in the East, and which was preserved in the religious systems of the Persians to the final overthrow of their Empire.... The flowers were formed by seven petals."[379]

This tree looks like a pillar, and is thrice crossed by conventionalized bull's horns tipped with ring symbols which may be stars, the highest pair of horns having a larger ring between them, but only partly shown as if it were a crescent. The tree with its many "sevenfold" designs may have been a symbol of the "Sevenfold-one-are-ye" deity. This is evidently the Assyrian tree which was called "the rod" or "staff".

What mythical animals did this tree shelter? Layard found that "the four creatures continually introduced on the sculptured walls", were "a man, a lion, an ox, and an eagle".[380]

In Sumeria the gods were given human form, but before this stage was reached the bull symbolized Nannar (Sin), the moon god, Ninip (Saturn, the old sun), and Enlil, while Nergal was a lion, as a tribal sun god. The eagle is represented by the Zu bird, which symbolized the storm and a phase of the sun, and was also a deity of fertility. On the silver vase of Lagash the lion and eagle were combined as the lion-headed eagle, a form of Nin-Girsu (Tammuz), and it was associated with wild goats, stags, lions, and bulls. On a mace head dedicated to Nin-Girsu, a lion slays a bull as the Zu bird slays serpents in the folk tale, suggesting the wars of totemic deities, according to one "school", and the battle of the sun with the storm clouds according to another. Whatever the explanation may be of one animal deity of fertility slaying another, it seems certain that the conflict was associated with the idea of sacrifice to procure the food supply.

In Assyria the various primitive gods were combined as a winged bull, a winged bull with human head (the king's), a winged lion with human head, a winged man, a deity with lion's head, human body, and eagle's legs with claws, and also as a deity with eagle's head and feather headdress, a human body, wings, and feather-fringed robe, carrying in one hand a metal basket on which two winged men adored the holy tree, and in the other a fir cone.[381]

Layard suggested that the latter deity, with eagle's head, was Nisroch, "the word Nisr signifying, in all Semitic languages, an eagle".[382] This deity is referred to in the Bible: "Sennacherib, king of Assyria, ... was worshipping in the house of Nisroch, his god".[383] Professor Pinches is certain that Nisroch is Ashur, but considers that the "ni" was attached to "Ashur" (Ashuraku or Ashurachu), as it was to "Marad" (Merodach) to give the reading Ni-Marad = Nimrod. The names of heathen deities were thus made "unrecognizable, and in all probability ridiculous as well.... Pious and orthodox lips could pronounce them without fear of defilement."[384] At the same time the "Nisr" theory is probable: it may represent another phase of this process. The names of heathen gods were not all treated in like manner by the Hebrew teachers. Abed-*nebo*, for instance, became Abed-*nego*, *Daniel*, i, 7), as Professor Pinches shows.

Seeing that the eagle received prominence in the mythologies of Sumeria and Assyria, as a deity of fertility with solar and atmospheric attributes, it is highly probable that the Ashur symbol, like the Egyptian Horus solar disk, is a winged symbol of life, fertility, and destruction. The idea that it represents the sun in eclipse, with protruding rays, seems rather far-fetched, because eclipses were disasters and indications of divine wrath;[385] it certainly does not explain why the "rays" should only stretch out sideways, like wings, and downward like a tail, why the "rays" should be double, like the double wings of cherubs, bulls, &c, and divided into sections suggesting feathers, or why the disk is surmounted by conventionalized horns, tipped with star-like ring symbols, identical with those depicted in the holy tree. What particular connection the five small rings within the disk were supposed to have with the eclipse of the sun is difficult to discover.

In one of the other symbols in which appears a feather-robed archer, it is significant to find that the arrow he is about to discharge has a head shaped like a trident; it is evidently a lightning symbol.

When Ezekiel prophesied to the Israelitish captives at Tel-abib, "by the river of Chebar" in Chaldea (Kheber, near Nippur), he appears to have utilized Assyrian symbolism. Probably he came into contact in Babylonia with fugitive priests from Assyrian cities.

This great prophet makes interesting references to "four living creatures", with "four faces"--the face of a man, the face of a lion, the face of an ox, and the face of an eagle; "they had the hands of a man under their wings, ... their wings were joined one to another; ... their wings were stretched upward: two wings of every one were joined one to another.... Their appearance was like burning coals of fire and like the appearance of lamps.... The living creatures ran and returned as the appearance of a flash of lightning."[386]

Elsewhere, referring to the sisters, Aholah and Aholibah, who had been in Egypt and had adopted unmoral ways of life Ezekiel tells that when Aholibah "doted upon the Assyrians" she "saw men pourtrayed upon the wall, the images of the Chaldeans pourtrayed with vermilion, girded with girdles upon their loins".[387] Traces of the red colour on the walls of Assyrian temples and palaces have been observed by excavators. The winged gods "like burning coals" were probably painted in vermilion.

Ezekiel makes reference to "ring" and "wheel" symbols. In his vision he saw "one wheel upon the earth by the living creatures, with his four faces. The appearance of the wheels and their work was like unto the colour of beryl; and they four had one likeness; and their appearance and their work was as it were a wheel in the middle of a wheel.... As for their rings, they were so high that they were dreadful; and their rings were full of eyes round about them four. And when the living creatures went, the wheels went by them; and when the living creatures were lifted up from the earth, the wheels were lifted up. Whithersoever the spirit was to go, they went, thither was their spirit to go; and the wheels were lifted up over against them; *for the spirit of the living creature was in the wheels*....[388] And the likeness of the firmament upon the heads of the living creature was as the colour of terrible crystal, stretched forth over their heads above.... And when they went I heard the noise of their wings, like the noise of great waters, as the voice of the Almighty, the voice of speech, as the noise of an host; when they stood they let down their wings...."[389]

Another description of the cherubs states: "Their whole body, and their backs, and their hands, and their wings, and the wheels, were full of eyes (? stars) round about, even the wheels that they four had. As for the wheels, it was cried unto them in my hearing, O wheel!" -- or, according to a marginal rendering, "they were called in my hearing, wheel, or Gilgal," i.e. move round.... "And the cherubims were lifted up."[390]

It would appear that the wheel (or hoop, a variant rendering) was a symbol of life, and that the Assyrian feather-robed figure which it enclosed was a god, not of war only, but also of fertility. His trident-headed arrow resembles, as has been suggested, a lightning symbol. Ezekiel's references are suggestive in this connection. When the cherubs "ran and returned" they had "the appearance of a flash of lightning", and "the noise of their wings" resembled "the noise of great waters". Their bodies were "like burning coals of fire". Fertility gods were associated with fire, lightning, and water. Agni of India, Sandan of Asia Minor, and Melkarth of Phoenicia were highly developed fire gods of fertility. The fire cult was also represented in Sumeria (pp. 49-51).

In the Indian epic, the *Mahabharata*, the revolving ring or wheel protects the Soma[391] (ambrosia) of the gods, on which their existence depends. The eagle giant Garuda sets forth to steal it. The gods, fully armed, gather round to protect the life-giving drink. Garuda approaches "darkening the worlds by the dust raised by the hurricane of his wings". The celestials, "overwhelmed by that dust", swoon away. Garuda afterwards assumes a fiery shape, then looks "like masses of black clouds", and in the end its body becomes golden and bright "as the rays of the sun". The Soma is protected by fire, which the bird quenches after "drinking in many rivers" with the numerous mouths it has assumed. Then Garuda finds that right above the Soma is "a wheel of steel, keen edged, and sharp as a razor, revolving incessantly. That fierce instrument, of the lustre of the blazing sun and of terrible form, was devised by the gods for cutting to pieces all robbers of the Soma." Garuda passes "through the spokes of the wheel", and has then to contend against "two great snakes of the lustre of blazing fire, of tongues bright as the lightning flash, of great energy, of mouth emitting fire, of blazing eyes". He slays the snakes.... The gods afterwards recover the stolen Soma.

Garuda becomes the vehicle of the god Vishnu, who carries the discus, another fiery wheel which revolves and returns to the thrower like lightning. "And he (Vishnu) made the bird sit on the flagstaff of his car, saying: 'Even thus thou shalt stay above me'."[392]

The Persian god Ahura Mazda hovers above the king in sculptured representations of that high dignitary, enclosed in a winged wheel, or disk, like Ashur, grasping a ring in one hand, the other being lifted up as if blessing those who adore him.

Shamash, the Babylonian sun god; Ishtar, the goddess of heaven; and other Babylonian deities carried rings as the Egyptian gods carried the ankh, the symbol of life. Shamash was also depicted sitting on his throne in a pillar-supported pavilion, in front of which is a sun wheel. The spokes of the wheel are formed by a star symbol and threefold rippling "water rays".

In Hittite inscriptions there are interesting winged emblems; "the central portion" of one "seems to be composed of two crescents underneath a disk (which is also divided like a crescent). Above the emblem there appear the symbol of sanctity (the divided oval) and the hieroglyph which Professor Sayce interprets as the name of the god Sandes." In another instance "the centre of the winged emblem may be seen to be a rosette, with a curious spreading object below. Above, two dots follow the name of Sandes, and a human arm bent 'in adoration' is by the side...." Professor Garstang is here dealing with sacred places "on rocky points or hilltops, bearing out the suggestion of the sculptures near Boghaz-Keui[393], in which there may be reasonably suspected the surviving traces of mountain cults, or cults of mountain deities, underlying the newer religious symbolism". Who the deity is it is impossible to say, but "he was identified at some time or other with Sandes".[394] It would appear, too, that the god may have been "called by a name which was that used also by the priest". Perhaps the priest king was believed to be an incarnation of the deity.

Sandes or Sandan was identical with Sandon of Tarsus, "the prototype of Attis",[395] who links with the Babylonian Tammuz. Sandon's animal symbol was the lion, and he carried the "double axe" symbol of the god of fertility and thunder. As Professor Frazer has shown in *The Golden Bough*, he links with Hercules and Melkarth.[396]

All the younger gods, who displaced the elder gods as one year displaces another, were deities of fertility, battle, lightning, fire, and the sun; it is possible, therefore, that Ashur was like Merodach, son of Ea, god of the deep, a form of Tammuz in origin. His spirit was in the solar wheel which revolved at times of seasonal change. In Scotland it was believed that on the morning of May Day (Beltaine) the rising sun revolved three times. The younger god was a spring sun god and fire god. Great bonfires were lit to strengthen him, or as a ceremony of riddance; the old year was burned out. Indeed the god himself might be burned (that is, the old god), so that he might renew his youth. Melkarth was burned at Tyre. Hercules burned himself on a mountain top, and his soul ascended to heaven as an eagle.

These fiery rites were evidently not unknown in Babylonia and Assyria. When, according to Biblical narrative, Nebuchadnezzar "made an image of gold" which he set up "in the plain of Dura, in the province of Babylon", he commanded: "O people, nations, and languages... at the time ye hear the sound of the cornet, flute, harp, sackbut, psaltery, dulcimer, and all kinds of musick... fall down and worship the golden image". Certain Jews who had been "set over the affairs of the province of Babylonia", namely, "Shadrach, Meshach, and Abed-nego", refused to adore the idol. They were punished by being thrown into "a burning fiery furnace", which was heated "seven times more than it was wont to be heated". They came forth uninjured.[397]

In the Koran it is related that Abraham destroyed the images of Chaldean gods; he "brake them all in pieces except the biggest of them; that they might lay the blame on that".[398] According to the commentators the Chaldaeans were at the time "abroad in the fields, celebrating a great festival". To punish the offender Nimrod had a great pyre erected at Cuthah. "Then they bound Abraham, and putting him into an engine, shot him into the midst of the fire, from which he was preserved by the angel Gabriel, who was sent to his assistance." Eastern Christians were wont to set apart in the Syrian calendar the 25th of January to commemorate Abraham's escape from Nimrod's pyre.[399]

It is evident that the Babylonian fire ceremony was observed in the spring season, and that human beings were sacrificed to the sun god. A mock king may have been burned to perpetuate the ancient sacrifice of real kings, who were incarnations of the god.

Isaiah makes reference to the sacrificial burning of kings in Assyria: "For through the voice of the Lord shall the Assyrian be beaten down, which smote with a rod. And in every place where the grounded staff shall pass, which the Lord shall lay upon him, it shall be with tabrets and harps: and in battles of shaking will he fight with it. For Tophet is ordained of old; yea, for the king it is prepared: he hath made it deep and large: the pile thereof is fire and much wood: the breath of the Lord, like a stream of brimstone, doth kindle it."[400] When Nineveh was about to fall, and with it the Assyrian Empire, the legendary king, Sardanapalus, who was reputed to have founded Tarsus, burned himself, with his wives, concubines, and eunuchs, on a pyre in his palace. Zimri, who reigned over Israel for seven days, "burnt the king's house over him with fire"[401]. Saul, another fallen king, was burned after death, and his bones were buried "under the oak in Jabesh".[402] In Europe the oak was associated with gods of fertility and lightning, including Jupiter and Thor. The ceremony of burning Saul is of special interest. Asa, the orthodox king of Judah, was, after death, "laid in the bed which was filled with sweet odours and divers kinds of spices prepared by the apothecaries' art: and they made a very great burning for him" (2 *Chronicles*, xvi, 14). Jehoram, the heretic king of Judah, who "walked in the way of the kings of Israel", died of "an incurable disease. And his people made no burning for him like the burning of his fathers" (2 *Chronicles*, xxi, 18, 19).

The conclusion suggested by the comparative study of the beliefs of neighbouring peoples, and the evidence afforded by Assyrian sculptures, is that Ashur was a highly developed form of the god of fertility, who was sustained, or aided in his conflicts with demons, by the fires and sacrifices of his worshippers.

It is possible to read too much into his symbols. These are not more complicated and vague than are the symbols on the standing stones of Scotland--the crescent with the "broken" arrow; the trident with the double rings, or wheels, connected by two crescents; the circle with the dot in its centre; the triangle with the dot; the large disk with two small rings on either side crossed by double straight lines; the so-called "mirror", and so on. Highly developed symbolism may not indicate a process of spiritualization so much, perhaps, as the persistence of magical beliefs and practices. There is really no direct evidence to support the theory that the Assyrian winged disk, or disk "with protruding rays", was of more spiritual character than the wheel which encloses the feather-robed archer with his trident-shaped arrow.

The various symbols may have represented phases of the god. When the spring fires were lit, and the god "renewed his life like the eagle", his symbol was possibly the solar wheel or disk with eagle's wings, which became regarded as a symbol of life. The god brought life and light to the world; he caused the crops to grow; he gave increase; he sustained his worshippers. But he was also the god who slew the demons of darkness and storm. The Hittite winged disk was Sandes or Sandon, the god of lightning, who stood on the back of a bull. As the lightning god was a war god, it was in keeping with his character to find him represented in Assyria as "Ashur the archer" with the bow and lightning arrow. On the disk of the Assyrian standard the lion and the bull appear with "the archer" as symbols of the war god Ashur, but they were also symbols of Ashur the god of fertility.

The life or spirit of the god was in the ring or wheel, as the life of the Egyptian and Indian gods, and of the giants of folk tales, was in "the egg". The "dot within the circle", a widespread symbol, may have represented the seed within "the egg" of more than one mythology, or the thorn within the egg of more than one legendary story. It may be that in Assyria, as in India, the crude beliefs and symbols of the masses were spiritualized by the speculative thinkers in the priesthood, but no literary evidence has survived to justify us in placing the Assyrian teachers on the same level as the Brahmans who composed the Upanishads.

Temples were erected to Ashur, but he might be worshipped anywhere, like the Queen of Heaven, who received offerings in the streets of Jerusalem, for "he needed no temple", as Professor Pinches says. Whether this was because he was a highly developed deity or a product of folk religion it is difficult to decide. One important fact is that the ruling king of Assyria was more closely connected with the worship of Ashur than the king of Babylonia was with the worship of Merodach. This may be because the Assyrian king was regarded as an incarnation of his god, like the Egyptian Pharaoh. Ashur accompanied the monarch on his campaigns: he was their conquering war god. Where the king was, there was Ashur also. No images were made of him, but his symbols were carried aloft, as were the symbols of Indian gods in the great war of the *Mahabharata* epic.

It would appear that Ashur was sometimes worshipped in the temples of other gods. In an interesting inscription he is associated with the moon god Nannar (Sin) of Haran. Esarhaddon, the Assyrian king, is believed to have been crowned in that city. "The writer", says Professor Pinches, "is apparently addressing Assur-bani-apli, 'the great and noble Asnapper':

"When the father of my king my lord went to Egypt, he was crowned (?) in the *ganni* of Harran, the temple (lit. 'Bethel') of cedar. The god Sin remained over the (sacred) standard, two crowns upon his head, (and) the god Nusku stood beside him. The father of the king my lord entered, (and) he (the priest of Sin) placed (the crown?) upon his head, (saying) thus: 'Thou shalt go and capture the lands in the midst'. (He we)nt, he captured the land of Egypt. The rest of the lands not submitting (?) to Assur (Ashur) and Sin, the king, the lord of kings, shall capture (them)."[403]

133

Ashur and Sin are here linked as equals. Associated with them is Nusku, the messenger of the gods, who was given prominence in Assyria. The kings frequently invoked him. As the son of Ea he acted as the messenger between Merodach and the god of the deep. He was also a son of Bel Enlil, and like Anu was guardian or chief of the Igigi, the "host of heaven". Professor Pinches suggests that he may have been either identical with the Sumerian fire god Gibil, or a brother of the fire god, and an impersonation of the light of fire and sun. In Haran he accompanied the moon god, and may, therefore, have symbolized the light of the moon also. Professor Pinches adds that in one inscription "he is identified with Nirig or En-reshtu" (Nin-Girsu = Tammuz).[404] The Babylonians and Assyrians associated fire and light with moisture and fertility.

The astral phase of the character of Ashur is highly probable. As has been indicated, the Greek rendering of Anshar as "Assoros", is suggestive in this connection. Jastrow, however, points out that the use of the characters Anshar for Ashur did not obtain until the eighth century B.C. "Linguistically", he says, "the change of Ashir to Ashur can be accounted for, but not the transformation of An-shar to Ashur or Ashir; so that we must assume the 'etymology' of Ashur, proposed by some learned scribe, to be the nature of a play upon the name."[405] On the other hand, it is possible that what appears arbitrary to us may have been justified in ancient Assyria on perfectly reasonable, or at any rate traditional, grounds. Professor Pinches points out that as a sun god, and "at the same time not Shamash", Ashur resembled Merodach. "His identification with Merodach, if that was ever accepted, may have been due to the likeness of the word to Asari, one of the deities' names."[406] As Asari, Merodach has been compared to the Egyptian Osiris, who, as the Nile god, was Asar-Hapi. Osiris resembles Tammuz and was similarly a corn deity and a ruler of the living and the dead, associated with sun, moon, stars, water, and vegetation. We may consistently connect Ashur with Aushar, "water field", Anshar, "god of the height", or "most high", and with the eponymous King Asshur who went out on the land of Nimrod and "builded Nineveh", if we regard him as of common origin with Tammuz, Osiris, and Attis--a developed and localized form of the ancient deity of fertility and corn.

Ashur had a spouse who is referred to as Ashuritu, or Beltu, "the lady". Her name, however, is not given, but it is possible that she was identified with the Ishtar of Nineveh. In the historical texts Ashur, as the royal god, stands alone. Like the Hittite Great Father, he was perhaps regarded as the origin of life. Indeed, it may have been due to the influence of the northern hillmen in the early Assyrian period, that Ashur was developed as a father god--a Baal. When the Hittite inscriptions are read, more light may be thrown on the Ashur problem. Another possible source of cultural influence is Persia. The supreme god Ahura-Mazda (Ormuzd) was, as has been indicated, represented, like Ashur, hovering over the king's head, enclosed in a winged disk or wheel, and the sacred tree figured in Persian mythology. The early Assyrian kings had non-Semitic and non-Sumerian names. It seems reasonable to assume that the religious culture of the ethnic elements they represented must have contributed to the development of the city god of Asshur.

[355] *Genesis*, x, 11.

[356] "A number of tablets have been found in Cappadocia of the time of the Second Dynasty of Ur which show marked affinities with Assyria. The divine name Ashir, as in early Assyrian texts, the institution of eponyms and many personal names which occur in Assyria, are so characteristic that we must assume kinship of peoples. But whether they witness to a settlement in Cappadocia from Assyria, or vice versa, is not yet clear." *Ancient Assyria*, C.H.W. Johns (Cambridge, 1912), pp. 12-13.

[357] Sumerian Ziku, apparently derived from Zi, the spiritual essence of life, the "self power" of the Universe.

[358] *Peri Archon*, cxxv.

[359] *Religion of Babylonia and Assyria*, p. 197 et seq.

[360] *Julius Caesar*, act iii, scene I.

[361] *Isaiah*, xiv, 4-14.

[362] *Edduhrott*, ii.

[363] *Religion of the Ancient Egyptians*, A. Wiedemann, pp. 289-90.

[364] *Ibid.*, p. 236. Atlas was also believed to be in the west.

[365] *Primitive Constellations*, vol. ii, p. 184.

[366] *Cuneiform Inscriptions of Western Asia*, xxx, II.

[367] *Isaiah*, xiii, 21. For "Satyrs" the Revised Version gives the alternative translation, "or he-goats".

[368] *Aspects of Religious Belief and Practice in Babylonia and Assyria*, p. 120, plate 18 and note.

[369] *Satapatha Brahmana*, translated by Professor Eggeling, part iv, 1897, p. 371. *(Sacred Books of the East.)*

[370] *Egyptian Myth and Legend*, pp. 165 et seq.

[371] *Classic Myth and Legend*, p. 105. The birds were called "Stymphalides".

[372] The so-called "shuttle" of Neith may be a thunderbolt. Scotland's archaic thunder deity is a goddess. The bow and arrows suggest a lightning goddess who was a deity of war because she was a deity of fertility.

[373] *Vedic Index*, Macdonell & Keith, vol. ii, pp. 125-6, and vol. i, 168-9.

[374] *Ezekiel*, xxxi, 3-8.

[375] *Ezekiel*, xxvii, 23, 24.

[376] *Isaiah*, xxxvii, 11.

[377] *Ibid.*, x, 5, 6.

[378] A winged human figure, carrying in one hand a basket and in another a fir cone.

[379] Layard's *Nineveh* (1856), p. 44.

[380] *Ibid.*, p. 309.

[381] The fir cone was offered to Attis and Mithra. Its association with Ashur suggests that the great Assyrian deity resembled the gods of corn and trees and fertility.

[382] *Nineveh*, p. 47.

[383] *Isaiah*, xxxvii, 37-8.

[384] *The Old Testament in the Light of the Historical Records and Legends of Assyria and Babylonia*, pp. 129-30.

[385] An eclipse of the sun in Assyria on June 15, 763 B.C., was followed by an outbreak of civil war.

[386] *Ezekiel*, i, 4-14.

[387] *Ezekiel*, xxiii, 1-15.

[388] As the soul of the Egyptian god was in the sun disk or sun egg.

[389] *Ezekiel,*, i, 15-28.

[390] *Ezekiel*, x, 11-5.

[391] Also called "Amrita".

[392] The *Mahabharata* (*Adi Parva*), Sections xxxiii-iv.

[393] Another way of spelling the Turkish name which signifies "village of the pass". The deep "gh" guttural is not usually attempted by English speakers. A common rendering is "Bog-haz' Kay-ee", a slight "oo" sound being given to the "a" in "Kay"; the "z" sound is hard and hissing.

[394] *The Land of the Hittites*, J. Garstang, pp. 178 et seq.

[395] *Ibid.*, p. 173.

[396] *Adonis, Attis, Osiris*, chaps. v and vi.

[397] *Daniel*, iii, 1-26.

[398] The story that Abraham hung an axe round the neck of Baal after destroying the other idols is of Jewish origin.

[399] *The Koran*, George Sale, pp. 245-6.

[400] *Isaiah*, xxx, 31-3. See also for Tophet customs *2 Kings*, xxiii, 10; *Jeremiah*, vii, 31, 32 and xix, 5-12.

[401] *1 Kings*, xvi, 18.

[402] *1 Samuel*, xxxi, 12, 13 and *1 Chronicles*, x, 11, 12.

[403] *The Old Testament in the Light of the Historical Records and Legends of Assyria and Babylonia*, pp. 201-2.

[404] *Babylonian and Assyrian Religion*, pp. 57-8.

[405] *Aspects of Religious Belief and Practice in Babylonia and Assyria*, p. 121.

[406] *Babylonian and Assyrian Religion*, p. 86.

Chapter XV. Conflicts for Trade and Supremacy

Abstract

Modern Babylonia--History repeating itself--Babylonian Trade Route in Mesopotamia--Egyptian Supremacy in Syria--Mitanni and Babylonia--Bandits who plundered Caravans--Arabian Desert Trade Route opened--Assyrian and Elamite Struggles with Babylonia--Rapid Extension of Assyrian Empire--Hittites control Western Trade Routes--Egypt's Nineteenth Dynasty Conquests--Campaigns of Rameses II--Egyptians and Hittites become Allies--Babylonian Fears of Assyria--Shalmaneser's Triumphs--Assyria Supreme in Mesopotamia--Conquest of Babylonia--Fall of a Great King--Civil War in Assyria--Its Empire goes to pieces--

Babylonian Wars with Elam--Revival of Babylonian Power--Invasions of Assyrians and Elamites--End of the Kassite Dynasty--Babylonia contrasted with Assyria.

It is possible that during the present century Babylonia may once again become one of the great wheat-producing countries of the world. A scheme of land reclamation has already been inaugurated by the construction of a great dam to control the distribution of the waters of the Euphrates, and, if it is energetically promoted on a generous scale in the years to come, the ancient canals, which are used at present as caravan roads, may yet be utilized to make the whole country as fertile and prosperous as it was in ancient days. When that happy consummation is reached, new cities may grow up and flourish beside the ruins of the old centres of Babylonian culture.

With the revival of agriculture will come the revival of commerce. Ancient trade routes will then be reopened, and the slow-travelling caravans supplanted by speedy trains. A beginning has already been made in this direction. The first modern commercial highway which is crossing the threshold of Babylonia's new Age is the German railway through Asia Minor, North Syria, and Mesopotamia to Baghdad.[407] It brings the land of Hammurabi into close touch with Europe, and will solve problems which engaged the attention of many rival monarchs for long centuries before the world knew aught of "the glory that was Greece and the grandeur that was Rome".

These sudden and dramatic changes are causing history to repeat itself. Once again the great World Powers are evincing much concern regarding their respective "spheres of influence" in Western Asia, and pressing together around the ancient land of Babylon. On the east, where the aggressive Elamites and Kassites were followed by the triumphant Persians and Medes, Russia and Britain have asserted themselves as protectors of Persian territory, and the influence of Britain is supreme in the Persian Gulf. Turkey controls the land of the Hittites, while Russia looms like a giant across the Armenian highlands; Turkey is also the governing power in Syria and Mesopotamia, which are being crossed by Germany's Baghdad railway. France is constructing railways in Syria, and will control the ancient "way of the Philistines". Britain occupies Cyprus on the Mediterranean coast, and presides over the destinies of the ancient land of Egypt, which, during the brilliant Eighteenth Dynasty, extended its sphere of influence to the borders of Asia Minor. Once again, after the lapse of many centuries, international politics is being strongly influenced by the problems connected with the development of trade in Babylonia and its vicinity.

The history of the ancient rival States, which is being pieced together by modern excavators, is, in view of present-day political developments, invested with special interest to us. We have seen Assyria rising into prominence. It began to be a great Power when Egypt was supreme in the "Western Land" (the land of the Amorites) as far north as the frontiers of Cappadocia. Under the Kassite regime Babylonia's political influence had declined in Mesopotamia, but its cultural influence remained, for its language and script continued in use among traders and diplomatists.

At the beginning of the Pharaoh Akhenaton period, the supreme power in Mesopotamia was Mitanni. As the ally of Egypt it constituted a buffer state on the borders of North Syria, which prevented the southern expansion from Asia Minor of the Hittite confederacy and the western expansion of aggressive Assyria, while it also held in check the ambitions of Babylonia, which still claimed the "land of the Amorites". So long as Mitanni was maintained as a powerful kingdom the Syrian possessions of Egypt were easily held in control, and the Egyptian merchants enjoyed preferential treatment compared with those of Babylonia. But when Mitanni was overcome, and its territories were divided between the Assyrians and the Hittites, the North Syrian Empire of Egypt went to pieces. A great struggle then ensued between the nations of western Asia for political supremacy in the "land of the Amorites".

Babylonia had been seriously handicapped by losing control of its western caravan road. Prior to the Kassite period its influence was supreme in Mesopotamia and middle Syria; from the days of Sargon of Akkad and of Naram-Sin until the close of the Hammurabi Age its merchants had naught to fear from bandits or petty kings between the banks of the Euphrates and the Mediterranean coast. The city of Babylon had grown rich and powerful as the commercial metropolis of Western Asia.

Separated from the Delta frontier by the broad and perilous wastes of the Arabian desert, Babylonia traded with Egypt by an indirect route. Its caravan road ran northward along the west bank of the Euphrates towards Haran, and then southward through Palestine. This was a long detour, but it was the only possible way.

During the early Kassite Age the caravans from Babylon had to pass through the area controlled by Mitanni, which was therefore able to impose heavy duties and fill its coffers with Babylonian gold. Nor did the situation improve when the influence of Mitanni suffered decline in southern Mesopotamia. Indeed the difficulties under which traders operated were then still further increased, for the caravan roads were infested by plundering bands of "Suti", to whom references are made in the Tell-el-Amarna letters. These bandits defied all the great powers, and became so powerful that even the messengers sent from one king to another were liable to be robbed and murdered without discrimination. When war broke out between powerful States they harried live stock and sacked towns in those areas which were left unprotected.

The "Suti" were Arabians of Aramaean stock. What is known as the "Third Semitic Migration" was in progress during this period. The nomads gave trouble to Babylonia and Assyria, and, penetrating Mesopotamia and Syria, sapped the power of Mitanni, until it was unable to resist the onslaughts of the Assyrians and the Hittites.

The Aramaean tribes are referred to, at various periods and by various peoples, not only as the "Suti", but also as the "Achlame", the "Arimi", and the "Khabiri". Ultimately they were designated simply as "Syrians", and under that name became the hereditary enemies of the Hebrews, although Jacob was regarded as being of their stock: "A Syrian ready to perish", runs a Biblical reference, "was my father (ancestor), and he went down into Egypt and sojourned there with a few, and became there a nation, great, mighty, and populous".[408]

An heroic attempt was made by one of the Kassite kings of Babylonia to afford protection to traders by stamping out brigandage between Arabia and Mesopotamia, and opening up a new and direct caravan road to Egypt across the Arabian desert. The monarch in question was Kadashman-Kharbe, the grandson of Ashur-uballit of Assyria. As we have seen, he combined forces with his distinguished and powerful kinsman, and laid a heavy hand on the "Suti". Then he dug wells and erected a chain of fortifications, like "block-houses", so that caravans might come and go without interruption, and merchants be freed from the imposts of petty kings whose territory they had to penetrate when travelling by the Haran route.

This bold scheme, however, was foredoomed to failure. It was shown scant favour by the Babylonian Kassites. No record survives to indicate the character of the agreement between Kadashman-Kharbe and Ashur-uballit, but there can be little doubt that it involved the abandonment by Babylonia of its historic claim upon Mesopotamia, or part of it, and the recognition of an Assyrian sphere of influence in that region. It was probably on account of his pronounced pro-Assyrian tendencies that the Kassites murdered Kadashman-Kharbe, and set the pretender, known as "the son of nobody", on the throne for a brief period.

Kadashman-Kharbe's immediate successors recognized in Assyria a dangerous and unscrupulous rival, and resumed the struggle for the possession of Mesopotamia. The trade route across the Arabian desert had to be abandoned. Probably it required too great a force to keep it open. Then almost every fresh conquest achieved by Assyria involved it in war with Babylonia, which appears to have been ever waiting for a suitable opportunity to cripple its northern rival.

But Assyria was not the only power which Babylonia had to guard itself against. On its eastern frontier Elam was also panting for expansion. Its chief caravan roads ran from Susa through Assyria towards Asia Minor, and through Babylonia towards the Phoenician coast. It was probably because its commerce was hampered by the growth of Assyrian power in the north, as Servia's commerce in our own day has been hampered by Austria, that it cherished dreams of conquering Babylonia. In fact, as Kassite influence suffered decline, one of the great problems of international politics was whether Elam or Assyria would enter into possession of the ancient lands of Sumer and Akkad.

Ashur-uballit's vigorous policy of Assyrian expansion was continued, as has been shown, by his son Bel-nirari. His grandson, Arik-den-ilu, conducted several successful campaigns, and penetrated westward as far as Haran, thus crossing the Babylonian caravan road. He captured great herds of cattle and flocks of sheep, which were transported to Asshur, and on one occasion carried away 250,000 prisoners.

Meanwhile Babylonia waged war with Elam. It is related that Khur-batila, King of Elam, sent a challenge to Kurigalzu III, a descendant of Kadashman-Kharbe, saying: "Come hither; I will fight with thee". The Babylonian monarch accepted the challenge, invaded the territory of his rival, and won a great victory. Deserted by his troops, the Elamite king was taken prisoner, and did not secure release until he had ceded a portion of his territory and consented to pay annual tribute to Babylonia.

Flushed with his success, the Kassite king invaded Assyria when Adad-nirari I died and his son Arik-den-ilu came to the throne. He found, however, that the Assyrians were more powerful than the Elamites, and suffered defeat. His son, Na´zi-mar-ut´tash[409], also made an unsuccessful attempt to curb the growing power of the northern Power.

These recurring conflicts were intimately associated with the Mesopotamian question. Assyria was gradually expanding westward and shattering the dreams of the Babylonian statesmen and traders who hoped to recover control of the caravan routes and restore the prestige of their nation in the west.

Like his father, Adad-nirari I of Assyria had attacked the Aramaean "Suti" who were settling about Haran. He also acquired a further portion of the ancient kingdom of Mitanni, with the result that he exercised sway over part of northern Mesopotamia. After defeating Na´zi-mar-ut´tash, he fixed the boundaries of the Assyrian and Babylonian spheres of influence much to the advantage of his own country.

At home Adad-nirari conducted a vigorous policy. He developed the resources of the city state of Asshur by constructing a great dam and quay wall, while he contributed to the prosperity of the priesthood and the growth of Assyrian culture by extending the temple of the god Ashur. Ere he died, he assumed the proud title of "Shar Kishshate", "king of the world", which was also used by his son Shalmaneser I. His reign extended over a period of thirty years and terminated about 1300 B.C.

Soon after Shalmaneser came to the throne his country suffered greatly from an earthquake, which threw down Ishtar's temple at Nineveh and Ashur's temple at Asshur. Fire broke out in the latter building and destroyed it completely.

These disasters did not dismay the young monarch. Indeed, they appear to have stimulated him to set out on a career of conquest, to secure treasure and slaves, so as to carry out the work of reconstructing the temples without delay. He became as great a builder, and as tireless a campaigner as Thothmes III of Egypt, and under his guidance Assyria became the most powerful nation in Western Asia. Ere he died his armies were so greatly dreaded that the Egyptians and Assyrians drew their long struggle for supremacy in Syria to a close, and formed an alliance for mutual protection against their common enemy.

It is necessary at this point to review briefly the history of Palestine and north Syria after the period of Hittite expansion under King Subbi-luliuma and the decline of Egyptian power under Akhenaton. The western part of Mitanni and the most of northern Syria had been colonized by the Hittites.[410] Farther south, their allies, the Amorites, formed a buffer State on the borders of Egypt's limited sphere of influence in southern Palestine, and of Babylonia's sphere in southern Mesopotamia. Mitanni was governed by a subject king who was expected to prevent the acquisition by Assyria of territory in the north-west.

Subbi-luliuma was succeeded on the Hittite throne by his son, King Mursil, who was known to the Egyptians as "Meraser", or "Maurasar". The greater part of this monarch's reign appears to have been peaceful and prosperous. His allies protected his frontiers, and he was able to devote himself to the work of consolidating his empire in Asia Minor and North Syria. He erected a great palace at Boghaz Köi, and appears to have had dreams of imitating the splendours of the royal Courts of Egypt, Assyria, and Babylon.

At this period the Hittite Empire was approaching the zenith of its power. It controlled the caravan roads of Babylonia and Egypt, and its rulers appear not only to have had intimate diplomatic relations with both these countries, but even to have concerned themselves regarding their internal affairs. When Rameses I came to the Egyptian throne, at the beginning of the Nineteenth Dynasty, he sealed an agreement with the Hittites, and at a later date the Hittite ambassador at Babylon, who represented Hattusil II, the second son of King Mursil, actually intervened in a dispute regarding the selection of a successor to the throne.

The closing years of King Mursil's reign were disturbed by the military conquests of Egypt, which had renewed its strength under Rameses I. Seti I, the son of Rameses I, and the third Pharaoh of the powerful Nineteenth Dynasty, took advantage of the inactivity of the Hittite ruler by invading southern Syria. He had first to grapple with the Amorites, whom he successfully defeated. Then he pressed northward as far as Tunip, and won a decisive victory over a Hittite army, which secured to Egypt for a period the control of Palestine as far north as Phoenicia.

When Mursil died he was succeeded on the Hittite throne by his son Mutallu, whom the Egyptians referred to as "Metella" or "Mautinel". He was a vigorous and aggressive monarch, and appears to have lost no time in compelling the Amorites to throw off their allegiance to Egypt and recognize him as their overlord. As a result, when Rameses II ascended the Egyptian throne he had to undertake the task of winning back the Asiatic possessions of his father.

The preliminary operations conducted by Rameses on the Palestinian coast were attended with much success. Then, in his fifth year, he marched northward with a great army, with purpose, it would appear, to emulate the achievements of Thothmes III and win fame as a mighty conqueror. But he underestimated the strength of his rival and narrowly escaped disaster. Advancing impetuously, with but two of his four divisions, he suddenly found himself surrounded by the army of the wily Hittite, King Mutallu, in the vicinity of the city of Kadesh, on the Orontes. His first division remained intact, but his second was put to flight by an intervening force of the enemy. From this perilous position Rameses extricated himself by leading a daring charge against the Hittite lines on the river bank, which proved successful. Thrown into confusion, his enemies sought refuge in the city, but the Pharaoh refrained from attacking them there.

Although Rameses boasted on his return home of having achieved a great victory, there is nothing more certain than that this campaign proved a dismal failure. He was unable to win back for Egypt the northern territories which had acknowledged the suzerainty of Egypt during the Eighteenth Dynasty. Subsequently he was kept fully engaged in maintaining his prestige in northern Palestine and the vicinity of Phoenicia. Then his Asiatic military operations, which extended altogether over a period of about twenty years, were brought to a close in a dramatic and unexpected manner. The Hittite king Mutallu had died in battle, or by the hand of an assassin, and was succeeded by his brother Hattusil II (Khetasar), who sealed a treaty of peace with the great Rameses.

An Egyptian copy of this interesting document can still be read on the walls of a Theban temple, but it is lacking in certain details which interest present-day historians. No reference, for instance, is made to the boundaries of the Egyptian Empire in Syria, so that it is impossible to estimate the degree of success which attended the campaigns of Rameses. An interesting light, however, is thrown on the purport of the treaty by a tablet letter which has been discovered by Professor Hugo Winckler at Boghaz Köi. It is a copy of a communication addressed by Hattusil II to the King of Babylonia, who had made an enquiry regarding it. "I will inform my brother," wrote the Hittite monarch; "the King of Egypt and I have made an alliance, and made ourselves brothers. Brothers we are and will [unite against] a common foe, and with friends in common."[411] The common foe could have been no other than Assyria, and the Hittite king's letter appears to convey a hint to Kadashman-turgu of Babylon that he should make common cause with Rameses II and Hattusil.

Shalmaneser I of Assyria was pursuing a determined policy of western and northern expansion. He struck boldly at the eastern Hittite States and conquered Malatia, where he secured great treasure for the god Ashur. He even founded colonies within the Hittite sphere of influence on the borders of Armenia. Shalmaneser's second campaign was conducted against the portion of ancient Mitanni which was under Hittite control. The vassal king, Sattuari, apparently a descendant of Tushratta's, endeavoured to resist the Assyrians with the aid of Hittites and Aramaeans, but his army of allies was put to flight. The victorious Shalmaneser was afterwards able to penetrate as far westward as Carchemish on the Euphrates.

Having thus secured the whole of Mitanni, the Assyrian conqueror attacked the Aramaean hordes which were keeping the territory round Haran in a continuous state of unrest, and forced them to recognize him as their overlord.

Shalmaneser thus, it would appear, gained control of northern Mesopotamia and consequently of the Babylonian caravan route to Haran. As a result Hittite prestige must have suffered decline in Babylon. For a generation the Hittites had had the Babylonian merchants at their mercy, and apparently compelled them to pay heavy duties. Winckler has found among the Boghaz Köi tablets several letters from the king of Babylon, who made complaints regarding robberies committed by Amoritic bandits, and requested that they should be punished and kept in control. Such a communication is a clear indication that he was entitled, in lieu of payment, to have an existing agreement fulfilled.

Shalmaneser found that Asshur, the ancient capital, was unsuitable for the administration of his extended empire, so he built a great city at Kalkhi (Nimrud), the Biblical Calah, which was strategically situated amidst fertile meadows on the angle of land formed by the Tigris and the Upper Zab. Thither to a new palace he transferred his brilliant Court.

He was succeeded by his son, Tukulti-Ninip I, who was the most powerful of the Assyrian monarchs of the Old Empire. He made great conquests in the north and east, extended and strengthened Assyrian influence in Mesopotamia, and penetrated into Hittite territory, bringing into subjection no fewer than forty kings, whom he compelled to pay annual tribute. It was inevitable that he should be drawn into conflict with the Babylonian king, who was plotting with the Hittites against him. One of the tablet letters found by Winckler at Boghaz Köi is of special interest in this connection. Hattusil advises the young monarch of Babylonia to "go and plunder the land of the foe". Apparently he sought to be freed from the harassing attention of the Assyrian conqueror by prevailing on his Babylonian royal friend to act as a "cat's paw".

It is uncertain whether or not Kashtiliash II of Babylonia invaded Assyria with purpose to cripple his rival. At any rate war broke out between the two countries, and Tukulti-Ninip proved irresistible in battle. He marched into Babylonia, and not only defeated Kashtiliash, but captured him and carried him off to Asshur, where he was presented in chains to the god Ashur.

The city of Babylon was captured, its wall was demolished, and many of its inhabitants were put to the sword. Tukulti-Ninip was evidently waging a war of conquest, for he pillaged E-sagila, "the temple of the high head", and removed the golden statue of the god Merodach to Assyria, where it remained for about sixteen years. He subdued the whole of Babylonia as far south as the Persian Gulf, and ruled it through viceroys.

Tukulti-Ninip, however, was not a popular emperor even in his own country. He offended national susceptibilities by showing preference for Babylonia, and founding a new city which has not been located. There he built a great palace and a temple for Ashur and his pantheon. He called the city after himself, Kar-Tukulti-Ninip[412].

Seven years after the conquest of Babylonia revolts broke out against the emperor in Assyria and Babylonia, and he was murdered in his palace, which had been besieged and captured by an army headed by his own son, Ashur-natsir-pal I, who succeeded him. The Babylonian nobles meantime drove the Assyrian garrisons from their cities, and set on the throne the Kassite prince Adad-shum-utsur.

Thus in a brief space went to pieces the old Assyrian Empire, which, at the close of Tukulti-Ninip's thirty years' reign, embraced the whole Tigro-Euphrates valley from the borders of Armenia to the Persian Gulf. An obscure century followed, during which Assyria was raided by its enemies and broken up into petty States.

The Elamites were not slow to take advantage of the state of anarchy which prevailed in Babylonia during the closing years of Assyrian rule. They overran a part of ancient Sumer, and captured Nippur, where they slew a large number of inhabitants and captured many prisoners. On a subsequent occasion they pillaged Isin. When, however, the Babylonian king had cleared his country of the Assyrians, he attacked the Elamites and drove them across the frontier.

Nothing is known regarding the reign of the parricide Ashur-natsir-pal I of Assyria. He was succeeded by Ninip-Tukulti-Ashur and Adad-shum-lishir, who either reigned concurrently or were father and son. After a brief period these were displaced by another two rulers, Ashur-nirari III and Nabu-dan.

It is not clear why Ninip-Tukulti-Ashur was deposed. Perhaps he was an ally of Adad-shum-utsur, the Babylonian king, and was unpopular on that account. He journeyed to Babylon on one occasion, carrying with him the statue of Merodach, but did not return. Perhaps he fled from the rebels. At any rate Adad-shum-utsur was asked to send him back, by an Assyrian dignitary who was probably Ashur-nirari III. The king of Babylon refused this request, nor would he give official recognition to the new ruler or rulers.

Soon afterwards another usurper, Bel-kudur-utsur, led an Assyrian army against the Babylonians, but was slain in battle. He was succeeded by Ninip-apil-esharia, who led his forces back to Asshur, followed by Adad-shum-utsur. The city was besieged but not captured by the Babylonian army.

Under Adad-shum-utsur, who reigned for thirty years, Babylonia recovered much of its ancient splendour. It held Elam in check and laid a heavy hand on Assyria, which had been paralysed by civil war. Once again it possessed Mesopotamia and controlled its caravan road to Haran and Phoenicia, and apparently its relations with the Hittites and Syrians were of a cordial character. The next king, Meli-shipak, assumed the Assyrian title "Shar Kishshati", "king of the world", and had a prosperous reign of fifteen years. He was succeeded by Marduk-aplu-iddin I, who presided over the destinies of Babylonia for about thirteen years. Thereafter the glory of the Kassite Dynasty passed away. King Zamama-shum-iddin followed with a twelvemonth's reign, during which his kingdom was successfully invaded from the north by the Assyrians under King Ashur-dan I, and from the east by the Elamites under a king whose name has not been traced. Several towns were captured and pillaged, and rich booty was carried off to Asshur and Susa.

Bel-shum-iddin succeeded Zamama-shum-iddin, but three years afterwards he was deposed by a king of Isin. So ended the Kassite Dynasty of Babylonia, which had endured for a period of 576 years and nine months.

Babylonia was called Karduniash during the Kassite Dynasty. This name was originally applied to the district at the river mouths, where the alien rulers appear to have first achieved ascendancy. Apparently they were strongly supported by the non-Semitic elements in the population, and represented a popular revolt against the political supremacy of the city of Babylon and its god Merodach. It is significant to find in this connection that the early Kassite kings showed a preference for Nippur as their capital and promoted the worship of Enlil, the elder Bel, who was probably identified with their own god of fertility and battle. Their sun god, Sachi, appears to have been merged in Shamash. In time, however, the kings followed the example of Hammurabi by exalting Merodach.

The Kassite language added to the "Babel of tongues" among the common people, but was never used in inscriptions. At an early period the alien rulers became thoroughly

Babylonianized, and as they held sway for nearly six centuries it cannot be assumed that they were unpopular. They allowed their mountain homeland, or earliest area of settlement in the east, to be seized and governed by Assyria, and probably maintained as slight a connection with it after settlement in Babylonia as did the Saxons of England with their Continental area of origin.

Although Babylonia was not so great a world power under the Kassites as it had been during the Hammurabi Dynasty, it prospered greatly as an industrial, agricultural, and trading country. The Babylonian language was used throughout western Asia as the language of diplomacy and commerce, and the city of Babylon was the mostimportant commercial metropolis of the ancient world. Its merchants traded directly and indirectly with far-distant countries. They imported cobalt--which was used for colouring glass a vivid blue--from China, and may have occasionally met Chinese traders who came westward with their caravans, while a brisk trade in marble and limestone was conducted with and through Elam. Egypt was the chief source of the gold supply, which was obtained from the Nubian mines; and in exchange for this precious metal the Babylonians supplied the Nilotic merchants with lapis-lazuli from Bactria, enamel, and their own wonderful coloured glass, which was not unlike the later Venetian, as well as chariots and horses. The Kassites were great horse breeders, and the battle steeds from the Babylonian province of Namar were everywhere in great demand. They also promoted the cattle trade. Cattle rearing was confined chiefly to the marshy districts at the head of the Persian Gulf, and the extensive steppes on the borders of the Arabian desert, so well known to Abraham and his ancestors, which provided excellent grazing. Agriculture also flourished; as in Egypt it constituted the basis of national and commercial prosperity.

It is evident that great wealth accumulated in Karduniash during the Kassite period. When the images of Merodach and Zerpanitum were taken back to Babylon, from Assyria, they were clad, as has been recorded, in garments embroidered with gold and sparkling with gems, while E-sagila was redecorated on a lavish scale with priceless works of art.

Assyria presented a sharp contrast to Babylonia, the mother land, from which its culture was derived. As a separate kingdom it had to develop along different lines. In fact, it was unable to exist as a world power without the enforced co-operation of neighbouring States. Babylonia, on the other hand, could have flourished in comparative isolation, like Egypt during the Old Kingdom period, because it was able to feed itself and maintain a large population so long as its rich alluvial plain was irrigated during its dry season, which extended over about eight months in the year.

The region north of Baghdad was of different geographical formation to the southern plain, and therefore less suitable for the birth and growth of a great independent civilization. Assyria embraced a chalk plateau of the later Mesozoic period, with tertiary deposits, and had an extremely limited area suitable for agricultural pursuits. Its original inhabitants were nomadic pastoral and hunting tribes, and there appears to be little doubt that agriculture was introduced along the banks of the Tigris by colonists from Babylonia, who formed city States which owed allegiance to the kings of Sumer and Akkad.

After the Hammurabi period Assyria rose into prominence as a predatory power, which depended for its stability upon those productive countries which it was able to conquer and hold in sway. It never had a numerous peasantry, and such as it had ultimately vanished, for the kings pursued the short-sighted policy of colonizing districts on the borders of their empire with their loyal subjects, and settling aliens in the heart of the homeland, where they were controlled by the military. In this manner they built up an artificial empire, which suffered at critical periods in its history because it lacked the great driving and sustaining force of a population welded together by immemorial native traditions and the love of country which is the essence of true patriotism. National sentiment was chiefly confined to the military aristocracy and the priests; the enslaved and uncultured masses of aliens were concerned mainly with their daily duties, and no doubt included communities, like the Israelites in captivity, who longed to return to their native lands.

Assyria had to maintain a standing army, which grew from an alliance of brigands who first enslaved the native population, and ultimately extended their sway over neighbouring States. The successes of the army made Assyria powerful. Conquering kings accumulated rich booty by pillaging alien cities, and grew more and more wealthy as they were able to impose annual tribute on those States which came under their sway. They even regarded Babylonia with avaricious eyes. It was to achieve the conquest of the fertile and prosperous mother State that the early Assyrian emperors conducted military operations in the north-west and laid hands on Mesopotamia. There was no surer way of strangling it than by securing control of its trade routes. What the command of the sea is to Great Britain at the present day, the command of the caravan roads was to ancient Babylonia.

Babylonia suffered less than Assyria by defeat in battle; its natural resources gave it great recuperative powers, and the native population was ever so intensely patriotic that centuries of alien sway could not obliterate their national aspirations. A conqueror of Babylon had to become a Babylonian. The Amorites and Kassites had in turn to adopt the modes of life and modes of thought of the native population. Like the Egyptians, the Babylonians ever achieved the intellectual conquest of their conquerors.

The Assyrian Empire, on the other hand, collapsed like a house of cards when its army of mercenaries suffered a succession of disasters. The kings, as we have indicated, depended on the tribute of subject States to pay their soldiers and maintain the priesthood; they were faced with national bankruptcy when their vassals successfully revolted against them.

The history of Assyria as a world power is divided into three periods: (1) the Old Empire; (2) the Middle Empire; (3) the New or Last Empire.

We have followed the rise and growth of the Old Empire from the days of Ashur-uballit until the reign of Tukulti-Ninip, when it flourished in great splendour and suddenly went to pieces. Thereafter, until the second period of the Old Empire, Assyria comprised but a few city States which had agricultural resources and were trading centres. Of these the most enterprising was Asshur. When a ruler of Asshur was able, by conserving his revenues, to command sufficient capital with purpose to raise a strong army of mercenaries as a business speculation, he set forth to build up a new empire on the ruins of the old. In its early stages, of course, this process was slow and difficult. It necessitated the adoption of a military career by native Assyrians, who officered the troops, and these troops had to be trained and disciplined by engaging in brigandage, which also brought them rich rewards for their services. Babylonia became powerful by developing the arts of peace; Assyria became powerful by developing the science of warfare.

---

[407] At Carchemish a railway bridge spans the mile-wide river ferry which Assyria's soldiers were wont to cross with the aid of skin floats. The engineers have found it possible to utilize a Hittite river wall about 3000 years old--the oldest engineering structure in the world. The ferry was on the old trade route.

[408] *Deuteronomy*, xxvi, 5

[409] Pr. *u* as *oo*.

[410] The chief cities of North Syria were prior to this period Hittite. This expansion did not change the civilization but extended the area of occupation and control.

[411] Garstang's *The Land of the Hittites*, p. 349.

[412] "Burgh of Tukulti-Ninip."

Chapter XVI. Race Movements that Shattered Empires
Abstract

The Third Semitic Migration--Achaean Conquest of Greece--Fall of Crete--Tribes of Raiders--European Settlers in Asia Minor--The Muski overthrow the Hittites--Sea Raids on Egypt--The Homeric Age--Israelites and Philistines in Palestine--Culture of Philistines--Nebuchadrezzar I of Babylonia--Wars against Elamites and Hittites--Conquests in Mesopotamia and Syria--Assyrians and Babylonians at War--Tiglath-pileser I of Assyria--His Sweeping Conquests--Muski Power broken--Big-game Hunting in Mesopotamia--Slaying of a Sea Monster--Decline of Assyria and Babylonia--Revival of Hittite Civilization--An Important Period in History--Philistines as Overlords of Hebrews--Kingdom of David and Saul--Solomon's Relations with Egypt and Phoenicia--Sea Trade with India--Aramaean Conquests--The Chaldaeans--Egyptian King plunders Judah and Israel--Historical Importance of Race Movements.

Great changes were taking place in the ancient world during the period in which Assyria rose into prominence and suddenly suffered decline. These were primarily due to widespread migrations of pastoral peoples from the steppe lands of Asia and Europe, and the resulting displacement of settled tribes. The military operations of the great Powers were also a disturbing factor, for they not only propelled fresh movements beyond their spheres of influence, but caused the petty States to combine against a common enemy and foster ambitions to achieve conquests on a large scale.

Towards the close of the Eighteenth Dynasty of Egypt, of which Amenhotep III and Akhenaton were the last great kings, two well-defined migrations were in progress. The Aramaean folk-waves had already begun to pour in increasing volume into Syria from Arabia, and in Europe the pastoral fighting folk from the mountains were establishing themselves along the south-eastern coast and crossing the Hellespont to overrun the land of the Hittites. These race movements were destined to exercise considerable influence in shaping the history of the ancient world.

The Aramaean, or Third Semitic migration, in time swamped various decaying States. Despite the successive efforts of the great Powers to hold it in check, it ultimately submerged the whole of Syria and part of Mesopotamia. Aramaean speech then came into common use among the mingled peoples over a wide area, and was not displaced until the time of the Fourth Semitic or Moslem migration from Arabia, which began in the seventh century of the Christian era, and swept northward through Syria to Asia Minor, eastward across Mesopotamia into Persia and India, and westward through Egypt along the north African coast to Morocco, and then into Spain.

When Syria was sustaining the first shocks of Aramaean invasion, the last wave of Achaeans, "the tamers of horses" and "shepherds of the people", had achieved the conquest of Greece, and contributed to the overthrow of the dynasty of King Minos of Crete. Professor Ridgeway identifies this stock, which had been filtering southward for several centuries, with the tall, fair-haired, and grey-eyed "Keltoi" (Celts),[413] who, Dr. Haddon believes, were representatives of "the mixed peoples of northern and Alpine descent".[414] Mr. Hawes, following Professor Sergi, holds, on the other hand, that the Achaeans were "fair in comparison with the native (Pelasgian-Mediterranean) stock, but not necessarily blonde".[415] The earliest Achaeans were rude, uncultured barbarians, but the last wave came from some unknown centre of civilization, and probably used iron as well as bronze weapons.

The old Cretans were known to the Egyptians as the "Keftiu", and traded on the Mediterranean and the Black Sea. It is significant to find, however, that no mention is made of them in the inscriptions of the Pharaohs after the reign of Amenhotep III. In their place appear the Shardana, the Mykenaean people who gave their name to Sardinia, the Danauna, believed to be identical with the Danaoi of Homer, the Akhaivasha, perhaps the Achaeans, and the Tursha and Shakalsha, who may have been of the same stock as the piratical Lycians.

When Rameses II fought his famous battle at Kadesh the Hittite king included among his allies the Aramaeans from Arabia, and other mercenaries like the Dardanui and Masa, who represented the Thraco-Phrygian peoples who had overrun the Balkans, occupied Thrace and Macedonia, and crossed into Asia Minor. In time the Hittite confederacy was broken up by the migrating Europeans, and their dominant tribe, the Muski[416]--the Moschoi of the Greeks and the Meshech of the Old Testament--came into conflict with the Assyrians. The Muski were forerunners of the Phrygians, and were probably of allied stock.

Pharaoh Meneptah, the son of Rameses II, did not benefit much by the alliance with the Hittites, to whom he had to send a supply of grain during a time of famine. He found it necessary, indeed, to invade Syria, where their influence had declined, and had to beat back from the Delta region the piratical invaders of the same tribes as were securing a footing in Asia Minor. In Syria, Meneptah fought with the Israelites, who apparently had begun their conquest of Canaan during his reign.

Before the Kassite Dynasty had come to an end, Rameses III of Egypt (1198-1167 B.C.) freed his country from the perils of a great invasion of Europeans by land and sea. He scattered a fleet on the Delta coast, and then arrested the progress of a strong force which was pressing southward through Phoenicia towards the Egyptian frontier. These events occurred at the beginning of the Homeric Age, and were followed by the siege of Troy, which, according to the Greeks, began about 1194 B.C.

The land raiders who were thwarted by Rameses III were the Philistines, a people from Crete.[417] When the prestige of Egypt suffered decline they overran the coastline of Canaan, and that country was then called Palestine, "the land of the Philistines", while the Egyptian overland trade route to Phoenicia became known as "the way of the Philistines". Their conflicts with the Hebrews are familiar to readers of the Old Testament. "The only contributions the Hebrews made to the culture of the country", writes Professor Macalister, "were their simple desert customs and their religious organization. On the other hand, the Philistines, sprung from one of the great homes of art of the ancient world, had brought with them the artistic instincts of their race: decayed no doubt, but still superior to anything they met with in the land itself. Tombs to be ascribed to them, found in Gezer, contained beautiful jewellery and ornaments. The Philistines, in fact, were the only cultured or artistic race who ever occupied the soil of Palestine, at least until the time when the influence of classical Greece asserted itself too strongly to be withstood. Whatsoever things raised life in the country above the dull animal existence of fellahin were due to this people.... The peasantry of the modern villages ... still tell of the great days of old when it (Palestine) was inhabited by the mighty race of the 'Fenish'."[418]

When the Kassite Dynasty of Babylonia was extinguished, about 1140 B.C., the Amorites were being displaced in Palestine by the Philistines and the Israelitish tribes; the Aramaeans were extending their conquests in Syria and Mesopotamia; the Muski were the overlords of the Hittites; Assyrian power was being revived at the beginning of the second period of the Old Empire; and Egypt was governed by a weakly king, Rameses VIII, a puppet in the hands of the priesthood, who was unable to protect the rich tombs of the Eighteenth Dynasty Pharaohs against the bands of professional robbers who were plundering them.

A new dynasty--the Dynasty of Pashe--had arisen at the ancient Sumerian city of Isin. Its early kings were contemporary with some of the last Kassite monarchs, and they engaged in conflicts with the Elamites, who were encroaching steadily upon Babylonian territory, and were ultimately able to seize the province of Namar, famous for its horses, which was situated to the east of Akkad. The Assyrians, under Ashur-dan I, were not only reconquering lost territory, but invading Babylonia and carrying off rich plunder. Ashur-dan inflicted a crushing defeat upon the second-last Kassite ruler.

There years later Nebuchadrezzar I, of the Dynasty of Pashe, seized the Babylonian throne. He was the most powerful and distinguished monarch of his line--an accomplished general and a wise statesman. His name signifies: "May the god Nebo protect my boundary". His first duty was to drive the Elamites from the land, and win back from them the statue of Merodach which they had carried off from E-sagila. At first he suffered a reverse, but although the season was midsummer, and the heat overpowering, he persisted in his campaign. The Elamites were forced to retreat, and following up their main force he inflicted upon them a shattering defeat on the banks of the Ula, a tributary of the Tigris. He then invaded Elam and returned with rich booty. The province of Namar was recovered, and its governor, Ritti Merodach, who was Nebuchadrezzar's battle companion, was restored to his family possessions and exempted from taxation. A second raid to Elam resulted in the recovery of the statue of Merodach. The Kassite and Lullume mountaineers also received attention, and were taught to respect the power of the new monarch.

Having freed his country from the yoke of the Elamites, and driven the Assyrians over the frontier, Nebuchadrezzar came into conflict with the Hittites, who appear to have overrun Mesopotamia. Probably the invaders were operating in conjunction with the Muski, who were extending their sway over part of northern Assyria. They were not content with securing control of the trade route, but endeavoured also to establish themselves permanently in Babylon, the commercial metropolis, which they besieged and captured. This happened in the third year of Nebuchadrezzar, when he was still reigning at Isin. Assembling a strong force, he hastened northward and defeated the Hittites, and apparently followed up his victory. Probably it was at this time that he conquered the "West Land" (the land of the Amorites) and penetrated to the Mediterranean coast. Egyptian power had been long extinguished in that region.

The possession of Mesopotamia was a signal triumph for Babylonia. As was inevitable, however, it brought Nebuchadrezzar into conflict some years later with the Assyrian king, Ashur-resh-ishi I, grandson of Ashur-dan, and father of the famous Tiglath-pileser I. The northern monarch had engaged himself in subduing the Lullume and Akhlami hill tribes in the south-east, whose territory had been conquered by Nebuchadrezzar. Thereafter he crossed the Babylonian frontier. Nebuchadrezzar drove him back and then laid siege to the border fortress of Zanki, but the Assyrian king conducted a sudden and successful reconnaissance in force which rendered perilous the position of the attacking force. By setting fire to his siege train the Babylonian war lord was able, however, to retreat in good order.

Some time later Nebuchadrezzar dispatched another army northward, but it suffered a serious defeat, and its general, Karashtu, fell into the hands of the enemy.

Nebuchadrezzar reigned less than twenty years, and appears to have secured the allegiance of the nobility by restoring the feudal system which had been abolished by the Kassites. He boasted that he was "the sun of his country, who restored ancient landmarks and boundaries", and promoted the worship of Ishtar, the ancient goddess of the people. By restoring the image of Merodach he secured the support of Babylon, to which city he transferred his Court.

Nebuchadrezzar was succeeded by his son Ellil-nadin-apil, who reigned a few years; but little or nothing is known regarding him. His grandson, Marduk-nadin-akhe, came into conflict with Tiglath-pileser I of Assyria, and suffered serious reverses, from the effects of which his country did not recover for over a century.

Tiglath-pileser I, in one of his inscriptions, recorded significantly: "The feet of the enemy I kept from my country". When he came to the throne, northern Assyria was menaced by the Muski and their allies, the Hittites and the Shubari of old Mitanni. The Kashiari hill tribes to the north of Nineveh, whom Shalmaneser I subdued, had half a century before thrown off the yoke of Assyria, and their kings were apparently vassals of the Muski.

Tiglath-pileser first invaded Mitanni, where he routed a combined force of Shubari hillmen and Hittites. Thereafter a great army of the Muski and their allies pressed southward with purpose to deal a shattering blow against the Assyrian power. The very existence of Assyria as a separate power was threatened by this movement. Tiglath-pileser, however, was equal to the occasion. He surprised the invaders among the Kashiari mountains and inflicted a crushing defeat, slaying about 14,000 and capturing 6000 prisoners, who were transported to Asshur. In fact, he wiped the invading army out of existence and possessed himself of all its baggage. Thereafter he captured several cities, and extended his empire beyond the Kashiari hills and into the heart of Mitanni.

His second campaign was also directed towards the Mitanni district, which had been invaded during his absence by a force of Hittites, about 4000 strong. The invaders submitted to him as soon as he drew near, and he added them to his standing army.

Subsequent operations towards the north restored the pre-eminence of Assyria in the Nairi country, on the shores of Lake Van, in Armenia, where Tiglath-pileser captured no fewer than twenty-three petty kings. These he liberated after they had taken the oath of allegiance and consented to pay annual tribute.

In his fourth year the conqueror learned that the Aramaeans were crossing the Euphrates and possessing themselves of Mitanni, which he had cleared of the Hittites. By a series of forced marches he caught them unawares, scattered them in confusion, and entered Carchemish, which he pillaged. Thereafter his army crossed the Euphrates in boats of skin, and plundered and destroyed six cities round the base of the mountain of Bishru.

While operating in this district, Tiglath-pileser engaged in big-game hunting. He recorded: "Ten powerful bull elephants in the land of Haran and on the banks of the Khabour I killed; four elephants alive I took. Their skins, their teeth, with the living elephants, I brought to my city of Asshur."[419] He also claimed to have slain 920 lions, as well as a number of wild oxen, apparently including in his record the "bags" of his officers and men. A later king credited him with having penetrated to the Phoenician coast, where he put to sea and slew a sea monster called the "nakhiru". While at Arvad, the narrative continues, the King of Egypt, who is not named, sent him a hippopotamus (pagutu). This story, however, is of doubtful authenticity. About this time the prestige of Egypt was at so low an ebb that its messengers were subjected to indignities by the Phoenician kings.

The conquests of Tiglath-pileser once more raised the Mesopotamian question in Babylonia, whose sphere of influence in that region had been invaded. Marduk-nadin-akhe, the grandson of Nebuchadrezzar I, "arrayed his chariots" against Tiglath-pileser, and in the first conflict achieved some success, but subsequently he was defeated in the land of Akkad. The Assyrian army afterwards captured several cities, including Babylon and Sippar.

Thus once again the Assyrian Empire came into being as the predominant world Power, extending from the land of the Hittites into the heart of Babylonia. Its cities were enriched by the immense quantities of booty captured by its warrior king, while the coffers of state were glutted with the tribute of subject States. Fortifications were renewed, temples were built, and great gifts were lavished on the priesthood. Artists and artisans were kept fully employed restoring the faded splendours of the Old Empire, and everywhere thousands of slaves laboured to make the neglected land prosperous as of old. Canals were repaired and reopened; the earthworks and quay wall of Ashur were strengthened, and its great wall was entirely rebuilt, faced with a rampart of earth, and protected once again by a deep moat. The royal palace was enlarged and redecorated.

Meanwhile Babylonia was wasted by civil war and invasions. It was entered more than once by the Aramaeans, who pillaged several cities in the north and the south. Then the throne was seized by Adad-aplu-iddina, the grandson of "a nobody", who reigned for about ten years. He was given recognition, however, by the Assyrian king, Ashur-bel-kala, son of Tiglath-pileser I, who married his daughter, and apparently restored to him Sippar and Babylon after receiving a handsome dowry. Ashur-bel-kala died without issue, and was succeeded by his brother, Shamshi-Adad.

An obscure period followed. In Babylonia there were two weak dynasties in less than half a century, and thereafter an Elamite Dynasty which lasted about six years. An Eighth Dynasty ensued, and lasted between fifty and sixty years. The records of its early kings are exceedingly meagre and their order uncertain. During the reign of Nabu-mukin-apli, who was perhaps the fourth monarch, the Aramaeans constantly raided the land and hovered about Babylon. The names of two or three kings who succeeded Nabu-mukin-apli are unknown.

A century and a half after Tiglath-pileser I conquered the north Syrian possessions of the Hittites, the Old Assyrian Empire reached the close of its second and last period. It had suffered gradual decline, under a series of inert and luxury-loving kings, until it was unable to withstand the gradual encroachment on every side of the restless hill tribes, who were ever ready to revolt when the authority of Ashur was not asserted at the point of the sword.

After 950 B.C. the Hittites of North Syria, having shaken off the last semblance of Assyrian authority, revived their power, and enjoyed a full century of independence and prosperity. In Cappadocia their kinsmen had freed themselves at an earlier period from the yoke of the Muski, who had suffered so severely at the hands of Tiglath-pileser I. The Hittite buildings and rock sculptures of this period testify to the enduring character of the ancient civilization of the "Hatti". Until the hieroglyphics can be read, however, we must wait patiently for the detailed story of the pre-Phrygian period, which was of great historical importance, because the tide of cultural influence was then flowing at its greatest volume from the old to the new world, where Greece was emerging in virgin splendour out of the ruins of the ancient Mykenaean and Cretan civilizations.

It is possible that the conquest of a considerable part of Palestine by the Philistines was not unconnected with the revival of Hittite power in the north. They may have moved southward as the allies of the Cilician State which was rising into prominence. For a period they were the overlords of the Hebrews, who had been displacing the older inhabitants of the "Promised Land", and appear to have been armed with weapons of iron. In fact, as is indicated by a passage in the Book of Samuel, they had made a "corner" in that metal and restricted its use among their vassals. "Now", the Biblical narrative sets forth, "there was no smith found throughout all the land of Israel; for the Philistines said, Lest the Hebrews make them swords and spears; but all the Israelites went down to the Philistines, to sharpen every man his share, and his coulter, and his axe, and his mattock".[420] "We are inclined", says Professor Macalister, "to picture the West as a thing of yesterday, new fangled with its inventions and its progressive civilization, and the East as an embodiment of hoary and unchanging traditions. But when West first met East on the shores of the Holy Land, it was the former which represented the magnificent traditions of the past, and the latter which looked forward to the future. The Philistines were of the remnant of the dying glories of Crete; the Hebrews had no past to speak of, but were entering on the heritage they regarded as theirs, by right of a recently ratified divine covenant."[421]

Saul was the leader of a revolt against the Philistines in northern Palestine, and became the ruler of the kingdom of Israel. Then David, having liberated Judah from the yoke of the Philistines, succeeded Saul as ruler of Israel, and selected Jerusalem as his capital. He also conquered Edom and Moab, but was unsuccessful in his attempt to subjugate Ammon. The Philistines were then confined to a restricted area on the seacoast, where they fused with the Semites and ultimately suffered loss of identity. Under the famous Solomon the united kingdom of the Hebrews reached its highest splendour and importance among the nations.

If the Philistines received the support of the Hittites, the Hebrews were strengthened by an alliance with Egypt. For a period of two and a half centuries no Egyptian army had crossed the Delta frontier into Syria. The ancient land of the Pharaohs had been overshadowed meantime by a cloud of anarchy, and piratical and robber bands settled freely on its coast line. At length a Libyan general named Sheshonk (Shishak) seized the throne from the Tanite Dynasty. He was the Pharaoh with whom Solomon "made affinity",[422] and from whom he received the city of Gezer, which an Egyptian army had captured.[423] Solomon had previously married a daughter of Sheshonk's.

Phoenicia was also flourishing. Freed from Egyptian, Hittite, and Assyrian interference, Tyre and Sidon attained to a high degree of power as independent city States. During the reigns of David and Solomon, Tyre was the predominant Phoenician power. Its kings, Abibaal and his son Hiram, had become "Kings of the Sidonians", and are believed to have extended their sway over part of Cyprus. The relations between the Hebrews and the Phoenicians were of a cordial character, indeed the two powers became allies.

And Hiram king of Tyre sent his servants unto Solomon; for he had heard that they had anointed him king in the room of his father: for Hiram was ever a lover of David. And Solomon sent to Hiram, saying, Thou knowest how that David my father could not build an house unto the name of the Lord His God for the wars which were about him on every side, until the Lord put them under the soles of his feet. But now the Lord my God hath given me rest on every side, so that there is neither adversary nor evil occurrent. And, behold, I purpose to build an house unto the name of the Lord my God, as the Lord spake unto David my father, saying, Thy son, whom I will set upon thy throne in thy room, he shall build an house unto my name. Now therefore command thou that they hew me cedar trees out of Lebanon; and my servants shall be with thy servants: and unto thee will I give hire for thy servants according to all that thou shalt appoint: for thou knowest that there is not among us any that can skill to hew timber like unto the Sidonians. And it came to pass, when Hiram heard the words of Solomon, that he rejoiced greatly, and said, Blessed be the Lord this day, which hath given unto David a wise son over this great people. And Hiram sent to Solomon, saying, I have considered the things which thou sentest to me for: and I will do all thy desire concerning timber of cedar, and concerning timber of fir. My servants shall bring them down from Lebanon unto the sea: and I will convey them by sea in floats unto the place that thou shalt appoint me, and will cause them to be discharged there, and thou shalt receive them: and thou shalt accomplish my desire, in giving food for my household. So Hiram gave Solomon cedar trees and fir trees according to all his desire. And Solomon gave Hiram twenty thousand measures of wheat for food to his household, and twenty measures of pure oil: thus gave Solomon to Hiram year by year. And the Lord gave Solomon wisdom, as he promised him: and there was peace between Hiram and Solomon; and they two made a league together.[424]

Hiram also sent skilled workers to Jerusalem to assist in the work of building the temple and Solomon's palace, including his famous namesake, "a widow's son of the (Hebrew) tribe of Naphtali", who, like his father, "a man of Tyre", had "understanding and cunning to work all works in brass".[425]

Solomon must have cultivated good relations with the Chaldaeans, for he had a fleet of trading ships on the Persian Gulf which was manned by Phoenician sailors. "Once in three years", the narrative runs, "came the navy of Tharshish, bringing gold, and silver, ivory, and apes, and peacocks."[426] Apparently he traded with India, the land of peacocks, during the Brahmanical period, when the Sanskrit name "Samudra", which formerly signified the "collected waters" of the broadening Indus, was applied to the Indian Ocean.[427]

The Aramaeans of the Third Semitic migration were not slow to take advantage of the weakness of Assyria and Babylon. They overran the whole of Syria, and entered into the possession of Mesopotamia, thus acquiring full control of the trade routes towards the west. From time to time they ravaged Babylonia from the north to the south. Large numbers of them acquired permanent settlement in that country, like the Amorites of the Second Semitic migration in the pre-Hammurabi Age.

In Syria the Aramaeans established several petty States, and were beginning to grow powerful at Damascus, an important trading centre, which assumed considerable political importance after the collapse of Assyria's Old Empire.

At this period, too, the Chaldaeans came into prominence in Babylonia. Their kingdom of Chaldaea (Kaldu, which signifies Sealand) embraces a wide stretch of the coast land at the head of the Persian Gulf between Arabia and Elam. As we have seen, an important dynasty flourished in this region in the time of Hammurabi. Although more than one king of Babylon recorded that he had extinguished the Sealand Power, it continued to exist all through the Kassite period. It is possible that this obscure kingdom embraced diverse ethnic elements, and that it was controlled in turn by military aristocracies of Sumerians, Elamites, Kassites, and Arabians. After the downfall of the Kassites it had become thoroughly Semitized, perhaps as a result of the Aramaean migration, which may have found one of its outlets around the head of the Persian Gulf. The ancient Sumerian city of Ur, which dominated a considerable area of steppe land to the west of the Euphrates, was included in the Sealand kingdom, and was consequently referred to in after-time as "Ur of the Chaldees".

When Solomon reigned over Judah and Israel, Babylonia was broken up into a number of petty States, as in early Sumerian times. The feudal revival of Nebuchadrezzar I had weakened the central power, with the result that the nominal high kings were less able to resist the inroads of invaders. Military aristocracies of Aramaeans, Elamites, and Chaldaeans held sway in various parts of the valley, and struggled for supremacy.

When Assyria began to assert itself again, it laid claim on Babylonia, ostensibly as the protector of its independence, and the Chaldaeans for a time made common cause with the Elamites against it. The future, however, lay with the Chaldaeans, who, like the Kassites, became the liberators of the ancient inhabitants. When Assyria was finally extinguished as a world power they revived the ancient glory of Babylonia, and supplanted the Sumerians as the scholars and teachers of Western Asia. The Chaldaeans became famous in Syria, and even in Greece, as "the wise men from the east", and were renowned as astrologers.

The prestige of the Hebrew kingdom suffered sharp and serious decline after Solomon's death. Pharaoh Sheshonk fostered the elements of revolt which ultimately separated Israel from Judah, and, when a favourable opportunity arose, invaded Palestine and Syria and reestablished Egypt's suzerainty over part of the area which had been swayed by Rameses II, replenishing his exhausted treasury with rich booty and the tribute he imposed. Phoenicia was able, however, to maintain its independence, but before the Assyrians moved westward again, Sidon had shaken off the yoke of Tyre and become an independent State.

It will be seen from the events outlined in this chapter how greatly the history of the ancient world was affected by the periodic migrations of pastoral folks from the steppe lands. These human tides were irresistible. The direction of their flow might be diverted for a time, but they ultimately overcame every obstacle by sheer persistency and overpowering volume. Great emperors in Assyria and Egypt endeavoured to protect their countries from the "Bedouin peril" by strengthening their frontiers and extending their spheres of influence, but the dammed-up floods of humanity only gathered strength in the interval for the struggle which might be postponed but could not be averted.

These migrations, as has been indicated, were due to natural causes. They were propelled by climatic changes which caused a shortage of the food supply, and by the rapid increase of population under peaceful conditions. Once a migration began to flow, it set in motion many currents and cross currents, but all these converged towards the districts which offered the most attractions to mankind. Prosperous and well-governed States were ever in peril of invasion by barbarous peoples. The fruits of civilization tempted them; the reward of conquest was quickly obtained in Babylon and Egypt with their flourishing farms and prosperous cities. Waste land was reclaimed then as now by colonists from centres of civilization; the migrating pastoral folks lacked the initiative and experience necessary to establish new communities in undeveloped districts. Highly civilized men sowed the harvest and the barbarians reaped it.

It must not be concluded, however, that the migrations were historical disasters, or that they retarded the general advancement of the human race. In time the barbarians became civilized and fused with the peoples whom they conquered. They introduced, too, into communities which had grown stagnant and weakly, a fresh and invigorating atmosphere that acted as a stimulant in every sphere of human activity. The Kassite, for instance, was a unifying and therefore a strengthening influence in Babylonia. He shook off the manacles of the past which bound the Sumerian and the Akkadian alike to traditional lines of policy based on unforgotten ancient rivalries. His concern was chiefly with the future. The nomads with their experience of desert wandering promoted trade, and the revival of trade inaugurated new eras of prosperity in ancient centres of culture, and brought them into closer touch than ever before with one another. The rise of Greece was due to the blending of the Achaeans and other pastoral fighting folks with the indigenous Pelasgians. Into the early States which fostered the elements of ancient Mykenaean civilization, poured the cultural influences of the East through Asia Minor and Phoenicia and from the Egyptian coast. The conquerors from the steppes meanwhile contributed their genius for organization, their simple and frugal habits of life, and their sterling virtues; they left a deep impress on the moral, physical, and intellectual life of Greece.

[413] Article "Celts" in *Encyclopaedia Britannica*, eleventh ed.

[414] *The Wanderings of Peoples*, p. 41.

[415] *Crete, the Forerunner of Greece*, p. 146.

[416] Pr. Moosh´kee.

[417] "Have I not brought up Israel out of the land of Egypt and the Philistines from Caphtor (Crete)?" *Amos*, viii, 7.

[418] *A History of Civilization in Palestine*, p. 58.

[419] Pinches' translation.

[420] *I Samuel*, xiii, 19.

[421] *A History of Civilization in Palestine*, p. 54.

[422] *1 Kings*, iii, 1.

[423] *Ibid.*, ix, 16.

[424] *1 Kings*, v, 1-12.

[425] *Ibid.*, vii, 14 *et seq.*

[426] *Ibid.*, x, 22-3.

[427] *Indian Myth and Legend*, pp. 83-4.

Chapter XVII. The Hebrews in Assyrian History

Abstract

Revival of Assyrian Power--The Syro-Cappadocian Hittites--The Aramaean State of Damascus--Reign of Terror in Mesopotamia--Barbarities of Ashur-natsir-pal III--Babylonia and Chaldaea subdued--Glimpse of the Kalkhi Valley--The Hebrew Kingdoms of Judah and Israel--Rival Monarchs and their Wars--How Judah became subject to Damascus--Ahab and the Phoenician Jezebel--Persecution of Elijah and other Prophets--Israelites fight against Assyrians--Shalmaneser as Overlord of Babylonia--Revolts of Jehu in Israel and Hazael in Damascus--Shalmaneser defeats Hazael--Jehu sends Tribute to Shalmaneser--Baal Worship Supplanted by Golden Calf Worship in Israel--Queen Athaliah of Judah--Crowning of the Boy King Joash--Damascus supreme in Syria and Palestine--Civil War in Assyria--Triumphs of Shamshi-Adad VII--Babylonia becomes an Assyrian Province.

In one of the Scottish versions of the Seven Sleepers legend a shepherd enters a cave, in which the great heroes of other days lie wrapped in magic slumber, and blows two blasts on the horn which hangs suspended from the roof. The sleepers open their eyes and raise themselves on their elbows. Then the shepherd hears a warning voice which comes and goes like the wind, saying: "If the horn is blown once again, the world will be upset altogether". Terrified by the Voice and the ferocious appearance of the heroes, the shepherd retreats hurriedly, locking the door behind him; he casts the key into the sea. The story proceeds: "If anyone should find the key and open the door, and blow but a single blast on the horn, Finn and all the Feans would come forth. And that would be a great day in Alban."[428]

After the lapse of an obscure century the national heroes of Assyria were awakened as if from sleep by the repeated blasts from the horn of the triumphant thunder god amidst the northern and western mountains--Adad or Rimmon of Syria, Teshup of Armenia, Tarku of the western Hittites. The great kings who came forth to "upset the world" bore the familiar names, Ashur-natsir-pal, Shalmaneser, Shamash-Adad, Ashur-dan, Adad-nirari, and Ashur-nirari. They revived and increased the ancient glory of Assyria during its Middle Empire period.

The Syro-Cappadocian Hittites had grown once again powerful and prosperous, but no great leader like Subbiluliuma arose to weld the various States into an Empire, so as to ensure the protection of the mingled peoples from the operations of the aggressive and ambitious war-lords of Assyria. One kingdom had its capital at Hamath and another at Carchemish on the Euphrates. The kingdom of Tabal flourished in Cilicia (Khilakku); it included several city States like Tarsus, Tiana, and Comana (Kammanu). Farther west was the dominion of the Thraco-Phrygian Muski. The tribes round the shores of Lake Van had asserted themselves and extended their sphere of influence. The State of Urartu was of growing importance, and the Nairi tribes had spread round the south-eastern shores of Lake Van. The northern frontier of Assyria was continually menaced by groups of independent hill States which would have been irresistible had they operated together against a common enemy, but were liable to be extinguished when attacked in detail.

A number of Aramaean kingdoms had come into existence in Mesopotamia and throughout Syria. The most influential of these was the State of Damascus, the king of which was the overlord of the Hebrew kingdoms of Israel and Judah when Ashur-natsir-pal III ascended the Assyrian throne about 885 B.C. Groups of the Aramaeans had acquired a high degree of culture and become traders and artisans. Large numbers had filtered, as well, not only into Babylonia but also Assyria and the north Syrian area of Hittite control. Accustomed for generations to desert warfare, they were fearless warriors. Their armies had great mobility, being composed mostly of mounted infantry, and were not easily overpowered by the Assyrian forces of footmen and charioteers. Indeed, it was not until cavalry was included in the standing army of Assyria that operations against the Aramaeans were attended with permanent success.

Ashur-natsir-pal III[429] was preceded by two vigorous Assyrian rulers, Adad-nirari III (911-890 B.C.) and Tukulti-Ninip II (890-885 B.C.). The former had raided North Syria and apparently penetrated as far as the Mediterranean coast. In consequence he came into conflict with Babylonia, but he ultimately formed an alliance with that kingdom. His son, Tukulti-Ninip, operated in southern Mesopotamia, and apparently captured Sippar. In the north he had to drive back invading bands of the Muski. Although, like his father, he carried out great works at Asshur, he appears to have transferred his Court to Nineveh, a sure indication that Assyria was once again becoming powerful in northern Mesopotamia and the regions towards Armenia.

Ashur-natsir-pal III, son of Tukulti-Ninip II, inaugurated a veritable reign of terror in Mesopotamia and northern Syria. His methods of dealing with revolting tribes were of a most savage character. Chiefs were skinned alive, and when he sacked their cities, not only fighting-men but women and children were either slaughtered or burned at the stake. It is not surprising to find therefore that, on more than one occasion, the kings of petty States made submission to him without resistance as soon as he invaded their domains.

In his first year he overran the mountainous district between Lake Van and the upper sources of the Tigris. Bubu, the rebel son of the governor of Nishtun, who had been taken prisoner, was transported to Arbela, where he was skinned alive. Like his father, Ashur-natsir-pal fought against the Muski, whose power was declining. Then he turned southward from the borders of Asia Minor and dealt with a rebellion in northern Mesopotamia.

An Aramaean pretender named Akhiababa had established himself at Suru in the region to the east of the Euphrates, enclosed by its tributaries the Khabar and the Balikh. He had come from the neighbouring Aramaean State of Bit-Adini, and was preparing, it would appear, to form a powerful confederacy against the Assyrians.

When Ashur-natsir-pal approached Suru, a part of its population welcomed him. He entered the city, seized the pretender and many of his followers. These he disposed of with characteristic barbarity. Some were skinned alive and some impaled on stakes, while others were enclosed in a pillar which the king had erected to remind the Aramaeans of his determination to brook no opposition. Akhiababa the pretender was sent to Nineveh with a few supporters; and when they had been flayed their skins were nailed upon the city walls.

Another revolt broke out in the Kirkhi district between the upper reaches of the Tigris and the southwestern shores of Lake Van. It was promoted by the Nairi tribes, and even supported by some Assyrian officials. Terrible reprisals were meted out to the rebels. When the city of Kinabu was captured, no fewer than 3000 prisoners were burned alive, the unfaithful governor being flayed. The city of Damdamusa was set on fire. Then Tela was attacked. Ashur-natsir-pal's own account of the operations runs as follows:--

The city (of Tello) was very strong; three walls surrounded it. The inhabitants trusted to their strong walls and numerous soldiers; they did not come down or embrace my feet. With battle and slaughter I assaulted and took the city. Three thousand warriors I slew in battle. Their booty and possessions, cattle, sheep, I carried away; many captives I burned with fire. Many of their soldiers I took alive; of some I cut off hands and limbs; of others the noses, ears, and arms; of many soldiers I put out the eyes. I reared a column of the living and a column of heads. I hung on high their heads on trees in the vicinity of their city. Their boys and girls I burned up in flames. I devastated the city, dug it up, in fire burned it; I annihilated it.[430]

The Assyrian war-lord afterwards forced several Nairi kings to acknowledge him as their overlord. He was so greatly feared by the Syro-Cappadocian Hittites that when he approached their territory they sent him tribute, yielding without a struggle.

For several years the great conqueror engaged himself in thus subduing rebellious tribes and extending his territory. His military headquarters were at Kalkhi, to which city the Court had been transferred. Thither he drafted thousands of prisoners, the great majority of whom he incorporated in the Assyrian army. Assyrian colonies were established in various districts for strategical purposes, and officials supplanted the petty kings in certain of the northern city States.

The Aramaeans of Mesopotamia gave much trouble to Ashur-natsir-pal. Although he had laid a heavy hand on Suru, the southern tribes, the Sukhi, stirred up revolts in Mesopotamia as the allies of the Babylonians. On one occasion Ashur-natsir-pal swept southward through this region, and attacked a combined force of Sukhi Aramaeans and Babylonians. The Babylonians were commanded by Zabdanu, brother of Nabu-aplu-iddin, king of Babylonia, who was evidently anxious to regain control of the western trade route. The Assyrian war-lord, however, proved to be too powerful a rival. He achieved so complete a victory that he captured the Babylonian general and 3000 of his followers. The people of Kashshi (Babylonia) and Kaldu (Chaldaea) were "stricken with terror", and had to agree to pay increased tribute.

Ashur-natsir-pal reigned for about a quarter of a century, but his wars occupied less than half of that period. Having accumulated great booty, he engaged himself, as soon as peace was secured throughout his empire, in rebuilding the city of Kalkhi, where he erected a great palace and made records of his achievements. He also extended and redecorated the royal palace at Nineveh, and devoted much attention to the temples.

Tribute poured in from the subject States. The mountain and valley tribes in the north furnished in abundance wine and corn, sheep and cattle and horses, and from the Aramaeans of Mesopotamia and the Syro-Cappadocian Hittites came much silver and gold, copper and lead, jewels and ivory, as well as richly decorated furniture, armour and weapons. Artists and artisans were also provided by the vassals of Assyria. There are traces of Phoenician influence in the art of this period.

Ashur-natsir-pal's great palace at Kalkhi was excavated by Layard, who has given a vivid description of the verdant plain on which the ancient city was situated, as it appeared in spring. "Its pasture lands, known as the 'Jaif', are renowned", he wrote, "for their rich and luxuriant herbage. In times of quiet, the studs of the Pasha and of the Turkish authorities, with the horses of the cavalry and of the inhabitants of Mosul, are sent here to graze.... Flowers of every hue enamelled the meadows; not thinly scattered over the grass as in northern climes, but in such thick and gathering clusters that the whole plain seemed a patchwork of many colours. The dogs, as they returned from hunting, issued from the long grass dyed red, yellow, or blue, according to the flowers through which they had last forced their way.... In the evening, after the labour of the day, I often sat at the door of my tent, giving myself up to the full enjoyment of that calm and repose which are imparted to the senses by such scenes as these.... As the sun went down behind the low hills which separate the river from the desert--even their rocky sides had struggled to emulate the verdant clothing of the plain--its receding rays were gradually withdrawn, like a transparent veil of light from the landscape. Over the pure cloudless sky was the glow of the last light. In the distance and beyond the Zab, Keshaf, another venerable ruin, rose indistinctly into the evening mist. Still more distant, and still more indistinct, was a solitary hill overlooking the ancient city of Arbela. The Kurdish mountains, whose snowy summits cherished the dying sunbeams, yet struggled with the twilight. The bleating of sheep and lowing of cattle, at first faint, became louder as the flocks returned from their pastures and wandered amongst the tents. Girls hurried over the greensward to seek their fathers' cattle, or crouched down to milk those which had returned alone to their well-remembered folds. Some were coming from the river bearing the replenished pitcher on their heads or shoulders; others, no less graceful in their form, and erect in their carriage, were carrying the heavy loads of long grass which they had cut in the meadows."[431]

Across the meadows so beautiful in March the great armies of Ashur-natsir-pal returned with the booty of great campaigns--horses and cattle and sheep, bales of embroidered cloth, ivory and jewels, silver and gold, the products of many countries; while thousands of prisoners were assembled there to rear stately buildings which ultimately fell into decay and were buried by drifting sands.

Layard excavated the emperor's palace and dispatched to London, among other treasures of antiquity, the sublime winged human-headed lions which guarded the entrance, and many bas reliefs.

The Assyrian sculptures of this period lack the technical skill, the delicacy and imagination of Sumerian and Akkadian art, but they are full of energy, dignified and massive, and strong and lifelike. They reflect the spirit of Assyria's greatness, which, however, had a materialistic basis. Assyrian art found expression in delineating the outward form rather than in striving to create a "thing of beauty" which is "a joy for ever".

When Ashur-natsir-pal died, he was succeeded by his son Shalmaneser III (860-825 B.C.), whose military activities extended over his whole reign. No fewer than thirty-two expeditions were recorded on his famous black obelisk.

As Shalmaneser was the first Assyrian king who came into direct touch with the Hebrews, it will be of interest here to review the history of the divided kingdoms of Israel and Judah, as recorded in the Bible, because of the light it throws on international politics and the situation which confronted Shalmaneser in Mesopotamia and Syria in the early part of his reign.

After Solomon died, the kingdom of his son Rehoboam was restricted to Judah, Benjamin, Moab, and Edom. The "ten tribes" of Israel had revolted and were ruled over by Jeroboam, whose capital was at Tirzah.[432] "There were wars between Rehoboam and Jeroboam continually."[433]

The religious organization which had united the Hebrews under David and Solomon was thus broken up. Jeroboam established the religion of the Canaanites and made "gods and molten images". He was condemned for his idolatry by the prophet Ahijah, who declared, "The Lord shall smite Israel, as a reed is shaken in the water; and he shall root up Israel out of this good land, which he gave to their fathers, and shall scatter them beyond the river, because they have made their groves, provoking the Lord to anger. And he shall give Israel up because of the sins of Jeroboam, who did sin, and who made Israel to sin."[434]

In Judah Rehoboam similarly "did evil in the sight of the Lord"; his subjects "also built them high places and images and groves, on every high hill, and under every green tree".[435] After the raid of the Egyptian Pharaoh Shishak (Sheshonk) Rehoboam repented, however. "And when he humbled himself, the wrath of the Lord turned from him, that he would not destroy him altogether: and also in Judah things went well."[436]

Rehoboam was succeeded by his son Abijah, who shattered the power of Jeroboam, defeating that monarch in battle after he was surrounded as Rameses II had been by the Hittite army. "The children of Israel fled before Judah: and God delivered them into their hand. And Abijah and his people slew them with a great slaughter: so there fell down slain in Israel five hundred thousand chosen men. Thus the children of Israel were brought under at that time, and the children of Judah prevailed, because they relied upon the Lord God of their fathers. And Abijah pursued after Jeroboam, and took cities from him, Bethel with the towns thereof, and Jeshanah with the towns thereof, and Ephraim with the towns thereof. Neither did Jeroboam recover strength again in the days of Abijah, and the Lord struck him and he died."[437]

Ere Jeroboam died, however, "Abijah slept with his fathers, and they buried him in the city of David: and Asa his son reigned in his stead. In his days the land was quiet ten years. And Asa did that which was good and right in the eyes of the Lord his God. For he took away the altars of the strange gods, and the high places, and brake down the images, and cut down the groves. And commanded Judah to seek the Lord God of their fathers and to do the law and the commandment. Also he took away out of all the cities of Judah the high places and the images:

and the kingdom was quiet before him. And he built fenced cities in Judah: for the land had rest, and he had no war in those years; because the Lord had given him rest."[438]

Jeroboam died in the second year of Asa's reign, and was succeeded by his son Nadab, who "did evil in the sight of the Lord, and walked in the way of his father, and in his sin wherewith he made Israel to sin".[439] Nadab waged war against the Philistines, and was besieging Gibbethon when Baasha revolted and slew him. Thus ended the First Dynasty of the Kingdom of Israel.

Baasha was declared king, and proceeded to operate against Judah. Having successfully waged war against Asa, he proceeded to fortify Ramah, a few miles to the north of Jerusalem, "that he might not suffer any to go out or come in to Asa king of Judah".[440]

Now Israel was at this time one of the allies of the powerful Aramaean State of Damascus, which had resisted the advance of the Assyrian armies during the reign of Ashur-natsir-pal I, and apparently supported the rebellions of the northern Mesopotamian kings. Judah was nominally subject to Egypt, which, however, was weakened by internal troubles, and therefore unable either to assert its authority in Judah or help its king to resist the advance of the Israelites.

In the hour of peril Judah sought the aid of the king of Damascus. "Asa took all the silver and the gold that were left in the treasures of the house of the Lord, and the treasures of the king's house, and delivered them into the hand of his servants: and King Asa sent them to Ben-hadad, the son of Tabrimon, the son of Hezion, king of Syria, that dwelt at Damascus, saying, There is a league between me and thee, and between my father and thy father: behold, I have sent unto thee a present of silver and gold: *come and break thy league with Baasha king of Israel, that he may depart from me*".[441]

Ben-hadad accepted the invitation readily. He waged war against Israel, and Baasha was compelled to abandon the building of the fortifications at Ramah. "Then king Asa made a proclamation throughout all Judah; none was exempted: and they took away the stones of Ramah, and the timber thereof, wherewith Baasha had builded; and king Asa built with them Geba of Benjamin, and Mizpah."[442]

Judah and Israel thus became subject to Damascus, and had to recognize the king of that city as arbiter in all their disputes.

After reigning about twenty-four years, Baasha of Israel died in 886 B.C. and was succeeded by his son Elah who came to the throne "in the twenty and sixth year of Asa". He had ruled a little over a year when he was murdered by "his servant Zimri, captain of half his chariots", while he was "drinking himself drunk in the house of Arza steward of his house in Tirzah".[443] Thus ended the Second Dynasty of the Kingdom of Israel.

Zimri's revolt was shortlived. He reigned only "seven days in Tirzah". The army was "encamped against Gibbethon, which belonged to the Philistines. And the people that were encamped heard say, Zimri hath conspired and hath also slain the king; wherefore all Israel made Omri, the captain of the host, king over Israel that day in the camp. And Omri went up from Gibbethon and all Israel with him, and they besieged Tirzah. And it came to pass when Zimri saw that the city was taken, that he went into the palace of the king's house, and burnt the king's house over him with fire, and died."[444]

Omri's claim to the throne was disputed by a rival named Tibni. "But the people that followed Omri prevailed against the people that followed Tibni, son of Ginath: so Tibni died, and Omri reigned."[445]

Omri was the builder of Samaria, whither his Court was transferred from Tirzah towards the close of his six years reign. He was followed by his son Ahab, who ascended the throne "in the thirty and eighth year of Asa king of Judah.... And Ahab ... did evil in the sight of the Lord above all that were before him." So notorious indeed were father and son that the prophet Micah declared to the backsliders of his day, "For the statutes of Omri are kept, and all the works of the house of Ahab, and ye walk in their counsel; that I should make thee a desolation, and the inhabitants thereof an hissing: therefore ye shall bear the reproach of my people".[446]

Ahab was evidently an ally of Sidon as well as a vassal of Damascus, for he married the notorious princess Jezebel, the daughter of the king of that city State. He also became a worshipper of the Phoenician god Baal, to whom a temple had been erected in Samaria. "And Ahab made a grove; and Ahab did more to provoke the Lord God of Israel to anger than all the kings of Israel that were before him."[447] Obadiah, who "feared the Lord greatly", was the governor of Ahab's house, but the outspoken prophet Elijah, whose arch enemy was the notorious Queen Jezebel, was an outcast like the hundred prophets concealed by Obadiah in two mountain caves.[448]

152

Ahab became so powerful a king that Ben-hadad II of Damascus picked a quarrel with him, and marched against Samaria. It was on this occasion that Ahab sent the famous message to Ben-hadad: "Let not him that girdeth on his harness (armour) boast himself as he that putteth it off". The Israelites issued forth from Samaria and scattered the attacking force. "And Israel pursued them: and Ben-hadad the king of Syria escaped on a horse with the horseman. And the king of Israel went out, and smote the horses and chariots, and slew the Syrians with a great slaughter." Ben-hadad was made to believe afterwards by his counsellors that he owed his defeat to the fact that the gods of Israel were "gods of the hills; therefore they are stronger than we". They added: "Let us fight against them in the plain, and surely we shall be stronger than they". In the following year Ben-hadad fought against the Israelites at Aphek, but was again defeated. He then found it necessary to make "a covenant" with Ahab.[449]

In 854 B.C. Shalmaneser III of Assyria was engaged in military operations against the Aramaean Syrians. Two years previously he had broken the power of Akhuni, king of Bit-Adini in northern Mesopotamia, the leader of a strong confederacy of petty States. Thereafter the Assyrian monarch turned towards the south-west and attacked the Hittite State of Hamath and the Aramaean State of Damascus. The various rival kingdoms of Syria united against him, and an army of 70,000 allies attempted to thwart his progress at Qarqar on the Orontes. Although Shalmaneser claimed a victory on this occasion, it was of no great advantage to him, for he was unable to follow it up. Among the Syrian allies were Bir-idri (Ben-hadad II) of Damascus, and Ahab of Israel ("Akhabbu of the land of the Sir'ilites"). The latter had a force of 10,000 men under his command.

Four years after Ahab began to reign, Asa died at Jerusalem and his son Jehoshaphat was proclaimed king of Judah. "And he walked in all the ways of Asa his father; he turned not aside from it, doing that which was right in the eyes of the Lord: nevertheless the high places were not taken away; for the people offered and burnt incense yet in the high places."[450]

There is no record of any wars between Israel and Judah during this period, but it is evident that the two kingdoms had been drawn together and that Israel was the predominating power. Jehoshaphat "joined affinity with Ahab", and some years afterwards visited Samaria, where he was hospitably entertained.[451] The two monarchs plotted together. Apparently Israel and Judah desired to throw off the yoke of Damascus, which was being kept constantly on the defence by Assyria. It is recorded in the Bible that they joined forces and set out on an expedition to attack Ramoth in Gilead, which Israel claimed, and take it "out of the hand of the king of Syria".[452] In the battle which ensued (in 853 B.C.) Ahab was mortally wounded, "and about the time of the sun going down he died". He was succeeded by his son Ahaziah, who acknowledged the suzerainty of Damascus. After a reign of two years Ahaziah was succeeded by Joram.

Jehoshaphat did not again come into conflict with Damascus. He devoted himself to the development of his kingdom, and attempted to revive the sea trade on the Persian gulf which had flourished under Solomon. "He made ships of Tharshish to go to Ophir for gold; but they went not; for the ships were broken (wrecked) at Ezion-geber." Ahaziah offered him sailors-probably Phoenicians--but they were refused.[453] Apparently Jehoshaphat had close trading relations with the Chaldaeans, who were encroaching on the territory of the king of Babylon, and menacing the power of that monarch. Jehoram succeeded Jehoshaphat and reigned eight years.

After repulsing the Syrian allies at Qarqar on the Orontes in 854 B.C., Shalmaneser III of Assyria found it necessary to invade Babylonia. Soon after he came to the throne he had formed an alliance with Nabu-aplu-iddin of that kingdom, and was thus able to operate in the north-west without fear of complications with the rival claimant of Mesopotamia. When Nabu-aplu-iddin died, his two sons Marduk-zakir-shum and Marduk-bel-usate were rivals for the throne. The former, the rightful heir, appealed for help to Shalmaneser, and that monarch at once hastened to assert his authority in the southern kingdom. In 851 B.C. Marduk-bel-usate, who was supported by an Aramaean army, was defeated and put to death.

Marduk-zakir-shum afterwards reigned over Babylonia as the vassal of Assyria, and Shalmaneser, his overlord, made offerings to the gods at Babylon, Borsippa, and Cuthah. The Chaldaeans were afterwards subdued, and compelled to pay annual tribute.

In the following year Shalmaneser had to lead an expedition into northern Mesopotamia and suppress a fresh revolt in that troubled region. But the western allies soon gathered strength again, and in 846 B.C. he found it necessary to return with a great army, but was not successful in achieving any permanent success, although he put his enemies to flight. The various western kingdoms, including Damascus, Israel, and Tyre and Sidon, remained unconquered, and continued to conspire against him.

The resisting power of the Syrian allies, however, was being greatly weakened by internal revolts, which may have been stirred up by Assyrian emissaries. Edom threw off the yoke of Judah and became independent. Jehoram, who had married Athaliah, a royal princess of Israel, was dead. His son Ahaziah, who succeeded him, joined forces with his cousin and overlord, King Joram of Israel, to assist him in capturing Ramoth-gilead from the king of Damascus. Joram took possession of the city, but was wounded, and returned to Jezreel to be healed.[454] He was the last king of the Omri Dynasty of Israel. The prophet Elisha sent a messenger to Jehu, a military leader, who was at Ramoth-gilead, with a box of oil and the ominous message, "Thus saith the Lord, I have anointed thee king over Israel. And thou shalt smite the house of Ahab thy master, that I may avenge the blood of my servants the prophets, and the blood of all the servants of the Lord, at the hand of Jezebel.... And the dogs shall eat Jezebel in the portion of Jezreel, and there shall be none to bury her."

Jehu "conspired against Joram", and then, accompanied by an escort, "rode in a chariot and went to Jezreel", so that he might be the first to announce the revolt to the king whom he was to depose.

The watchman on the tower of Jezreel saw Jehu and his company approaching and informed Joram, who twice sent out a messenger to enquire, "Is it peace?" Neither messenger returned, and the watchman informed the wounded monarch of Israel, "He came even unto them, and cometh not again; and the driving is like the driving of Jehu the son of Nimshi; for he driveth furiously".

King Joram went out himself to meet the famous charioteer, but turned to flee when he discovered that he came as an enemy. Then Jehu drew his bow and shot Joram through the heart. Ahaziah endeavoured to conceal himself in Samaria, but was slain also. Jezebel was thrown down from a window of the royal harem and trodden under foot by the horsemen of Jehu; her body was devoured by dogs.[455]

The Syrian king against whom Joram fought at Ramoth-gilead was Hazael. He had murdered Ben-hadad II as he lay on a bed of sickness by smothering him with a thick cloth soaked in water. Then he had himself proclaimed the ruler of the Aramaean State of Damascus. The prophet Elisha had previously wept before him, saying, "I know the evil that thou wilt do unto the children of Israel; their strongholds wilt thou set on fire, and their young men wilt thou slay with the sword, and wilt dash their children and rip up their women with child".[456]

The time seemed ripe for Assyrian conquest. In 843 B.C. Shalmaneser III crossed the Euphrates into Syria for the sixteenth time. His first objective was Aleppo, where he was welcomed. He made offerings there to Hadad, the local Thor, and then suddenly marched southward. Hazael went out to oppose the advancing Assyrians, and came into conflict with them in the vicinity of Mount Hermon. "I fought with him", Shalmaneser recorded, "and accomplished his defeat; I slew with the sword 1600 of his warriors and captured 1121 chariots and 470 horses. He fled to save his life."

Hazael took refuge within the walls of Damascus, which the Assyrians besieged, but failed, however, to capture. Shalmaneser's soldiers meanwhile wasted and burned cities without number, and carried away great booty. "In those days", Shalmaneser recorded, "I received tribute from the Tyrians and Sidonians and from Yaua (Jehu) son (successor) of Khumri (Omri)." The following is a translation from a bas relief by Professor Pinches of a passage detailing Jehu's tribute:

The tribute of Yaua, son of Khumri: silver, gold, a golden cup, golden vases, golden vessels, golden buckets, lead, a staff for the hand of the king (and) sceptres, I received.[457]

The scholarly translator adds, "It is noteworthy that the Assyrian form of the name, Yaua, shows that the unpronounced aleph at the end was at that time sounded, so that the Hebrews must have called him Yahua (Jehua)".

Shalmaneser did not again attack Damascus. His sphere of influence was therefore confined to North Syria. He found it more profitable, indeed, to extend his territories into Asia Minor. For several years he engaged himself in securing control of the north-western caravan road, and did not rest until he had subdued Cilicia and overrun the Hittite kingdoms of Tabal and Malatia.

Hazael of Damascus avenged himself meanwhile on his unfaithful allies who had so readily acknowledged the shadowy suzerainty of Assyria. "In those days the Lord began to cut Israel short: and Hazael smote them in all the coasts of Israel; from Jordan eastward, all the land of Gilead, the Gadites, and the Reubenites, and the Manassites, from Aroer, which is by the river Arnon, even Gilead and Bashan."[458] Israel thus came completely under the sway of Damascus.

Jehu appears to have cherished the ambition of uniting Israel and Judah under one crown. His revolt received the support of the orthodox Hebrews, and he began well by inaugurating reforms in the northern kingdom with purpose apparently to re-establish the worship of David's God. He persecuted the prophets of Baal, but soon became a backslider, for although he stamped out the Phoenician religion he began to worship "the golden calves that

154

were in Bethel and that were in Dan.... He departed not from the sins of Jeroboam, which made Israel to sin."[459] Apparently he found it necessary to secure the support of the idolators of the ancient cult of the "Queen of Heaven".

The crown of Judah had been seized by the Israelitish Queen mother Athaliah after the death of her son Ahaziah at the hands of Jehu.[460] She endeavoured to destroy "all the seed royal of the house of Judah". But another woman thwarted the completion of her monstrous design. This was Jehoshabeath, sister of Ahaziah and wife of the priest Jehoiada, who concealed the young prince Joash "and put him and his nurse in a bedchamber", in "the house of God". There Joash was strictly guarded for six years.[461]

In time Jehoiada stirred up a revolt against the Baal-worshipping queen of Judah. Having secured the support of the captains of the royal guard and a portion of the army, he brought out from the temple the seven years old prince Joash, "the king's son, and put upon him the crown, and gave him the testimony, and made him king. And Jehoiada and his sons anointed him, and said, God save the king.

"Now when Athaliah heard the noise of the people running and praising the king, she came to the people into the house of the Lord: and she looked, and, behold the king stood at his pillar at the entering in, and the princes and the trumpets by the king: and all the people of the land rejoiced, and sounded with trumpets, also the singers with instruments of musick, and such as taught to sing praise. Then Athaliah rent her clothes, and said, Treason, Treason.

"Then Jehoiada the priest brought out the captains of hundreds that were set over the host, and said unto them, Have her forth of the ranges: and whoso followeth her, let him be slain by the sword. For the priest said, Slay her not in the house of the Lord. So they laid hands on her; and when she was come to the entering of the horse gate by the king's house, they slew her there.

"And Jehoiada made a covenant between him, and between all the people, and between the king, that they should be the Lord's people. Then all the people went to the house of Baal, and brake it down, and brake his altars and his images in pieces, and slew Mattan the priest of Baal before the altars."[462]

When Jehu of Israel died, he was succeeded by Jehoahaz. "The Lord was kindled against Israel, and he delivered them into the hand of Ben-hadad the son of Hazael all their days." Then Jehoahaz repented. He "besought the Lord, and the Lord hearkened unto him: for he saw the oppression of Israel, because the king of Syria oppressed them. And the Lord gave Israel a saviour, so that they went out from under the hands of the Syrians."[463] The "saviour", as will be shown, was Assyria. Not only Israel, but Judah, under King Joash, Edom, the Philistines and the Ammonites were compelled to acknowledge the suzerainty of Damascus.

Shalmaneser III swayed an extensive and powerful empire, and kept his generals continually employed suppressing revolts on his frontiers. After he subdued the Hittites, Kati, king of Tabal, sent him his daughter, who was received into the royal harem. Tribes of the Medes came under his power: the Nairi and Urartian tribes continued battling with his soldiers on his northern borders like the frontier tribes of India against the British troops. The kingdom of Urartu was growing more and more powerful.

In 829 B.C. the great empire was suddenly shaken to its foundations by the outbreak of civil war. The party of rebellion was led by Shalmaneser's son Ashur-danin-apli, who evidently desired to supplant the crown prince Shamshi-Adad. He was a popular hero and received the support of most of the important Assyrian cities, including Nineveh, Asshur, Arbela, Imgurbel, and Dur-balat, as well as some of the dependencies. Shalmaneser retained Kalkhi and the provinces of northern Mesopotamia, and it appears that the greater part of the army also remained loyal to him.

After four years of civil war Shalmaneser died. His chosen heir, Shamshi-Adad VII, had to continue the struggle for the throne for two more years.

When at length the new king had stamped out the last embers of revolt within the kingdom, he had to undertake the reconquest of those provinces which in the interval had thrown off their allegiance to Assyria. Urartu in the north had grown more aggressive, the Syrians were openly defiant, the Medes were conducting bold raids, and the Babylonians were plotting with the Chaldaeans, Elamites, and Aramaeans to oppose the new ruler. Shamshi-Adad, however, proved to be as great a general as his father. He subdued the Medes and the Nairi tribes, burned many cities and collected enormous tribute, while thousands of prisoners were taken and forced to serve the conqueror.

Having established his power in the north, Shamshi-Adad then turned attention to Babylonia. On his way southward he subdued many villages. He fell upon the first strong force of Babylonian allies at Dur-papsukal in Akkad, and achieved a great victory, killing 13,000 and taking 3000 captives. Then the Babylonian king, Marduk-balatsu-ikbi, advanced to meet him with his mixed force of Babylonians, Chaldaeans, Elamites, and Aramaeans, but was defeated in a fierce battle on the banks of the Daban canal. The Babylonian camp was captured, and the prisoners taken by the Assyrians included 5000 footmen, 200 horsemen, and 100 chariots.

Shamshi-Adad conducted in all five campaigns in Babylonia and Chaldaea, which he completely subdued, penetrating as far as the shores of the Persian Gulf. In the end he took prisoner the new king, Bau-akh-iddina, the successor of Marduk-balatsu-ikbi, and transported him to Assyria, and offered up sacrifices as the overlord of the ancient land at Babylon, Borsippa, and Cuthah. For over half a century after this disaster Babylonia was a province of Assyria. During that period, however, the influence which it exercised over the Assyrian Court was so great that it contributed to the downfall of the royal line of the Second Empire.

[428] *Finn and His Warrior Band*, pp. 245 *et seq.* (London, 1911).

[429] Also rendered Ashur-na'sir-pal.

[430] *A History of the Babylonians and Assyrians*, G.S. Goodspeed, p. 197.

[431] *Discoveries at Nineveh*, Sir A.H. Layard (London, 1856), pp. 55, 56.

[432] "Thou art beautiful, O my love, as Tirzah, comely as Jerusalem." *Solomon's Song*, vi, 4.

[433] *2 Chronicles*, xii, 15.

[434] *1 Kings*, xiv, 1-20.

[435] *Ibid.*, 21-3.

[436] *2 Chronicles*, xii, 1-12.

[437] *2 Chronicles*, xiii, 1-20.

[438] *Ibid.*, xiv, 1-6.

[439] *1 Kings*, xv, 25-6.

[440] *1 Kings*, xv, 16-7.

[441] *Ibid.*, 18-9.

[442] *Ibid.*, 20-2.

[443] *1 Kings*, xvi, 9-10.

[444] *Ibid.*, 15-8.

[445] *Ibid.*, 21-2.

[446] *Micah*, vi, 16.

[447] *1 Kings*, xvi, 29-33.

[448] *Ibid.*, xviii, 1-4.

[449] *1 Kings*, xx.

[450] *Ibid.*, xxii, 43.

[451] *2 Chronicles*, xviii, 1-2.

[452] *1 Kings*, xxii and *2 Chronicles*, xviii.

[453] *1 Kings*, xxii, 48-9.

[454] *1 Kings*, viii.

[455] *2 Kings*, ix and *2 Chronicles*, xxii.

[456] *2 Kings*, viii, 1-15.

[457] *The Old Testament in the Light of the Historical Records and Legends of Assyria and Babylonia*, pp. 337 *et seq.*

[458] *2 Kings*, x, 32-3.

[459] *Ibid.*, 1-31.

[460] *2 Kings*, xi, 1-3.

[461] *2 Chronicles*, xxii, 10-12.

[462] *2 Chronicles*, xxiii, 1-17.

[463] *2 Kings*, xiii, 1-5.

Chapter XVIII. The Age of Semiramis

Abstract

Queen Sammu-rammat the original of Semiramis--"Mother-right" among "Mother Worshippers"--Sammu-rammat compared to Queen Tiy--Popularity of Goddess Cults--Temple Worship and Domestic Worship--Babylonian Cultural Influence in Assyria--Ethical Tendency in Shamash Worship--The Nebo Religious Revolt--Aton Revolt in Egypt--The Royal Assyrian Library--Fish Goddess of Babylonia in Assyria--The Semiramis and Shakuntala Stories--The Mock King and Queen--Dove Goddesses of Assyria, Phoenicia, and Cyprus--Ishtar's Dove Form--St. Valentine's Day beliefs--Sacred Doves of Cretans, Hittites, and Egyptians--Pigeon Lore in Great Britain and Ireland--Deities associated with various Animals--The Totemic Theory-- Common Element in Ancient Goddess Cults--Influence of Agricultural Beliefs--Nebo a form of Ea--His Spouse Tashmit a Love Goddess and Interceder--Traditions of Famous Mother Deities--

Adad-nirari IV the "Saviour" of Israel--Expansion of the Urartian Empire--Its Famous Kings--Decline and Fall of Assyria's Middle Empire Dynasty.

One of the most interesting figures in Mesopotamian history came into prominence during the Assyrian Middle Empire period. This was the famous Sammu-rammat, the Babylonian wife of an Assyrian ruler. Like Sargon of Akkad, Alexander the Great, and Dietrich von Bern, she made, by reason of her achievements and influence, a deep impression on the popular imagination, and as these monarchs became identified in tradition with gods of war and fertility, she had attached to her memory the myths associated with the mother goddess of love and battle who presided over the destinies of mankind. In her character as the legendary Semiramis of Greek literature, the Assyrian queen was reputed to have been the daughter of Derceto, the dove and fish goddess of Askalon, and to have departed from earth in bird form.

It is not quite certain whether Sammu-rammat was the wife of Shamshi-Adad VII or of his son, Adad-nirari IV. Before the former monarch reduced Babylonia to the status of an Assyrian province, he had signed a treaty of peace with its king, and it is suggested that it was confirmed by a matrimonial alliance. This treaty was repudiated by King Bau-akh-iddina, who was transported with his palace treasures to Assyria.

As Sammu-rammat was evidently a royal princess of Babylonia, it seems probable that her marriage was arranged with purpose to legitimatize the succession of the Assyrian overlords to the Babylonian throne. The principle of "mother right" was ever popular in those countries where the worship of the Great Mother was perpetuated if not in official at any rate in domestic religion. Not a few Egyptian Pharaohs reigned as husbands or as sons of royal ladies. Succession by the female line was also observed among the Hittites. When Hattusil II gave his daughter in marriage to Putakhi, king of the Amorites, he inserted a clause in the treaty of alliance "to the effect that the sovereignty over the Amorite should belong to the son and descendants of his daughter for evermore".[464]

As queen or queen-mother, Sammu-rammat occupied as prominent a position in Assyria as did Queen Tiy of Egypt during the lifetime of her husband, Amenhotep III, and the early part of the reign of her son, Amenhotep IV (Akhenaton). The Tell-el-Amarna letters testify to Tiy's influence in the Egyptian "Foreign Office", and we know that at home she was joint ruler with her husband and took part with him in public ceremonials. During their reign a temple was erected to the mother goddess Mut, and beside it was formed a great lake on which sailed the "barque of Aton" in connection with mysterious religious ceremonials. After Akhenaton's religious revolt was inaugurated, the worship of Mut was discontinued and Tiy went into retirement. In Akhenaton's time the vulture symbol of the goddess Mut did not appear above the sculptured figures of royalty.

What connection the god Aton had with Mut during the period of the Tiy regime remains obscure. There is no evidence that Aton was first exalted as the son of the Great Mother goddess, although this is not improbable.

Queen Sammu-rammat of Assyria, like Tiy of Egypt, is associated with social and religious innovations. She was the first, and, indeed, the only Assyrian royal lady, to be referred to on equal terms with her royal husband in official inscriptions. In a dedication to the god Nebo, that deity is reputed to be the protector of "the life of Adad-nirari, king of the land of Ashur, his lord, and the life of Sammu-rammat, she of the palace, his lady".[465]

During the reign of Adad-nirari IV the Assyrian Court radiated Babylonian culture and traditions. The king not only recorded his descent from the first Shalmaneser, but also claimed to be a descendant of Bel-kap-kapu, an earlier, but, to us, unknown, Babylonian monarch than "Sulili", i.e. Sumu-la-ilu, the great-great-grandfather of Hammurabi. Bel-kap-kapu was reputed to have been an overlord of Assyria.

Apparently Adad-nirari desired to be regarded as the legitimate heir to the thrones of Assyria and Babylonia. His claim upon the latter country must have had a substantial basis. It is not too much to assume that he was a son of a princess of its ancient royal family. Sammurammat may therefore have been his mother. She could have been called his "wife" in the mythological sense, the king having become "husband of his mother". If such was the case, the royal pair probably posed as the high priest and high priestess of the ancient goddess cult--the incarnations of the Great Mother and the son who displaced his sire.

The worship of the Great Mother was the popular religion of the indigenous peoples of western Asia, including parts of Asia Minor, Egypt, and southern and western Europe. It appears to have been closely associated with agricultural rites practised among representative communities of the Mediterranean race. In Babylonia and Assyria the peoples of the goddess cult fused with the peoples of the god cult, but the prominence maintained by Ishtar, who absorbed many of the old mother deities, testifies to the persistence of immemorial habits of thought and antique religious ceremonials among the descendants of the earliest settlers in the Tigro-

Euphrates valley. Merodach's spouse Zerpanitum was not a shadowy deity but a goddess who exercised as much influence as her divine husband. As Aruru she took part with him in the creation of mankind. In Asia Minor the mother goddess was overshadowed by the father god during the period of Hatti predominance, but her worship was revived after the early people along the coast and in the agricultural valleys were freed from the yoke of the father-god worshippers.

It must be recognized, in this connection, that an official religion was not always a full reflection of popular beliefs. In all the great civilizations of antiquity it was invariably a compromise between the beliefs of the military aristocracy and the masses of mingled peoples over whom they held sway. Temple worship had therefore a political aspect; it was intended, among other things, to strengthen the position of the ruling classes. But ancient deities could still be worshipped, and were worshipped, in homes and fields, in groves and on mountain tops, as the case might be. Jeremiah has testified to the persistence of the folk practices in connection with the worship of the mother goddess among the inhabitants of Palestine. Sacrificial fires were lit and cakes were baked and offered to the "Queen of Heaven" in the streets of Jerusalem and other cities. In Babylonia and Egypt domestic religious practices were never completely supplanted by temple ceremonies in which rulers took a prominent part. It was always possible, therefore, for usurpers to make popular appeal by reviving ancient and persistent forms of worship. As we have seen, Jehu of Israel, after stamping out Phoenician Baal worship, secured a strong following by giving official recognition to the cult of the golden calf.

It is not possible to set forth in detail, or with intimate knowledge, the various innovations which Sammu-rammat introduced, or with which she was credited, during the reigns of Adad-nirari IV (810-782 B.C.) and his father. No discovery has been made of documents like the Tell-el-Amarna "letters", which would shed light on the social and political life of this interesting period. But evidence is not awanting that Assyria was being suffused with Babylonian culture. Royal inscriptions record the triumphs of the army, but suppress the details of barbarities such as those which sully the annals of Ashur-natsir-pal, who had boys and girls burned on pyres and the heroes of small nations flayed alive. An ethical tendency becomes apparent in the exaltation of the Babylonian Shamash as an abstract deity who loved law and order, inspired the king with wisdom and ordained the destinies of mankind. He is invoked on equal terms with Ashur.

The prominence given to Nebo, the god of Borsippa, during the reign of Adad-nirari IV is highly significant. He appears in his later character as a god of culture and wisdom, the patron of scribes and artists, and the wise counsellor of the deities. He symbolized the intellectual life of the southern kingdom, which was more closely associated with religious ethics than that of war-loving Assyria.

A great temple was erected to Nebo at Kalkhi, and four statues of him were placed within it, two of which are now in the British Museum. On one of these was cut the inscription, from which we have quoted, lauding the exalted and wise deity and invoking him to protect Adad-nirari and the lady of the palace, Sammu-rammat, and closing with the exhortation, "Whoso cometh in after time, let him trust in Nebo and trust in no other god".

The priests of Ashur in the city of Asshur must have been as deeply stirred by this religious revolt at Kalkhi as were the priests of Amon when Akhenaton turned his back on Thebes and the national god to worship Aton in his new capital at Tell-el-Amarna.

It would appear that this sudden stream of Babylonian culture had begun to flow into Assyria as early as the reign of Shalmaneser III, and it may be that it was on account of that monarch's pro-Babylonian tendencies that his nobles and priests revolted against him. Shalmaneser established at Kalkhi a royal library which was stocked with the literature of the southern kingdom. During the reign of Adad-nirari IV this collection was greatly increased, and subsequent additions were made to it by his successors, and especially Ashur-nirari IV, the last monarch of the Middle Empire. The inscriptions of Shamshi-Adad, son of Shalmaneser III, have literary qualities which distinguish them from those of his predecessors, and may be accounted for by the influence exercised by Babylonian scholars who migrated northward.

To the reign of Adad-nirari belongs also that important compilation the "Synchronistic History of Assyria and Babylonia", which deals with the relations of the two kingdoms and refers to contemporary events and rulers.

The legends of Semiramis indicate that Sammu-rammat was associated like Queen Tiy with the revival of mother worship. As we have said, she went down to tradition as the daughter of the fish goddess, Derceto. Pliny identified that deity with Atargatis of Hierapolis.[466]

In Babylonia the fish goddess was Nina, a developed form of Damkina, spouse of Ea of Eridu. In the inscription on the Nebo statue, that god is referred to as the "son of

Nudimmud" (Ea). Nina was the goddess who gave her name to Nineveh, and it is possible that Nebo may have been regarded as her son during the Semiramis period.

The story of Semiramis's birth is evidently of great antiquity. It seems to survive throughout Europe in the nursery tale of the "Babes in the Wood". A striking Indian parallel is afforded by the legend of Shakuntala, which may be first referred to for the purpose of comparative study. Shakuntala was the daughter of the rishi, Viswamitra, and Menaka, the Apsara (celestial fairy). Menaka gave birth to her child beside the sacred river Malini. "And she cast the new-born infant on the bank of that river and went away. And beholding the newborn infant lying in that forest destitute of human beings but abounding with lions and tigers, a number of vultures sat around to protect it from harm." A sage discovered the child and adopted her. "Because", he said, "she was surrounded by *Shakuntas* (birds), therefore hath she been named by me *Shakuntala* (bird protected)."[467]

Semiramis was similarly deserted at birth by her Celestial mother. She was protected by doves, and her Assyrian name, Sammu-rammat, is believed to be derived from "Summat"--"dove", and to signify "the dove goddess loveth her". Simmas, the chief of royal shepherds, found the child and adopted her. She was of great beauty like Shakuntala, the maiden of "perfect symmetry", "sweet smiles", and "faultless features", with whom King Dushyanta fell in love and married in Gandharva fashion.[468]

Semiramis became the wife of Onnes, governor of Nineveh, and one of the generals of its alleged founder, King Ninus. She accompanied her husband to Bactria on a military campaign, and is said to have instructed the king how that city should be taken. Ninus fell in love with Semiramis, and Onnes, who refused to give her up, went and hanged himself. The fair courtesan then became the wife of the king.

The story proceeds that Semiramis exercised so great an influence over the impressionable King Ninus, that she persuaded him to proclaim her Queen of Assyria for fivedays. She then ascended the throne decked in royal robes. On the first day she gave a great banquet, and on the second thrust Ninus into prison, or had him put to death. In this manner she secured the empire for herself. She reigned for over forty years.

Professor Frazer inclines to the view that the legend is a reminiscence of the custom of appointing a mock king and queen to whom the kingdom was yielded up for five days. Semiramis played the part of the mother goddess, and the priestly king died a violent death in the character of her divine lover. "The mounds of Semiramis which were pointed out all over Western Asia were said to have been the graves of her lovers whom she buried alive.... This tradition is one of the surest indications of the identity of the mythical Semiramis with the Babylonian goddess Ishtar or Astarte."[469] As we have seen, Ishtar and other mother goddesses had many lovers whom they deserted like La Belle Dame sans Merci (pp. 174-175).

As Queen of Assyria, Semiramis was said to have cut roads through mountainous districts and erected many buildings. According to one version of the legend she founded the city of Babylon. Herodotus, however, says in this connection: "Semiramis held the throne for five generations before the later princess (Nitocris).... She raised certain embankments, well worthy of inspection, in the plain near Babylon, to control the river (Euphrates), which, till then, used to overflow and flood the whole country round about."[470] Lucian, who associates the famous queen with "mighty works in Asia", states that she was reputed by some to be the builder of the ancient temple of Aphrodite in the Libanus, although others credited it to Cinyras, or Deukalion.[471] Several Median places bear her name, and according to ancient Armenian tradition she was the founder of Van, which was formerly called "Shamiramagerd". Strabo tells that unidentified mountains in Western Asia were named after Semiramis.[472] Indeed, many of the great works in the Tigro-Euphrates valley, not excepting the famous inscription of Darius, were credited to the legendary queen of Babylonia and Assyria.[473] She was the rival in tradition of the famous Sesostris of Egypt as a ruler, builder, and conqueror.

All the military expeditions of Semiramis were attended with success, except her invasion of India. She was supposed to have been defeated in the Punjab. After suffering this disaster she died, or abdicated the throne in favour of her son Ninyas. The most archaic form of the legend appears to be that she was turned into a dove and took flight to heaven in that form. After her death she was worshipped as a dove goddess like "Our Lady of Trees and Doves" in Cyprus, whose shrine at old Paphos was founded, Herodotus says, by Phoenician colonists from Askalon.[474] Fish and doves were sacred to Derceto (Attar),[475] who had a mermaid form. "I have beheld", says Lucian, "the image of Derceto in Phoenicia. A marvellous spectacle it is. One half is a woman, but the part which extends from thighs to feet terminates with the tail of a fish."[476]

Derceto was supposed to have been a woman who threw herself in despair into a lake. After death she was adored as a goddess and her worshippers abstained from eating fish, except sacrificially. A golden image of a fish was suspended in her temple. Atargatis, who was identical with Derceto, was reputed in another form of the legend to have been born of an egg which the sacred fishes found in the Euphrates and thrust ashore (p. 28). The Greek Aphrodite was born of the froth of the sea and floated in a sea-shell. According to Hesiod,

> The wafting waves
> First bore her to Cythera the divine:
> To wave-encircled Cyprus came she then,
> And forth emerged, a goddess, in the charms
> Of awful beauty. Where her delicate feet
> Had pressed the sands, green herbage flowering sprang.
> Her Aphrodite gods and mortals name,
> The foam-born goddess; and her name is known
> As Cytherea with the blooming wreath,
> For that she touched Cythera's flowery coast;
> And Cypris, for that on the Cyprian shore
> She rose, amid the multitude of waves. *Elton's translation.*

The animals sacred to Aphrodite included the sparrow, the dove, the swan, the swallow, and the wryneck.[477] She presided over the month of April, and the myrtle, rose, poppy, and apple were sacred to her.

Some writers connect Semiramis, in her character as a dove goddess, with Media and the old Persian mother goddess Anaitis, and regard as arbitrary her identification with the fish goddess Derceto or Atargatis. The dove was certainly not a popular bird in the religious art of Babylonia and Assyria, but in one of the hymns translated by Professor Pinches Ishtar says, "Like a lonely dove I rest". In another the worshipper tries to touch Ishtar's heart by crying, "Like the dove I moan". A Sumerian psalmist makes a goddess (Gula, who presided over Larak, a part of Isin) lament over the city after it was captured by the enemy:

> My temple E-aste, temple of Larak,
> Larak the city which Bel Enlil gave,
> Beneath are turned to strangeness, above are turned to strangeness,
> With wailings on the lyre my dwelling-place is surrendered to the stranger,
> *The dove cots they wickedly seized, the doves they entrapped....*
> The ravens he (Enlil) caused to fly.[478]

Apparently there were temple and household doves in Babylonia. The Egyptians had their household dovecots in ancient as in modern times. Lane makes reference to the large pigeon houses in many villages. They are of archaic pattern, "with the walls slightly inclining inwards (like many of the ancient Egyptian buildings)", and are "constructed upon the roofs of the huts with crude brick, pottery, and mud.... Each pair of pigeons occupies a separate (earthen) pot."[479] It may be that the dove bulked more prominently in domestic than in official religion, and had a special seasonal significance. Ishtar appears to have had a dove form. In the Gilgamesh epic she is said to have loved the "brilliant Allalu bird" (the "bright-coloured wood pigeon", according to Sayce), and to have afterwards wounded it by breaking its wings.[480] She also loved the lion and the horse, and must therefore have assumed the forms of these animals. The goddess Bau, "she whose city is destroyed", laments in a Sumerian psalm:

> Like a dove to its dwelling-place, how long to my dwelling-place will they pursue

me,

> To my sanctuary ... the sacred place they pursue me....
> My resting place, the brick walls of my city Isin, thou art destroyed;
> My sanctuary, shrine of my temple Galmah, thou art destroyed.

> *Langdon's translation.*

Here the goddess appears to be identified with the doves which rest on the walls and make their nests in the shrine. The Sumerian poets did not adorn their poems with meaningless picturesque imagery; their images were stern facts; they had a magical or religious significance like the imagery of magical incantations; the worshipper invoked the deity by naming his or her various attributes, forms, &c.

Of special interest are the references in Sumerian psalms to the ravens as well as the doves of goddesses. Throughout Asia and Europe ravens are birds of ill omen. In Scotland there still linger curious folk beliefs regarding the appearance of ravens and doves after death. Michael Scott, the great magician, when on his deathbed told his friends to place his body on a hillock. "Three ravens and three doves would be seen flying towards it. If the ravens were first the body was to be burned, but if the doves were first it was to receive Christian burial. The ravens were foremost, but in their hurry flew beyond their mark. So the devil, who had long been preparing a bed for Michael, was disappointed."[481]

In Indian mythology Purusha, the chaos giant, first divided himself. "Hence were husband and wife produced." This couple then assumed various animal forms and thus "created every living pair whatsoever down to the ants".[482] Goddesses and fairies in the folk tales of many countries sometimes assume bird forms. The "Fates" appear to Damayanti in the Nala story as swans which carry love messages.[483]

According to Aryo-Indian belief, birds were "blessed with fecundity". The Babylonian Etana eagle and the Egyptian vulture, as has been indicated, were deities of fertility. Throughout Europe birds, which were "Fates", mated, according to popular belief, on St. Valentine's Day in February, when lots were drawn for wives by rural folks. Another form of the old custom is referred to by the poet Gay:--

Last Valentine, the day when birds of kind
Their paramours with mutual chirpings find,
I early rose....
Thee first I spied, and the first swain we see,
In spite of fortune, shall our true love be.

The dove appears to have been a sacred bird in various areas occupied by tribes of the Mediterranean race. Models of a shrine found in two royal graves at Mycenae are surmounted by a pair of doves, suggesting twin goddesses like Isis and Nepthys of Egypt and Ishtar and Belitsheri of Babylonia. Doves and snakes were associated with the mother goddess of Crete, "typifying", according to one view, "her connection with air and earth. Although her character was distinctly beneficent and pacific, yet as Lady of the Wild Creatures she had a more fearful aspect, one that was often depicted on carved gems, where lions are her companions."[484] Discussing the attributes and symbols of this mother goddess, Professor Burrows says: "As the serpent, coming from the crevices of the earth, shows the possession of the tree or pillar from the underworld, so the dove, with which this goddess is also associated, shows its possession from the world of the sky".[485] Professor Robertson Smith has demonstrated that the dove was of great sanctity among the Semites.[486] It figures in Hittite sculptures and was probably connected with the goddess cult in Asia Minor. Although Egypt had no dove goddess, the bird was addressed by lovers--

I hear thy voice, O turtle dove--
The dawn is all aglow--
Weary am I with love, with love,
Oh, whither shall I go?[487]

Pigeons, as indicated, are in Egypt still regarded as sacred birds, and a few years ago British soldiers created a riot by shooting them. Doves were connected with the ancient Greek oracle at Dodona. In many countries the dove is closely associated with love, and also symbolizes innocence, gentleness, and holiness.

The pigeon was anciently, it would appear, a sacred bird in these islands, and Brand has recorded curious folk beliefs connected with it. In some districts the idea prevailed that no person could die on a bed which contained pigeon feathers: "If anybody be sick and lye a dying, if they lye upon pigeon feathers they will be languishing and never die, but be in pain and torment," wrote a correspondent. A similar superstition about the feathers of different varieties of wild fowl[488] obtained in other districts. Brand traced this interesting traditional belief in Yorkshire, Lancashire, Derbyshire, and some of the Welsh and Irish counties.[489] It still lingers in parts of the Scottish Highlands. In the old ballad of "The Bloody Gardener" the white dove appears to a young man as the soul of his lady love who was murdered by his mother. He first saw the bird perched on his breast and then "sitting on a myrtle tree".[490]

The dove was not only a symbol of Semiramis, but also of her mother Derceto, the Phoenician fish goddess. The connection between bird and fish may have been given an astral significance. In "Poor Robin's Almanack" for 1757 a St. Valentine rhyme begins:--

This month bright Phoebus enters Pisces,
The maids will have good store of kisses,
For always when the sun comes there,
Valentine's day is drawing near,
And both the men and maids incline
To choose them each a Valentine.

As we have seen, the example was set by the mating birds. The "Almanack" poet no doubt versified an old astrological belief: when the spring sun entered the sign of the Fishes, the love goddess in bird form returned to earth.

Advocates of the Totemic theory, on the other hand, may hold that the association of doves with snake goddesses and fish goddesses of fertility was due to the fusion of tribes who had various animal totems. "The Pelew Islanders believed", says Professor Frazer, "that the souls of their forefathers lived in certain species of animals, which accordingly they held sacred and would not injure. For this reason one man would not kill snakes, another would not harm pigeons, and so on; but everyone was quite ready to kill and eat the sacred animals of his neighbours."[491] That the Egyptians had similar customs is suggested by what Herodotus tells us regarding their sacred animals: "Those who live near Thebes and the lake Moeris hold the crocodile in religious veneration.... Those who live in or near Elephantine, so far from considering these beasts as sacred, make them an article of food.... The hippopotamus is esteemed sacred in the district of Papremis, but in no other part of Egypt.... They roast and boil ... birds and fishes ... excepting those which are preserved for sacred purposes."[492] Totemic animals controlled the destinies of tribes and families. "Grose tells us", says Brand, "that, besides general notices of death, many families have particular warnings or notices: some by the appearance of a bird, and others by the figure of a tall woman, dressed all in white.... Pennant says that many of the great families in Scotland had their demon or genius, who gave them monitions of future events."[493] Members of tribes which venerated the pigeon therefore invoked it like the Egyptian love poet and drew omens from its notes, or saw one appearing as the soul of the dead like the lover in the ballad of "The Bloody Gardener". They refrained also from killing the pigeon except sacrificially, and suffered agonies on a deathbed which contained pigeon feathers, the "taboo" having been broken.

Some such explanation is necessary to account for the specialization of certain goddesses as fish, snake, cat, or bird deities. Aphrodite, who like Ishtar absorbed the attributes of several goddesses of fertility and fate, had attached to her the various animal symbols which were prominent in districts or among tribes brought into close contact, while the poppy, rose, myrtle, &c., which were used as love charms, or for making love potions, were also consecrated to her. Anthropomorphic deities were decorated with the symbols and flowers of folk religion.

From the comparative evidence accumulated here, it will be seen that the theory of the mythical Semiramis's Median or Persian origin is somewhat narrow. It is possible that the dove was venerated in Cyprus, as it certainly was in Crete, long centuries before Assyrian and Babylonian influence filtered westward through Phoenician and Hittite channels. In another connection Sir Arthur Evans shows that the resemblance between Cretan and early Semitic beliefs "points rather to some remote common element, the nature of which is at present obscure, than to any definite borrowing by one side or another".[494]

From the evidence afforded by the Semiramis legends and the inscriptions of the latter half of the Assyrian Middle Empire period, it may be inferred that a renascence of "mother worship" was favoured by the social and political changes which were taking place. In the first place the influence of Babylon must have been strongly felt in this connection. The fact that Adadnirari found it necessary to win the support of the Babylonians by proclaiming his descent from one of their ancient royal families, suggests that he was not only concerned about the attitude assumed by the scholars of the southern kingdom, but also that of the masses of old Sumerian and Akkadian stocks who continued to bake cakes to the Queen of Heaven so as to ensure good harvests. In the second place it is not improbable that even in Assyria the introduction of Nebo and his spouse made widespread appeal. That country had become largely peopled by an alien population; many of these aliens came from districts where "mother worship" prevailed, and had no traditional respect for Ashur, while they regarded with hostility the military aristocracy who conquered and ruled in the name of that dreaded deity. Perhaps, too, the influence of the Aramaeans, who in Babylonia wrecked the temples of the sun god, tended to revive the ancient religion of the Mediterranean race. Jehu's religious revolt in Israel, which established once again the cult of Ashtoreth, occurred after he came under the sway of Damascus, and may have not been unconnected with the political ascendancy elsewhere of the goddess cult.

Nebo, whom Adad-nirari exalted at Kalkhi, was more than a local god of Borsippa. "The most satisfactory view", says Jastrow, "is to regard him as a counterpart of Ea. Like Ea, he is the embodiment and source of wisdom.... The study of the heavens formed part of the wisdom which is traced back to Nebo, and the temple school at Borsippa became one of the chief centres for the astrological, and, subsequently, for the astronomical lore of Babylonia.... Like Nebo, Ea is also associated with the irrigation of the fields and with their consequent fertility. A hymn praises him as the one who fills the canals and the dikes, who protects the fields and brings the crops to maturity." Nebo links with Merodach (Marduk), who is sometimes referred to as his father. Jastrow assumes that the close partnership between Nebo and Merodach "had as a consequence a transfer of some of the father Marduk's attributes as a solar deity to Nebo,[495] his son, just as Ea passed his traits on to his son, Marduk".[496]

As the "recorder" or "scribe" among the gods, Nebo resembles the Egyptian god Thoth, who links with Khonsu, the lunar and spring sun god of love and fertility, and with Osiris. In Borsippa he had, like Merodach in Babylon, pronounced Tammuz traits. Nebo, in fact, appears to be the Tammuz of the new age, the son of the ancient goddess, who became "Husband of his Mother". If Nebo had no connection with Great Mother worship, it is unlikely that his statue would have borne an inscription referring to King Adad-nirari and Queen Sammu-rammat on equal terms. The Assyrian spouse of Nebo was called Tashmit. This "goddess of supplication and love" had a lunar significance. A prayer addressed to her in association with Nannar (Sin) and Ishtar, proceeds:

In the evil of the eclipse of the moon which ... has taken place,

In the evil of the powers, of the portents, evil and not good, which are in my palace and my land,

(I) have turned towards thee!...

Before Nabu (Nebo) thy spouse, thy lord, the prince, the first-born of E-sagila, intercede for me!

May he hearken to my cry at the word of thy mouth; may he remove my sighing, may he learn my supplication!

Damkina is similarly addressed in another prayer:

O Damkina, mighty queen of all the gods,

O wife of Ea, valiant art thou,

O Ir-nina, mighty queen of all the gods ...

Thou that dwellest in the Abyss, O lady of heaven and earth!...

In the evil of the eclipse of the moon, etc.

Bau is also prayed in a similar connection as "mighty lady that dwellest in the bright heavens", i.e. "Queen of heaven".[497]

Tashmit, whose name signifies "Obedience", according to Jastrow, or "Hearing", according to Sayce, carried the prayers of worshippers to Nebo, her spouse. As Isis interceded with Osiris, she interceded with Nebo, on behalf of mankind. But this did not signify that she was the least influential of the divine pair. A goddess played many parts: she was at once mother, daughter, and wife of the god; the servant of one god or the "mighty queen of all the gods". The Great Mother was, as has been indicated, regarded as the eternal and undecaying one; the gods passed away, son succeeding father; she alone remained. Thus, too, did Semiramis survive in the popular memory, as the queen-goddess of widespread legends, after kings and gods had been forgotten. To her was ascribed all the mighty works of other days in the lands where the indigenous peoples first worshipped the Great Mother as Damkina, Nina, Bau, Ishtar, or Tashmit, because the goddess was anciently believed to be the First Cause, the creatrix, the mighty one who invested the ruling god with the powers he possessed--the god who held sway because he was her husband, as did Nergal as the husband of Eresh-ki-gal, queen of Hades.

The multiplication of well-defined goddesses was partly due to the tendency to symbolize the attributes of the Great Mother, and partly due to the development of the great "Lady" in a particular district where she reflected local phenomena and where the political influence achieved by her worshippers emphasized her greatness. Legends regarding a famous goddess were in time attached to other goddesses, and in Aphrodite and Derceto we appear to have mother deities who absorbed the traditions of more than one local "lady" of river and plain, forest and mountain. Semiramis, on the other hand, survived as a link between the old world and the new, between the country from which emanated the stream of ancient culture and the regions which received it. As the high priestess of the cult, she became identified with the goddess whose bird name she bore, as Gilgamesh and Etana became identified with the primitive culture-hero or patriarch of the ancient Sumerians, and Sargon became identified with Tammuz. No doubt the fame of Semiramis was specially emphasized because of her close association, as Queen Sammu-rammat, with the religious innovations which disturbed the land of the god Ashur during the Middle Empire period.

Adad-nirari IV, the son or husband of Sammu-rammat, was a vigorous and successful campaigner. He was the Assyrian king who became the "saviour" of Israel. Although it is not possible to give a detailed account of his various expeditions, we find from the list of these which survives in the Eponym Chronicle that he included in the Assyrian Empire a larger extent of territory than any of his predecessors. In the north-east he overcame the Median and other tribes, and acquired a large portion of the Iranian plateau; he compelled Edom to pay tribute, and established his hold in Babylonia by restricting the power of the Chaldaeans in Sealand. In the north he swayed--at least, so he claimed--the wide domains of the Nairi people. He also confirmed his supremacy over the Hittites.

The Aramaean state of Damascus, which had withstood the attack of the great Shalmaneser and afterwards oppressed, as we have seen, the kingdoms of Israel and Judah, was completely overpowered by Adad-nirari. The old king, Hazael, died when Assyria's power was being strengthened and increased along his frontiers. He was succeeded by his son Mari, who is believed to be identical with the Biblical Ben-Hadad III.[498]

Shortly after this new monarch came to the throne, Adad-nirari IV led a great army against him. The Syrian ruler appears to have been taken by surprise; probably his kingdom was suffering from the three defeats which had been previously administered by the revolting Israelites.[499] At any rate Mari was unable to gather together an army of allies to resist the Assyrian advance, and took refuge behind the walls of Damascus. This strongly fortified city was closely invested, and Mari had at length to submit and acknowledge Adad-nirari as his overlord. The price of peace included 23,000 talents of silver, 20 of gold, 3000 of copper, and 5000 of iron, as well as ivory ornaments and furniture, embroidered materials, and other goods "to a countless amount". Thus "the Lord gave Israel a saviour, so that they went out from under the hand of the Syrians: and the children of Israel dwelt in their tents, as beforetime". This significant reference to the conquest of Damascus by the Assyrian king is followed by another which throws light on the religious phenomena of the period: "Nevertheless they departed not from the sins of the house of Jeroboam, who made Israel sin, but walked therein: and there remained the grove also in Samaria".[500] Ashtoreth and her golden calf continued to be venerated, and doves were sacrificed to the local Adonis.

It is not certain whether Adad-nirari penetrated farther than Damascus. Possibly all the states which owed allegiance to the king of that city became at once the willing vassals of Assyria, their protector. The tribute received by Adad-nirari from Tyre, Sidon, the land of Omri (Israel), Edom, and Palastu (Philistia) may have been gifted as a formal acknowledgment of his suzerainty and with purpose to bring them directly under Assyrian control, so that Damascus might be prevented from taking vengeance against them.

Meagre details survive regarding the reign of the next king, Shalmaneser IV (781-772 B.C). These are, however, supplemented by the Urartian inscriptions. Although Adad-nirari boasted that he had subdued the kingdom of Urartu in the north, he appears to have done no more than limit its southern expansion for a time.

The Urarti were, like the Mitanni, a military aristocracy[501] who welded together by conquest the tribes of the eastern and northern Highlands which several Assyrian monarchs included in their Empire. They acquired the elements of Assyrian culture, and used the Assyrian script for their own language. Their god was named Khaldis, and they called their nation Khaldia. During the reign of Ashur-natsir-pal their area of control was confined to the banks of the river Araxes, but it was gradually extended under a succession of vigorous kings towards the south-west until they became supreme round the shores of Lake Van. Three of their early kings were Lutipris, Sharduris I, and Arame.

During the reign of Shamshi-Adad the Assyrians came into conflict with the Urarti, who were governed at the time by "Ushpina of Nairi" (Ishpuinis, son of Sharduris II). The Urartian kingdom had extended rapidly and bordered on Assyrian territory. To the west were the tribes known as the Mannai, the northern enemies of the Medes, a people of Indo-European speech.

When Adad-nirari IV waged war against the Urarti, their king was Menuas, the son of Ishpuinis. Menuas was a great war-lord, and was able to measure his strength against Assyria on equal terms. He had nearly doubled by conquest the area controlled by his predecessors. Adad-nirari endeavoured to drive his rival northward, but all along the Assyrian frontier from the Euphrates to the Lower Zab, Menuas forced the outposts of Adad-nirari to retreat southward. The Assyrians, in short, were unable to hold their own.

Having extended his kingdom towards the south, Menuas invaded Hittite territory, subdued Malatia and compelled its king to pay tribute. He also conquered the Mannai and other tribes. Towards the north and north-west he added a considerable area to his kingdom, which became as large as Assyria.

Menuas's capital was the city of Turushpa or Dhuspas (Van), which was called Khaldinas[502] after the national god. For a century it was the seat of Urartian administration. The buildings erected there by Menuas and his successors became associated in after-time with the traditions of Semiramis, who, as Queen Sammu-rammat of Assyria, was a contemporary of the great Urartian conqueror. Similarly a sculptured representation of the Hittite god was referred to by Herodotus as a memorial of the Egyptian king Sesostris.

164

The strongest fortification at Dhuspas was the citadel, which was erected on a rocky promontory jutting into Lake Van. A small garrison could there resist a prolonged siege. The water supply of the city was assured by the construction of subterranean aqueducts. Menuas erected a magnificent palace, which rivalled that of the Assyrian monarch at Kalkhi, and furnished it with the rich booty brought back from victorious campaigns. He was a lover of trees and planted many, and he laid out gardens which bloomed with brilliant Asian flowers. The palace commanded a noble prospect of hill and valley scenery on the south-western shore of beautiful Lake Van.

Menuas was succeeded by his son Argistis, who ascended the throne during the lifetime of Adad-nirari of Assyria. During the early part of his reign he conducted military expeditions to the north beyond the river Araxes. He afterwards came into conflict with Assyria, and acquired more territory on its northern frontier. He also subdued the Mannai, who had risen in revolt.

For three years (781-778 B.C.) the general of Shalmaneser IV waged war constantly with Urartu, and again in 776 B.C. and 774 B.C. attempts were made to prevent the southern expansion of that Power. On more than one occasion the Assyrians were defeated and compelled to retreat.

Assyria suffered serious loss of prestige on account of its inability to hold in check its northern rival. Damascus rose in revolt and had to be subdued, and northern Syria was greatly disturbed. Hadrach was visited in the last year of the king's reign.

Ashur-dan III (771-763 B.C.) occupied the Assyrian throne during a period of great unrest. He was unable to attack Urartu. His army had to operate instead on his eastern and southern frontiers. A great plague broke out in 765 B.C., the year in which Hadrach had again to be dealt with. On June 15, 763 B.C., there was a total eclipse of the sun, and that dread event was followed by a revolt at Asshur which was no doubt of priestly origin. The king's son Adad-nirari was involved in it, but it is not certain whether or not he displaced his father for a time. In 758 B.C. Ashur-dan again showed signs of activity by endeavouring to suppress the revolts which during the period of civil war had broken out in Syria.

Adad-nirari V came to the throne in 763 B.C. He had to deal with revolts in Asshur in other cities. Indeed for the greater part of his reign he seems to have been kept fully engaged endeavouring to establish his authority within the Assyrian borders. The Syrian provinces regained their independence.

During the first four years of his successor Ashurnirari IV (753-746 B.C.) the army never left Assyria. Namri was visited in 749-748 B.C., but it is not certain whether he fought against the Urartians, or the Aramaeans who had become active during this period of Assyrian decline. In 746 B.C. a revolt broke out in the city of Kalkhi and the king had to leave it. Soon afterwards he died--perhaps he was assassinated--and none of his sons came to the throne. A year previously Nabu-natsir, known to the Greeks as Nabonassar, was crowned king of Babylonia.

Ashur-nirari IV appears to have been a monarch of somewhat like character to the famous Akhenaton of Egypt--an idealist for whom war had no attractions. He kept his army at home while his foreign possessions rose in revolt one after another. Apparently he had dreams of guarding Assyria against attack by means of treaties of peace. He arranged one with a Mesopotamian king, Mati-ilu of Agusi, who pledged himself not to go to war without the consent of his Assyrian overlord, and it is possible that there were other documents of like character which have not survived to us. During his leisure hours the king engaged himself in studious pursuits and made additions to the royal library. In the end his disappointed soldiers found a worthy leader in one of its generals who seized the throne and assumed the royal name of Tiglath-pileser.

Ashur-nirari IV was the last king of the Middle Empire of Assyria. He may have been a man of high character and refinement and worthy of our esteem, although an unsuitable ruler for a predatory State.

---

[464] *The Land of the Hittites*, J. Garstang, p. 354.

[465] *The Old Testament in the Light of the Historical Records and Legends of Assyria and Babylonia*, T.G. Pinches, p. 343.

[466] *Nat. Hist.*, v, 19 and *Strabo* xvi, 1-27.

[467] *The Mahabharata: Adi Parva*, sections lxxi and lxxii (Roy's translation, pp. 213 216, and *Indian Myth and Legend*, pp. 157 *et seq.*

[468] That is, without ceremony but with consent.

[469] *The Golden Bough (The Scapegoat)*, pp. 369 *et seq.*, (3rd edition). Perhaps the mythic Semiramis and legends connected were in existence long before the historic Sammu-rammat, though the two got mixed up.

[470] *Herodotus*, i, 184.

[471] *De dea Syria*, 9-14.

[472] *Strabo*, xvi, 1, 2.

[473] *Diodorus Siculus*, ii, 3.

[474] *Herodotus*, i, 105.

[475] *Diodorus Siculus*, ii, 4.

[476] *De dea Syria*, 14.

[477] This little bird allied to the woodpecker twists its neck strangely when alarmed. It may have symbolized the coquettishness of fair maidens. As love goddesses were "Fates", however, the wryneck may have been connected with the belief that the perpetrator of a murder, or a death spell, could be detected when he approached his victim's corpse. If there was no wound to "bleed afresh", the "death thraw" (the contortions of death) might indicate who the criminal was. In a Scottish ballad regarding a lady, who was murdered by her lover, the verse occurs:

> 'Twas in the middle o' the night
> The cock began to craw;
> And at the middle o' the night
> The corpse began to thraw.

[478] Langdon's *Sumerian and Babylonian Psalms*, pp. 133, 135.

[479] Introduction to Lane's *Manners and Customs of the Modern Egyptians*.

[480] Tammuz is referred to in a Sumerian psalm as "him of the dovelike voice, yea, dovelike". He may have had a dove form. Angus, the Celtic god of spring, love, and fertility, had a swan form; he also had his seasonal period of sleep like Tammuz.

[481] Campbell's *Superstitions of the Scottish Highlands*, p. 288.

[482] *Indian Myth and Legend*, p. 95.

[483] *Ibid.*, pp. 329-30.

[484] *Crete, the Forerunner of Greece*, C.H. and H.B. Hawes, p. 139

[485] *The Discoveries in Crete*, pp. 137-8.

[486] *Religion of the Semites*, p. 294.

[487] *Egyptian Myth and Legend*, p. 59.

[488] Including the goose, one of the forms of the harvest goddess.

[489] *Brand's Popular Antiquities*, vol. ii, 230-1 and vol. iii, 232 (1899 ed.).

[490] *Ibid.*, vol. iii, 217. The myrtle was used for love charms.

[491] *The Golden Bough (Spirits of the Corn and of the Wild)*, vol. ii, p. 293 (3rd ed.).

[492] *Herodotus*, ii, 69, 71, and 77.

[493] *Brand's Popular Antiquities*, vol. iii, p. 227.

[494] Cited by Professor Burrows in *The Discoveries in Crete*, p. 134.

[495] Like the Egyptian Horus, Nebo had many phases: he was connected with the sun and moon, the planet Mercury, water and crops; he was young and yet old--a mystical god.

[496] *Aspects of Religious Belief and Practice in Babylonia and Assyria*, pp. 94 *et seq.*

[497] *Babylonian Magic and Sorcery*, L.W. King, pp. 6-7 and 26-7.

[498] *2 Kings*, xiii, 3.

[499] *2 Kings*, xiii, 14-25.

[500] *3 Kings*, xiii, 5, 6.

[501] The masses of the Urartian folk appear to have been of Hatti stock--"broad heads", like their descendants, the modern Armenians.

[502] It is uncertain whether this city or Kullani in north Syria it the Biblical Calno. *Isaiah*, x, 9.

Chapter XIX. Assyria's Age of Splendour

Abstract

Tiglath-pileser IV, the Biblical Pul--Babylonian Campaign--Urartian Ambitions in North Syria--Battle of Two Kings and Flight of Sharduris-- Conquest of Syro-Cappadocian States--Hebrew History from Jehu to Menahem --Israel subject to Assyria--Urartu's Power broken--Ahaz's Appeal to Assyria--Damascus and Israel subdued--Babylonia united to Assyria--Shalmaneser and Hoshea--Sargon deports the "Lost Ten Tribes"--Merodach Baladan King of Babylonia--Egyptian Army of Allies routed--Ahaz and Isaiah--Frontier Campaigns--Merodach Baladan overthrown--Sennacherib and the Hittite States--Merodach Baladan's second and brief Reign--Hezekiah and Sennacherib--Destruction of Assyrian Army--Sack of Babylon--Esarhaddon--A Second Semiramis--Raids of Elamites, Cimmerians, Scythians, and Medes--Sack of Sidon--Manasseh and Isaiah's Fate--Esarhaddon conquers Lower Egypt--Revolt of Assyrian Nobles--Ashurbanipal.

We now enter upon the last and most brilliant phase of Assyrian civilization--the period of the Third or New Empire during which flourished Tiglath-pileser IV, the mighty conqueror; the Shalmaneser of the Bible; "Sargon the Later", who transported the "lost ten tribes" of Israel; Sennacherib, the destroyer of Babylon, and Esarhaddon, who made Lower Egypt an Assyrian province. We also meet with notable figures of Biblical fame, including Ahaz, Hezekiah, Isaiah, and the idolatrous Manasseh.

Tiglath-pileser IV, who deposed Ashur-nirari IV, was known to the Babylonians as Pulu, which, some think, was a term of contempt signifying "wild animal". In the Bible he is referred to as Pul, Tiglath-pilneser, and Tiglath-pileser.[503] He came to the Assyrian throne towards the end of April in 745 B.C. and reigned until 727 B.C. We know nothing regarding his origin, but it seems clear that he was not of royal descent. He appears to have been a popular leader of the revolt against Ashur-nirari, who, like certain of his predecessors, had pronounced pro-Babylonian tendencies. It is significant to note in this connection that the new king was an unswerving adherent of the cult of Ashur, by the adherents of which he was probably strongly supported.

Tiglath-pileser combined in equal measure those qualities of generalship and statesmanship which were necessary for the reorganization of the Assyrian state and the revival of its military prestige. At the beginning of his reign there was much social discontent and suffering. The national exchequer had been exhausted by the loss of tribute from revolting provinces, trade was paralysed, and the industries were in a languishing condition. Plundering bands of Aramaeans were menacing the western frontiers and had overrun part of northern Babylonia. New political confederacies in Syria kept the north-west regions in a constant state of unrest, and the now powerful Urartian kingdom was threatening the Syro-Cappadocian states as if its rulers had dreams of building up a great world empire on the ruins of that of Assyria.

Tiglath-pileser first paid attention to Babylonia, and extinguished the resistance of the Aramaeans in Akkad. He appears to have been welcomed by Nabonassar, who became his vassal, and he offered sacrifices in the cities of Babylon, Sippar, Cuthah, and Nippur. Sippar had been occupied by Aramaeans, as on a previous occasion when they destroyed the temple of the sun god Shamash which was restored by Nabu-aplu-iddina of Babylon.

Tiglath-pileser did not overrun Chaldaea, but he destroyed its capital, Sarrabanu, and impaled King Nabu-ushabshi. He proclaimed himself "King of Sumer and Akkad" and "King of the Four Quarters". The frontier states of Elam and Media were visited and subdued.

Having disposed of the Aramaeans and other raiders, the Assyrian monarch had next to deal with his most powerful rival, Urartu. Argistis I had been succeeded by Sharduris III, who had formed an alliance with the north Mesopotamian king, Mati-ilu of Agusi, on whom Ashur-nirari had reposed his faith. Ere long Sharduris pressed southward from Malatia and compelled the north Syrian Hittite states, including Carchemish, to acknowledge his suzerainty. A struggle then ensued between Urartu and Assyria for the possession of the Syro-Cappadocian states.

At this time the reputation of Tiglath-pileser hung in the balance. If he failed in his attack on Urartu, his prestige would vanish at home and abroad and Sharduris might, after establishing himself in northern Syria, invade Assyria and compel its allegiance.

Two courses lay before Tiglath-pileser. He could either cross the mountains and invade Urartu, or strike at his rival in north Syria, where the influence of Assyria had been completely extinguished. The latter appeared to him to be the most feasible and judicious procedure, for if he succeeded in expelling the invaders he would at the same time compel the allegiance of the rebellious Hittite states.

In the spring of 743 B.C. Tiglath-pileser led his army across the Euphrates and reached Arpad without meeting with any resistance. The city appears to have opened its gates to him although it was in the kingdom of Mati-ilu, who acknowledged Urartian sway. Its foreign garrison was slaughtered. Well might Sharduris exclaim, in the words of the prophet, "Where is the king of Arpad? where are the gods of Arpad?"[504]

Leaving Arpad, Tiglath-pileser advanced to meet Sharduris, who was apparently hastening southward to attack the Assyrians in the rear. Tiglath-pileser, however, crossed the Euphrates and, moving northward, delivered an unexpected attack on the Urartian army in Qummukh. A fierce battle ensued, and one of its dramatic incidents was a single combat between the rival kings. The tide of battle flowed in Assyria's favour, and when evening was falling the chariots and cavalry of Urartu were thrown into confusion. An attempt was made to capture King Sharduris, who leapt from his chariot and made hasty escape on horseback, hotly pursued in the gathering darkness by an Assyrian contingent of cavalry. Not until "the bridge of the Euphrates" was reached was the exciting night chase abandoned.

Tiglath-pileser had achieved an overwhelming victory against an army superior to his own in numbers. Over 70,000 of the enemy were slain or taken captive, while the Urartian camp with its stores and horses and followers fell into the hands of the triumphant Assyrians. Tiglath-pileser burned the royal tent and throne as an offering to Ashur, and carried Sharduris's bed to the temple of the goddess of Nineveh, whither he returned to prepare a new plan of campaign against his northern rival.

Despite the blow dealt against Urartu, Assyria did not immediately regain possession of north Syria. The shifty Mati-ilu either cherished the hope that Sharduris would recover strength and again invade north Syria, or that he might himself establish an empire in that region. Tiglath-pileser had therefore to march westward again. For three years he conducted vigorous campaigns in "the western land", where he met with vigorous resistance. In 740 B.C. Arpad was captured and Mati-ilu deposed and probably put to death. Two years later Kullani and Hamath fell, and the districts which they controlled were included in the Assyrian empire and governed by Crown officials.

Once again the Hebrews came into contact with Assyria. The Dynasty of Jehu had come to an end by this time. Its fall may not have been unconnected with the trend of events in Assyria during the closing years of the Middle Empire.

Supported by Assyria, the kings of Israel had become powerful and haughty. Jehoash, the grandson of Jehu, had achieved successes in conflict with Damascus. In Judah the unstable Amaziah, son of Joash, was strong enough to lay a heavy hand on Edom, and flushed with triumph then resolved to readjust his relations with his overlord, the king of Israel. Accordingly he sent a communication to Jehoash which contained some proposal regarding their political relations, concluding with the offer or challenge, "Come, let us look one another in the face". A contemptuous answer was returned.

Jehoash the king of Israel sent to Amaziah king of Judah, saying, The thistle that was in Lebanon sent to the cedar that was in Lebanon, saying, Give thy daughter to my son to wife: and there passed by a wild beast that was in Lebanon, and trode down the thistle. Thou hast indeed smitten Edom, and thine heart hath lifted thee up: glory of this, and tarry at home, for why shouldest thou meddle to thy hurt, that thou shouldest fall, even thou, and Judah with thee? But Amaziah would not hear. Therefore Jehoash king of Israel went up; and he and Amaziah king of Judah looked one another in the face at Beth-shemesh [city of Shamash, the sun god], which belongeth to Judah. And Judah was put to the worse before Israel; and they fled every man to their tents.

Jehoash afterwards destroyed a large portion of the wall of Jerusalem and plundered the temple and palace, returning home to Samaria with rich booty and hostages.[505]Judah thus remained a vassal state of Israel's.

Jeroboam, son of Jehoash, had a long and prosperous reign. About 773 B.C. he appears to have co-operated with Assyria and conquered Damascus and Hamath. His son Zachariah, the last king of the Jehu Dynasty of Israel, came to the throne in 740 B.C. towards the close of the reign of Azariah, son of Amaziah, king of Judah. Six months afterwards he was assassinated by Shallum. This usurper held sway at Samaria for only a month. "For Menahem the son of Gadi went up from Tirzah, and came to Samaria, and smote Shallum the son of Jabesh in Samaria, and slew him, and reigned in his stead."[506]

Tiglath-pileser was operating successfully in middle Syria when he had dealings with, among others, "Menihimme (Menahem) of the city of the Samarians", who paid tribute. No resistance was possible on the part of Menahem, the usurper, who was probably ready to welcome the Assyrian conqueror, so that, by arranging an alliance, he might secure his own position. The Biblical reference is as follows: "And Pul the king of Assyria came against the land: and Menahem gave Pul a thousand talents of silver, that his hand might be with him to confirm the kingdom in his hand. And Menahem exacted the money of Israel, even of all the mighty men of wealth, of each man fifty shekels of silver, to give to the king of Assyria. So the king of Assyria turned back, and stayed not there in the land."[507] Rezin of Damascus, Hiram of Tyre, and Zabibi, queen of the Arabians, also sent gifts to Tiglath-pileser at this time (738 B.C.). Aramaean revolts on the borders of Elam were suppressed by Assyrian governors, and large numbers of the inhabitants were transported to various places in Syria.

Tiglath-pileser next operated against the Median and other hill tribes in the north-east. In 735 B.C. he invaded Urartu, the great Armenian state which had threatened the supremacy of Assyria in north Syria and Cappadocia. King Sharduris was unable to protect his frontier or hamper the progress of the advancing army, which penetrated to his capital. Dhuspas was soon captured, but Sharduris took refuge in his rocky citadel which he and his predecessors had laboured to render impregnable. There he was able to defy the might of Assyria, for the fortress could be approached on the western side alone by a narrow path between high walls and towers, so that only a small force could find room to operate against the numerous garrison.

Tiglath-pileser had to content himself by devastating the city on the plain and the neighbouring villages. He overthrew buildings, destroyed orchards, and transported to Nineveh those of the inhabitants he had not put to the sword, with all the live stock he could lay hands on. Thus was Urartu crippled and humiliated: it never regained its former prestige among the northern states.

In the following year Tiglath-pileser returned to Syria. The circumstances which made this expedition necessary are of special interest on account of its Biblical associations. Menahem, king of Israel, had died, and was succeeded by his son Pekahiah. "But Pekah the son of Remaliah, a captain of his, conspired against him and smote him in Samaria, in the palace of the king's house, ... and he killed him, and reigned in his room."[508] When Pekah was on the throne, Ahaz began to reign over Judah.

Judah had taken advantage of the disturbed conditions in Israel to assert its independence. The walls of Jerusalem were repaired by Jotham, father of Ahaz, and a tunnel constructed to supply it with water. Isaiah refers to this tunnel: "Go forth and meet Ahaz ... at the end of the conduit of the upper pool in the highway of the fuller's field" (*Isaiah*, vii, 3).

Pekah had to deal with a powerful party in Israel which favoured the re-establishment of David's kingdom in Palestine. Their most prominent leader was the prophet Amos, whose eloquent exhortations were couched in no uncertain terms. He condemned Israel for its idolatries, and cried:

For thus saith the Lord unto the house of Israel, Seek ye me and ye shall live.... Have ye offered unto me sacrifices and offerings in the wilderness forty years, O house of Israel? But ye have borne the tabernacle of your Moloch and Chiun your images, the star of your god, which ye made to yourselves.[509]

Pekah sought to extinguish the orthodox party's movement by subduing Judah. So he plotted with Rezin, king of Damascus. Amos prophesied,

Thus saith the Lord.... I will send a fire into the house of Hazael, which will devour the palaces of Ben-hadad. I will break also the bar of Damascus ... and the people of Syria shall go into captivity unto Kir.... The remnant of the Philistines shall perish.

Tyre, Edom, and Ammon would also be punished.[510] Judah was completely isolated by the allies who acknowledged the suzerainty of Damascus. Soon after Ahaz came to the throne he found himself hemmed in on every side by adversaries who desired to accomplish his fall. "At that time Rezin, king of Syria, and Pekah ...came up to Jerusalem to war: and they besieged Ahaz, but could not overcome him."[511] Judah, however, was overrun; the city of Elath was captured and restored to Edom, while the Philistines were liberated from the control of Jerusalem.

Isaiah visited Ahaz and said,

Take heed, and be quiet; fear not, neither be faint-hearted for the two tails of these smoking firebrands, for the fierce anger of Rezin with Syria, and of the son of Remaliah. Because Syria, Ephraim, and the son of Remaliah, have taken evil counsel against thee, saying, Let us go up against Judah, and vex it, and let us make a breach therein for us, and set a king in the midst of it, even the son of Tabeal: Thus saith the Lord God, It shall not stand, neither shall it come to pass.[512]

The unstable Ahaz had sought assistance from the Baal, and "made his son to pass through the fire, according to the abominations of the heathen".[513] Then he resolved to purchase the sympathy of one of the great Powers. There was no hope of assistance from "the fly that is in the uttermost part of the rivers of Egypt", for the Ethiopian Pharaohs had not yet conquered the Delta region, so he turned to "the bee that is in the land of Assyria".[514] Assyria was the last resource of the king of Judah.

So Ahaz sent messengers to Tiglath-pileser king of Assyria, saying, I am thy servant and thy son: come up and save me out of the hand of Syria and out of the hand of the king of Israel, which rise up against me. And Ahaz took the silver and gold that was found in the house of the Lord, and in the treasures of the king's house, and sent it for a present to the king of Assyria. And the king of Assyria hearkened unto him: for the king of Assyria went up against Damascus, and took it, and carried the people of it captive to Kir[515] and slew Rezin.[516]

Tiglath-pileser recorded that Rezin took refuge in his city like "a mouse". Israel was also dealt with.

In the days of Pekah king of Israel came Tiglath-pileser king of Assyria, and took Ijon and Abel-beth-maachah, and Janoah and Kedesh, and Hazor, and Gilead, and Galilee, all the land of Naphtali, and carried them captive to Assyria. And Hoshea the son of Elah made a conspiracy against Pekah the son of Remaliah, and smote him, and slew him, and reigned in his stead.[517]

Tiglath-pileser recorded: "They overthrew Paqaha (Pekah), their king, and placed Ausi'a (Hoshea) over them". He swept through Israel "like a hurricane". The Philistines and the Arabians of the desert were also subdued. Tribute was sent to the Assyrian monarch by Phoenicia, Moab, Ammon, and Edom. It was a proud day for Ahaz when he paid a visit to Tiglath-pileser at Damascus.[518] An Assyrian governor was appointed to rule over Syria and its subject states.

Babylon next claimed the attention of Tiglath-pileser. Nabonassar had died and was succeeded by his son Nabu-nadin-zeri, who, after reigning for two years, was slain in a rebellion. The throne was then seized by Nabu-shum-ukin, but in less than two months this usurper was assassinated and the Chaldaeans had one of their chiefs, Ukinzer, proclaimed king (732 B.C.).

When the Assyrian king returned from Syria in 731 B.C. he invaded Babylonia. He was met with a stubborn resistance. Ukinzer took refuge in his capital, Shapia, which held out successfully, although the surrounding country was ravaged and despoiled. Two years afterwards Tiglath-pileser returned, captured Shapia, and restored peace throughout Babylonia. He was welcomed in Babylon, which opened its gates to him, and he had himself proclaimed king of Sumer and Akkad. The Chaldaeans paid tribute.

Tiglath-pileser had now reached the height of his ambition. He had not only extended his empire in the west from Cappadocia to the river of Egypt, crippled Urartu and pacified his eastern frontier, but brought Assyria into close union with Babylonia, the mother land, the home of culture and the land of the ancient gods. He did not live long, however, to enjoy his final triumph, for he died a little over twelve months after he "took the hands of Bel (Merodach)" at Babylon.

He was succeeded by Shalmaneser V (727-722 B.C.), who may have been his son, but this is not quite certain. Little is known regarding his brief reign. In 725 B.C. he led an expedition to Syria and Phoenicia. Several of the vassal peoples had revolted when they heard of the death of Tiglath-pileser. These included the Phoenicians, the Philistines, and the Israelites who were intriguing with either Egypt or Mutsri.

Apparently Hoshea, king of Israel, pretended when the Assyrians entered his country that he remained friendly. Shalmaneser, however, was well informed, and made Hoshea a prisoner. Samaria closed its gates against him although their king had been dispatched to Assyria.

The Biblical account of the campaign is as follows: "Against him (Hoshea) came up Shalmaneser king of Assyria; and Hoshea became his servant, and gave him presents. And the king of Assyria found conspiracy in Hoshea: for he had sent messengers to So king of Egypt,[519] and brought no present to the king of Assyria, as he had done year by year; therefore the king of Assyria shut him up and bound him in prison.

"Then the king of Assyria came up throughout all the land, and went up to Samaria, and besieged it three years."[520]

Shalmaneser died before Samaria was captured, and may have been assassinated. The next Assyrian monarch, Sargon II (722-705 B.C.), was not related to either of his two predecessors. He is referred to by Isaiah,[521] and is the Arkeanos of Ptolemy. He was the Assyrian monarch who deported the "Lost Ten Tribes".

"In the ninth year of Hoshea" (and the first of Sargon) "the king of Assyria took Samaria, and carried Israel away into Assyria, and placed them in Halah and in Habor by the river of Gozan, and in the cities of the Medes."[522] In all, according to Sargon's record, "27,290 people dwelling in the midst of it (Samaria) I carried off".

They (the Israelites) left all the commandments of the Lord their God, and made them molten images, even two calves, and made a grove, and worshipped all the host of heaven (the stars), and served Baal. And they caused their sons and their daughters to pass through the fire, and used divination and enchantments, and sold themselves to do evil in the sight of the Lord, to provoke him to anger. Therefore the Lord was very angry with Israel, and removed them out of his sight: there was none left but the tribe of Judah only. And the king of Assyria brought men from Babylon, and from Cuthah, and from Ava, and from Hamath, and from Sepharvaim, and placed them in the cities of Samaria instead of the children of Israel: and they possessed Samaria, and dwelt in the cities thereof.... And the men of Babylon made Succoth-benoth, and the men of Cuth (Cuthah) made Nergal, and the men of Hamath made Ashima, and the Avites made Nibhaz and Tartak, and the Sepharites burnt their children in fire to Adram-melech and Anam-melech, the gods of Sepharvaim.

A number of the new settlers were slain by lions, and the king of Assyria ordered that a Samaritan priest should be sent to "teach them the manner of the God of the land". This man was evidently an orthodox Hebrew, for he taught them "how they should fear the Lord.... So they feared the Lord", but also "served their own gods ... their graven images".[523]

There is no evidence to suggest that the "Ten Lost Tribes", "regarding whom so many nonsensical theories have been formed", were not ultimately absorbed by the peoples among whom they settled between Mesopotamia and the Median Highlands.[524] The various sections must have soon lost touch with one another. They were not united like the Jews (the people of Judah), who were transported to Babylonia a century and a half later, by a common religious bond, for although a few remained faithful to Abraham's God, the majority of the Israelites worshipped either the Baal or the Queen of Heaven.

The Assyrian policy of transporting the rebellious inhabitants of one part of their empire to another was intended to break their national spirit and compel them to become good and faithful subjects amongst the aliens, who must have disliked them. "The colonists," says Professor Maspero, "exposed to the same hatred as the original Assyrian conquerors, soon forgot to look upon the latter as the oppressors of all, and, allowing their present grudge to efface the memory of past injuries, did not hesitate to make common cause with them. In time of peace the (Assyrian) governor did his best to protect them against molestation on the part of the natives, and in return for this they rallied round him whenever the latter threatened to get out of hand, and helped him to stifle the revolt, or hold it in check until the arrival of reinforcements. Thanks to their help, the empire was consolidated and maintained without too many violent outbreaks in regions far removed from the capital, and beyond the immediate reach of the sovereign."[525]

While Sargon was absent in the west, a revolt broke out in Babylonia. A Chaldaean king, Merodach Baladan III, had allied himself with the Elamites, and occupied Babylon. A battle was fought at Dur-ilu and the Elamites retreated. Although Sargon swept triumphantly through the land, he had to leave his rival, the tyrannous Chaldaean, in possession of the capital, and he reigned there for over eleven years.

Trouble was brewing in Syria. It was apparently fostered by an Egyptian king-- probably Bocchoris of Sais, the sole Pharaoh so far as can be ascertained of the Twenty-fourth Dynasty, who had allied himself with the local dynasts of Lower Egypt and apparently sought to extend his sway into Asia, the Ethiopians being supreme in Upper Egypt. An alliance had been formed to cast off the yoke of Assyria. The city states involved Arpad, Simirra, Damascus, Samaria, and Gaza. Hanno of Gaza had fled to Egypt after Tiglath-pileser came to the relief of Judah and broke up the league of conspirators by capturing Damascus, and punishing Samaria, Gaza, and other cities. His return in Sargon's reign was evidently connected with the new rising in which he took part. The throne of Hamath had been seized by an adventurer, named Ilu-bi´di, a smith. The Philistines of Ashdod and the Arabians being strongly pro-Egyptian in tendency, were willing sympathizers and helpers against the hated Assyrians.

Sargon appeared in the west with a strong army before the allies had matured their plans. He met the smith king of Hamath in battle at Qarqar, and, having defeated him, had him skinned alive. Then he marched southward. At Rapiki (Raphia) he routed an army of allies. Shabi (?So), the Tartan (commander-in-chief) of Pi´ru[526](Pharaoh), King of Mutsri (an Arabian state confused, perhaps, with Misraim = Egypt), escaped "like to a shepherd whose sheep have been taken". Piru and other two southern kings, Samsi and Itamara, afterwards paid tribute to Sargon. Hanno of Gaza was transported to Asshur.

In 715 B.C. Sargon, according to his records, appeared with his army in Arabia, and received gifts in token of homage from Piru of Mutsri, Samsi of Aribi, and Itamara of Saba.

Four years later a revolt broke out in Ashdod which was, it would appear, directly due to the influence of Shabaka, the Ethiopian Pharaoh, who had deposed Bocchoris of Sais. Another league was about to be formed against Assyria. King Azuri of Ashdod had been deposed because of his Egyptian sympathies by the Assyrian governor, and his brother Akhimiti was placed on the throne. The citizens, however, overthrew Akhimiti, and an adventurer from Cyprus was proclaimed king (711 B.C.)

It would appear that advances were made by the anti-Assyrians to Ahaz of Judah. That monarch was placed in a difficult position. He knew that if the allies succeeded in stamping out Assyrian authority in Syria and Palestine they would certainly depose him, but if on the other hand he joined them and Assyria triumphed, its emperor would show him small mercy. As Babylon defied Sargon and received the active support of Elam, and there were rumours of risings in the north, it must have seemed to the western kings as if the Assyrian empire was likely once again to go to pieces.

Fortunately for Ahaz he had a wise counsellor at this time in the great statesman and prophet, the scholarly Isaiah. The Lord spake by Isaiah saying, "Go and loose the sackcloth from off thy loins, and put off thy shoe from thy foot. And he did so, walking naked and barefoot. And the Lord said, Like as my servant Isaiah hath walked naked and barefoot three years for a sign and wonder upon Egypt and upon Ethiopia; so shall the king of Assyria lead away the Egyptians prisoners.... And they (the allies) shall be afraid and ashamed of Ethiopia their expectation, and of Egypt their glory."[527]

Isaiah warned Ahaz against joining the league, "in the year that Tartan[528] came unto Ashdod (when Sargon the king of Assyria sent him)". The Tartan "fought against Ashdod and took it".[529] According to Sargon's record the Pretender of Ashdod fled to Arabia, where he was seized by an Arabian chief and delivered up to Assyria. The pro-Egyptian party in Palestine went under a cloud for a period thereafter.

Before Sargon could deal with Merodach Baladan of Babylon, he found it necessary to pursue the arduous task of breaking up a powerful league which had been formed against him in the north. The Syro-Cappadocian Hittite states, including Tabal in Asia Minor and Carchemish in north Syria, were combining for the last time against Assyria, supported by Mita (Midas), king of the Muski-Phrygians, and Rusas, son of Sharduris III, king of Urartu.

Urartu had recovered somewhat from the disasters which it had suffered at the hands of Tiglath-pileser, and was winning back portions of its lost territory on the north-east frontier of Assyria. A buffer state had been formed in that area by Tiglath-pileser, who had assisted the king of the Mannai to weld together the hill tribesmen between Lake Van and Lake Urmia into an organized nation. Iranzu, its ruler, remained faithful to Assyria and consequently became involved in war with Rusas of Urartu, who either captured or won over several cities of the Mannai. Iranzu was succeeded by his son Aza, and this king was so pronounced a pro-Assyrian that his pro-Urartian subjects assassinated him and set on the throne Bagdatti of Umildish.

Soon after Sargon began his operations in the north he captured Bagdatti and had him skinned alive. The flag of revolt, however, was kept flying by his brother, Ullusunu, but ere long this ambitious man found it prudent to submit to Sargon on condition that he would retain the throne as a faithful Assyrian vassal. His sudden change of policy appears to have been due to the steady advance of the Median tribes into the territory of the Mannai. Sargon conducted a vigorous and successful campaign against the raiders, and extended Ullusunu's area of control.

The way was now clear to Urartu. In 714 B.C. Sargon attacked the revolting king of Zikirtu, who was supported by an army led by Rusas, his overlord. A fierce battle was fought in which the Assyrians achieved a great victory. King Rusas fled, and when he found that the Assyrians pressed home their triumph by laying waste the country before them, he committed suicide, according to the Assyrian records, although those of Urartu indicate that he subsequently took part in the struggle against Sargon. The Armenian peoples were compelled to acknowledge the suzerainty of Assyria, and the conqueror received gifts from various tribes between Lake Van and the Caspian Sea, and along the frontiers from Lake Van towards the south-east as far as the borders of Elam.

Rusas of Urartu was succeeded by Argistes II, who reigned over a shrunken kingdom. He intrigued with neighbouring states against Assyria, but was closely watched. Ere long he found himself caught between two fires. During his reign the notorious Cimmerians and Scythians displayed much activity in the north and raided his territory.

The pressure of fresh infusions of Thraco-Phrygian tribes into western Asia Minor had stirred Midas of the Muski to co-operate with the Urartian power in an attempt to stamp out Assyrian influence in Cilicia, Cappadocia, and north Syria. A revolt in Tabal in 718 B.C. was extinguished by Sargon, but in the following year evidences were forthcoming of a more serious and widespread rising. Pisiris, king of Carchemish, threw off the Assyrian yoke. Before, however, his allies could hasten to his assistance he was overcome by the vigilant Sargon, who deported a large proportion of the city's inhabitants and incorporated it in an Assyrian province. Tabal revolted in 713 B.C. and was similarly dealt with. In 712 B.C. Milid had to be overcome. The inhabitants were transported, and "Suti" Aramaean settlers settled in their homes. The king of Commagene, having remained faithful, received large extensions of territory. Finally in 709 B.C. Midas of the Muski-Phrygians was compelled to acknowledge the suzerainty of Assyria. The northern confederacy was thus completely worsted and broken up. Tribute was paid by many peoples, including the rulers of Cyprus.

Sargon was now able to deal with Babylonia, which for about twelve years had been ruled by Merodach Baladan, who oppressed the people and set at defiance ancient laws by seizing private estates and transferring them to his Chaldaean kinsmen. He still received the active support of Elam.

Sargon's first move was to interpose his army between those of the Babylonians and Elamites. Pushing southward, he subdued the Aramaeans on the eastern banks of the Tigris, and drove the Elamites into the mountains. Then he invaded middle Babylonia from the east. Merodach Baladan hastily evacuated Babylon, and, moving southward, succeeded in evading

Sargon's army. Finding Elam was unable to help him, he took refuge in the Chaldaean capital, Bit Jakin, in southern Babylonia.

Sargon was visited by the priests of Babylon and Borsippa, and hailed as the saviour of the ancient kingdom. He was afterwards proclaimed king at E-sagila, where he "took the hands of Bel". Then having expelled the Aramaeans from Sippar, he hastened southward, attacked Bit Jakin and captured it. Merodach Baladan escaped into Elam. The whole of Chaldaea was subdued.

Thus "Sargon the Later" entered at length into full possession of the empire of Sargon of Akkad. In Babylonia he posed as an incarnation of his ancient namesake, and had similarly Messianic pretensions which were no doubt inspired by the Babylonian priesthood. Under him Assyria attained its highest degree of splendour.

He recorded proudly not only his great conquests but also his works of public utility: he restored ancient cities, irrigated vast tracts of country, fostered trade, and promoted the industries. Like the pious Pharaohs of Egypt he boasted that he fed the hungry and protected the weak against the strong.

Sargon found time during his strenuous career as a conqueror to lay out and build a new city, called Dur-Sharrukin, "the burgh of Sargon", to the north of Nineveh. It was completed before he undertook the Babylonian campaign. The new palace was occupied in 708 B.C. Previous to that period he had resided principally at Kalkhi, in the restored palace of Ashur-natsir-pal III.

He was a worshipper of many gods. Although he claimed to have restored the supremacy of Asshur "which had come to an end", he not only adored Ashur but also revived the ancient triad of Anu, Bel, and Ea, and fostered the growth of the immemorial "mother-cult" of Ishtar. Before he died he appointed one of his sons, Sennacherib, viceroy of the northern portion of the empire. He was either assassinated at a military review or in some frontier war. As much is suggested by the following entry in an eponym list.

Eponymy of Upahhir-belu, prefect of the city of Amedu ... According to the oracle of the Kulummite(s).... A soldier (entered) the camp of the king of Assyria (and killed him?), month Ab, day 12th, Sennacherib (sat on the throne).[530]

The fact that Sennacherib lamented his father's sins suggests that the old king had in some manner offended the priesthood. Perhaps, like some of the Middle Empire monarchs, he succumbed to the influence of Babylon during the closing years of his life. It is stated that "he was not buried in his house", which suggests that the customary religious rites were denied him, and that his lost soul was supposed to be a wanderer which had to eat offal and drink impure water like the ghost of a pauper or a criminal.

The task which lay before Sennacherib (705-680 B.C.) was to maintain the unity of the great empire of his distinguished father. He waged minor wars against the Kassite and Illipi tribes on the Elamite border, and the Muski and Hittite tribes in Cappadocia and Cilicia. The Kassites, however, were no longer of any importance, and the Hittite power had been extinguished, for ere the states could recover from the blows dealt by the Assyrians the Cimmerian hordes ravaged their territory. Urartu was also overrun by the fierce barbarians from the north. It was one of these last visits of the Assyrians to Tabal of the Hittites and the land of the Muski (Meshech) which the Hebrew prophet referred to in after-time when he exclaimed:

Asshur is there and all her company: his graves are about him: all of them slain, fallen by the sword.... There is Meshech, Tubal, and all her multitude: her graves are round about him: all of them uncircumcised, slain by the sword, though they caused their terror in the land of the living.... (*Ezekiel*, xxxii.)

Sennacherib found that Ionians had settled in Cilicia, and he deported large numbers of them to Nineveh. The metal and ivory work at Nineveh show traces of Greek influence after this period.

A great conspiracy was fomented in several states against Sennacherib when the intelligence of Sargon's death was bruited abroad. Egypt was concerned in it. Taharka (the Biblical Tirhakah[531]), the last Pharaoh of the Ethiopian Dynasty, had dreams of re-establishing Egyptian supremacy in Palestine and Syria, and leagued himself with Luli, king of Tyre, Hezekiah, king of Judah, and others. Merodach Baladan, the Chaldaean king, whom Sargon had deposed, supported by Elamites and Aramaeans, was also a party to the conspiracy. "At that time Merodach Baladan, the son of Baladan, king of Babylon, sent letters and a present to Hezekiah.... And Hezekiah was glad of them."[532]

Merodach Baladan again seized the throne of Babylon. Sargon's son, who had been appointed governor, was murdered and a pretender sat on the throne for a brief period, but Merodach Baladan thrust him aside and reigned for nine months, during which period he busied himself by encouraging the kings of Judah and Tyre to revolt. Sennacherib invaded Babylonia with a strong army, deposed Merodach Baladan, routed the Chaldaeans and Aramaeans, and appointed as vassal king Bel-ibni, a native prince, who remained faithful to Assyria for about three years.

In 707 B.C. Sennacherib appeared in the west. When he approached Tyre, Luli, the king, fled to Cyprus. The city was not captured, but much of its territory was ceded to the king of Sidon. Askalon was afterwards reduced. At Eltekeh Sennacherib came into conflict with an army of allies, including Ethiopian, Egyptian, and Arabian Mutsri forces, which he routed. Then he captured a number of cities in Judah and transported 200,150 people. He was unable, however, to enter Jerusalem, in which Hezekiah was compelled to remain "like a bird in a cage". It appears that Hezekiah "bought off" the Assyrians on this occasion with gifts of gold and silver and jewels, costly furniture, musicians, and female slaves.

In 689 B.C. Sennacherib found it necessary to penetrate Arabia. Apparently another conspiracy was brewing, for Hezekiah again revolted. On his return from the south--according to Berosus he had been in Egypt--the Assyrian king marched against the king of Judah.

And when Hezekiah saw that Sennacherib was come, and that he was purposed to fight against Jerusalem, he took counsel with the princes and his mighty men to stop the waters of the fountains which were without the city: and they did help him.... Why should the kings of Assyria come and find much water?

Sennacherib sent messengers to Jerusalem to attempt to stir up the people against Hezekiah. "He wrote also letters to rail on the Lord God of Israel, and to speak against him, saying, As the gods of the nations of other lands have not delivered their people out of mine hand, so shall not the God of Hezekiah deliver his people out of mine hand."[533]

Hezekiah sent his servants to Isaiah, who was in Jerusalem at the time, and the prophet said to them:

Thus shall ye say to your master. Thus saith the Lord, Be not afraid of the words which thou hast heard, with which the servants of the king of Assyria have blasphemed me. Behold, I will send a blast upon him, and he shall hear a rumour, and shall return to his own land; and I will cause him to fall by the sword in his own land.[534]

According to Berosus, the Babylonian priestly historian, the camp of Sennacherib was visited in the night by swarms of field mice which ate up the quivers and bows and the (leather) handles of shields. Next morning the army fled.

The Biblical account of the disaster is as follows:

And it came to pass that night, that the angel of the Lord went out, and smote the camp of the Assyrians an hundred and four score and five thousand: and when they arose early in the morning, behold, they were all dead corpses. So Sennacherib king of Assyria departed, and went and returned and dwelt at Nineveh.[535]

A pestilence may have broken out in the camp, the infection, perhaps, having been carried by field mice. Byron's imagination was stirred by the vision of the broken army of Assyria.

The Assyrian came down like a wolf on the fold,
And his cohorts were gleaming with purple and gold;
And the sheen of their spears was like stars of the sea,
When the blue wave rolls nightly on deep Galilee.

Like the leaves of the forest when summer is green,
That host with their banners at sunset were seen;
Like the leaves of the forest when autumn hath blown,
That host on the morrow lay withered and strown.

For the Angel of Death spread his wings on the blast,
And breathed on the face of the foe as he passed;
And the eyes of the sleepers waxed deadly and chill,
And their hearts but once heaved--and forever grew still!

And there lay the steed with his nostril all wide,
But through it there rolled not the breath of his pride;
And the foam of his gasping lay white on the turf,
And cold as the spray of the rock-beating surf.

And there lay the rider distorted and pale,
With the dew on his brow, and the rust on his mail;
And the tents were all silent--the banners alone--
Thelances uplifted--the trumpet unblown.

174

And the widows of Asshur are loud in their wail,
And the idols are broke in the temple of Baal;
And the might of the Gentile, unsmote by the sword,
Hath melted like snow in the glance of the Lord.

Before this disaster occurred Sennacherib had to invade Babylonia again, for the vassal king, Bel-ibni, had allied himself with the Chaldaeans and raised the standard of revolt. The city of Babylon was besieged and captured, and its unfaithful king deported with a number of nobles to Assyria. Old Merodach Baladan was concerned in the plot and took refuge on the Elamite coast, where the Chaldaeans had formed a colony. He died soon afterwards.

Sennacherib operated in southern Babylonia and invaded Elam. But ere he could return to Assyria he was opposed by a strong army of allies, including Babylonians, Chaldaeans, Aramaeans, Elamites, and Persians, led by Samunu, son of Merodach Baladan. A desperate battle was fought. Although Sennacherib claimed a victory, he was unable to follow it up. This was in 692 B.C. A Chaldaean named Mushezib-Merodach seized the Babylonian throne.

In 691 B.C. Sennacherib again struck a blow for Babylonia, but was unable to depose Mushezib-Merodach. His opportunity came, however, in 689 B.C. Elam had been crippled by raids of the men of Parsua (Persia), and was unable to co-operate with the Chaldaean king of Babylon. Sennacherib captured the great commercial metropolis, took Mushezib-Merodach prisoner, and dispatched him to Nineveh. Then he wreaked his vengeance on Babylon. For several days the Assyrian soldiers looted the houses and temples, and slaughtered the inhabitants without mercy. E-sagila was robbed of its treasures, images of deities were either broken in pieces or sent to Nineveh: the statue of Bel-Merodach was dispatched to Asshur so that he might take his place among the gods who were vassals of Ashur. "The city and its houses," Sennacherib recorded, "from foundation to roof, I destroyed them, I demolished them, I burned them with fire; walls, gateways, sacred chapels, and the towers of earth and tiles, I laid them low and cast them into the Arakhtu."[536]

"So thorough was Sennacherib's destruction of the city in 689 B.C.," writes Mr. King, "that after several years of work, Dr. Koldewey concluded that all traces of earlier buildings had been destroyed on that occasion. More recently some remains of earlier strata have been recognized, and contract-tablets have been found which date from the period of the First Dynasty. Moreover, a number of earlier pot-burials have been unearthed, but a careful examination of the greater part of the ruins has added little to our knowledge of this most famous city before the Neo-Babylonian period."[537]

It is possible that Sennacherib desired to supplant Babylon as a commercial metropolis by Nineveh. He extended and fortified that city, surrounding it with two walls protected by moats. According to Diodorus, the walls were a hundred feet high and about fifty feet wide. Excavators have found that at the gates they were about a hundred feet in breadth. The water supply of the city was ensured by the construction of dams and canals, and strong quays were erected to prevent flooding. Sennacherib repaired a lofty platform which was isolated by a canal, and erected upon it his great palace. On another platform he had an arsenal built.

Sennacherib's palace was the most magnificent building of its kind ever erected by an Assyrian emperor. It was lavishly decorated, and its bas-reliefs display native art at its highest pitch of excellence. The literary remains of the time also give indication of the growth of culture: the inscriptions are distinguished by their prose style. It is evident that men of culture and refinement were numerous in Assyria. The royal library of Kalkhi received many additions during the reign of the destroyer of Babylon.

Like his father, Sennacherib died a violent death. According to the Babylonian Chronicle he was slain in a revolt by his son "on the twentieth day of Tebet" (680 B.C). The revolt continued from the "20th of Tebet" (early in January) until the 2nd day of Adar (the middle of February). On the 18th of Adar, Esarhaddon, son of Sennacherib, was proclaimed king.

Berosus states that Sennacherib was murdered by two of his sons, but Esarhaddon was not one of the conspirators. The Biblical reference is as follows: "Sennacherib ... dwelt at Nineveh. And it came to pass, as he was worshipping in the house of Nisroch (?Ashur) his god, that Adrammelech and Sharezer (Ashur-shar-etir) his sons smote him with the sword: and they escaped into the land of Armenia (Urartu). And Esarhaddon his son reigned in his stead." Ashur-shar-etir appears to have been the claimant to the throne.

Esarhaddon (680-668 B.C.) was a man of different type from his father. He adopted towards vassal states a policy of conciliation, and did much to secure peace within the empire by his magnanimous treatment of rebel kings who had been intimidated by their neighbours and forced to entwine themselves in the meshes of intrigue. His wars were directed mainly to secure the protection of outlying provinces against aggressive raiders.

The monarch was strongly influenced by his mother, Naki'a, a Babylonian princess who appears to have been as distinguished a lady as the famous Sammu-rammat. Indeed, it is possible that traditions regarding her contributed to the Semiramis legends. But it was not only due to her that Esarhaddon espoused the cause of the pro-Babylonian party. He appears to be identical with the Axerdes of Berosus, who ruled over the southern kingdom for eight years. Apparently he had been appointed governor by Sennacherib after the destruction of Babylon, and it may be that during his term of office in Babylonia he was attracted by its ethical ideals, and developed those traits of character which distinguished him from his father and grandfather. He married a Babylonian princess, and one of his sons, Shamash-shum-ukin, was born in a Babylonian palace, probably at Sippar. He was a worshipper of the mother goddess Ishtar of Nineveh and Ishtar of Arbela, and of Shamash, as well as of the national god Ashur.

As soon as Esarhaddon came to the throne he undertook the restoration of Babylon, to which many of the inhabitants were drifting back. In three years the city resumed its pre-eminent position as a trading and industrial centre. Withal, he won the hearts of the natives by expelling Chaldaeans from the private estates which they had seized during the Merodach-Baladan regime, and restoring them to the rightful heirs.

A Chaldaean revolt was inevitable. Two of Merodach Baladan's sons gave trouble in the south, but were routed in battle. One fled to Elam, where he was assassinated; the other sued for peace, and was accepted by the diplomatic Esarhaddon as a vassal king.

Egypt was intriguing in the west. Its Ethiopian king, Taharka (the Biblical Tirhakah) had stirred up Hezekiah to revolt during Sennacherib's reign. An Assyrian ambassador who had visited Jerusalem "heard say concerning Tirhakah.... He sent messengers to Hezekiah saying.... Let not thy God, in whom thou trustest, deceive thee saying, Jerusalem shall not be given into the hand of the king of Assyria. Behold, thou hast heard what the kings of Assyria have done to all lands by destroying them utterly; and shalt thou be delivered? Have the gods of the nations delivered them which my fathers have destroyed, as Gozan, and Haran, and Rezeph, and the children of Eden which were in Telassar? Where is the king of Hamath, and the king of Arphad, and the king of the city of Sepharvaim, Hena, and Ivah?"[538] Sidon was a party to the pro-Egyptian league which had been formed in Palestine and Syria.

Early in his reign Esarhaddon conducted military operations in the west, and during his absence the queen-mother Naki'a held the reins of government. The Elamites regarded this innovation as a sign of weakness, and invaded Babylon. Sippar was plundered, and its gods carried away. The Assyrian governors, however, ultimately repulsed the Elamite king, who was deposed soon after he returned home. His son, who succeeded him, restored the stolen gods, and cultivated good relations with Esarhaddon. There was great unrest in Elam at this period: it suffered greatly from the inroads of Median and Persian pastoral fighting folk.

In the north the Cimmerians and Scythians, who were constantly warring against Urartu, and against each other, had spread themselves westward and east. Esarhaddon drove Cimmerian invaders out of Cappadocia, and they swamped Phrygia.

The Scythian peril on the north-east frontier was, however, of more pronounced character. The fierce mountaineers had allied themselves with Median tribes and overrun the buffer State of the Mannai. Both Urartu and Assyria were sufferers from the brigandage of these allies. Esarhaddon's generals, however, were able to deal with the situation, and one of the notable results of the pacification of the north-eastern area was the conclusion of an alliance with Urartu.

The most serious situation with which the emperor had to deal was in the west. The King of Sidon, who had been so greatly favoured by Sennacherib, had espoused the Egyptian cause. He allied himself with the King of Cilicia, who, however, was unable to help him much. Sidon was besieged and captured; the royal allies escaped, but a few years later were caught and beheaded. The famous seaport was destroyed, and its vast treasures deported to Assyria (about 676 B.C). Esarhaddon replaced it by a new city called Kar-Esarhaddon, which formed the nucleus of the new Sidon.

It is believed that Judah and other disaffected States were dealt with about this time. Manasseh had succeeded Hezekiah at Jerusalem when but a boy of twelve years. He appears to have come under the influence of heathen teachers.

For he built up again the high places which Hezekiah his father had destroyed; and he reared up altars for Baal, and made a grove, as did Ahab king of Israel; and worshipped all the host of heaven, and served them.... And he built altars for all the host of heaven in the two courts of the house of the Lord. And he made his son pass through the fire, and observed times, and used enchantments, and dealt with familiar spirits and wizards: he wrought much wickedness in the sight of the Lord, to provoke him to anger. And he set a graven image of the grove that he had made in the house, of which the Lord said to David, and to Solomon his son, In this house, and in Jerusalem, which I have chosen out of all tribes of Israel, will I put my name for ever.[539]

Isaiah ceased to prophesy after Manasseh came to the throne. According to Rabbinic traditions he was seized by his enemies and enclosed in the hollow trunk of a tree, which was sawn through. Other orthodox teachers appear to have been slain also. "Manasseh shed innocent blood very much, till he had filled Jerusalem from one end to another."[540] It is possible that there is a reference to Isaiah's fate in an early Christian lament regarding the persecutions of the faithful: "Others had trial of cruel mockings and scourgings, yea, moreover of bonds and imprisonment: they were stoned, *they were sawn asunder*, were tempted, were slain with the sword".[541] There is no Assyrian evidence regarding the captivity of Manasseh. "Wherefore the Lord brought upon them (the people of Judah) the captains of the host of the king of Assyria, which took Manasseh among the thorns, and bound him with fetters, and carried him to Babylon. And when he was in affliction, he besought the Lord his God, and humbled himself greatly before the God of his fathers, and prayed unto him: and he was intreated of him, and heard his supplication, and brought him again to Jerusalem into his kingdom."[542] It was, however, in keeping with the policy of Esarhaddon to deal in this manner with an erring vassal. The Assyrian records include Manasseh of Judah (Menasê of the city of Yaudu) with the kings of Edom, Moab, Ammon, Tyre, Ashdod, Gaza, Byblos, &c, and "twenty-two kings of Khatti" as payers of tribute to Esarhaddon, their overlord. Hazael of Arabia was conciliated by having restored to him his gods which Sennacherib had carried away.

Egypt continued to intrigue against Assyria, and Esarhaddon resolved to deal effectively with Taharka, the last Ethiopian Pharaoh. In 674 B.C. he invaded Egypt, but suffered a reverse and had to retreat. Tyre revolted soon afterwards (673 B.C).

Esarhaddon, however, made elaborate preparations for his next campaign. In 671 B.C. he went westward with a much more powerful army. A detachment advanced to Tyre and invested it. The main force meanwhile pushed on, crossed the Delta frontier, and swept victoriously as far south as Memphis, where Taharka suffered a crushing defeat. That great Egyptian metropolis was then occupied and plundered by the soldiers of Esarhaddon. Lower Egypt became an Assyrian province; the various petty kings, including Necho of Sais, had set over them Assyrian governors. Tyre was also captured.

When he returned home Esarhaddon erected at the Syro-Cappadocian city of Singirli[543] a statue of victory, which is now in the Berlin museum. On this memorial the Assyrian "King of the kings of Egypt" is depicted as a giant. With one hand he pours out an oblation to a god; in the other he grasps his sceptre and two cords attached to rings, which pierce the lips of dwarfish figures representing the Pharaoh Taharka of Egypt and the unfaithful King of Tyre.

In 668 B.C. Taharka, who had fled to Napata in Ethiopia, returned to Upper Egypt, and began to stir up revolts. Esarhaddon planned out another expedition, so that he might shatter the last vestige of power possessed by his rival. But before he left home he found it necessary to set his kingdom in order.

During his absence from home the old Assyrian party, who disliked the emperor because of Babylonian sympathies, had been intriguing regarding the succession to the throne. According to the Babylonian Chronicle, "the king remained in Assyria" during 669 B.C., "and he slew with the sword many noble men". Ashur-bani-pal was evidently concerned in the conspiracy, and it is significant to find that he pleaded on behalf of certain of the conspirators. The crown prince Sinidinabal was dead: perhaps he had been assassinated.

At the feast of the goddess Gula (identical with Bau, consort of Ninip), towards the end of April in 668 B.C., Esarhaddon divided his empire between two of his sons. Ashur-bani-pal was selected to be King of Assyria, and Shamash-shum-ukin to be King of Babylon and the vassal of Ashur-banipal. Other sons received important priestly appointments.

Soon after these arrangements were completed Esarhaddon, who was suffering from bad health, set out for Egypt. He died towards the end of October, and the early incidents of his campaign were included in the records of Ashur-bani-pal's reign. Taharka was defeated at Memphis, and retreated southward to Thebes.

So passed away the man who has been eulogized as "the noblest and most sympathetic figure among the Assyrian kings". There was certainly much which was attractive in his character. He inaugurated many social reforms, and appears to have held in check his overbearing nobles. Trade flourished during his reign. He did not undertake the erection of a new city, like his father, but won the gratitude of the priesthood by his activities as a builder and restorer of temples. He founded a new "house of Ashur" at Nineveh, and reconstructed several temples in Babylonia. His son Ashur-bani-pal was the last great Assyrian ruler.

[503] *2 Kings*, xv, 19 and 29; *2 Chronicles*, xxviii, 20.

[504] *2 Kings*, xviii, 34 and xix, 13.

[505] *2 Kings*, xiv, 1-14.

[506] *2 Kings*, xv, 1-14.

[507] *2 Kings*, xv, 19, 20.

[508] *2 Kings*, xv, 25.

[509] *Amos*, v.

[510] *Amos*, i.

[511] *2 Kings*, xvi, 5.

[512] *Isaiah*, vii, 3-7.

[513] *2 Kings*, xv, 3.

[514] *Isaiah*, vii, 18.

[515] Kir was probably on the borders of Elam.

[516] *2 Kings*, xvi, 7-9.

[517] *2 Kings*, xv, 29, 30.

[518] *2 Kings*, xvi, 10.

[519] In the Hebrew text this monarch is called Sua, Seveh, and So, says Maspero. The Assyrian texts refer to him as Sebek, Shibahi, Shabè, &c. He has been identified with Pharaoh Shabaka of the Twenty-fifth Egyptian Dynasty; that monarch may have been a petty king before he founded his Dynasty. Another theory is that he was Seve, king of Mutsri, and still another that he was a petty king of an Egyptian state in the Delta and not Shabaka.

[520] *2 Kings*, xvii, 3-5.

[521] *Isaiah*, xx, 1.

[522] *2 Kings*, xvii, 6.

[523] *2 Kings*, xvii, 16-41.

[524] The people carried away would not be the whole of the inhabitants--only, one would suppose, the more important personages, enough to make up the number 27,290 given above.

[525] *Passing of the Empires*, pp. 200-1.

[526] Those who, like Breasted, identify "Piru of Mutsri" with "Pharaoh of Egypt" adopt the view that Bocchoris of Sais paid tribute to Sargon. Piru, however, is subsequently referred to with two Arabian kings as tribute payers to Sargon apparently after Lower Egypt had come under the sway of Shabaka, the first king of the Ethiopian or Twenty-fifth Dynasty.

[527] *Isaiah*, xx, 2-5.

[528] Commander-in-chief.

[529] *Isaiah*, xx, 1.

[530] *The Old Testament in the Light of the Historical Records and Legends of Assyria and Babylonia*, T.G. Pinches, p. 372.

[531] *Isaiah*, xxxvii, 9.

[532] *Isaiah*, xxix, 1, 2.

[533] *2 Chronicles*, xxxii, 9-17.

[534] *2 Kings*, xix, 6, 7.

[535] *2 Kings*, xix, 35, 36.

[536] Smith-Sayce, *History of Sennacherib*, pp. 132-5.

[537] *A History of Sumer and Akkad*, p. 37.

[538] *Isaiah*, xxxvii, 8-13.

[539] *2 Kings*, xxi, 3-7.

[540] *2 Kings*, xxi, 16.

[541] *Hebrews*, xi, 36, 37.

[542] *2 Chronicles*, xxxiii, 11-3. It may be that Manasseh was taken to Babylon during Ashur-bani-pal's reign. See next chapter.

[543] Pronounce *g* as in *gem*.

Chapter XX. The Last Days of Assyria and Babylonia

Abstract

Doom of Nineveh and Babylon--Babylonian Monotheism--Ashur-banipal and his Brother, King of Babylon--Ceremony of "Taking the Hands of Bel"--Merodach restored to E-sagila--Assyrian Invasion of Egypt and Sack of Thebes--Lydia's Appeal to Assyria--Elam subdued--Revolt of Babylon--Death of Babylonian King--Sack of Susa--Psamtik of Egypt--Cimmerians crushed--Ashur-bani-pal's Literary Activities--The Sardanapalus Legend--Last Kings of Assyria--Fall of Nineveh--The New Babylonian Empire--Necho of Egypt expelled from Syria-

The burden of Nineveh.... The Lord is slow to anger, and great in power, and will not at all acquit the wicked: the Lord hath his way in the whirlwind and in the storm, and the clouds are the dust of his feet. He rebuketh the sea, and maketh it dry, and drieth up all the rivers: Bashan languisheth, and Carmel, and the flower of Lebanon languisheth.... He that dasheth in pieces is come up before thy face.... The gates of the rivers shall be opened, and the palace shall be dissolved. And Huzzab shall be led away captive, she shall be brought up, and her maids shall lead her as with the voice of doves, tabering upon their breasts.... Draw thee waters for the siege, fortify thy strong holds: go into clay, and tread the morter, make strong the brick-kiln. There shall the fire devour thee; the sword shall cut thee off.... Thy shepherds slumber, O king of Assyria: thy nobles shall dwell in the dust: thy people is scattered upon the mountains, and no man gathereth them. There is no healing of thy bruise; thy wound is grievous: all that hear the bruit of thee shall clap the hands over thee: for upon whom hath not thy wickedness passed continually?[544]

The doom of Babylon was also foretold:

Bel boweth down, Nebo stoopeth.... Come down, and sit in the dust, O virgin daughter of Babylon, sit on the ground: there is no throne, O daughter of the Chaldeans.... Stand now with thine enchantments, and with the multitude of thy sorceries, wherein thou hast laboured from thy youth; if so be thou shalt be able to profit, if so be thou mayest prevail. Thou art wearied in the multitude of thy counsels. Let now the astrologers, the star-gazers, the monthly prognosticators, stand up, and save thee from these things that shall come upon thee. Behold, they shall be as stubble; the fire shall burn them.... Thus shall they be unto thee with whom thou hast laboured, even thy merchants, from thy youth: they shall wander every one to his quarter; none shall save thee.[545]

Against a gloomy background, dark and ominous as a thundercloud, we have revealed in the last century of Mesopotamian glory the splendour of Assyria and the beauty of Babylon. The ancient civilizations ripened quickly before the end came. Kings still revelled in pomp and luxury. Cities resounded with "the noise of a whip, and the noise of the rattling of the wheels, and of the prancing horses, and of the jumping chariots. The horseman lifteth up both the bright sword and the glittering spear.... The valiant men are in scarlet."[546] But the minds of cultured men were more deeply occupied than ever with the mysteries of life and creation. In the libraries, the temples, and observatories, philosophers and scientists were shattering the unsubstantial fabric of immemorial superstition; they attained to higher conceptions of the duties and responsibilities of mankind; they conceived of divine love and divine guidance; they discovered, like Wordsworth, that the soul has--

An obscure sense
Of possible sublimity, whereto
With growing faculties she doth aspire.

One of the last kings of Babylon, Nebuchadrezzar, recorded a prayer which reveals the loftiness of religious thought and feeling attained by men to whom graven images were no longer worthy of adoration and reverence--men whose god was not made by human hands--

O eternal prince! Lord of all being!
As for the king whom thou lovest, and
Whose name thou hast proclaimed
As was pleasing to thee,
Do thou lead aright his life,
Guide him in a straight path.
I am the prince, obedient to thee,
The creature of thy hand;
Thou hast created me, and
With dominion over all people
Thou hast entrusted me.
According to thy grace, O Lord,
Which thou dost bestow on
All people,
Cause me to love thy supreme dominion,
And create in my heart
The worship of thy godhead

And grant whatever is pleasing to thee,
Because thou hast fashioned my life.[547]

The "star-gazers" had become scientists, and foretold eclipses: in every sphere of intellectual activity great men were sifting out truth from the debris of superstition. It seemed as if Babylon and Assyria were about to cross the threshold of a new age, when their doom was sounded and their power was shattered for ever. Nineveh perished with dramatic suddenness: Babylon died of "senile decay".

When, in 668 B.C., intelligence reached Nineveh that Esarhaddon had passed away, on the march through Egypt, the arrangements which he had made for the succession were carried out smoothly and quickly. Naki'a, the queen mother, was acting as regent, and completed her lifework by issuing a proclamation exhorting all loyal subjects and vassals to obey the new rulers, her grandsons, Ashur-bani-pal, Emperor of Assyria, and Shamash-shum-ukin, King of Babylon. Peace prevailed in the capital, and there was little or no friction throughout the provinces: new rulers were appointed to administer the States of Arvad and Ammon, but there were no changes elsewhere.

Babylon welcomed its new king--a Babylonian by birth and the son of a Babylonian princess. The ancient kingdom rejoiced that it was no longer to be ruled as a province; its ancient dignities and privileges were being partially restored. But one great and deep-seated grievance remained. The god Merodach was still a captive in the temple of Ashur. No king could reign aright if Merodach were not restored to E-sagila. Indeed he could not be regarded as the lord of the land until he had "taken the hands of Bel".

The ceremony of taking the god's hands was an act of homage. When it was consummated the king became the steward or vassal of Merodach, and every day he appeared before the divine one to receive instructions and worship him. The welfare of the whole kingdom depended on the manner in which the king acted towards the god. If Merodach was satisfied with the king he sent blessings to the land; if he was angry he sent calamities. A pious and faithful monarch was therefore the protector of the people.

This close association of the king with the god gave the priests great influence in Babylon. They were the power behind the throne. The destinies of the royal house were placed in their hands; they could strengthen the position of a royal monarch, or cause him to be deposed if he did not satisfy their demands. A king who reigned over Babylon without the priestly party on his side occupied an insecure position. Nor could he secure the co-operation of the priests unless the image of the god was placed in the temple. Where king was, there Merodach had to be also.

Shamash-shum-ukin pleaded with his royal brother and overlord to restore Bel Merodach to Babylon. Ashur-bani-pal hesitated for a time; he was unwilling to occupy a less dignified position, as the representative of Ashur, than his distinguished predecessor, in his relation to the southern kingdom. At length, however, he was prevailed upon to consult the oracle of Shamash, the solar lawgiver, the revealer of destiny. The god was accordingly asked if Shamash-shum-ukin could "take the hands of Bel" in Ashur's temple, and then proceed to Babylon as his representative. In response, the priests of Shamash informed the emperor that Bel Merodach could not exercise sway as sovereign lord so long as he remained a prisoner in a city which was not his own.

Ashur-bani-pal accepted the verdict, and then visited Ashur's temple to plead with Bel Merodach to return to Babylon. "Let thy thoughts", he cried, "dwell in Babylon, which in thy wrath thou didst bring to naught. Let thy face be turned towards E-sagila, thy lofty and divine temple. Return to the city thou hast deserted for a house unworthy of thee. O Merodach! lord of the gods, issue thou the command to return again to Babylon."

Thus did Ashur-bani-pal make pious and dignified submission to the will of the priests. A favourable response was, of course, received from Merodach when addressed by the emperor, and the god's image was carried back to E-sagila, accompanied by a strong force. Ashur-bani-pal and Shamash-shum-ukin led the procession of priests and soldiers, and elaborate ceremonials were observed at each city they passed, the local gods being carried forth to do homage to Merodach.

Babylon welcomed the deity who was thus restored to his temple after the lapse of about a quarter of a century, and the priests celebrated with unconcealed satisfaction and pride the ceremony at which Shamash-shum-ukin "took the hands of Bel". The public rejoicings were conducted on an elaborate scale. Babylon believed that a new era of prosperity had been inaugurated, and the priests and nobles looked forward to the day when the kingdom would once again become free and independent and powerful.

Ashur-bani-pal (668-626 B.C.) made arrangements to complete his father's designs regarding Egypt. His Tartan continued the campaign, and Taharka, as has been stated, was driven from Memphis. The beaten Pharaoh returned to Ethiopia and did not again attempt to expel the Assyrians. He died in 666 B.C. It was found that some of the petty kings of Lower Egypt had been intriguing with Taharka, and their cities were severely dealt with. Necho of Sais had to be arrested, among others, but was pardoned after he appeared before Ashur-bani-pal, and sent back to Egypt as the Assyrian governor.

Tanutamon, a son of Pharaoh Shabaka, succeeded Taharka, and in 663 B.C. marched northward from Thebes with a strong army. He captured Memphis. It is believed Necho was slain, and Herodotus relates that his son Psamtik took refuge in Syria. In 661 B.C. Ashur-bani-pal's army swept through Lower Egypt and expelled the Ethiopians. Tanutamon fled southward, but on this occasion the Assyrians followed up their success, and besieged and captured Thebes, which they sacked. Its nobles were slain or taken captive. According to the prophet Nahum, who refers to Thebes as No (Nu-Amon = city of Amon), "her young children also were dashed in pieces at the top of all the streets: and they (the Assyrians) cast lots for her honourable men, and all her great men were bound in chains".[548] Thebes never again recovered its prestige. Its treasures were transported to Nineveh. The Ethiopian supremacy in Egypt was finally extinguished, and Psamtik, son of Necho, who was appointed the Pharaoh, began to reign as the vassal of Assyria.

When the kings on the seacoasts of Palestine and Asia Minor found that they could no longer look to Egypt for help, they resigned themselves to the inevitable, and ceased to intrigue against Assyria. Gifts were sent to Ashur-bani-pal by the kings of Arvad, Tyre, Tarsus, and Tabal. The Arvad ruler, however, was displaced, and his son set on his throne. But the most extraordinary development was the visit to Nineveh of emissaries from Gyges, king of Lydia, who figures in the legends of Greece. This monarch had been harassed by the Cimmerians after they accomplished the fall of Midas of Phrygia in 676 B.C., and he sought the help of Ashur-bani-pal. It is not known whether the Assyrians operated against the Cimmerians in Tabal, but, as Gyges did not send tribute, it would appear that he held his own with the aid of mercenaries from the State of Caria in southwestern Asia Minor. The Greeks of Cilicia, and the Achaeans and Phoenicians of Cyprus remained faithful to Assyria.

Elam gave trouble in 665 B.C. by raiding Akkad, but the Assyrian army repulsed the invaders at Dur-ilu and pushed on to Susa. The Elamites received a crushing defeat in a battle on the banks of the River Ula. King Teumman was slain, and a son of the King of Urtagu was placed on his throne. Elam thus came under Assyrian sway.

The most surprising and sensational conspiracy against Ashur-bani-pal was fomented by his brother Shamash-shum-ukin of Babylon, after the two had co-operated peacefully for fifteen years. No doubt the priestly party at E-sagila were deeply concerned in the movement, and the king may have been strongly influenced by the fact that Babylonia was at the time suffering from severe depression caused by a series of poor harvests. Merodach, according to the priests, was angry; it was probably argued that he was punishing the people because they had not thrown off the yoke of Assyria.

The temple treasures of Babylon were freely drawn upon to purchase the allegiance of allies. Ere Ashur-bani-pal had any knowledge of the conspiracy his brother had won over several governors in Babylonia, the Chaldaeans, Aramaeans and Elamites, and many petty kings in Palestine and Syria: even Egypt and Libya were prepared to help him. When, however, the faithful governor of Ur was approached, he communicated with his superior at Erech, who promptly informed Ashur-bani-pal of the great conspiracy. The intelligence reached Nineveh like a bolt from the blue. The emperor's heart was filled with sorrow and anguish. In after-time he lamented in an inscription that his "faithless brother" forgot the favours he had shown him. "Outwardly with his lips he spoke friendly things, while inwardly his heart plotted murder."

In 652 B.C. Shamash-shum-ukin precipitated the crisis by forbidding Ashur-bani-pal to make offerings in the cities of Babylonia. He thus declared his independence.

War broke out simultaneously. Ur and Erech were besieged and captured by the Chaldaeans, and an Elamite army marched to the aid of the King of Babylon, but it was withdrawn before long on account of the unsettled political conditions at home. The Assyrian armies swept through Babylonia, and the Chaldeans in the south were completely subjugated before Babylon was captured. That great commercial metropolis was closely besieged for three years, and was starved into submission. When the Assyrians were entering the city gates a sensational happening occurred. Shamash-shum-ukin, the rebel king, shut himself up in his palace and set fire to it, and perished there amidst the flames with his wife and children, his slaves and all his treasures. Ashur-bani-pal was in 647 B.C. proclaimed King Kandalanu[549] of Babylon, and reigned over it until his death in 626 B.C.

Elam was severely dealt with. That unhappy country was terribly devastated by Assyrian troops, who besieged and captured Susa, which was pillaged and wrecked. It was recorded afterwards as a great triumph of this campaign that the statue of Nana of Erech, which had been carried off by Elamites 1635 years previously, was recovered and restored to the ancient Sumerian city. Elam's power of resistance was finally extinguished, and the country fell a ready prey to the Medes and Persians, who soon entered into possession of it. Thus, by destroying a buffer State, Ashur-bani-pal strengthened the hands of the people who were destined twenty years after his death to destroy the Empire of Assyria.

The western allies of Babylon were also dealt with, and it may be that at this time Manasseh of Judah was taken to Babylon (2 Chronicles, xxxiii, II), where, however, he was forgiven. The Medes and the Mannai in the north-west were visited and subdued, and a new alliance was formed with the dying State of Urartu.

Psamtik of Egypt had thrown off the yoke of Assyria, and with the assistance of Carian mercenaries received from his ally, Gyges, king of Lydia, extended his sway southward. He made peace with Ethiopia by marrying a princess of its royal line. Gyges must have weakened his army by thus assisting Psamtik, for he was severely defeated and slain by the Cimmerians. His son, Ardys, appealed to Assyria for help. Ashur-bani-pal dispatched an army to Cilicia. The joint operations of Assyria and Lydia resulted in the extinction of the kingdom of the Cimmerians about 645 B.C.

The records of Ashur-bani-pal cease after 640 B.C., so that we are unable to follow the events of his reign during its last fourteen years. Apparently peace prevailed everywhere. The great monarch, who was a pronounced adherent of the goddess cults, appears to have given himself up to a life of indulgence and inactivity. Under the name Sardanapalus he went down to tradition as a sensual Oriental monarch who lived in great pomp and luxury, and perished in his burning palace when the Medes revolted against him. It is evident, however, that the memory of more than one monarch contributed to the Sardanapalus legend, for Ashur-bani-pal had lain nearly twenty years in his grave before the siege of Nineveh took place.

In the Bible he is referred to as "the great and noble Asnapper", and he appears to have been the emperor who settled the Babylonian, Elamite, and other colonists "in the cities of Samaria".[550]

He erected at Nineveh a magnificent palace, which was decorated on a lavish scale. The sculptures are the finest productions of Assyrian art, and embrace a wide variety of subjects--battle scenes, hunting scenes, and elaborate Court and temple ceremonies. Realism is combined with a delicacy of touch and a degree of originality which raises the artistic productions of the period to the front rank among the artistic triumphs of antiquity.

Ashur-bani-pal boasted of the thorough education which he had received from the tutors of his illustrious father, Esarhaddon. In his palace he kept a magnificent library. It contained thousands of clay tablets on which were inscribed and translated the classics of Babylonia. To the scholarly zeal of this cultured monarch is due the preservation of the Babylonian story of creation, the Gilgamesh and Etana legends, and other literary and religious products of remote antiquity. Most of the literary tablets in the British Museum were taken from Ashur-bani-pal's library.

There are no Assyrian records of the reigns of Ashur-bani-pal's two sons, Ashur-etil-ilani--who erected a small palace and reconstructed the temple to Nebo at Kalkhi--and Sin-shar-ishkun, who is supposed to have perished in Nineveh. Apparently Ashur-etil-ilani reigned for at least six years, and was succeeded by his brother.

A year after Ashur-bani-pal died, Nabopolassar, who was probably a Chaldaean, was proclaimed king at Babylon. According to Babylonian legend he was an Assyrian general who had been sent southward with an army to oppose the advance of invaders from the sea. Nabopolassar's sway at first was confined to Babylon and Borsippa, but he strengthened himself by forming an offensive and defensive alliance with the Median king, whose daughter he had married to his son Nebuchadrezzar. He strengthened the fortifications of Babylon, rebuilt the temple of Merodach, which had been destroyed by Ashur-bani-pal, and waged war successfully against the Assyrians and their allies in Mesopotamia.

About 606 B.C. Nineveh fell, and Sin-shar-ishkun may have burned himself there in his palace, like his uncle, Shamash-shum-ukin of Babylon, and the legendary Sardanapalus. It is not certain, however, whether the Scythians or the Medes were the successful besiegers of the great Assyrian capital. "Woe to the bloody city! it is all full of lies and robbery", Nahum had cried."... The gates of the rivers shall be opened, and the palace shall be dissolved.... Take ye the spoil of silver, take the spoil of gold.... Behold, I am against thee, saith the Lord of hosts[551]."

According to Herodotus, an army of Medes under Cyaxares had defeated the Assyrians and were besieging Nineveh when the Scythians overran Media. Cyaxares raised the siege and went against them, but was defeated. Then the Scythians swept across Assyria and Mesopotamia, and penetrated to the Delta frontier of Egypt. Psamtik ransomed his kingdom with handsome gifts. At length, however, Cyaxares had the Scythian leaders slain at a banquet, and then besieged and captured Nineveh.

Assyria was completely overthrown. Those of its nobles and priests who escaped the sword no doubt escaped to Babylonia. Some may have found refuge also in Palestine and Egypt.

Necho, the second Pharaoh of the Twenty-sixth Egyptian Dynasty, did not hesitate to take advantage of Assyria's fall. In 609 B.C. he proceeded to recover the long-lost Asiatic possessions of Egypt, and operated with an army and fleet. Gaza and Askalon were captured. Josiah, the grandson of Manasseh, was King of Judah. "In his days Pharaoh-nechoh king of Egypt went up against the king of Assyria to the river Euphrates: and king Josiah went against him; and he (Necho) slew him at Megiddo."[552]His son, Jehoahaz, succeeded him, but was deposed three months later by Necho, who placed another son of Josiah, named Eliakim, on the throne, "and turned his name to Jehoiakim".[553] The people were heavily taxed to pay tribute to the Pharaoh.

When Necho pushed northward towards the Euphrates he was met by a Babylonian army under command of Prince Nebuchadrezzar.[554] The Egyptians were routed at Carchemish in 605 B.C. (*Jeremiah*, xvi, 2).

In 604 B.C. Nabopolassar died, and the famous Nebuchadrezzar II ascended the throne of Babylon. He lived to be one of its greatest kings, and reigned for over forty years. It was he who built the city described by Herodotus (pp. 219 *et seq.*), and constructed its outer wall, which enclosed so large an area that no army could invest it. Merodach's temple was decorated with greater magnificence than ever before. The great palace and hanging gardens were erected by this mighty monarch, who no doubt attracted to the city large numbers of the skilled artisans who had fled from Nineveh. He also restored temples at other cities, and made generous gifts to the priests. Captives were drafted into Babylonia from various lands, and employed cleaning out the canals and as farm labourers.

The trade and industries of Babylon flourished greatly, and Nebuchadrezzar's soldiers took speedy vengeance on roving bands which infested the caravan roads. "The king of Egypt", after his crushing defeat at Carchemish, "came not again any more out of his land: for the king of Babylon had taken from the river of Egypt unto the river Euphrates all that pertained to the king of Egypt."[555] Jehoiakim of Judah remained faithful to Necho until he was made a prisoner by Nebuchadrezzar, who "bound him in fetters to carry him to Babylon".[556] He was afterwards sent back to Jerusalem. "And Jehoiakim became his (Nebuchadrezzar's) servant three years: then he turned and rebelled against him."[557]

Bands of Chaldaeans, Syrians, Moabites, and Ammonites were harassing the frontiers of Judah, and it seemed to the king as if the Babylonian power had collapsed. Nebuchadrezzar hastened westward and scattered the raiders before him. Jehoiakim died, and his son Jehoiachan, a youth of eighteen years, succeeded him. Nebuchadrezzar laid siege to Jerusalem, and the young king submitted to him and was carried off to Babylon, with "all the princes, and all the mighty men of valour, even ten thousand captives, and all the craftsmen and smiths: none remained save the poorest sort of the people of the land".[558] Nebuchadrezzar had need of warriors and workmen.

Zedekiah was placed on the throne of Judah as an Assyrian vassal. He remained faithful for a few years, but at length began to conspire with Tyre and Sidon, Moab, Edom, and Ammon in favour of Egyptian suzerainty. Pharaoh Hophra (Apries), the fourth king of the Twenty-sixth Dynasty, took active steps to assist the conspirators, and "Zedekiah rebelled against the king of Babylon[559]".

Nebuchadrezzar led a strong army through Mesopotamia, and divided it at Riblah, on the Orontes River. One part of it descended upon Judah and captured Lachish and Azekah. Jerusalem was able to hold out for about eighteen months. Then "the famine was sore in the city, so that there was no bread for the people of the land. Then the city was broken up, and all the men of war fled, and went forth out of the city by night by way of the gate between the two walls, which was by the king's garden." Zedekiah attempted to escape, but was captured and carried before Nebuchadrezzar, who was at Riblah, in the land of Hamath.

And the king of Babylon slew the sons of Zedekiah before his eyes.... Then he put out the eyes of Zedekiah; and the king of Babylon bound him in chains and carried him to Babylon and put him in prison till the day of his death[560].

The majority of the Jews were deported to Babylonia, where they were employed as farm labourers. Some rose to occupy important official positions. A remnant escaped to Egypt with Jeremiah.

Jerusalem was plundered and desolated. The Assyrians "burned the house of the Lord and the king's house, and all the houses of Jerusalem", and "brake down all the walls of Jerusalem round about". Jeremiah lamented:

How doth the city sit solitary, that was full of people! how is she become as a widow! she that was great among the nations, and princess among the provinces, how is she become tributary! She weepeth sore in the night, and her tears are on her cheeks: among all her lovers she hath none to comfort her: all her friends have dealt treacherously with her, they are become her enemies. Judah is gone into captivity because of affliction, and because of great servitude: she dwelleth among the heathen, she findeth no rest: all her persecutors overtook her between the straits.... Jerusalem remembered in the days of her affliction and of her miseries all her pleasant things that she had in the days of old....[561]

Tyre was besieged, but was not captured. Its king, however, arranged terms of peace with Nebuchadrezzar.

Amel-Marduk, the "Evil Merodach" of the Bible, the next king of Babylon, reigned for a little over two years. He released Jehoiachin from prison, and allowed him to live in the royal palace.[562] Berosus relates that Amel-Marduk lived a dissipated life, and was slain by his brother-in-law, Nergal-shar-utsur, who reigned two years (559-6 B.C.). Labashi-Marduk, son of Nergal-shar-utsur, followed with a reign of nine months. He was deposed by the priests. Then a Babylonian prince named Nabu-na´id (Nabonidus) was set on the throne. He was the last independent king of Babylonia. His son Belshazzar appears to have acted as regent during the latter part of the reign.

Nabonidus engaged himself actively during his reign (556-540 B.C.) in restoring temples. He entirely reconstructed the house of Shamash, the sun god, at Sippar, and, towards the end of his reign, the house of Sin, the moon god, at Haran. The latter building had been destroyed by the Medes.

The religious innovations of Nabonidus made him exceedingly unpopular throughout Babylonia, for he carried away the gods of Ur, Erech, Larsa, and Eridu, and had them placed in E-sagila. Merodach and his priests were displeased: the prestige of the great god was threatened by the policy adopted by Nabonidus. As an inscription composed after the fall of Babylon sets forth; Merodach "gazed over the surrounding lands ... looking for a righteous prince, one after his own heart, who should take his hands.... He called by name Cyrus."

Cyrus was a petty king of the shrunken Elamite province of Anshan, which had been conquered by the Persians. He claimed to be an Achaemenian—that is a descendant of the semi-mythical Akhamanish (the Achaemenes of the Greeks), a Persian patriarch who resembled the Aryo-Indian Manu and the Germanic Mannus. Akhamanish was reputed to have been fed and protected in childhood by an eagle—the sacred eagle which cast its shadow on born rulers. Probably this eagle was remotely Totemic, and the Achaemenians were descendants of an ancient eagle tribe. Gilgamesh was protected by an eagle, as we have seen, as the Aryo-Indian Shakuntala was by vultures and Semiramis by doves. The legends regarding the birth and boyhood of Cyrus resemble those related regarding Sargon of Akkad and the Indian Karna and Krishna.

Cyrus acknowledged as his overlord Astyages, king of the Medes. He revolted against Astyages, whom he defeated and took prisoner. Thereafter he was proclaimed King of the Medes and Persians, who were kindred peoples of Indo-European speech. The father of Astyages was Cyaxares, the ally of Nabopolassar of Babylon. When this powerful king captured Nineveh he entered into possession of the northern part of the Assyrian Empire, which extended westward into Asia Minor to the frontier of the Lydian kingdom; he also possessed himself of Urartu (Armenia). Lydia had, after the collapse of the Cimmerian power, absorbed Phrygia, and its ambitious king, Alyattes, waged war against the Medes. At length, owing to the good offices of Nebuchadrezzar of Babylon and Syennesis of Cilicia, the Medes and Lydians made peace in 585 B.C. Astyages then married a daughter of the Lydian ruler.

When Cyrus overthrew Cyaxares, king of the Medes, Croesus, king of Lydia, formed an alliance against him with Amasis, king of Egypt, and Nabonidus, king of Babylon. The latter was at first friendly to Cyrus, who had attacked Cyaxares when he was advancing on Babylon to dispute Nabonidus's claim to the throne, and perhaps to win it for a descendant of Nebuchadrezzar, his father's ally. It was after the fall of the Median Dynasty that Nabonidus undertook the restoration of the moon god's temple at Haran.

Cyrus advanced westward against Croesus of Lydia before that monarch could receive assistance from the intriguing but pleasure-loving Amasis of Egypt; he defeated and overthrew him, and seized his kingdom (547-546 B.C.). Then, having established himself as supreme ruler in Asia Minor, he began to operate against Babylonia. In 539 B.C. Belshazzar was defeated near Opis. Sippar fell soon afterwards. Cyrus's general, Gobryas, then advanced upon Babylon, where Belshazzar deemed himself safe. One night, in the month of Tammuz—

Belshazzar the king made a great feast to a thousand of his lords, and drank wine before the thousand. Belshazzar, whiles he tasted the wine, commanded to bring the golden and silver vessels which his father Nebuchadnezzar had taken out of the temple which was in Jerusalem; that the king, and his princes, his wives, and his concubines, might drink therein.... They drank wine, and praised the gods of gold, and of silver, of brass, of iron, of wood, and of stone.... In that night was Belshazzar the king of the Chaldeans slain.[563]

On the 16th of Tammuz the investing army under Gobryas entered Babylon, the gates having been opened by friends within the city. Some think that the Jews favoured the cause of Cyrus. It is quite as possible, however, that the priests of Merodach had a secret understanding with the great Achaemenian, the "King of kings".

A few days afterwards Cyrus arrived at Babylon. Belshazzar had been slain, but Nabonidus still lived, and he was deported to Carmania. Perfect order prevailed throughout the city, which was firmly policed by the Persian soldiers, and there was no looting. Cyrus was welcomed as a deliverer by the priesthood. He "took the hands" of Bel Merodach at E-sagila, and was proclaimed "King of the world, King of Babylon, King of Sumer and Akkad, and King of the Four Quarters".

Cyrus appointed his son Cambyses as governor of Babylon. Although a worshipper of Ahura-Mazda and Mithra, Cambyses appears to have conciliated the priesthood. When he became king, and swept through Egypt, he was remembered as the madman who in a fit of passion slew a sacred Apis bull. It is possible, however, that he performed what he considered to be a pious act: he may have sacrificed the bull to Mithra.

The Jews also welcomed Cyrus. They yearned for their native land.

By the rivers of Babylon, there we sat down, yea, we wept, when we remembered Zion. We hanged our harps upon the willows in the midst thereof. For there they that carried us away captive required of us a song; and they that wasted us required of us mirth, saying, Sing us one of the songs of Zion. How shall we sing the Lord's song in a strange land? If I forget thee, O Jerusalem, let my right hand forget her cunning. If I do not remember thee, let my tongue cleave to the roof of my mouth; if I prefer not Jerusalem above my chief joy.[564]

Cyrus heard with compassion the cry of the captives.

Now in the first year of Cyrus king of Persia, that the word of the Lord by the mouth of Jeremiah might be fulfilled, the Lord stirred up the spirit of Cyrus king of Persia, that he made a proclamation throughout all his kingdom, and put it also in writing, saying, Thus saith Cyrus king of Persia, The Lord God of heaven hath given me all kingdoms of the earth; and he hath charged me to build him an house at Jerusalem, which is in Judah. Who is there among you of all his people? his God be with him, and let him go up to Jerusalem, which is in Judah, and build the house of the Lord God of Israel (he is the God) which is in Jerusalem.[565]

In 538 B.C. the first party of Jews who were set free saw through tears the hills of home, and hastened their steps to reach Mount Zion. Fifty years later Ezra led back another party of the faithful. The work of restoring Jerusalem was undertaken by Nehemiah in 445 B.C.

The trade of Babylon flourished under the Persians, and the influence of its culture spread far and wide. Persian religion was infused with new doctrines, and their deities were given stellar attributes. Ahura-Mazda became identified with Bel Merodach, as, perhaps, he had previously been with Ashur, and the goddess Anahita absorbed the attributes of Nina, Ishtar, Zerpanitum, and other Babylonian "mother deities".

Another "Semiramis" came into prominence. This was the wife and sister of Cambyses. After Cambyses died she married Darius I, who, like Cyrus, claimed to be an Achaemenian. He had to overthrow a pretender, but submitted to the demands of the orthodox Persian party to purify the Ahura-Mazda religion of its Babylonian innovations. Frequent revolts in Babylon had afterwards to be suppressed. The Merodach priesthood apparently suffered loss of prestige at Court. According to Herodotus, Darius plotted to carry away from E-sagila a great statue of Bel "twelve cubits high and entirely of solid gold". He, however, was afraid "to lay his hands upon it". Xerxes, son of Darius (485-465 B.C.), punished Babylon for revolting, when intelligence reached them of his disasters in Greece, by pillaging and partly destroying the temple. "He killed the priest who forbade him to move the statue, and took it away."[566] The city lost its vassal king, and was put under the control of a governor. It, however, regained some of its ancient glory after the burning of Susa palace, for the later Persian monarchs resided in it. Darius II died at Babylon, and Artaxerxes II promoted in the city the worship of Anaitis.

When Darius III, the last Persian emperor, was overthrown by Alexander the Great in 331 B.C., Babylon welcomed the Macedonian conqueror as it had welcomed Cyrus. Alexander was impressed by the wisdom and accomplishments of the astrologers and priests, who had become known as "Chaldaeans", and added Bel Merodach to his extraordinary pantheon, which already included Amon of Egypt, Melkarth, and Jehovah. Impressed by the antiquity and magnificence of Babylon, he resolved to make it the capital of his world-wide empire, and there he received ambassadors from countries as far east as India and as far west as Gaul.

The canals of Babylonia were surveyed, and building operations on a vast scale planned out. No fewer than ten thousand men were engaged working for two months reconstructing and decorating the temple of Merodach, which towered to a height of 607 feet. It looked as if Babylon were about to rise to a position of splendour unequalled in its history, when Alexander fell sick, after attending a banquet, and died on an evening of golden splendour sometime in June of 323 B.C.

One can imagine the feelings of the Babylonian priests and astrologers as they spent the last few nights of the emperor's life reading "the omens of the air"--taking note of wind and shadow, moon and stars and planets, seeking for a sign, but unable to discover one favourable. Their hopes of Babylonian glory were suspended in the balance, and they perished completely when the young emperor passed away in the thirty-third year of his life. For four days and four nights the citizens mourned in silence for Alexander and for Babylon.

The ancient city fell into decay under the empire of the Seleucidae. Seleucus I had been governor of Babylon, and after the break-up of Alexander's empire he returned to the ancient metropolis as a conqueror. "None of the persons who succeeded Alexander", Strabo wrote, "attended to the undertaking at Babylon"--the reconstruction of Merodach's temple. "Other works were neglected, and the city was dilapidated partly by the Persians and partly by time and through the indifference of the Greeks, particularly after Seleucus Nicator fortified Seleukeia on the Tigris."[567]

Seleucus drafted to the city which bore his name the great bulk of the inhabitants of Babylon. The remnant which was left behind continued to worship Merodach and other gods after the walls had crumbled and the great temple began to tumble down. Babylon died slowly, but at length the words of the Hebrew prophet were fulfilled:

The cormorant and the bittern shall possess it; the owl also and the raven shall dwell in it.... They shall call the nobles thereof to the kingdom, but none shall be there, and all her princes shall be nothing. And thorns shall come up in her palaces, nettles and brambles in the fortresses thereof: and it shall be an habitation of dragons, and a court for owls. The wild beasts of the desert shall also meet with the wild beasts of the island, and the satyr shall cry to his fellow: the screech owl also shall rest there, and find for herself a place of rest.[568]

---

[544] *Nahum*, i, ii, and iii.
[545] *Isaiah*, xlvi, 1; xlvii, 1-15.
[546] *Nahum*, iii, 2, 3; ii, 3.
[547] Goodspeed's *A History of the Babylonians and Assyrians*, p. 348.
[548] *Nahum*, iii, 8-11.
[549] Ptolemy's Kineladanus.
[550] *Ezra*, iv, 10.
[551] *Nahum*, iii and ii.
[552] 2 *Kings*, xxiii, 29.
[553] *Ibid.*, 33-5.
[554] Nebuchadrezzar is more correct than Nebuchadnezzar.
[555] 2 *Kings*, xxiv, 7.
[556] 2 *Chronicles*, xxxvi, 6.
[557] 2 *Kings*, xxiv, 1.
[558] 2 *Kings*, xxiv, 8-15.
[559] *Jeremiah*, lii, 3.
[560] *Jeremiah*, lii, 4-11.
[561] *The Lamentations of Jeremiah*, i, 1-7.
[562] *Jeremiah*, lii, 31-4.
[563] *Daniel*, v, I et seq.
[564] *Psalms*, cxxxvii, 1-6.
[565] *Ezra*, i, 1-3.
[566] *Herodotus*, i, 183; *Strabo*, xvi, 1, 5; and *Arrian*, vii, 17.
[567] *Strabo*, xvi, 1-5.
[568] *Isaiah*, xxiiv, 11-4.

CPSIA information can be obtained at www.ICGtesting.com
Printed in the USA
LVOW04s0759220215

427737LV00028B/751/P